I Was an Eighth-Grade Ninja

ZONDERVAN

I Was an Eighth-Grade Ninja
Copyright © 2007 by Funnypages Productions, LLC

Requests for information should be addressed to:
Zondervan, *Grand Rapids, Michigan* 49530

Library of Congress Cataloging-in-Publication Data

Simmons, Andy.
I was an eighth-grade ninja / written by Andrew Simmons and Rob Corley ; illustrated by
Ariel Padilla ; created by Tom Bancroft and Rob Corley.
     p. cm. — (Tomo book ; #1)
   "Published in association with Funnypages Productions, LLC."
   ISBN 978-0-310-71300-5 (pbk.)
   1. Graphic novels. I. Corley, Rob. II. Padilla, Ariel, 1968- III. Bancroft, Tom. IV. Title.
   PN6727.S51574I2 2007
   741.5'973 — dc22

2007005080

Any Internet addresses (websites, blogs, etc.) and telephone numbers printed in this
book are offered as a resource. They are not intended in any way to be or imply an
endorsement by Zondervan, nor does Zondervan vouch for the content of these sites
and numbers for the life of this book.

This book published in conjunction with Funnypages Productions, LLC, 106 Mission
Court, Suite 704, Franklin, TN 37067

Series Editor: Bud Rogers
Managing Editor: Bruce Nuffer
Managing Art Director: Merit Alderink

Printed in the United States of America

HB 11.18.2019

GRAPHIC NOVELS

TOMO

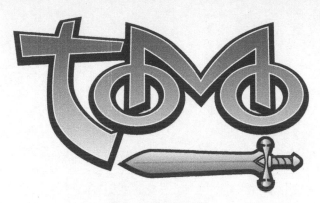

I Was an Eighth-Grade Ninja

SERIES EDITOR
BUD ROGERS

STORY BY
ANDREW SIMMONS
& ROB CORLEY

ART BY
ARIEL PADILLA

CREATED BY
TOM BANCROFT
& ROB CORLEY

funnypages PRODUCTIONS

ZONDERVAN®

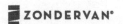

ZONDERVAN.com/
AUTHORTRACKER
follow your favorite authors

I WAS AN EIGHTH-GRADE NINJA

SERIES EDITOR
BUD ROGERS

STORY BY
ANDREW SIMMONS
& BOB CORLEY

ART BY
ARIEL PADILLA

CREATED BY
TOM BANCROFT
& BOB CORLEY

ZONDERVAN

ZONDERVAN.com/
AUTHORTRACKER

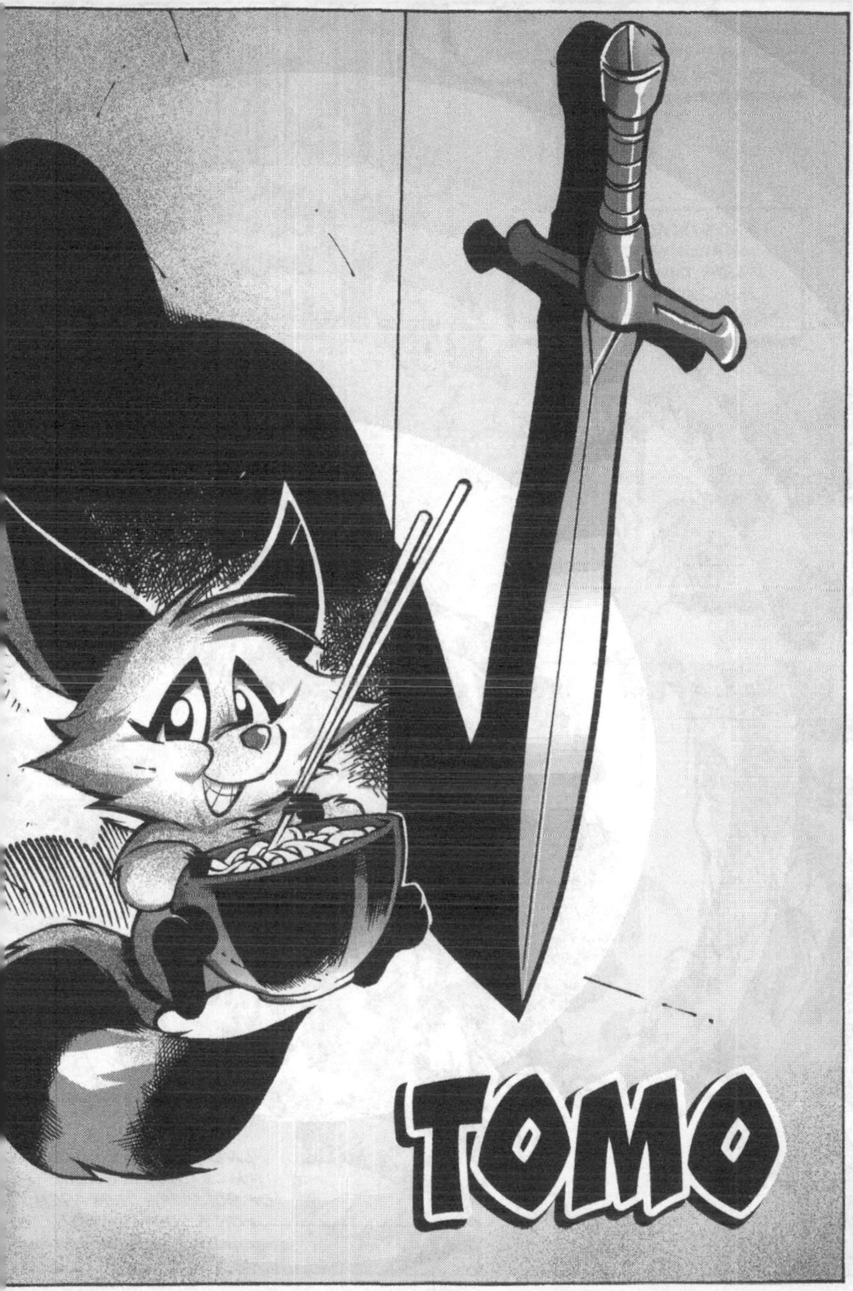
TOMO

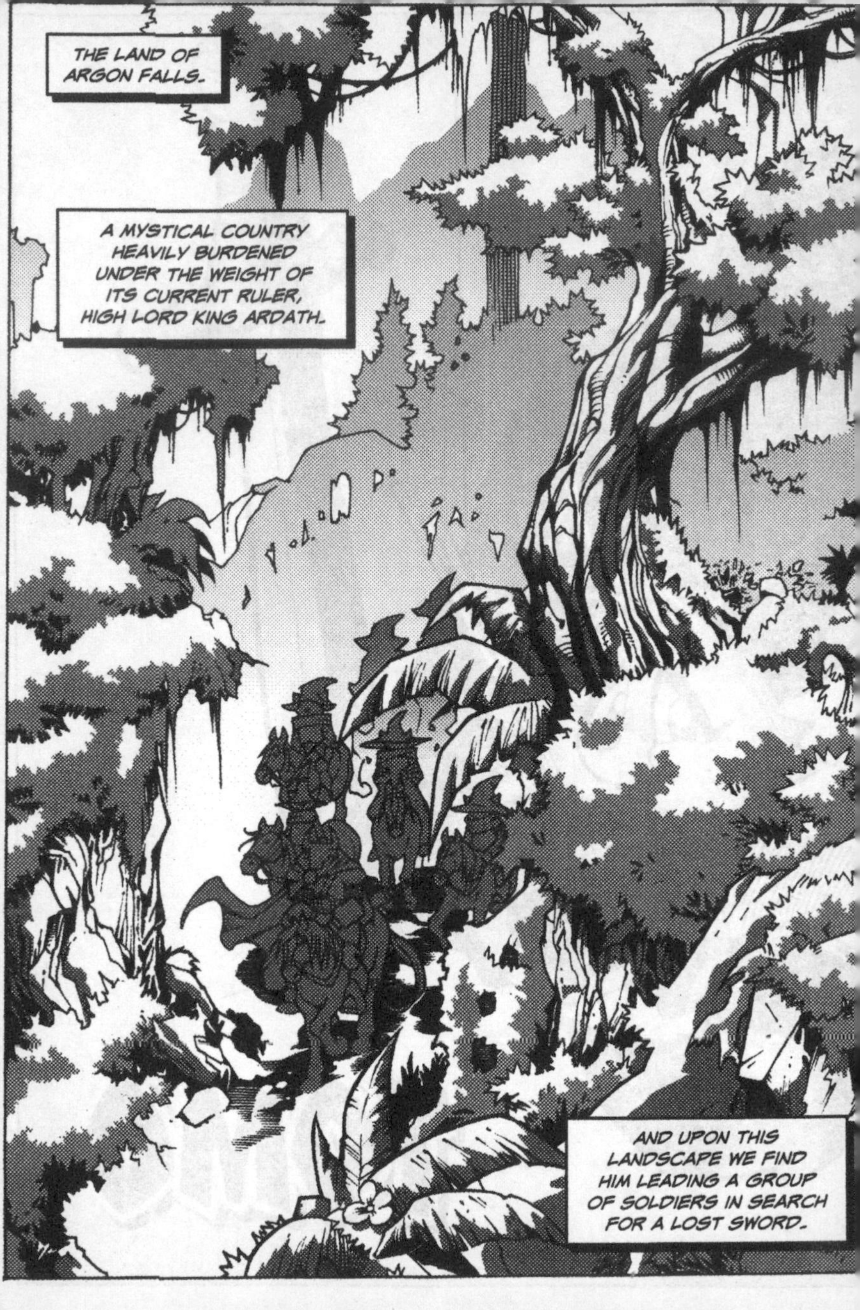
THE LAND OF ARGON FALLS.
A MYSTICAL COUNTRY HEAVILY BURDENED UNDER THE WEIGHT OF ITS CURRENT RULER, HIGH LORD KING ARDATH.
AND UPON THIS LANDSCAPE WE FIND HIM LEADING A GROUP OF SOLDIERS IN SEARCH FOR A LOST SWORD.

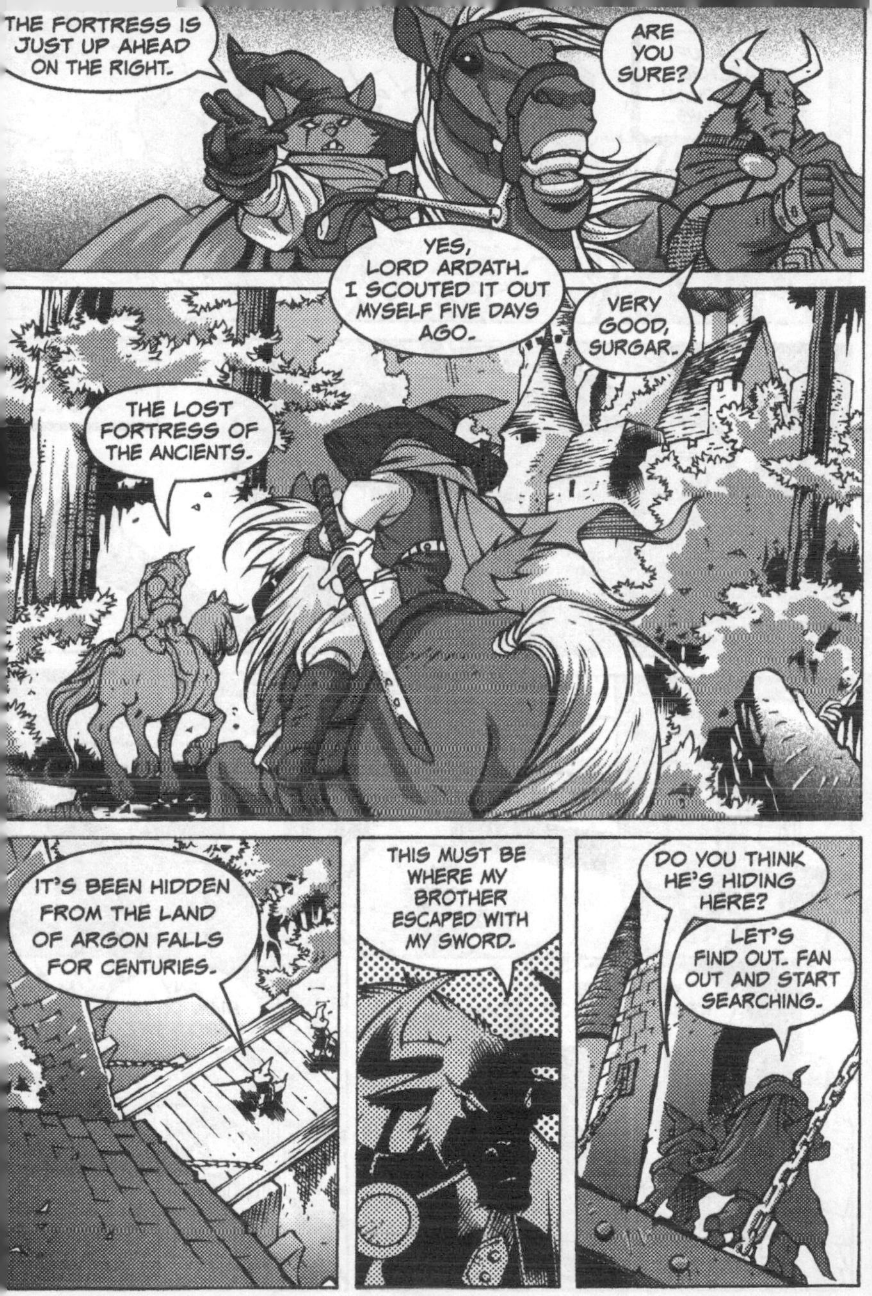
THE FORTRESS IS JUST UP AHEAD ON THE RIGHT.
ARE YOU SURE?
YES, LORD ARDATH. I SCOUTED IT OUT MYSELF FIVE DAYS AGO.
VERY GOOD, SURGAR.
THE LOST FORTRESS OF THE ANCIENTS.
IT'S BEEN HIDDEN FROM THE LAND OF ARGON FALLS FOR CENTURIES.
THIS MUST BE WHERE MY BROTHER ESCAPED WITH MY SWORD.
DO YOU THINK HE'S HIDING HERE?
LET'S FIND OUT. FAN OUT AND START SEARCHING.

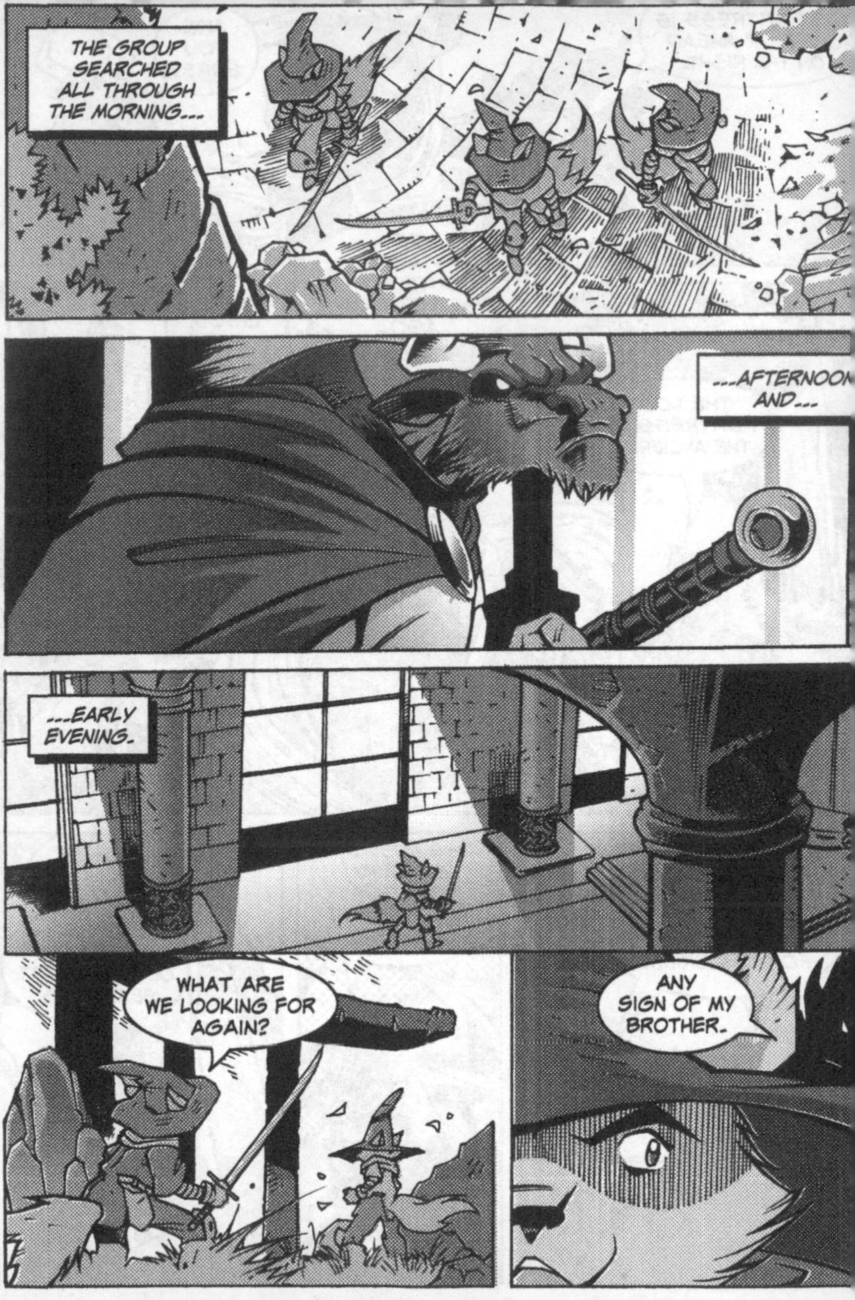
THE GROUP SEARCHED ALL THROUGH THE MORNING...
...AFTERNOON AND...
...EARLY EVENING.
WHAT ARE WE LOOKING FOR AGAIN?
ANY SIGN OF MY BROTHER.

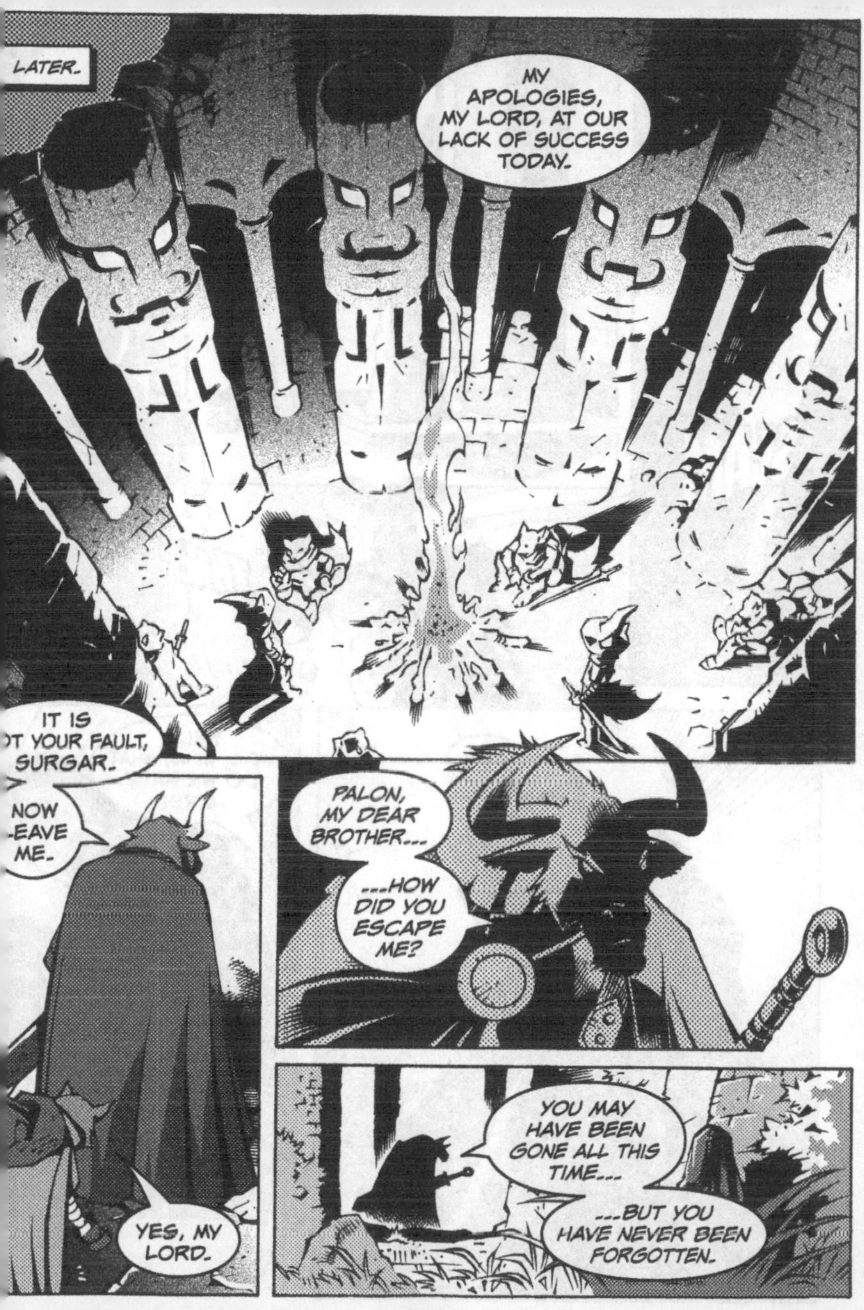
LATER.
MY APOLOGIES, MY LORD, AT OUR LACK OF SUCCESS TODAY.
IT IS OT YOUR FAULT, SURGAR.
NOW EAVE ME.
YES, MY LORD.
PALON, MY DEAR BROTHER...
...HOW DID YOU ESCAPE ME?
YOU MAY HAVE BEEN GONE ALL THIS TIME...
...BUT YOU HAVE NEVER BEEN FORGOTTEN.

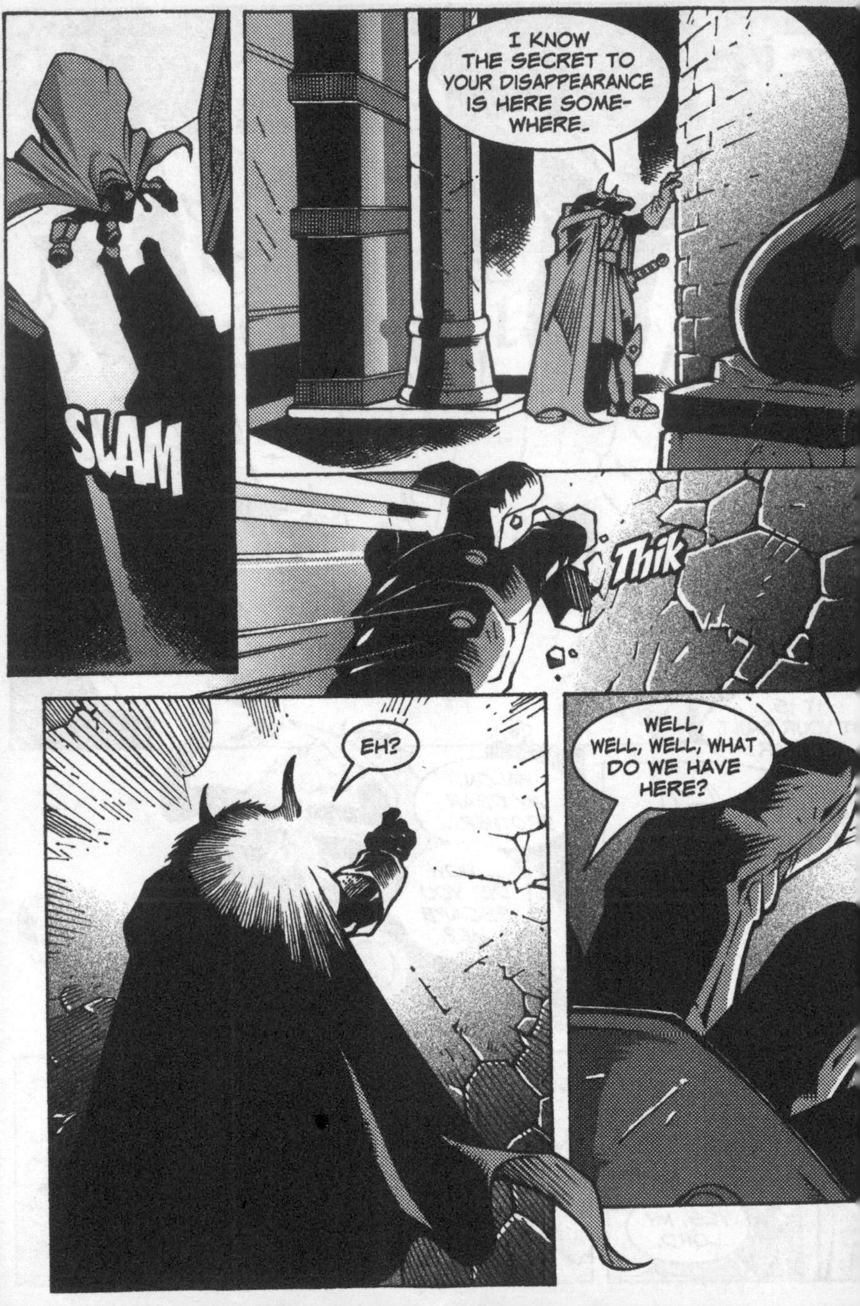
SLAM
I KNOW THE SECRET TO YOUR DISAPPEARANCE IS HERE SOME-WHERE.
THIK
EH?
WELL, WELL, WELL, WHAT DO WE HAVE HERE?

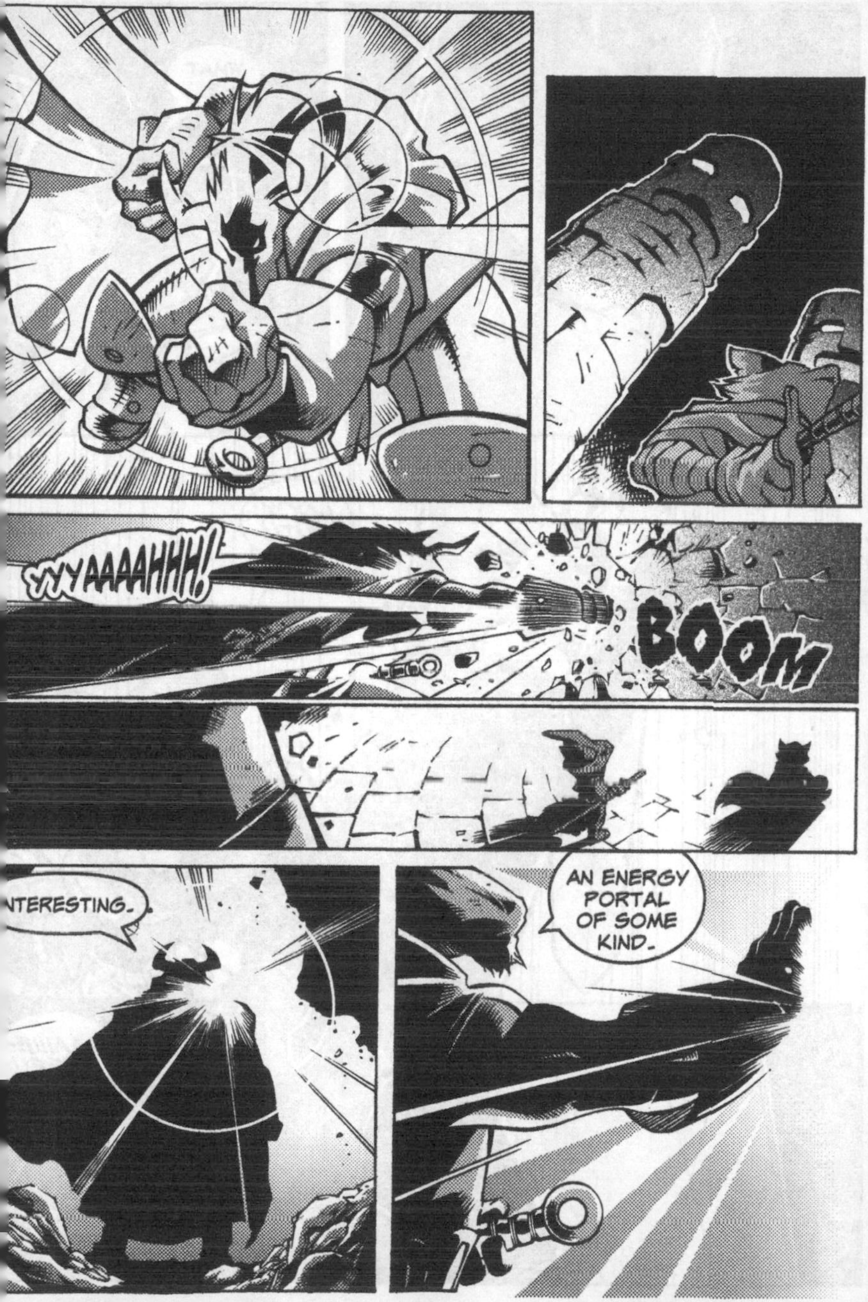
YYYAAAAHHH!
BOOM
NTERESTING...
AN ENERGY PORTAL OF SOME KIND...

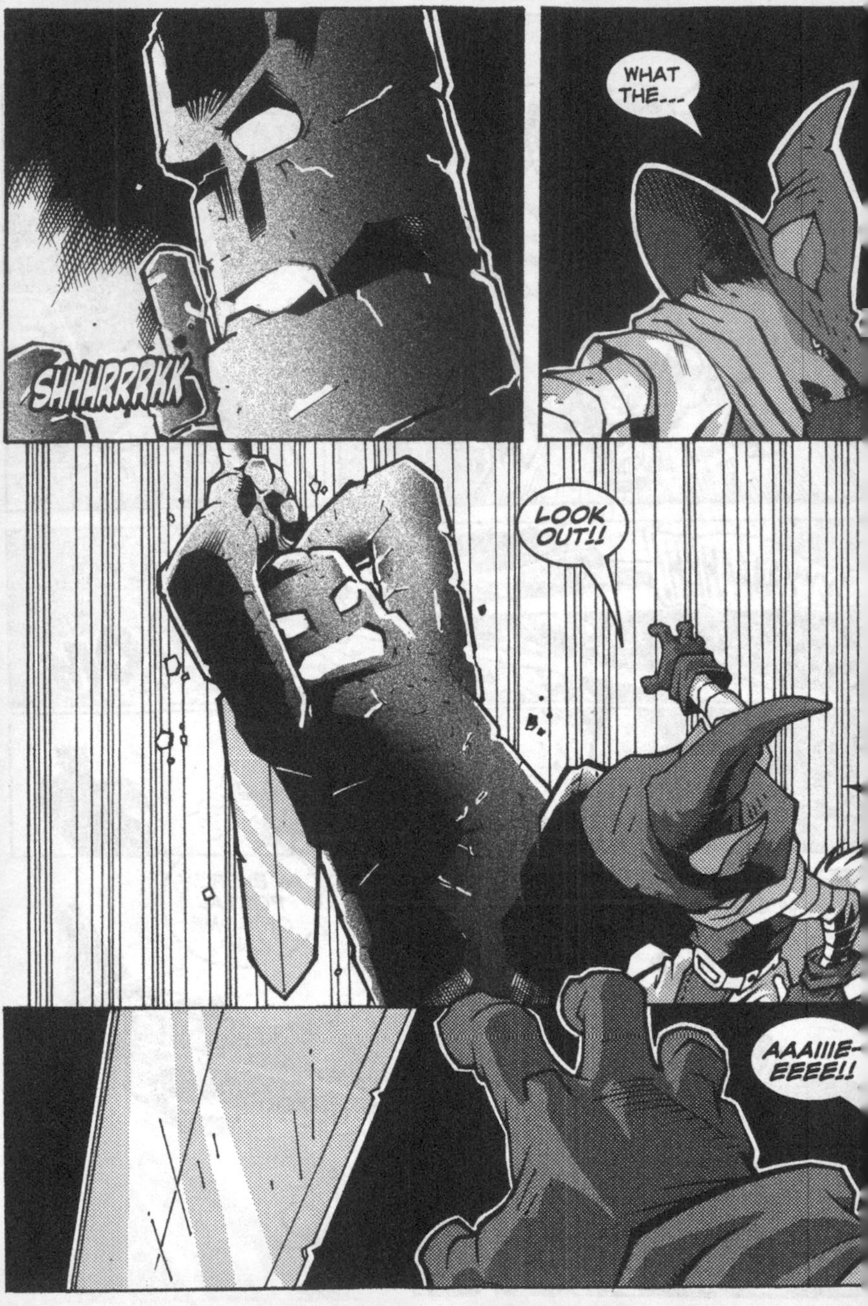
SHHHRRRKK
WHAT THE...
LOOK OUT!!
AAAIIIE-EEEE!!

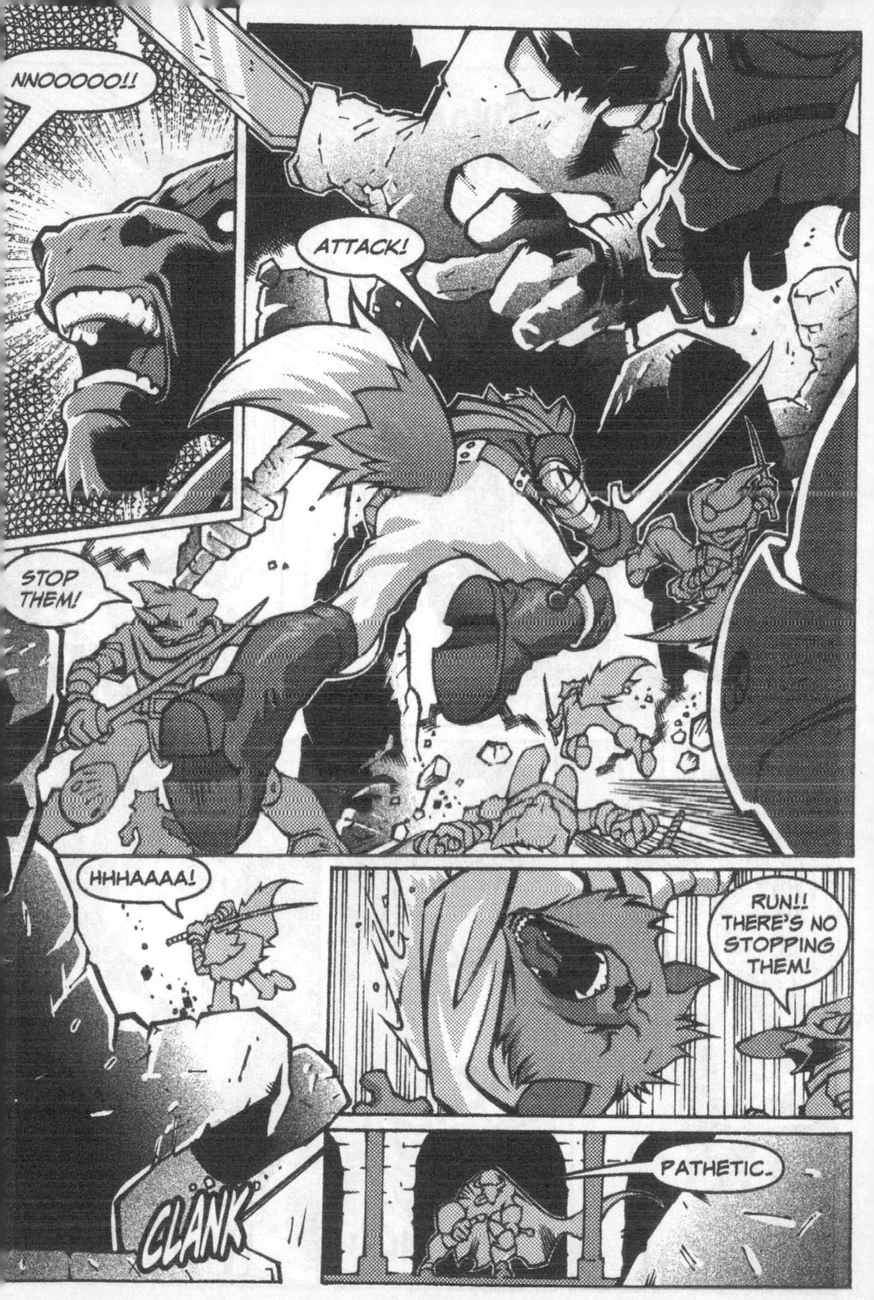
NNOOOOO!!
ATTACK!
STOP THEM!
HHHAAAA!
CLANK
RUN!! THERE'S NO STOPPING THEM!
PATHETIC.

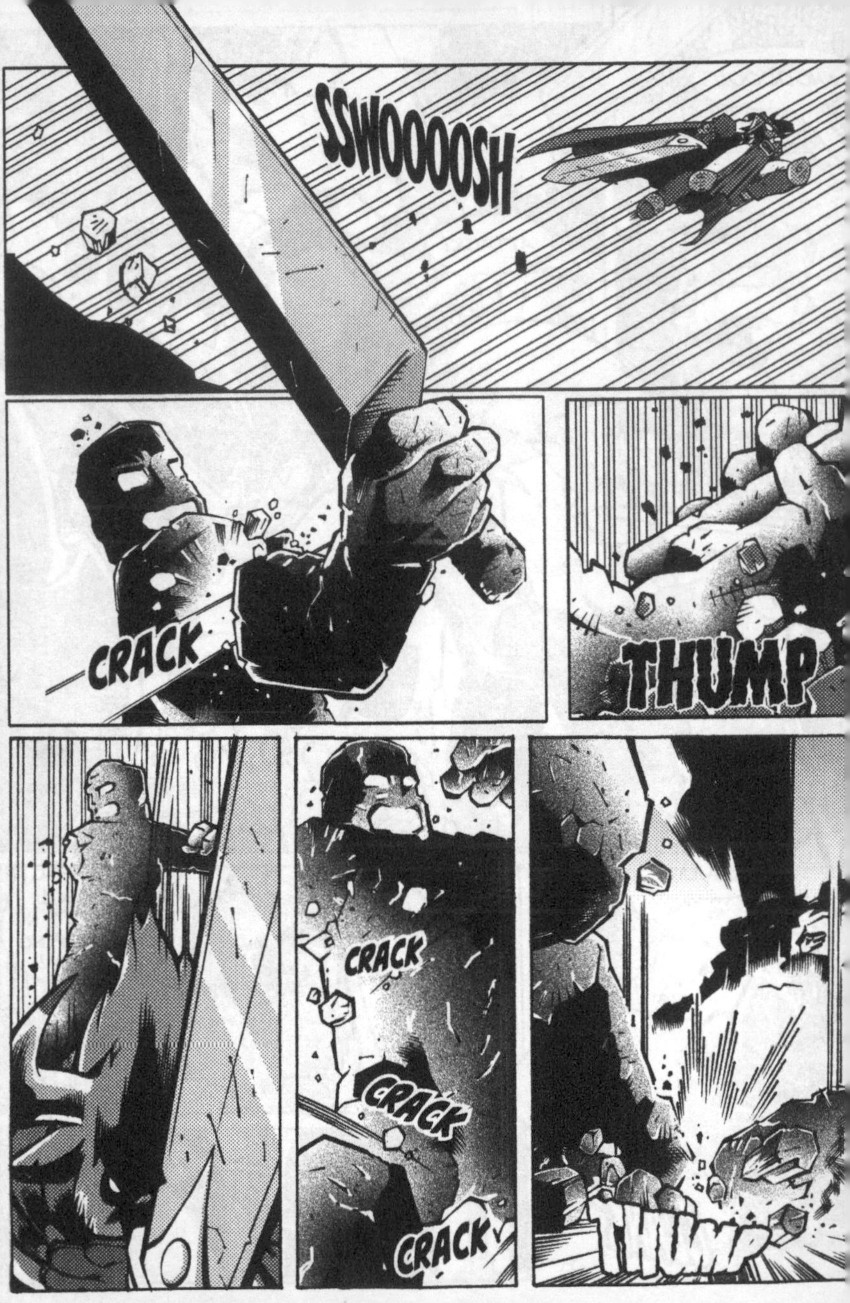
SSWOOOOSH
CRACK
THUMP
CRACK
CRACK
CRACK
THUMP

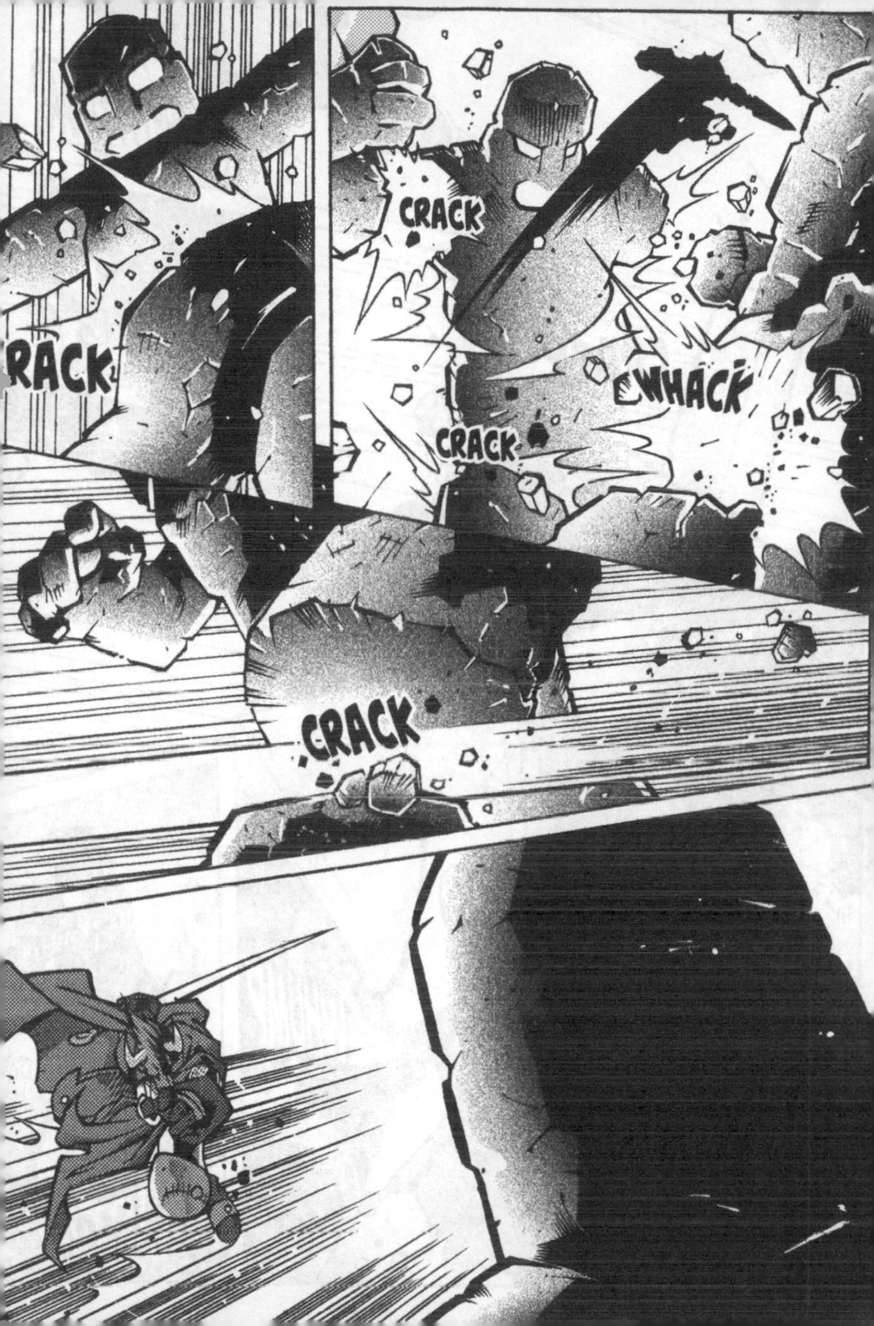
RACK
CRACK
WHACK
CRACK
CRACK

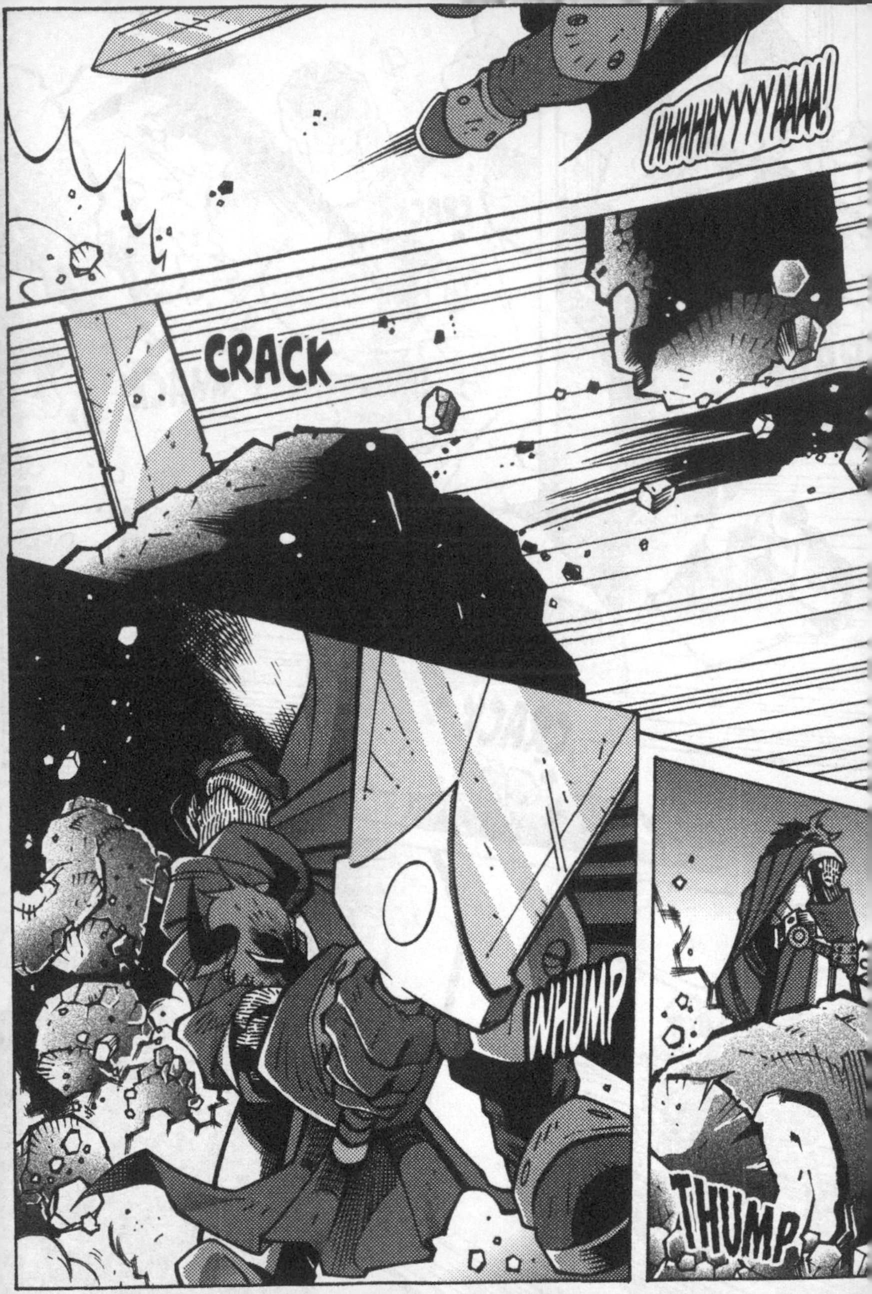
HHHHYYYYAAAA!
CRACK
WHUMP
THUMP

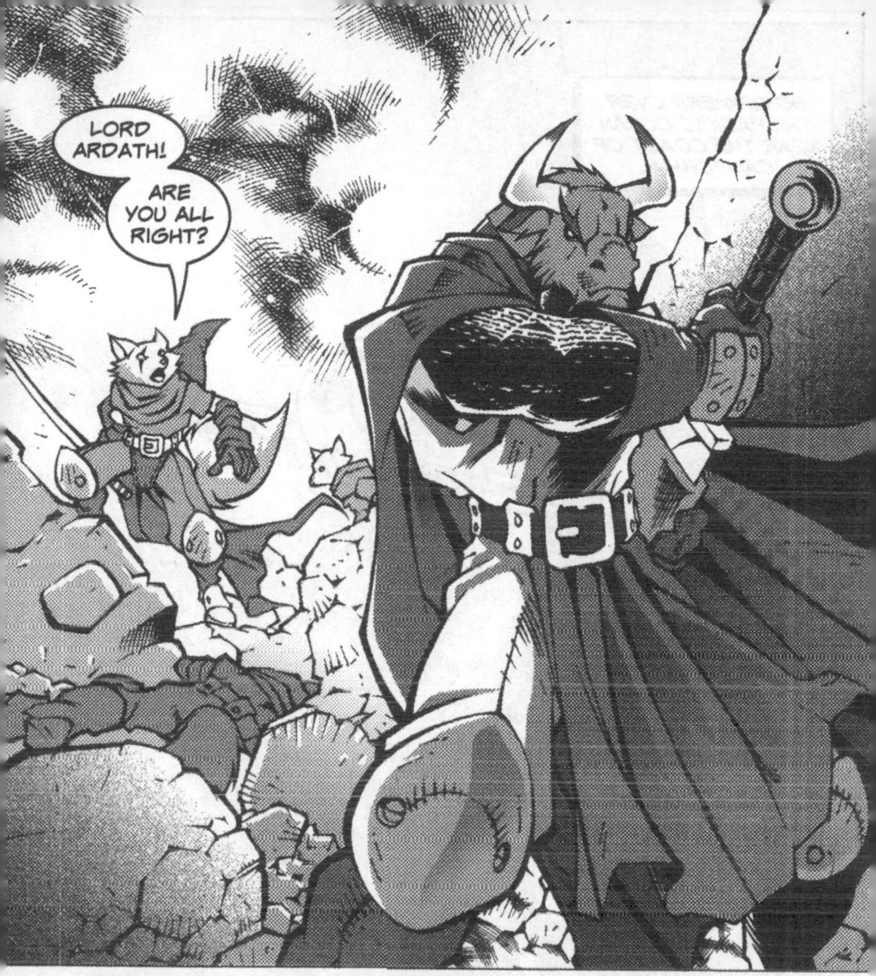
LORD ARDATH!
ARE YOU ALL RIGHT?

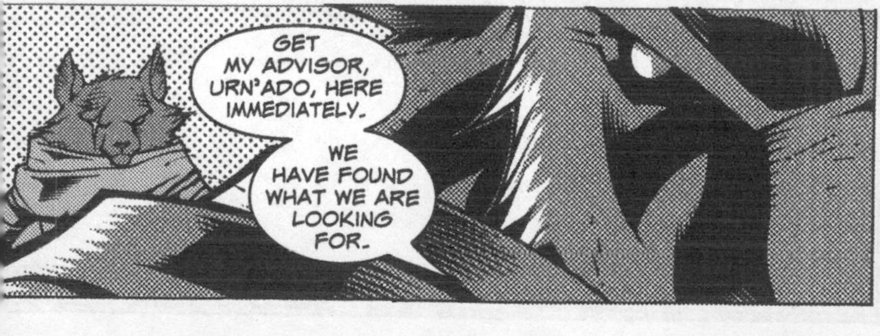
GET MY ADVISOR, URN'ADO, HERE IMMEDIATELY.
WE HAVE FOUND WHAT WE ARE LOOKING FOR.

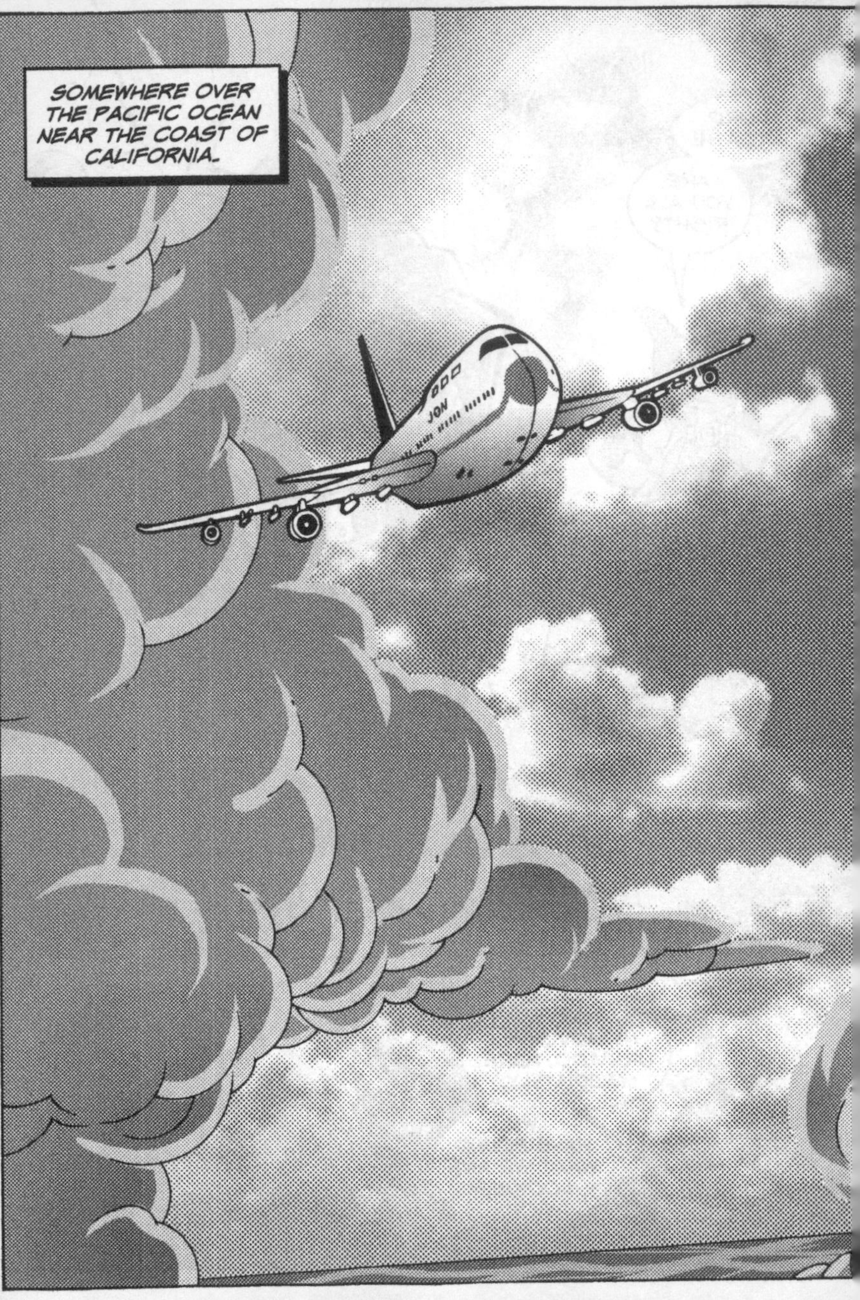
SOMEWHERE OVER THE PACIFIC OCEAN NEAR THE COAST OF CALIFORNIA.
JON

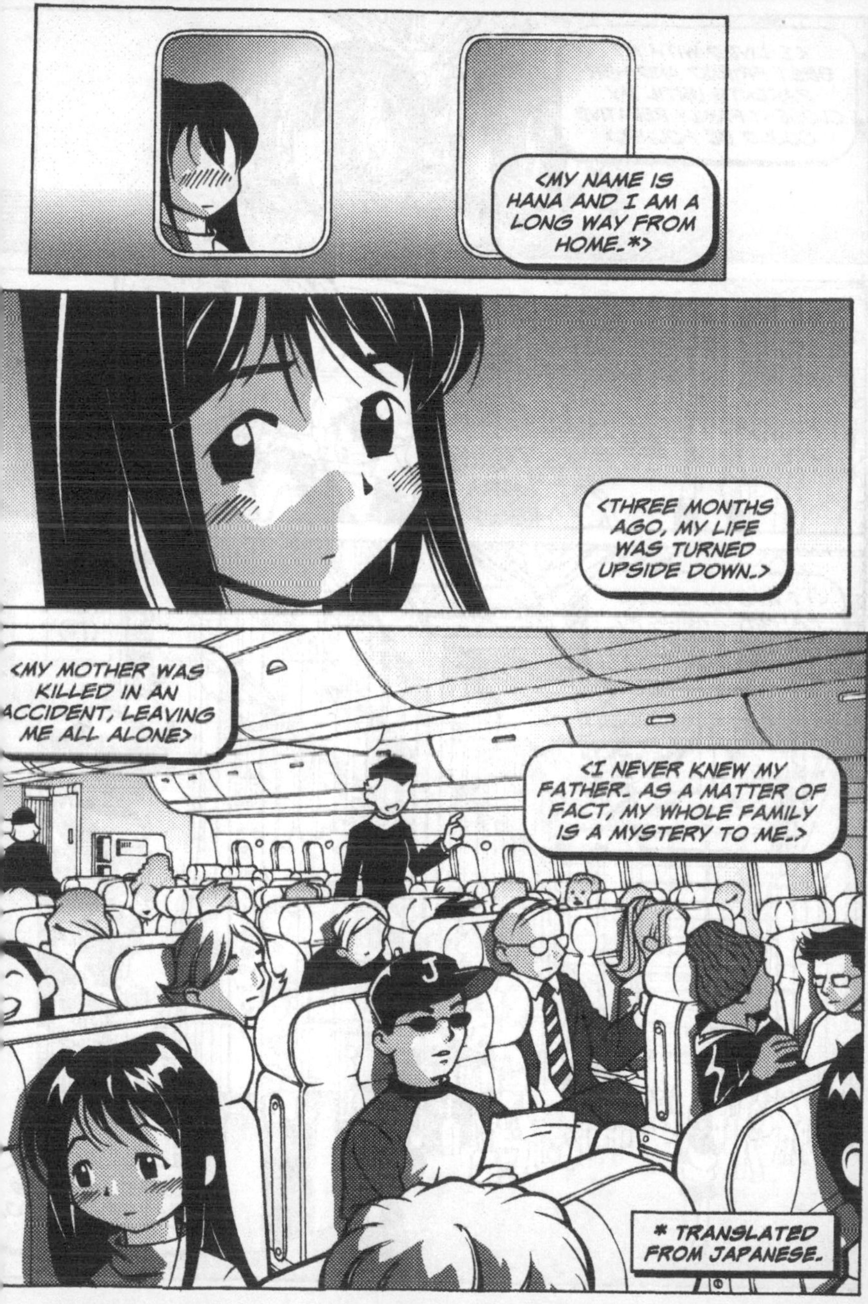
<MY NAME IS HANA AND I AM A LONG WAY FROM HOME.*>
<THREE MONTHS AGO, MY LIFE WAS TURNED UPSIDE DOWN.>
<MY MOTHER WAS KILLED IN AN ACCIDENT, LEAVING ME ALL ALONE>
<I NEVER KNEW MY FATHER. AS A MATTER OF FACT, MY WHOLE FAMILY IS A MYSTERY TO ME.>
* TRANSLATED FROM JAPANESE.

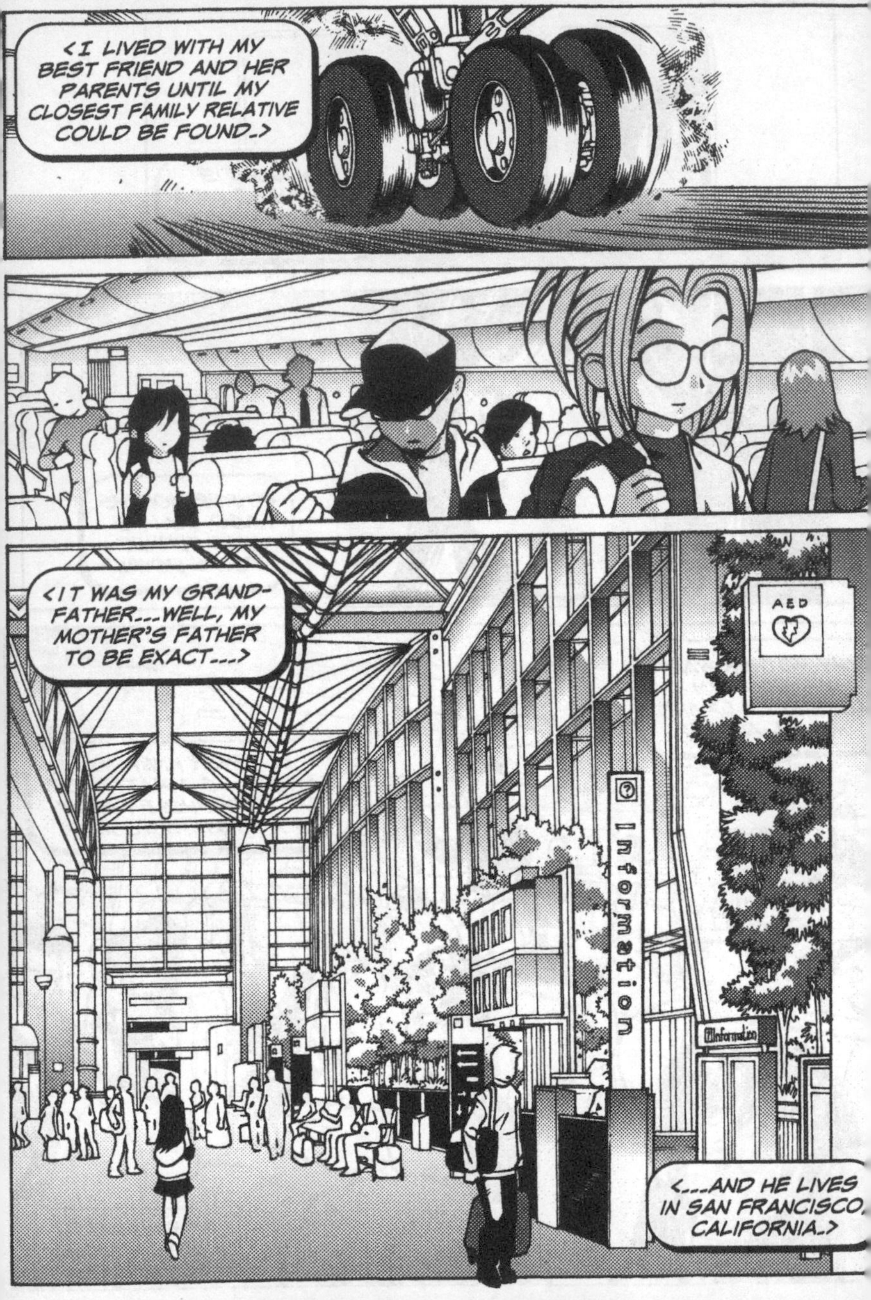

<I LIVED WITH MY BEST FRIEND AND HER PARENTS UNTIL MY CLOSEST FAMILY RELATIVE COULD BE FOUND.>
<IT WAS MY GRAND-FATHER...WELL, MY MOTHER'S FATHER TO BE EXACT...>
AED
Information
Information
<...AND HE LIVES IN SAN FRANCISCO, CALIFORNIA.>

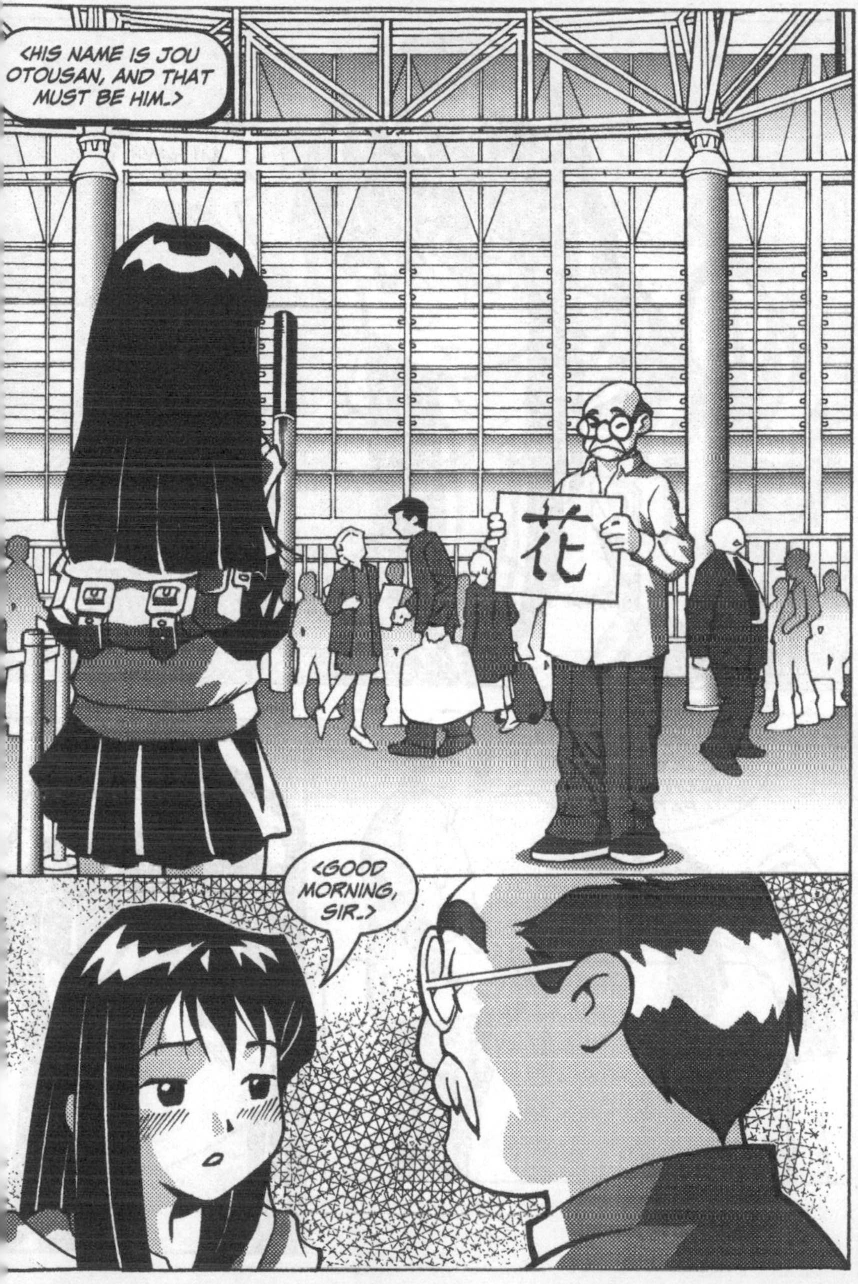
<HIS NAME IS JOU OTOUSAN, AND THAT MUST BE HIM.>
花
<GOOD MORNING, SIR.>

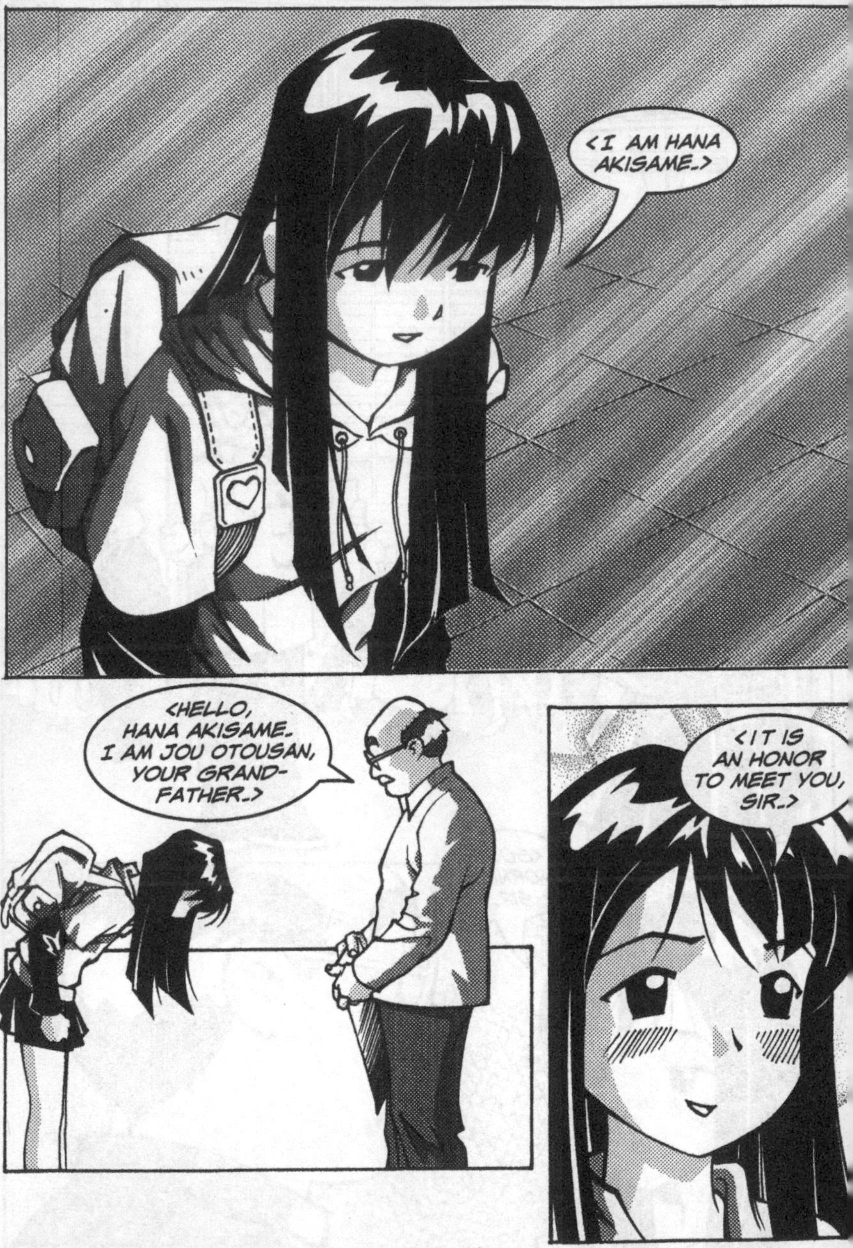
<I AM HANA AKISAME.>
<HELLO, HANA AKISAME. I AM JOU OTOUSAN, YOUR GRAND-FATHER.>
<IT IS AN HONOR TO MEET YOU, SIR.>

<THE HONOR IS ALL MINE, LITTLE FLOWER.*>
* HANA MEANS FLOWER IN JAPANESE.
<VERY WELL, LET'S GO GET YOUR BAGS.>

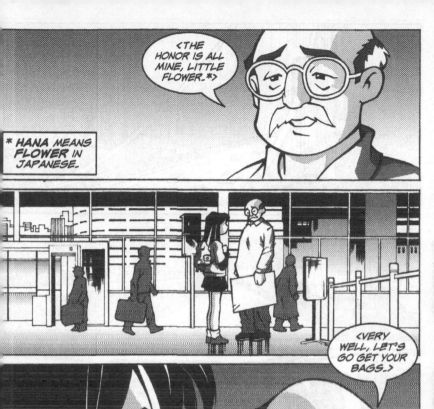

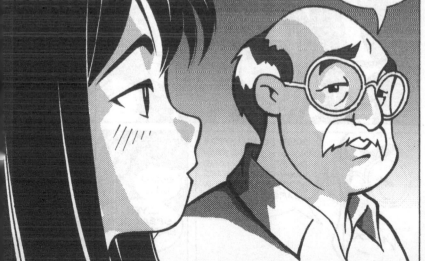

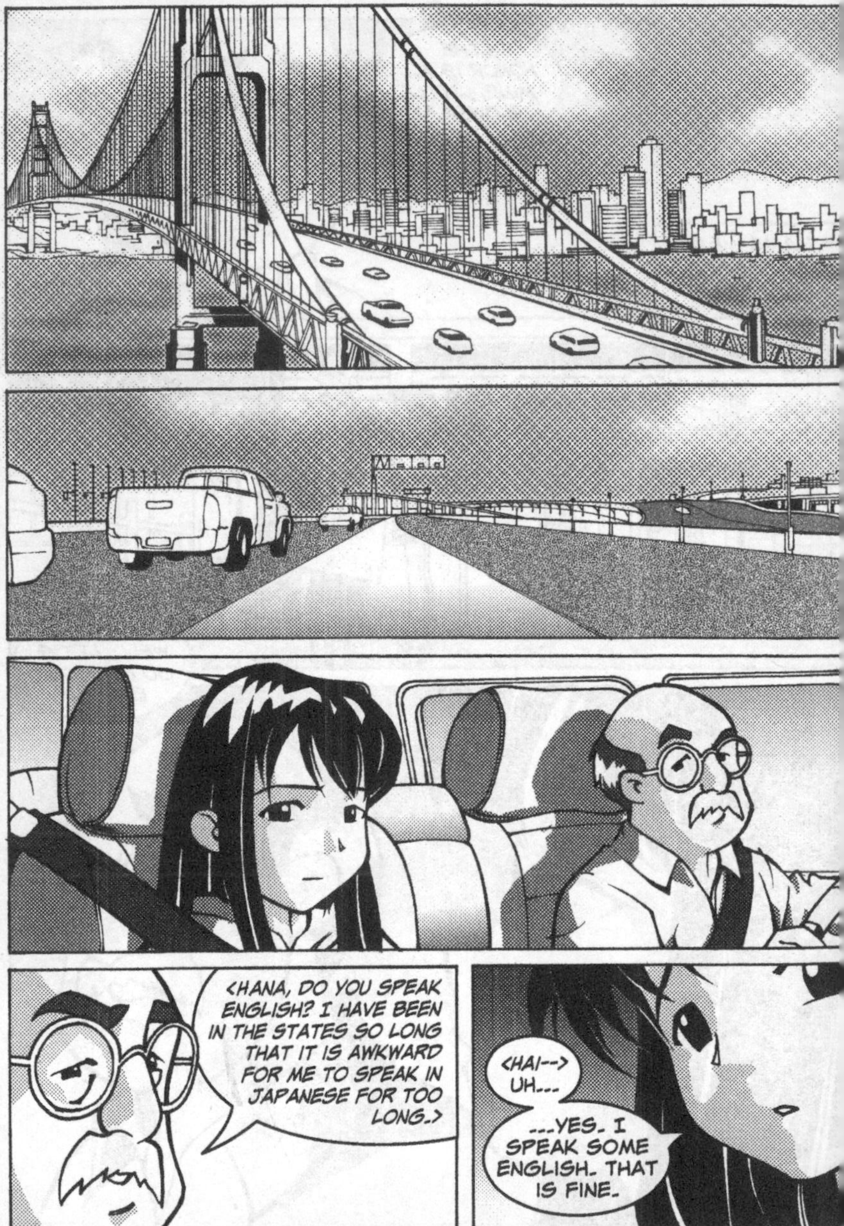
<HANA, DO YOU SPEAK ENGLISH? I HAVE BEEN IN THE STATES SO LONG THAT IT IS AWKWARD FOR ME TO SPEAK IN JAPANESE FOR TOO LONG.>
<HAI--> UH...
...YES. I SPEAK SOME ENGLISH. THAT IS FINE.

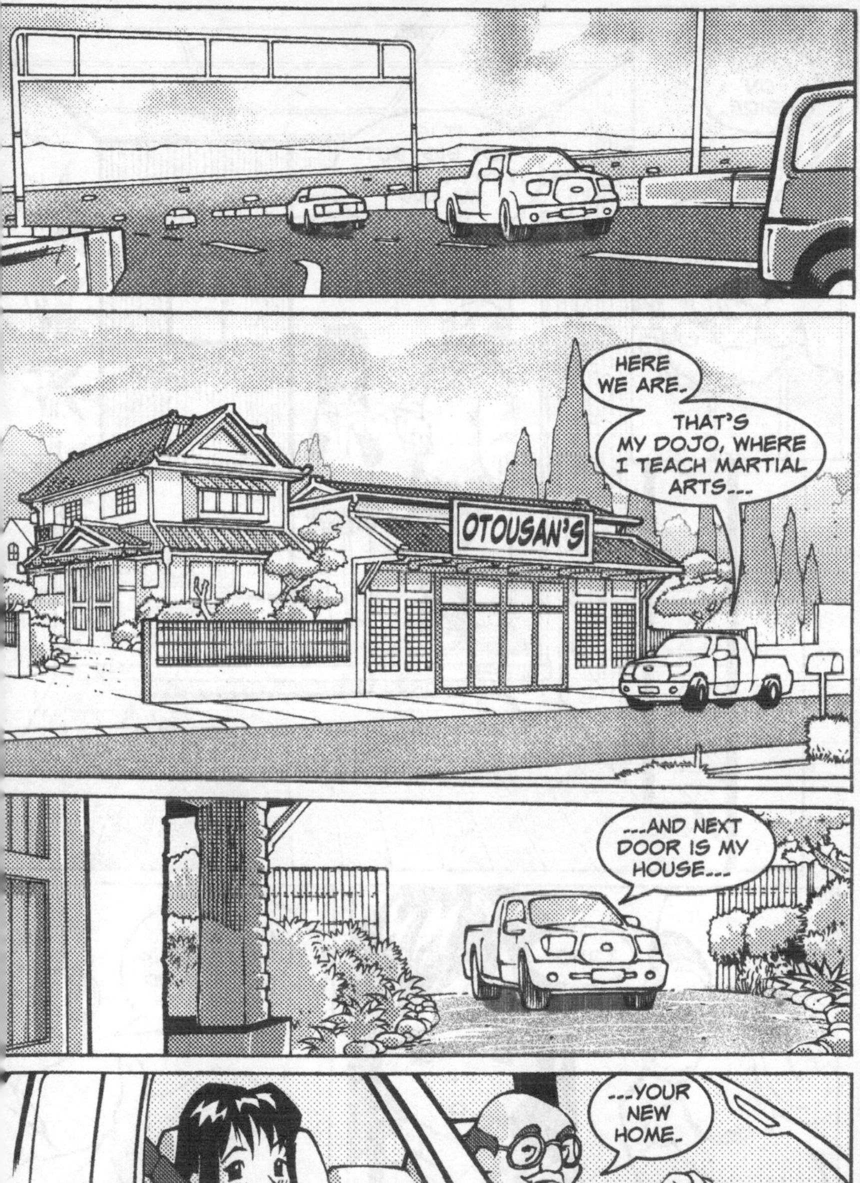
HERE WE ARE.
THAT'S MY DOJO, WHERE I TEACH MARTIAL ARTS...
OTOUSAN'S
...AND NEXT DOOR IS MY HOUSE...
...YOUR NEW HOME.

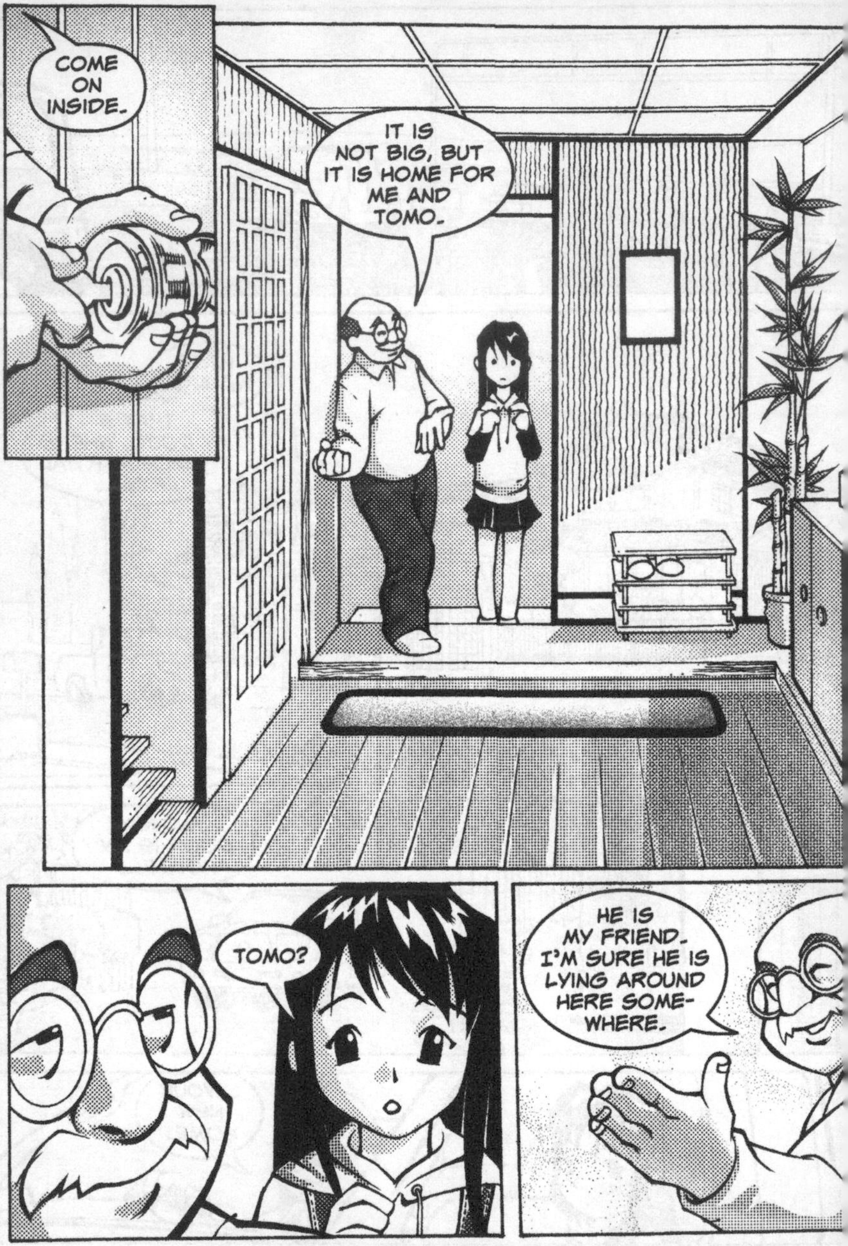
COME ON INSIDE.
IT IS NOT BIG, BUT IT IS HOME FOR ME AND TOMO.
TOMO?
HE IS MY FRIEND. I'M SURE HE IS LYING AROUND HERE SOME-WHERE.

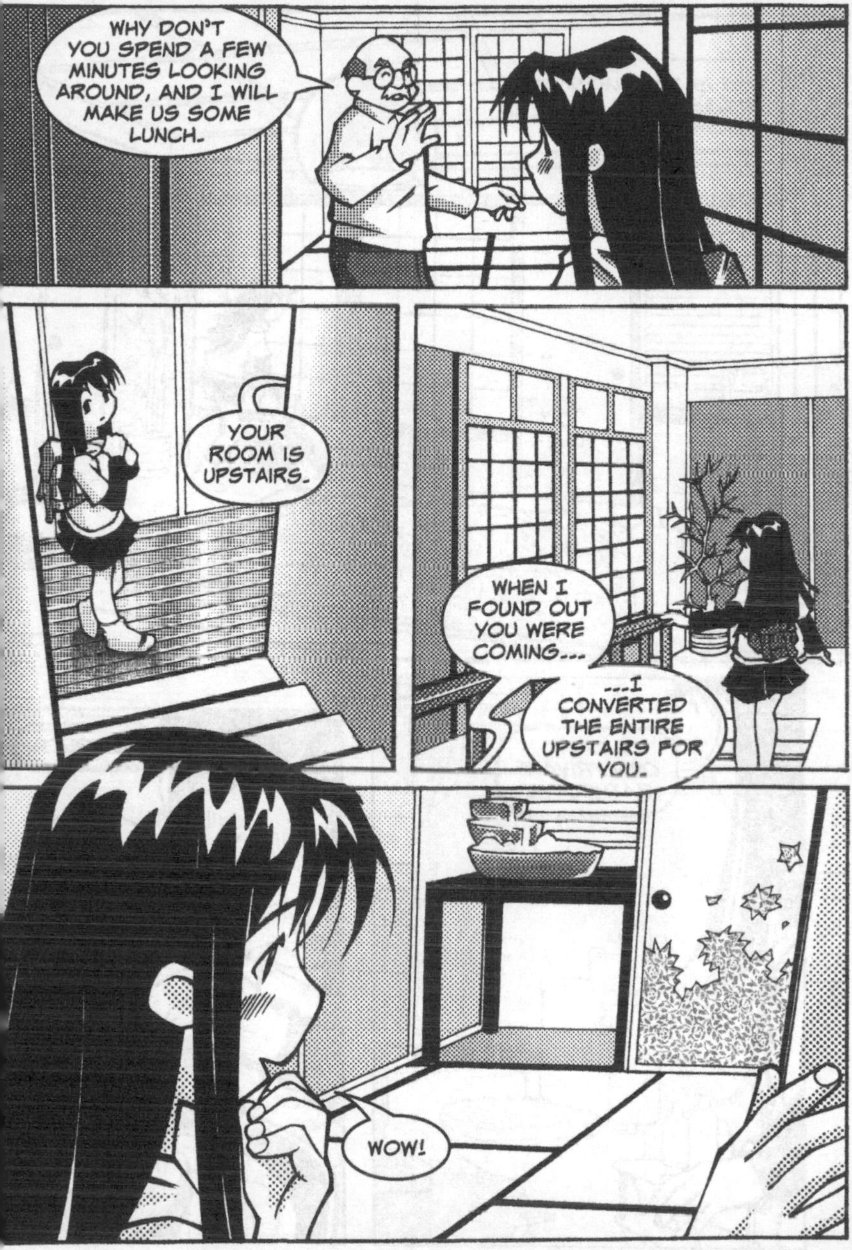
WHY DON'T YOU SPEND A FEW MINUTES LOOKING AROUND, AND I WILL MAKE US SOME LUNCH.
YOUR ROOM IS UPSTAIRS.
WHEN I FOUND OUT YOU WERE COMING...
...I CONVERTED THE ENTIRE UPSTAIRS FOR YOU.
WOW!

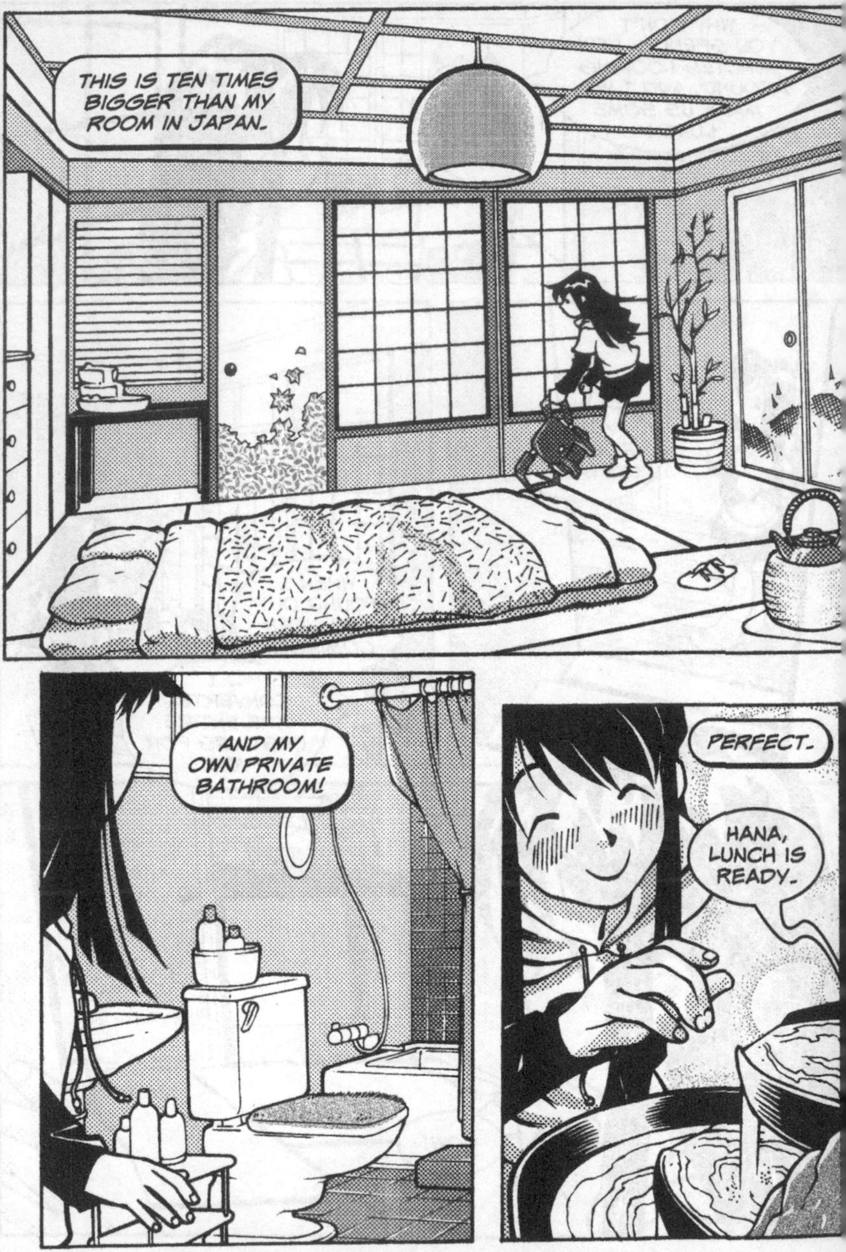
THIS IS TEN TIMES BIGGER THAN MY ROOM IN JAPAN.
AND MY OWN PRIVATE BATHROOM!
PERFECT.
HANA, LUNCH IS READY.

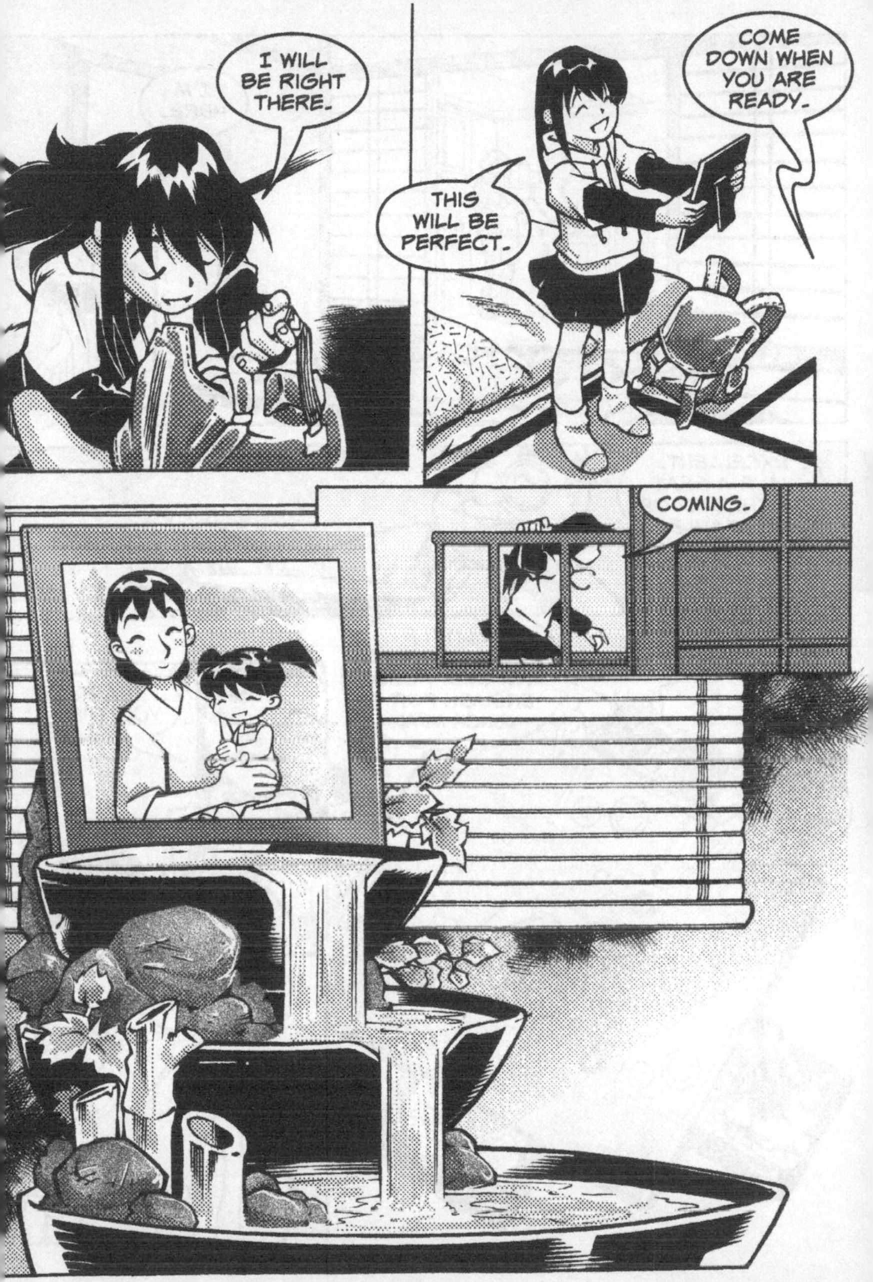
I WILL BE RIGHT THERE.
THIS WILL BE PERFECT.
COME DOWN WHEN YOU ARE READY.
COMING.

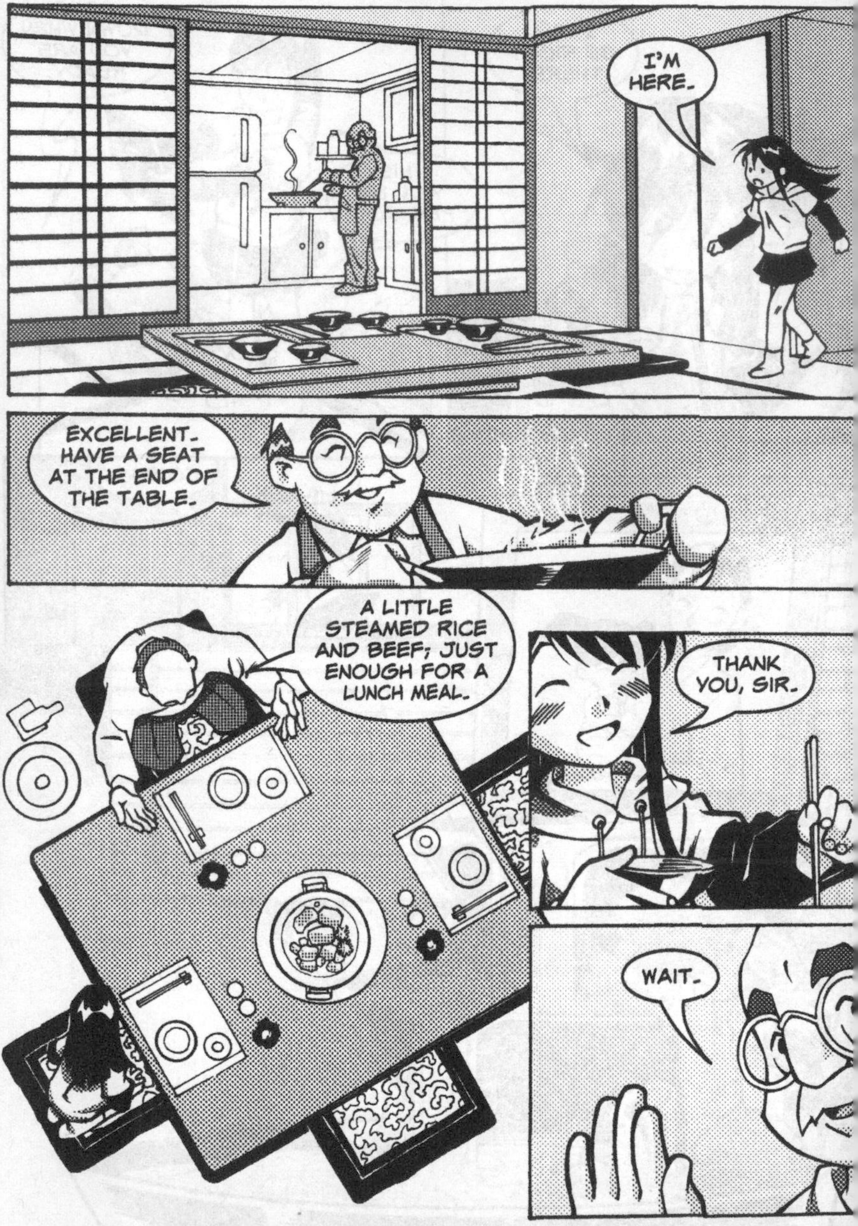
I'M HERE.
EXCELLENT. HAVE A SEAT AT THE END OF THE TABLE.
A LITTLE STEAMED RICE AND BEEF; JUST ENOUGH FOR A LUNCH MEAL.
THANK YOU, SIR.
WAIT.

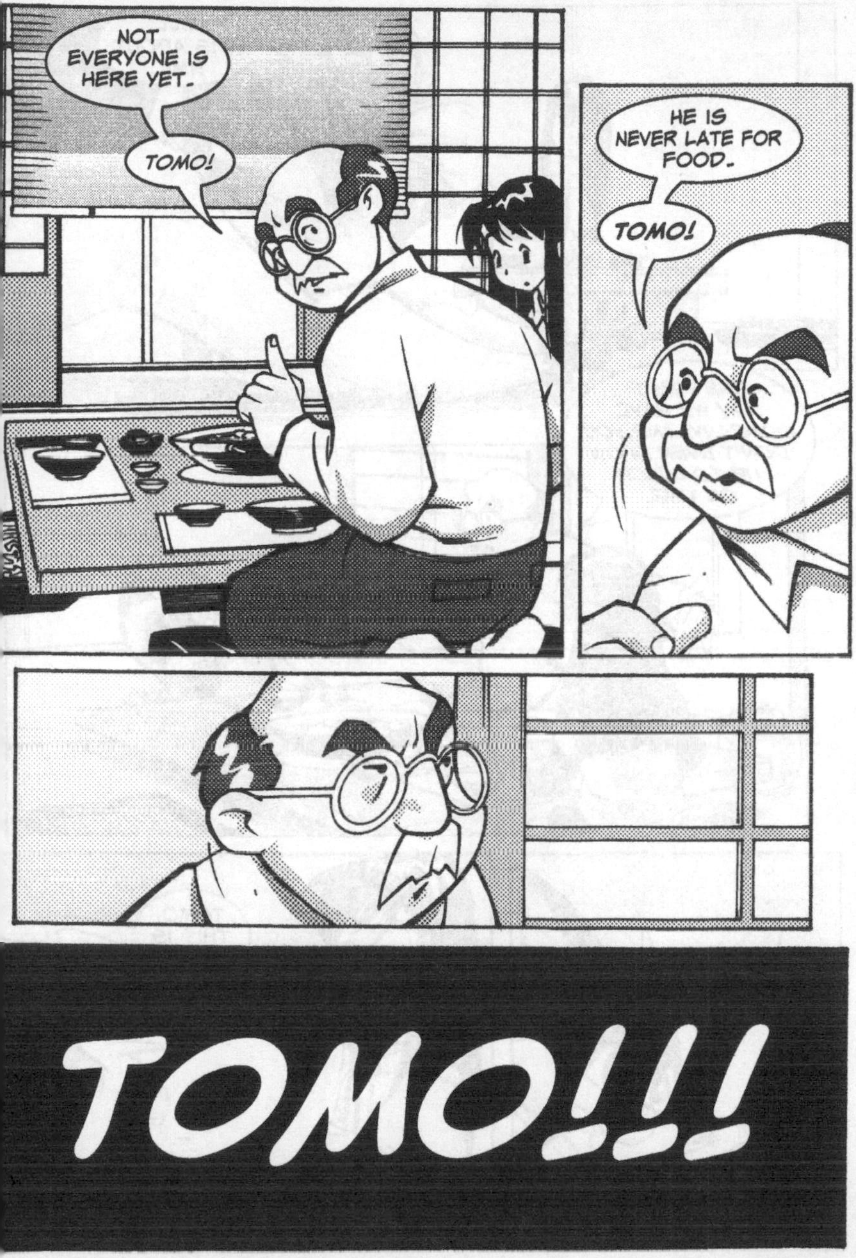
NOT EVERYONE IS HERE YET.
TOMO!
HE IS NEVER LATE FOR FOOD.
TOMO!
TOMO!!!

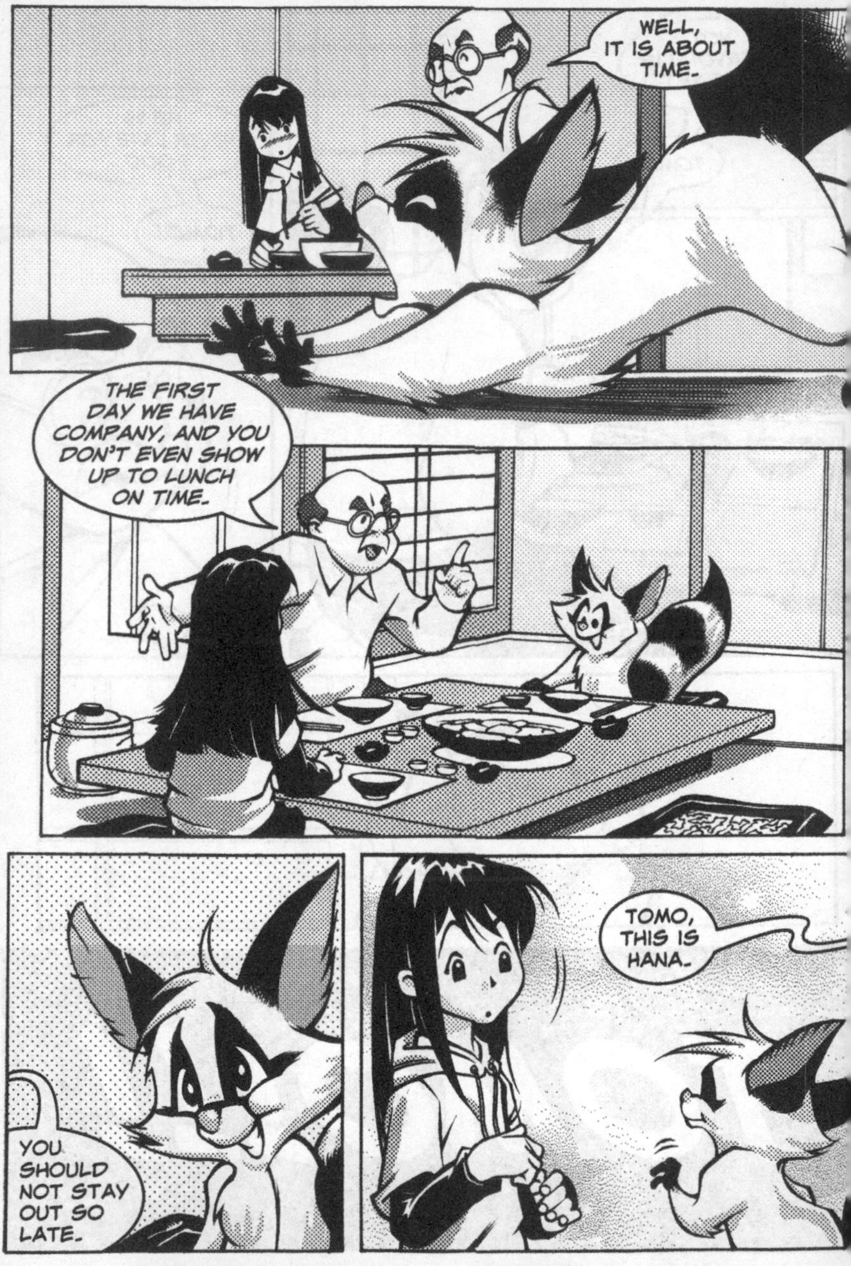
WELL, IT IS ABOUT TIME.
THE FIRST DAY WE HAVE COMPANY, AND YOU DON'T EVEN SHOW UP TO LUNCH ON TIME.
YOU SHOULD NOT STAY OUT SO LATE.
TOMO, THIS IS HANA.

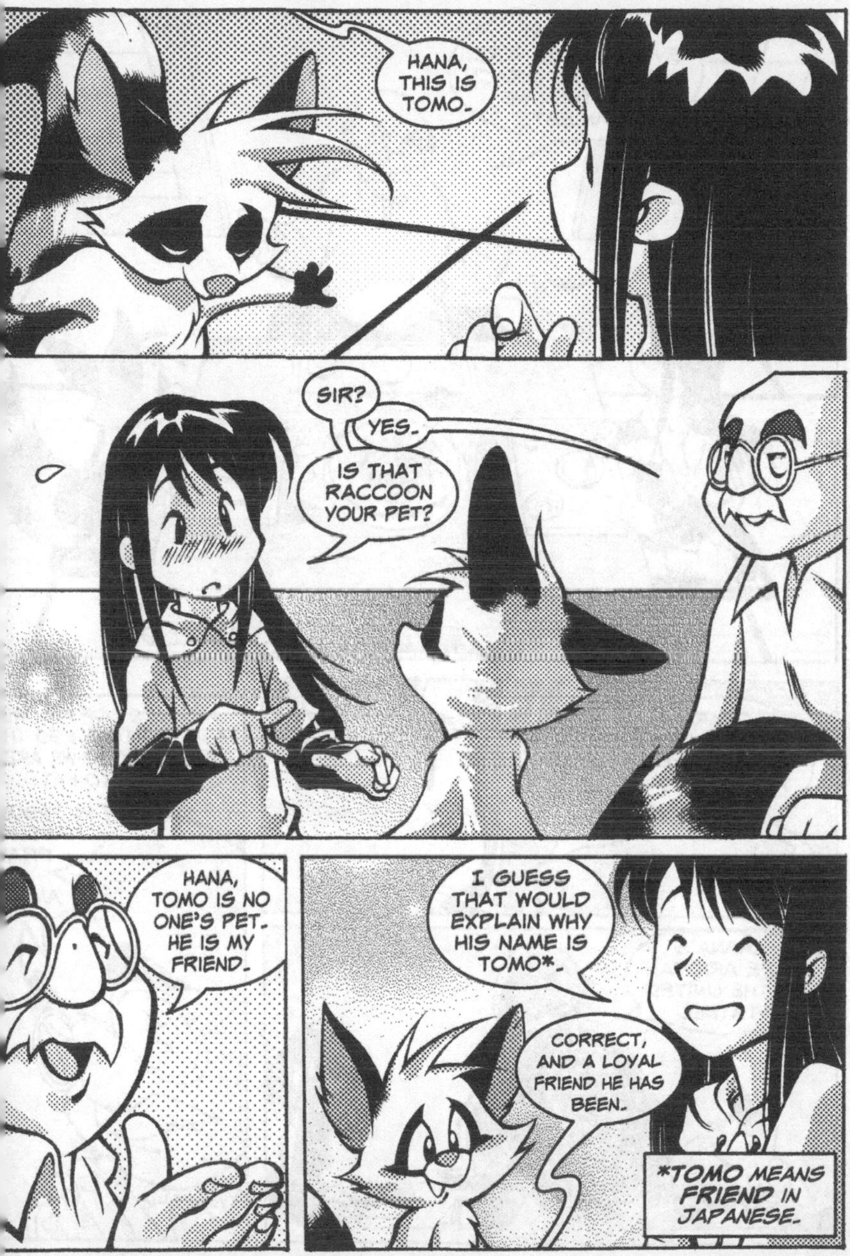
HANA, THIS IS TOMO.
SIR?
YES.
IS THAT RACCOON YOUR PET?
HANA, TOMO IS NO ONE'S PET. HE IS MY FRIEND.
I GUESS THAT WOULD EXPLAIN WHY HIS NAME IS TOMO*.
CORRECT, AND A LOYAL FRIEND HE HAS BEEN.
*TOMO MEANS FRIEND IN JAPANESE.

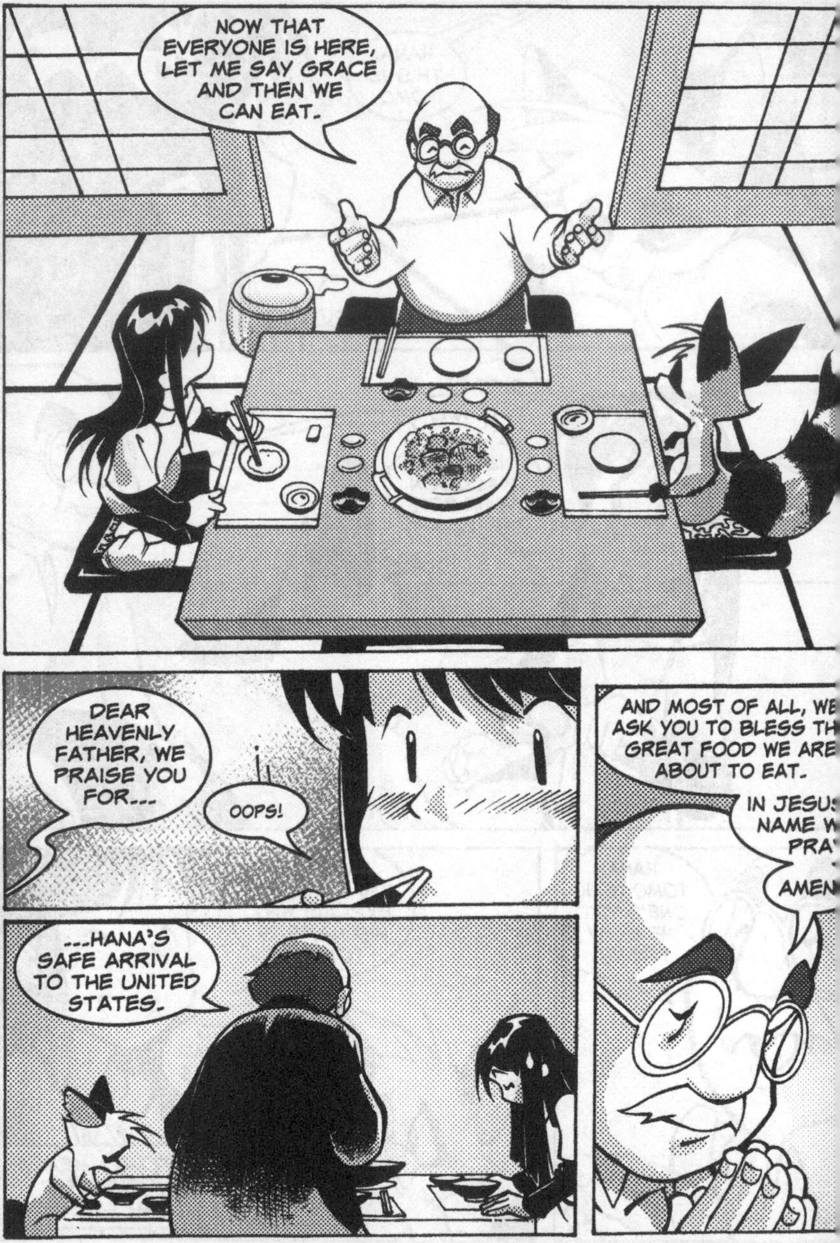
NOW THAT EVERYONE IS HERE, LET ME SAY GRACE AND THEN WE CAN EAT.
DEAR HEAVENLY FATHER, WE PRAISE YOU FOR...
OOPS!
...HANA'S SAFE ARRIVAL TO THE UNITED STATES.
AND MOST OF ALL, WE ASK YOU TO BLESS TH GREAT FOOD WE ARE ABOUT TO EAT.
IN JESUS NAME W PRA
AMEN

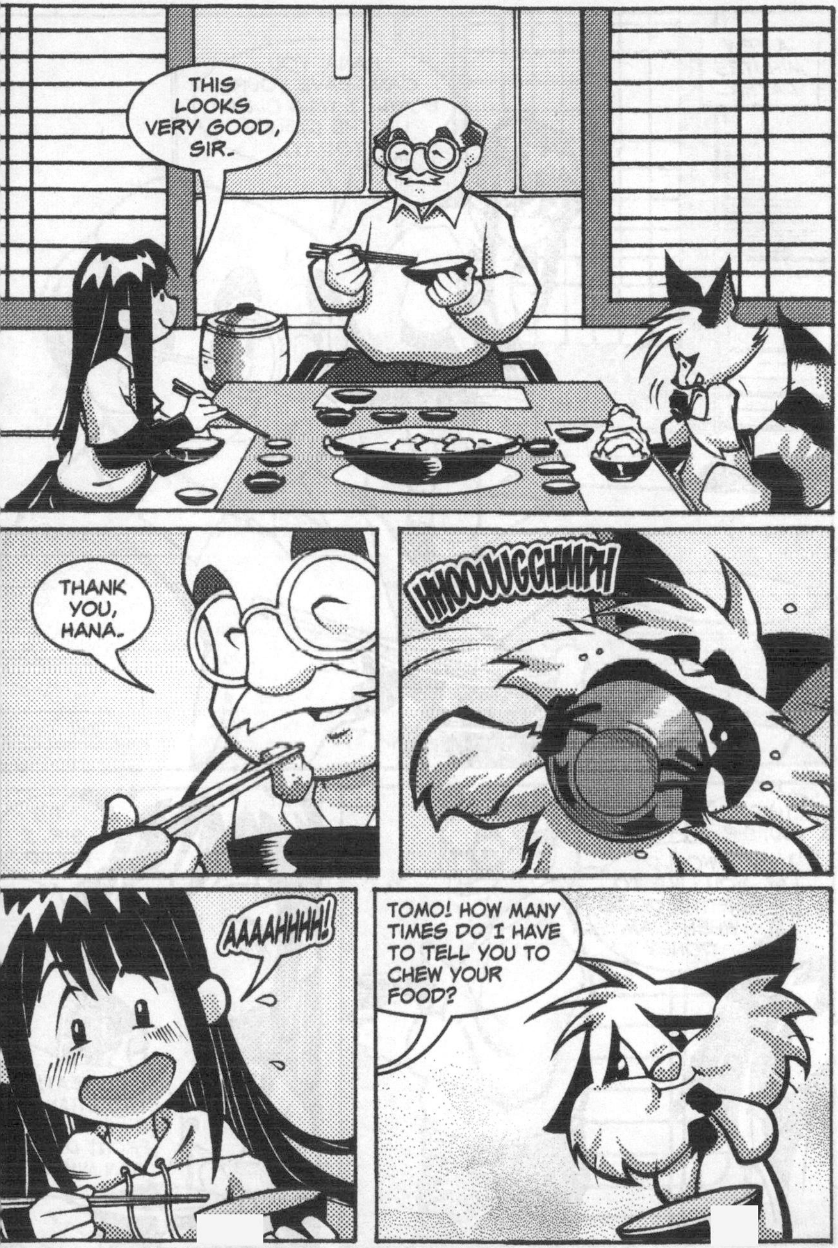
THIS LOOKS VERY GOOD, SIR.
THANK YOU, HANA.
HMOOOUGGHMPH
AAAAHHHH!
TOMO! HOW MANY TIMES DO I HAVE TO TELL YOU TO CHEW YOUR FOOD?

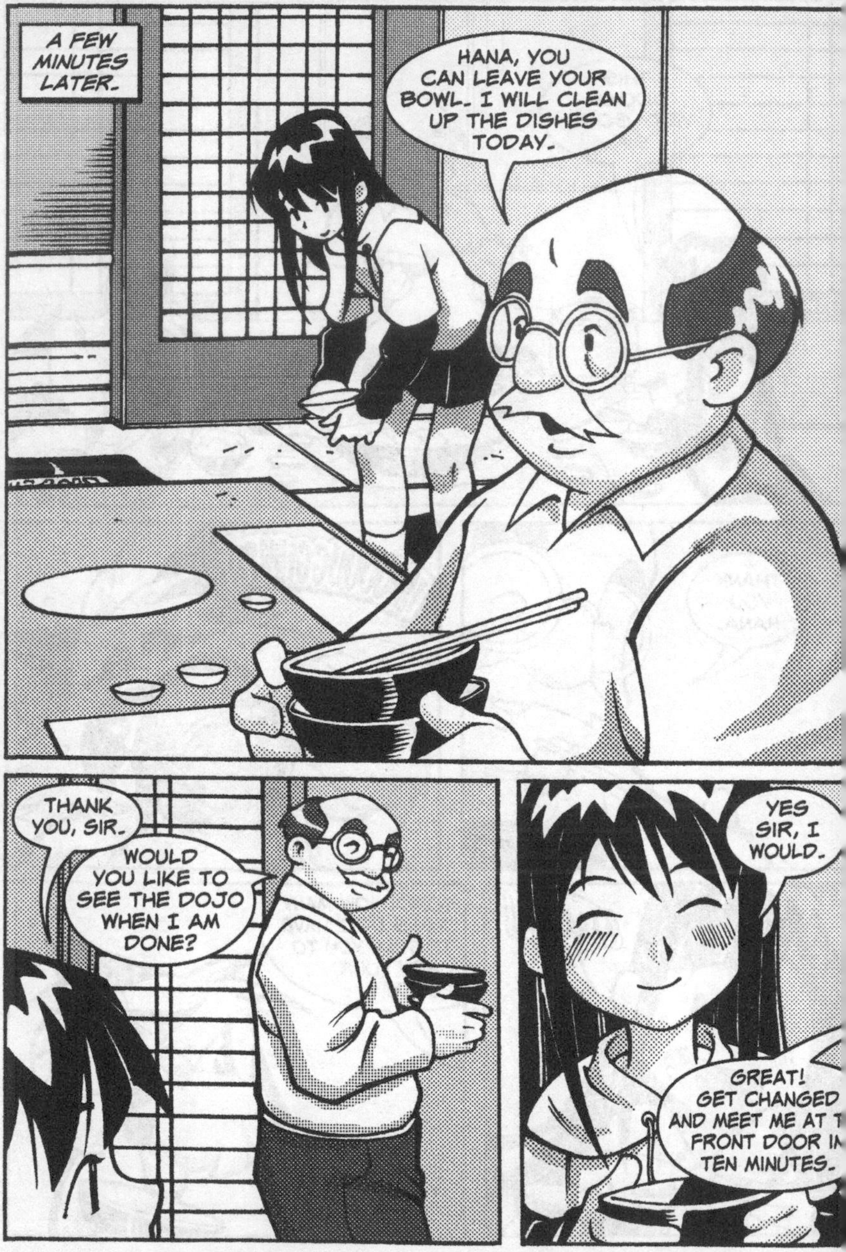
A FEW MINUTES LATER.
HANA, YOU CAN LEAVE YOUR BOWL. I WILL CLEAN UP THE DISHES TODAY.
THANK YOU, SIR.
WOULD YOU LIKE TO SEE THE DOJO WHEN I AM DONE?
YES SIR, I WOULD.
GREAT! GET CHANGED AND MEET ME AT T FRONT DOOR IN TEN MINUTES.

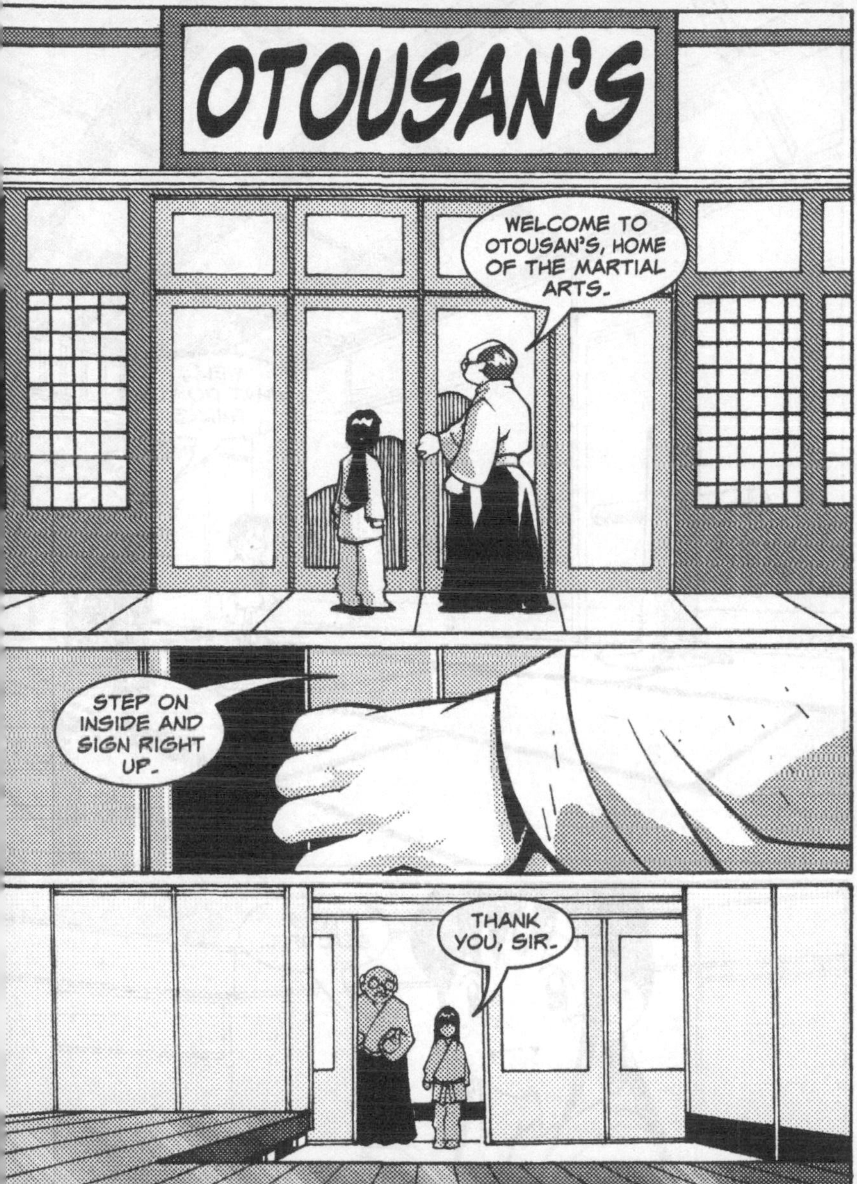
OTOUSAN'S
WELCOME TO OTOUSAN'S, HOME OF THE MARTIAL ARTS.
STEP ON INSIDE AND SIGN RIGHT UP.
THANK YOU, SIR.

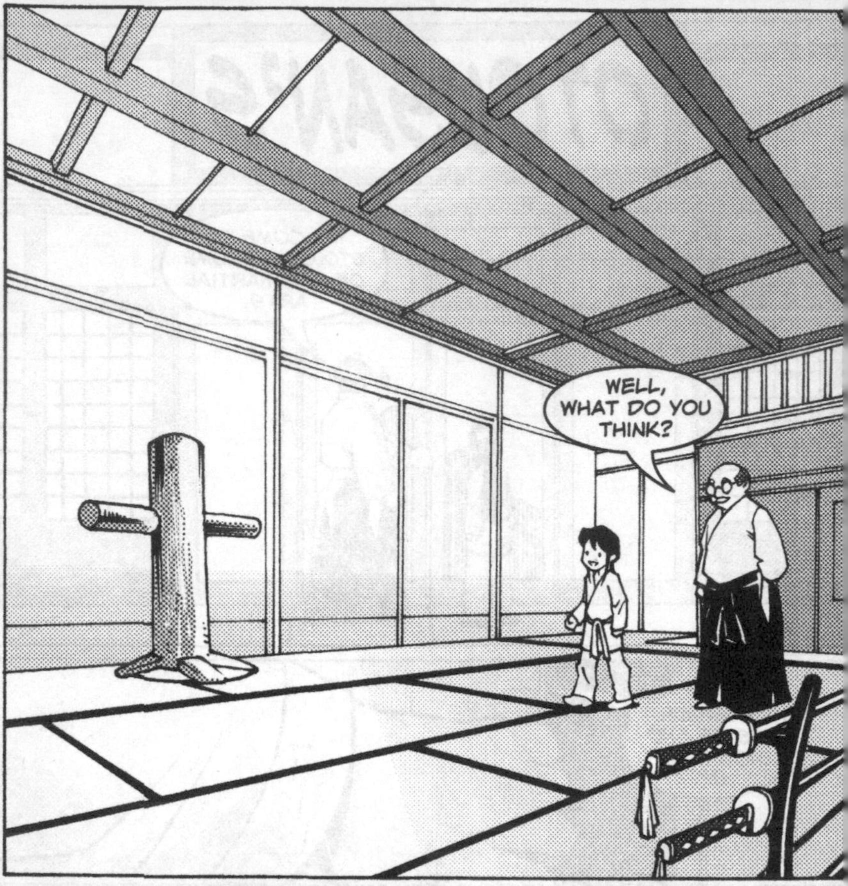
WELL, WHAT DO YOU THINK?

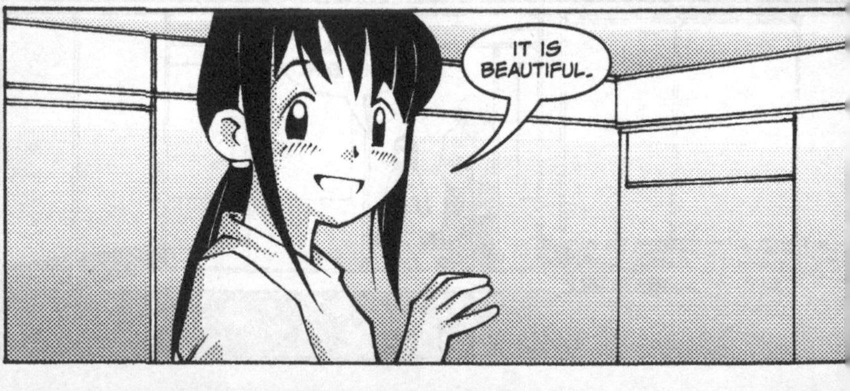
IT IS BEAUTIFUL.

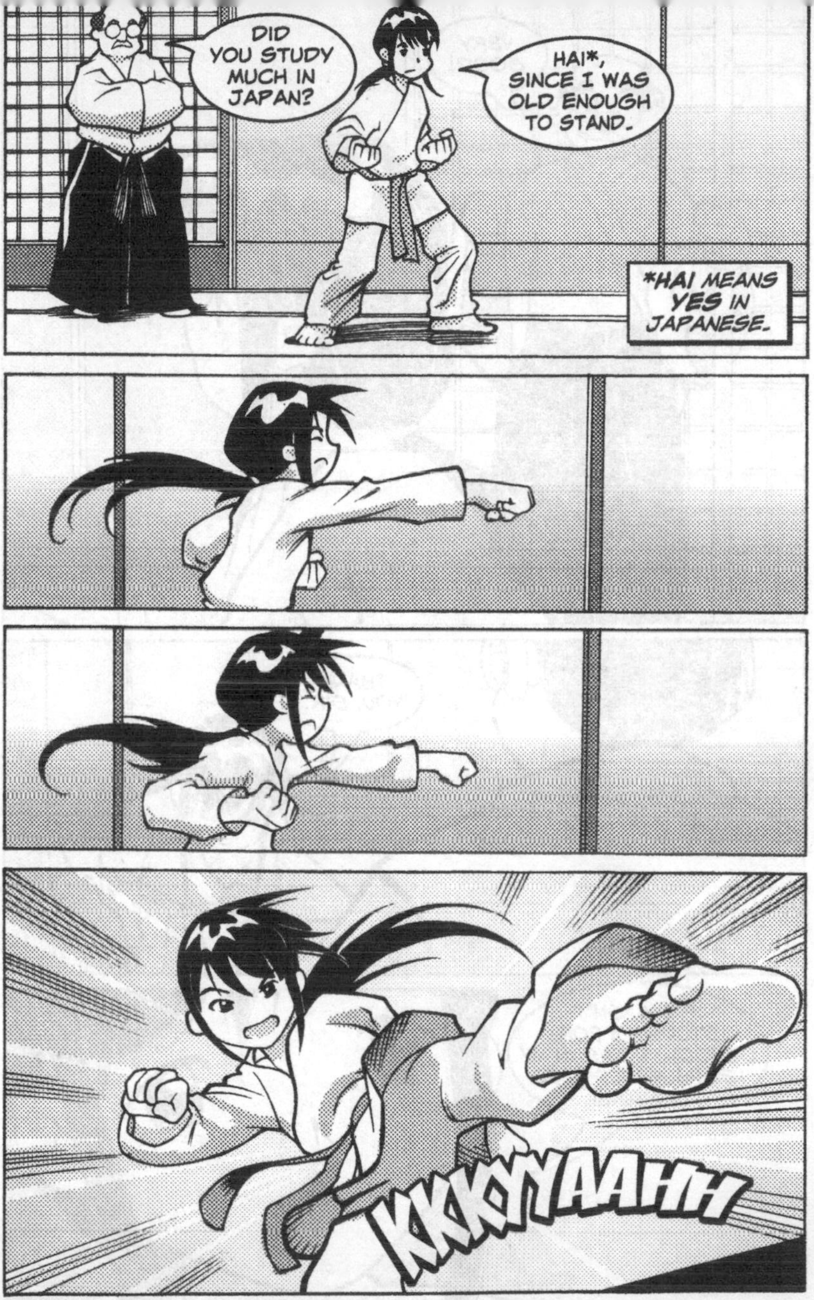
DID YOU STUDY MUCH IN JAPAN?
HAI*, SINCE I WAS OLD ENOUGH TO STAND.
*HAI MEANS YES IN JAPANESE.
KKKYYAAHH

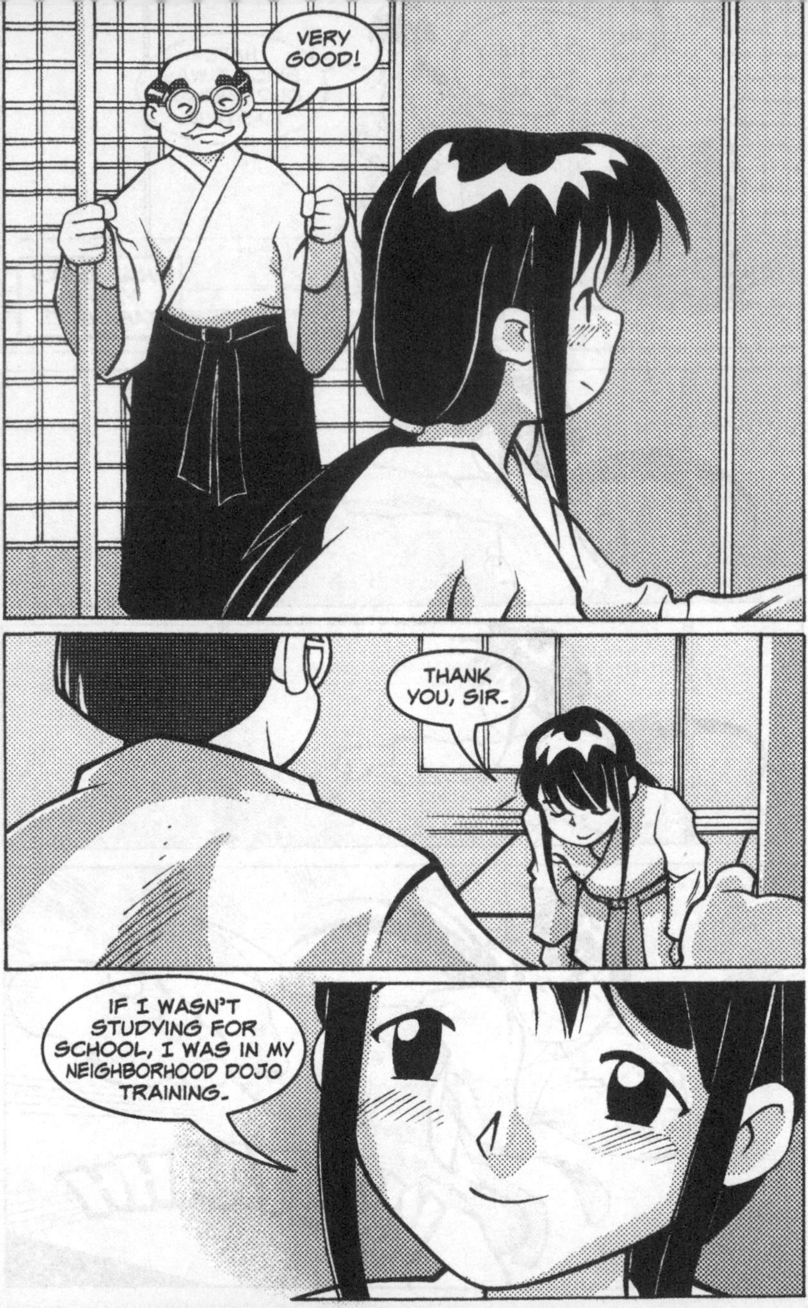
VERY GOOD!
THANK YOU, SIR.
IF I WASN'T STUDYING FOR SCHOOL, I WAS IN MY NEIGHBORHOOD DOJO TRAINING.

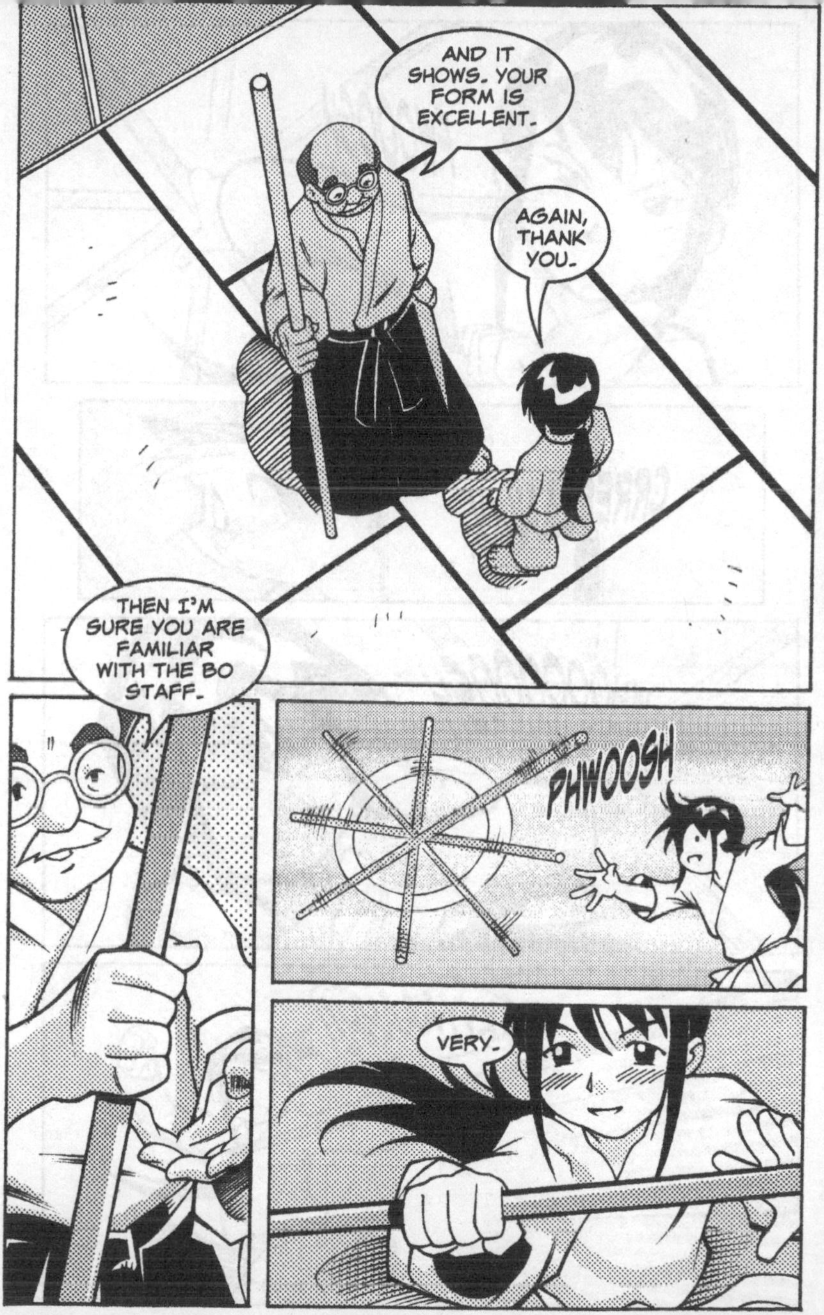
AND IT SHOWS. YOUR FORM IS EXCELLENT.
AGAIN, THANK YOU.
THEN I'M SURE YOU ARE FAMILIAR WITH THE BO STAFF.
PHWOOSH
VERY.

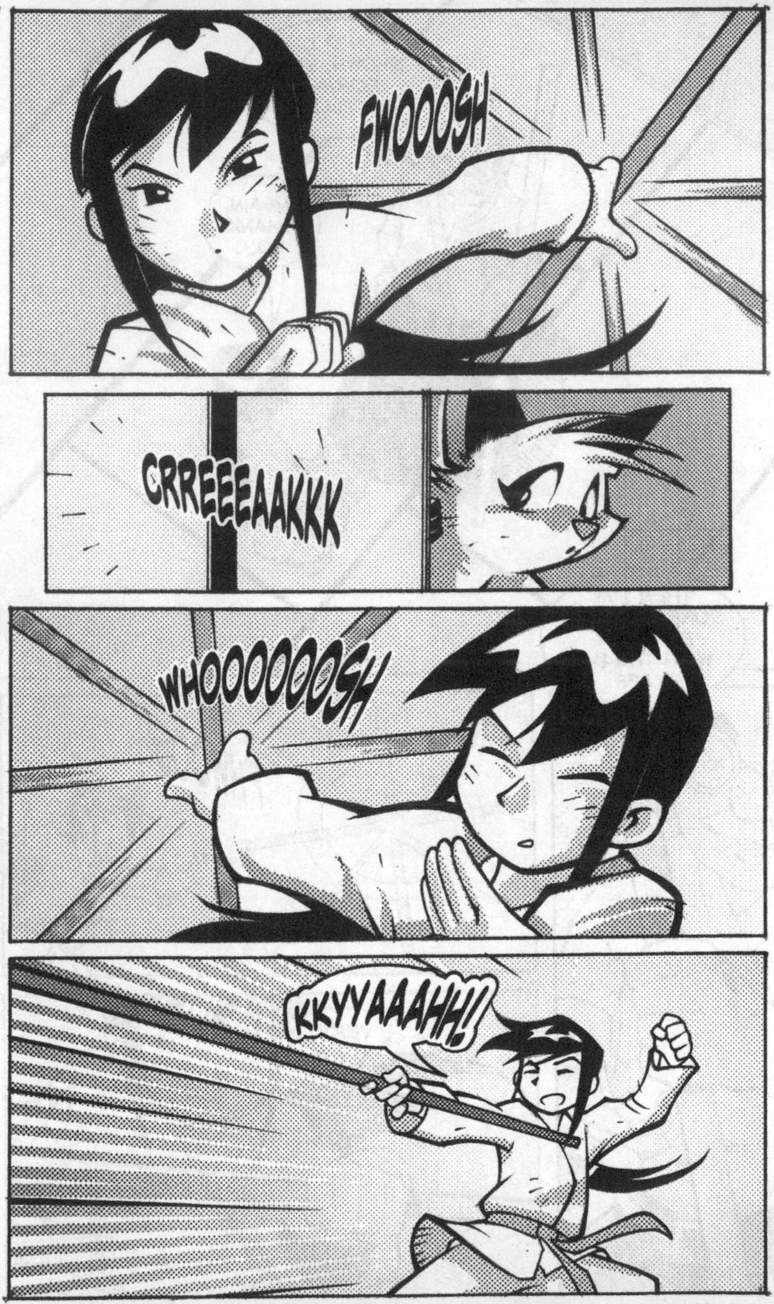
FWOOOSH
CRREEEAAKKK
WHOOOOOOSH
KKYYAAAHH!!

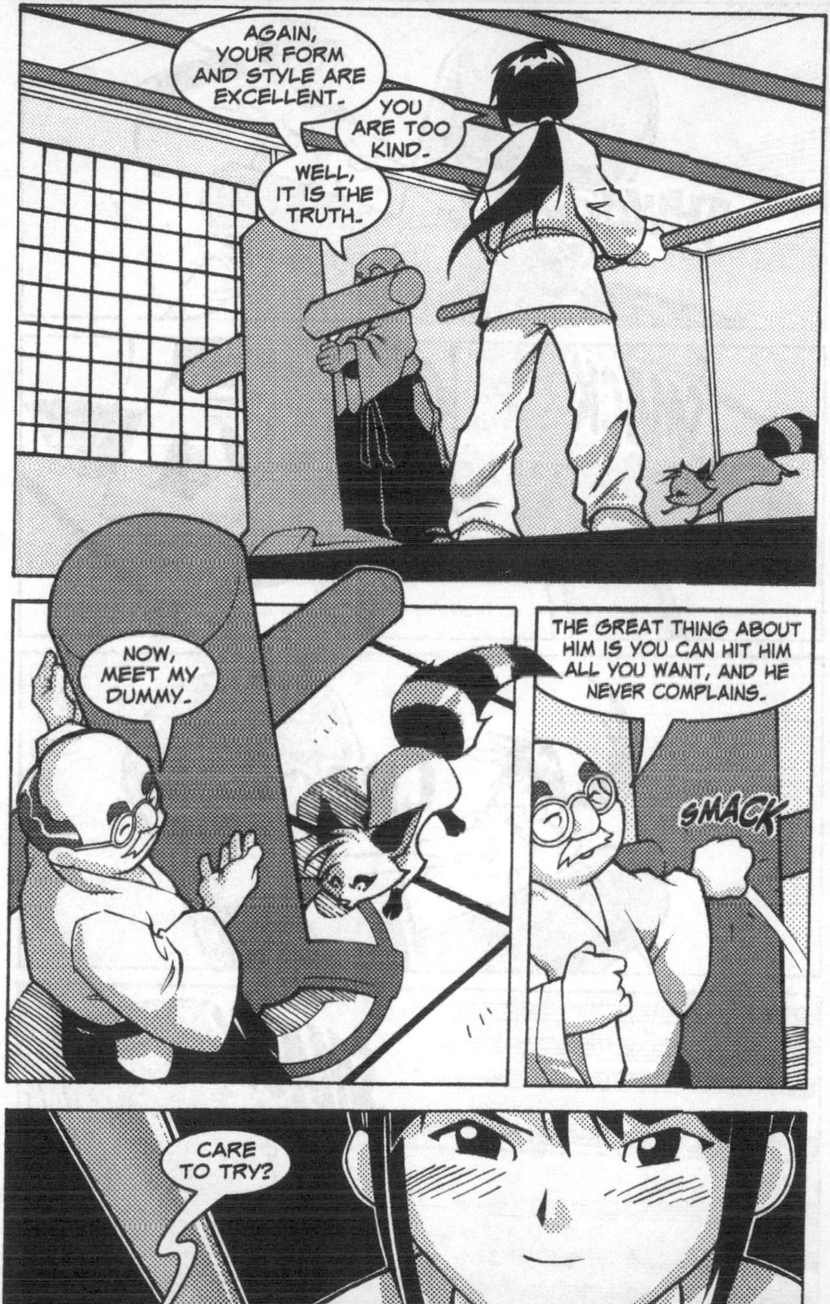
AGAIN, YOUR FORM AND STYLE ARE EXCELLENT.
YOU ARE TOO KIND.
WELL, IT IS THE TRUTH.
NOW, MEET MY DUMMY.
THE GREAT THING ABOUT HIM IS YOU CAN HIT HIM ALL YOU WANT, AND HE NEVER COMPLAINS.
SMACK
CARE TO TRY?

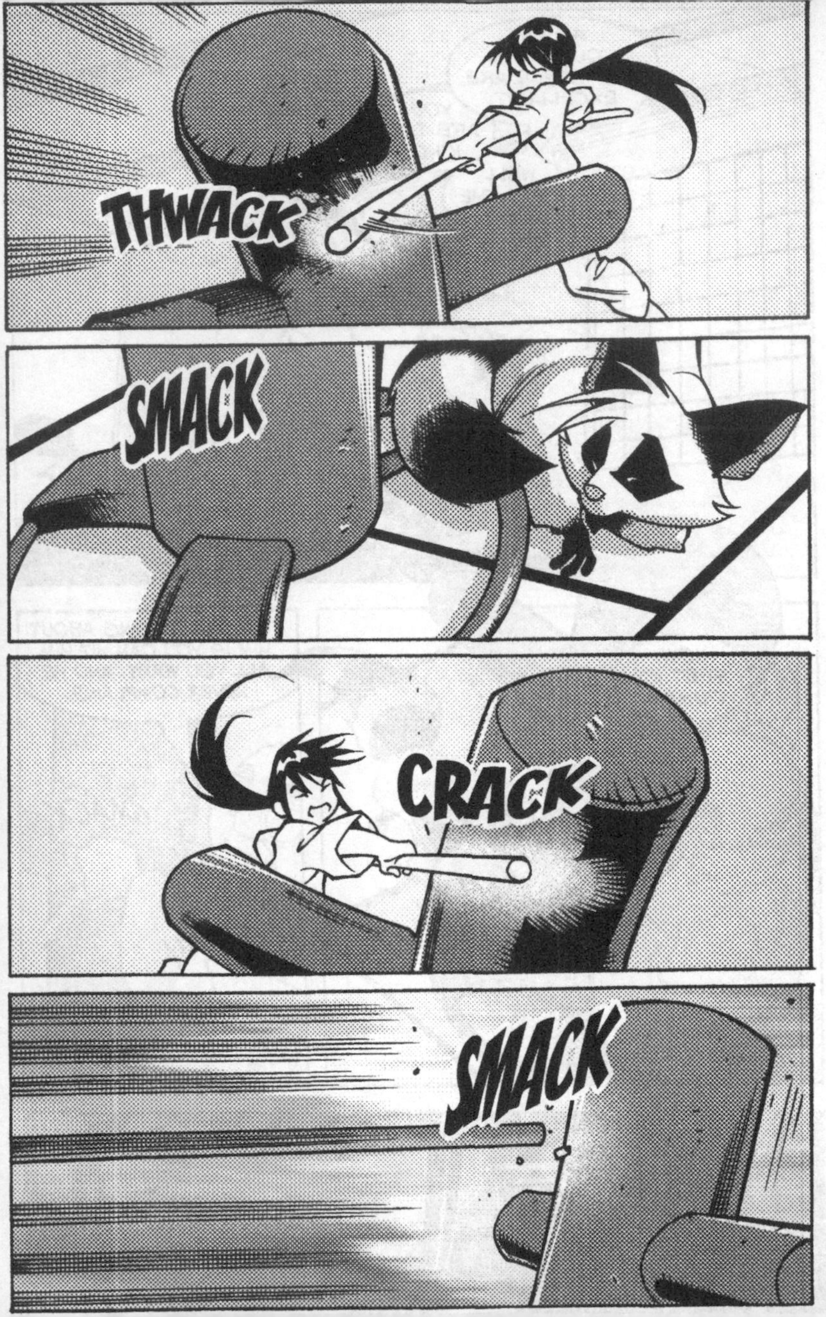
THWACK
SMACK
CRACK
SMACK

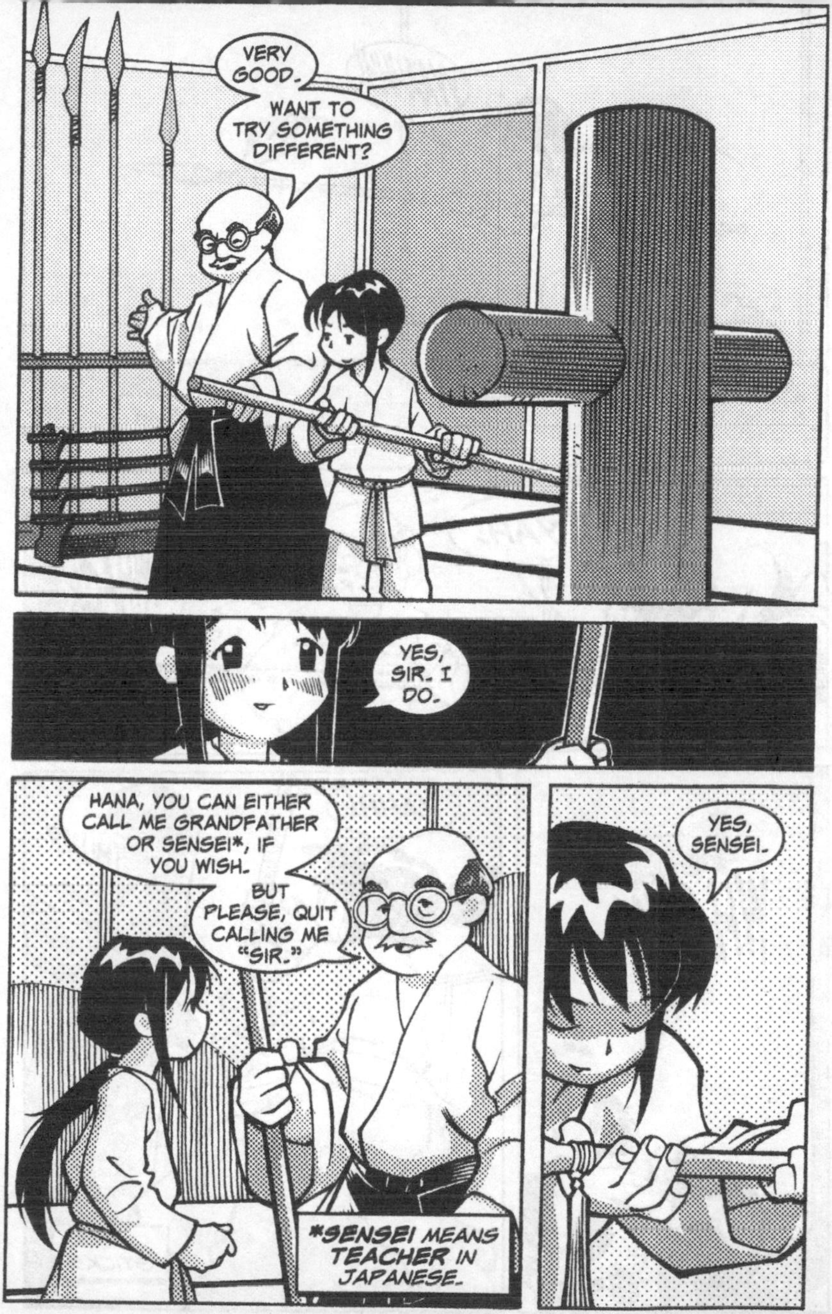
VERY GOOD.
WANT TO TRY SOMETHING DIFFERENT?
YES, SIR. I DO.
HANA, YOU CAN EITHER CALL ME GRANDFATHER OR SENSEI*, IF YOU WISH.
BUT PLEASE, QUIT CALLING ME "SIR."
*SENSEI MEANS TEACHER IN JAPANESE.
YES, SENSEI.

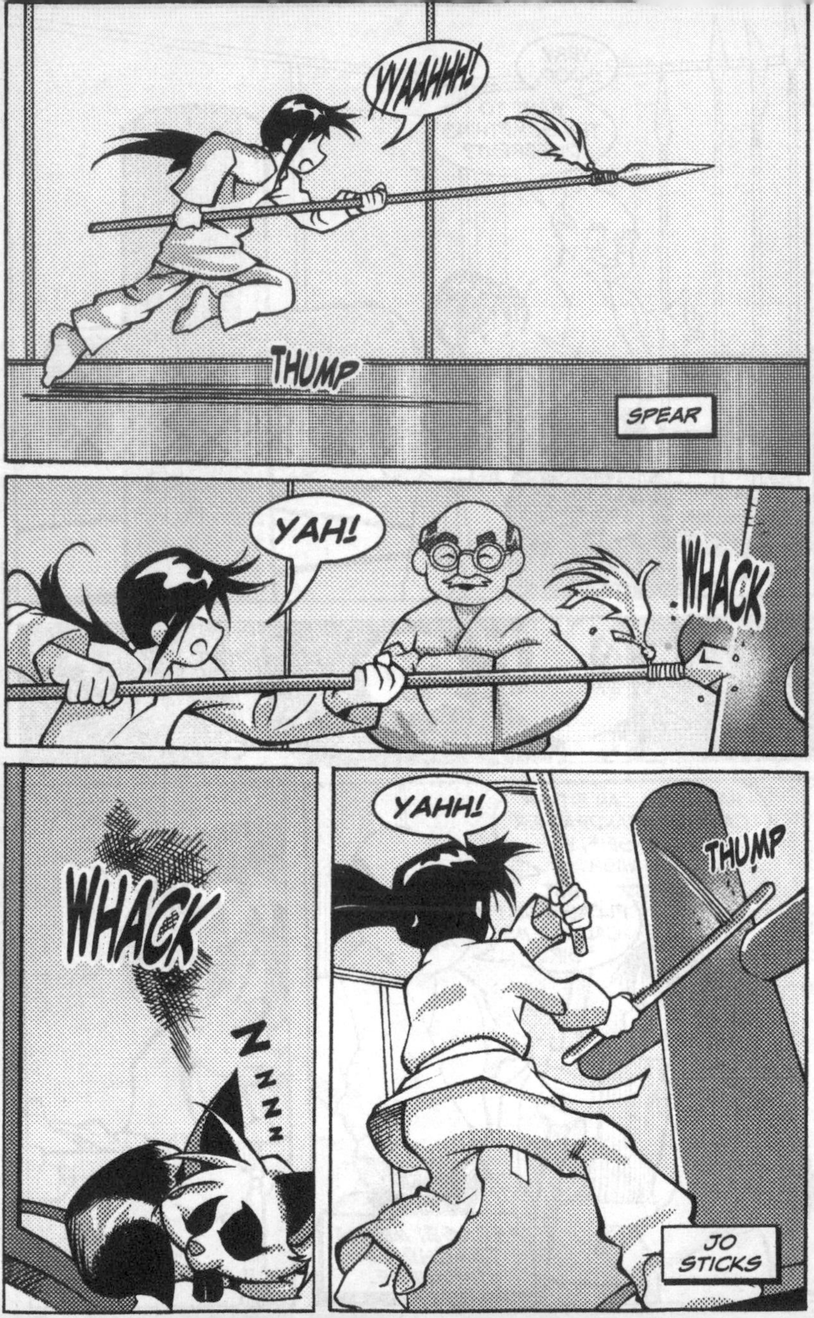
YYAAHHH!
THUMP
SPEAR
YAH!
WHACK
WHACK
Z
Z Z Z Z
YAHH!
THUMP
JO STICKS

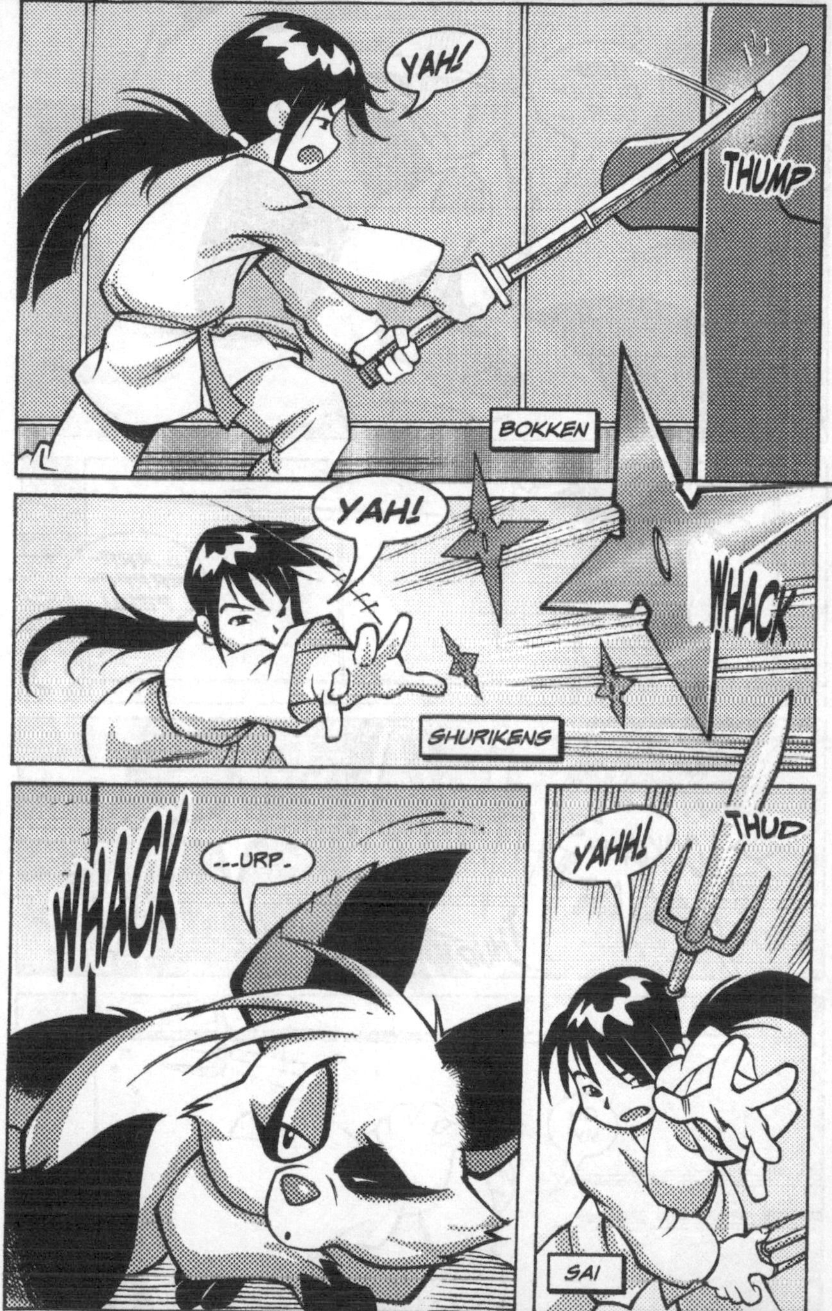
YAH!
THUMP
BOKKEN
YAH!
WHACK
SHURIKENS
WHACK
---URP-
YAHH!
THUD
SAI

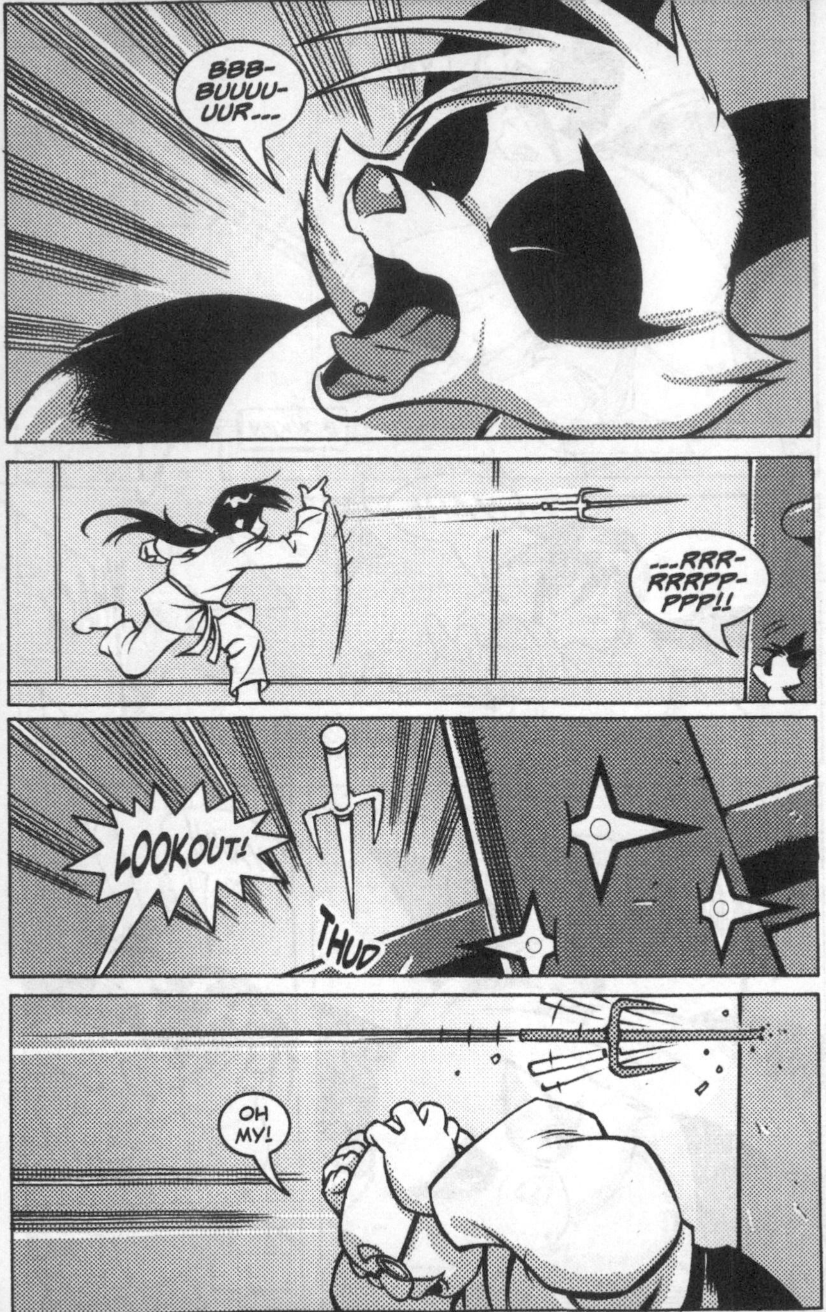
BBB-
BUUUU-
UUR---
---RRR-
RRRPP-
PPP!!
LOOKOUT!
THUD
OH
MY!

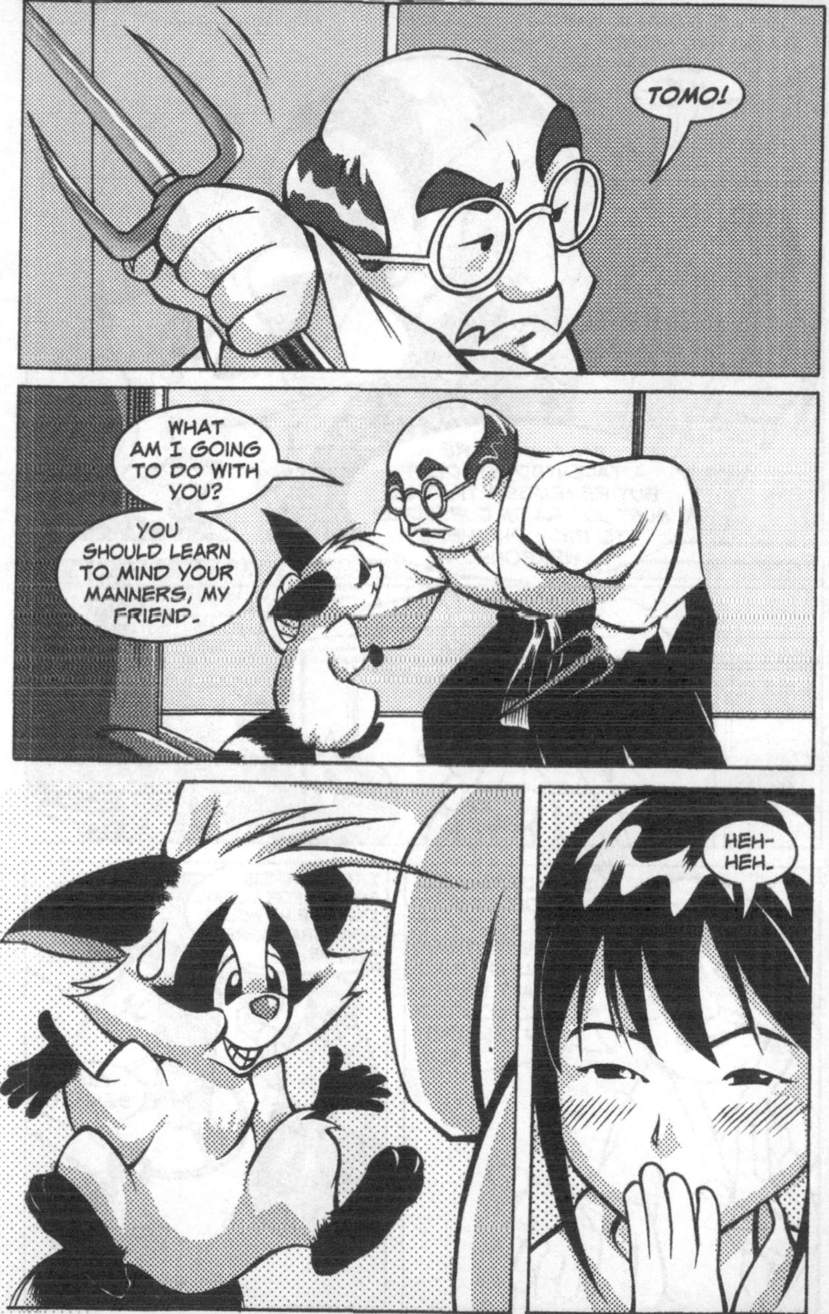
TOMO!
WHAT AM I GOING TO DO WITH YOU?
YOU SHOULD LEARN TO MIND YOUR MANNERS, MY FRIEND.
HEH-HEH.

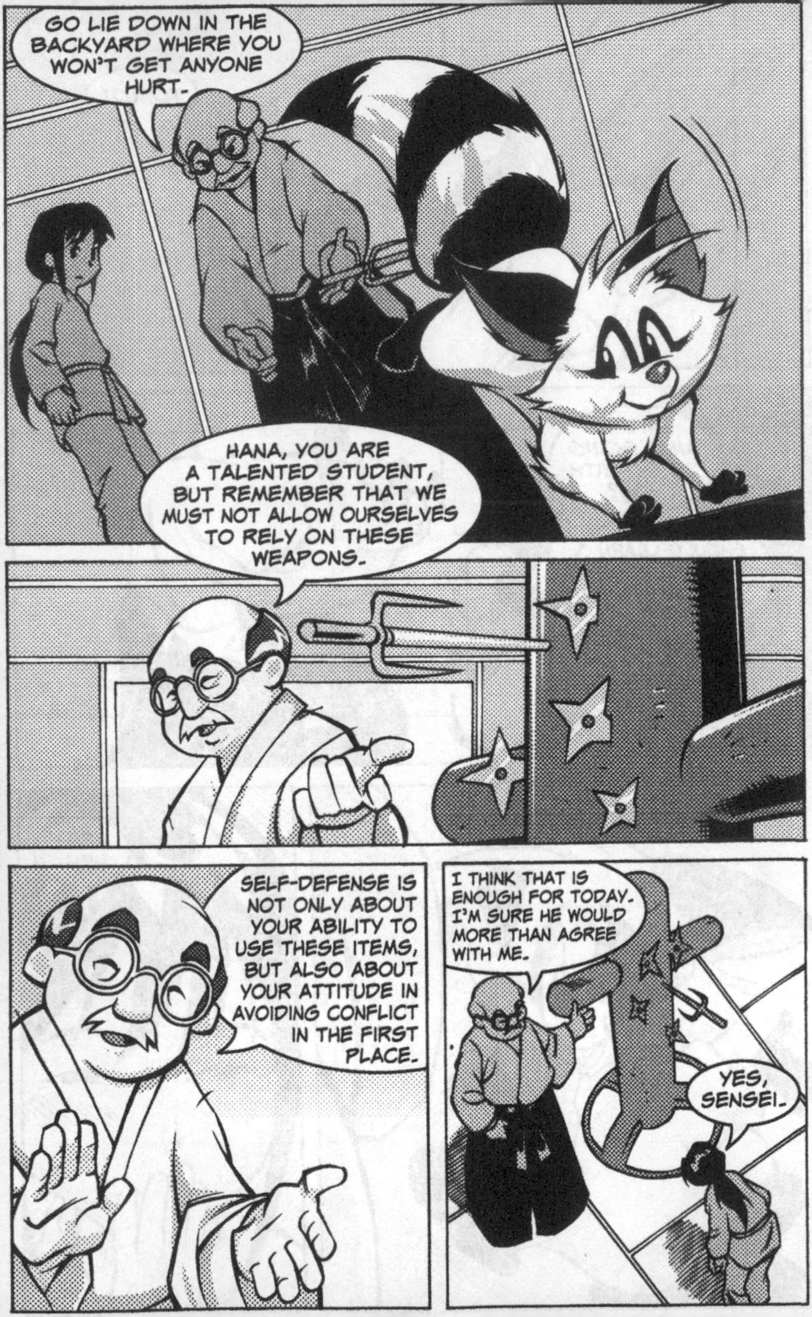
GO LIE DOWN IN THE BACKYARD WHERE YOU WON'T GET ANYONE HURT.
HANA, YOU ARE A TALENTED STUDENT, BUT REMEMBER THAT WE MUST NOT ALLOW OURSELVES TO RELY ON THESE WEAPONS.
SELF-DEFENSE IS NOT ONLY ABOUT YOUR ABILITY TO USE THESE ITEMS, BUT ALSO ABOUT YOUR ATTITUDE IN AVOIDING CONFLICT IN THE FIRST PLACE.
I THINK THAT IS ENOUGH FOR TODAY. I'M SURE HE WOULD MORE THAN AGREE WITH ME.
YES, SENSEI.

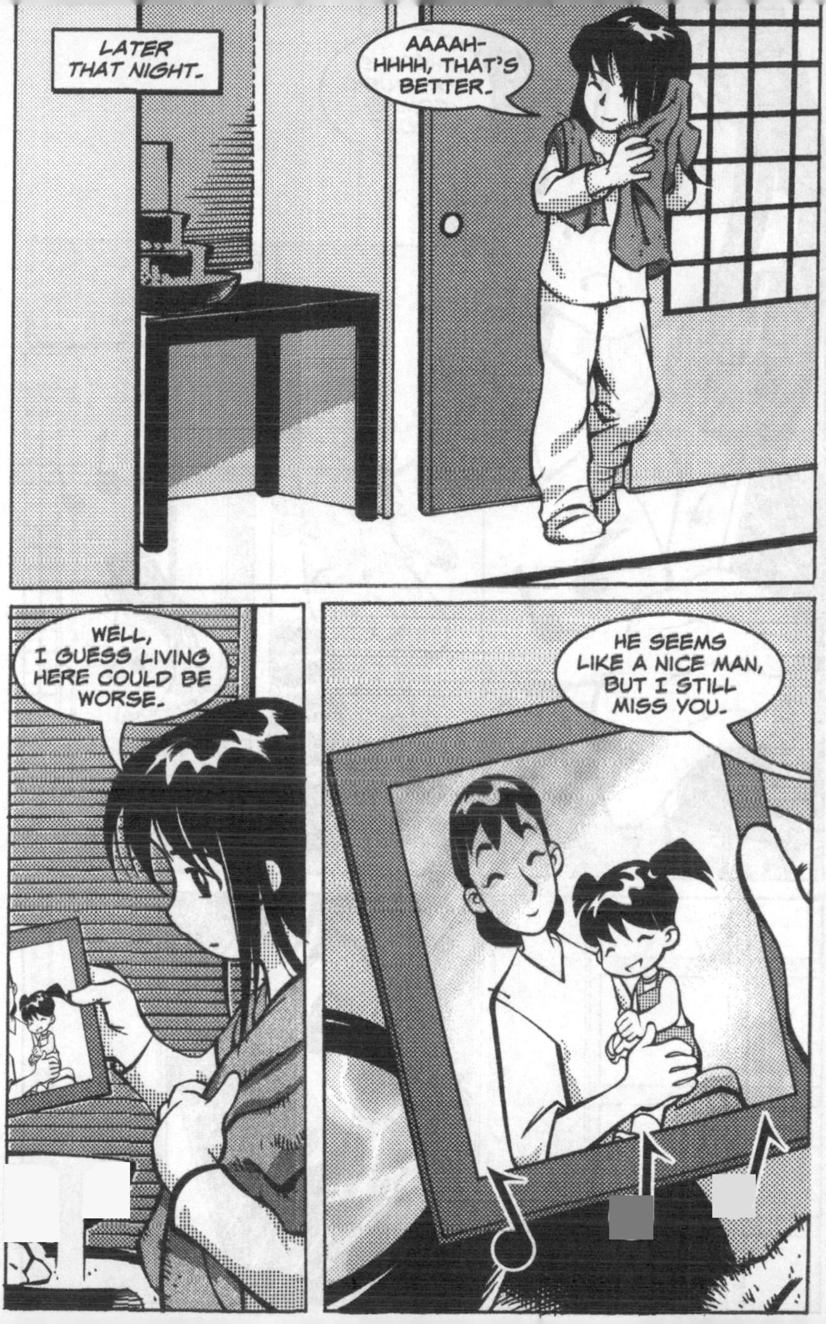
LATER THAT NIGHT...
AAAAH-HHHH, THAT'S BETTER...
WELL, I GUESS LIVING HERE COULD BE WORSE...
HE SEEMS LIKE A NICE MAN, BUT I STILL MISS YOU...

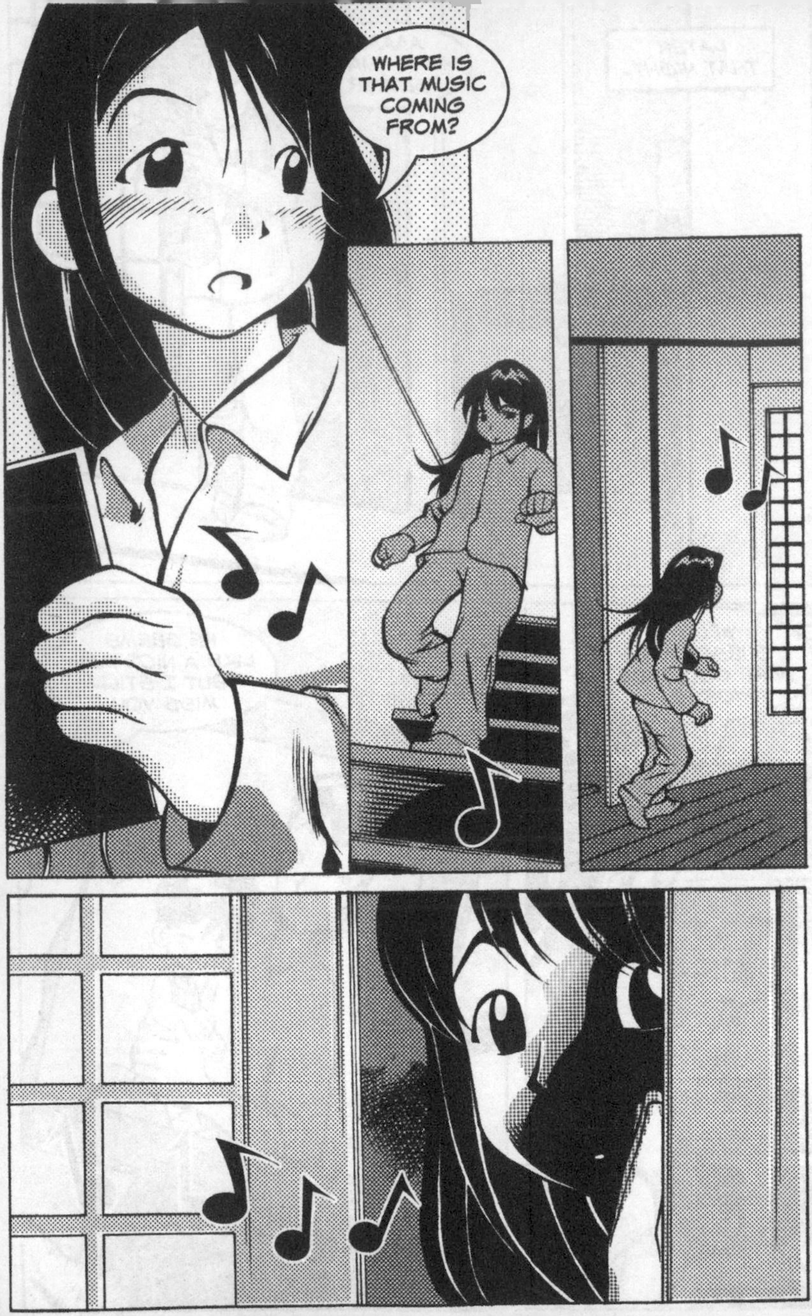
WHERE IS THAT MUSIC COMING FROM?

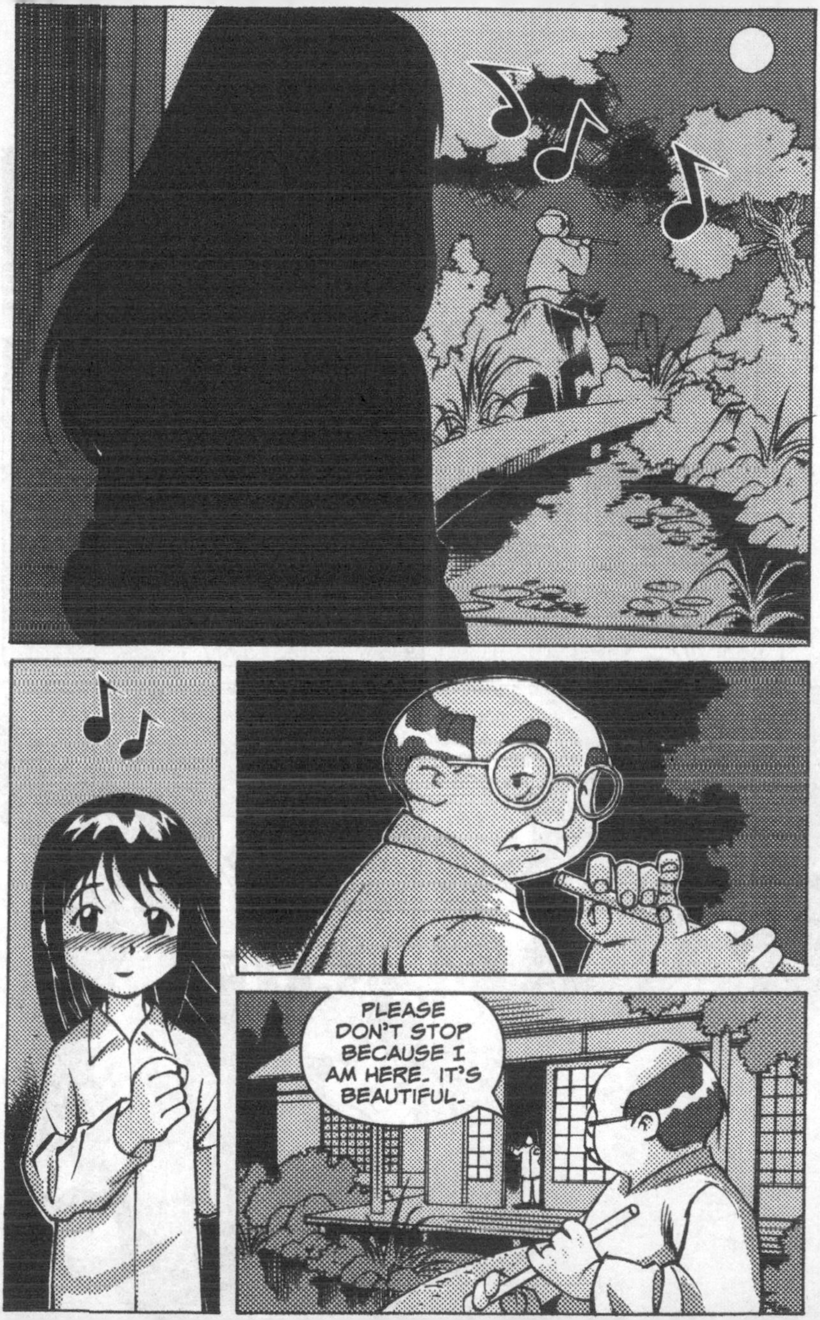
PLEASE DON'T STOP BECAUSE I AM HERE. IT'S BEAUTIFUL.

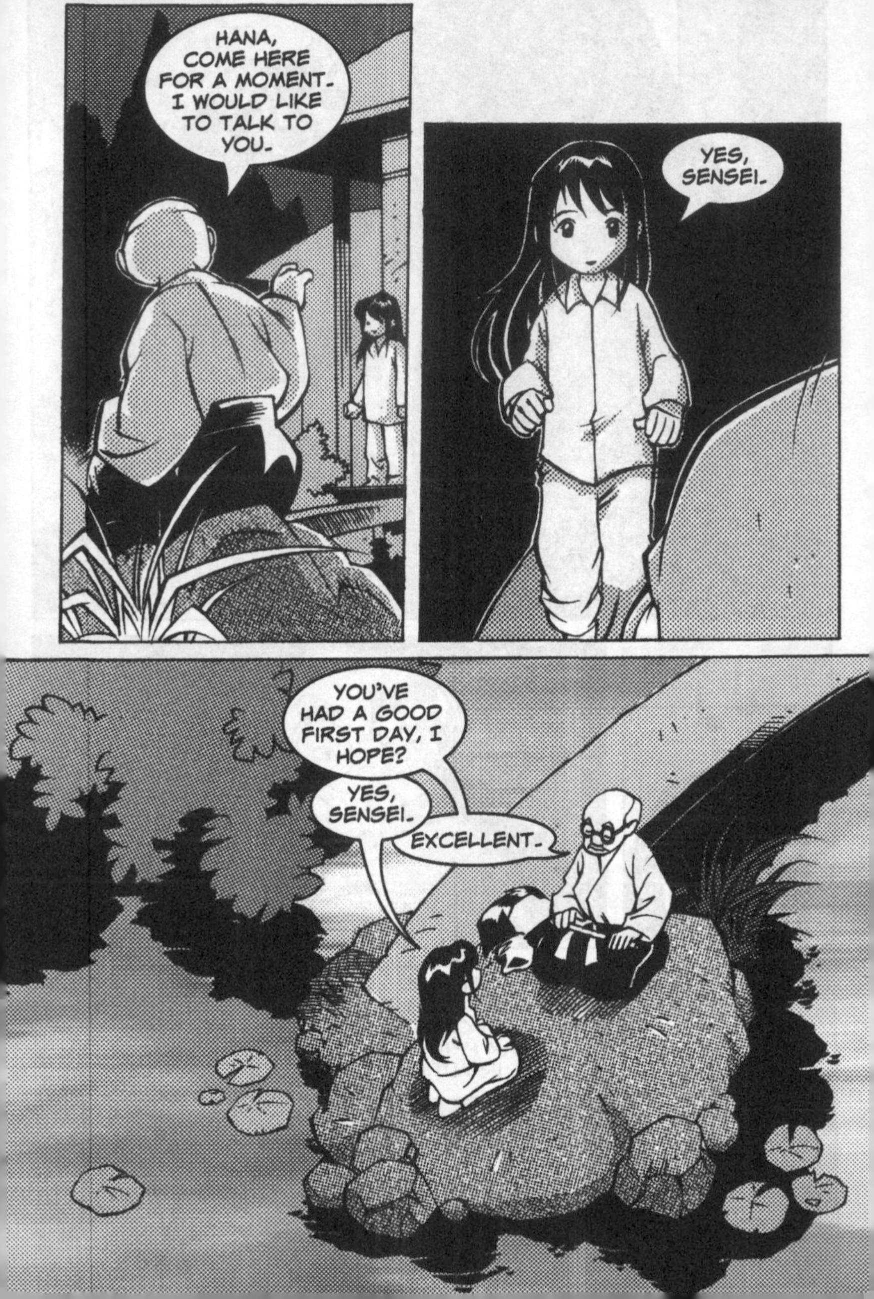
HANA, COME HERE FOR A MOMENT. I WOULD LIKE TO TALK TO YOU.
YES, SENSEI.
YOU'VE HAD A GOOD FIRST DAY, I HOPE?
YES, SENSEI.
EXCELLENT.

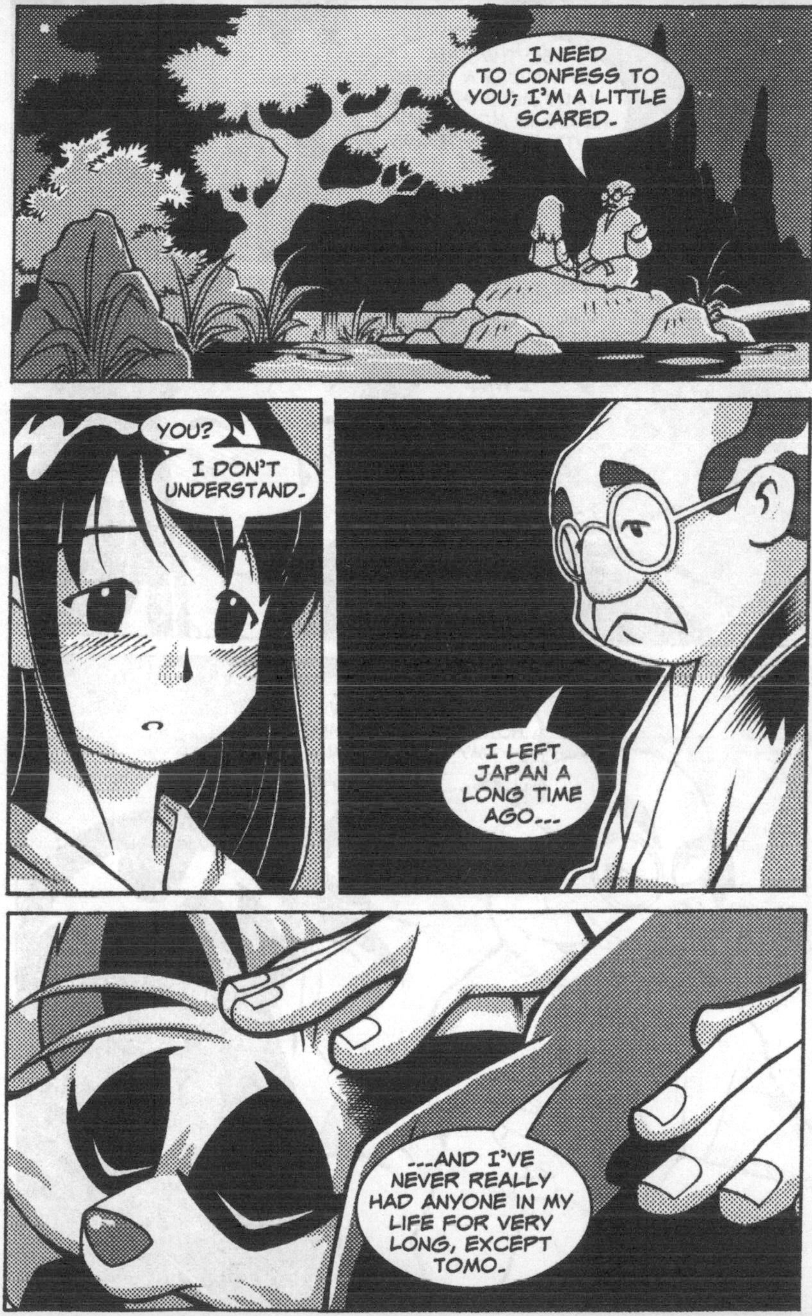
I NEED TO CONFESS TO YOU; I'M A LITTLE SCARED.
YOU?
I DON'T UNDERSTAND.
I LEFT JAPAN A LONG TIME AGO...
...AND I'VE NEVER REALLY HAD ANYONE IN MY LIFE FOR VERY LONG, EXCEPT TOMO.

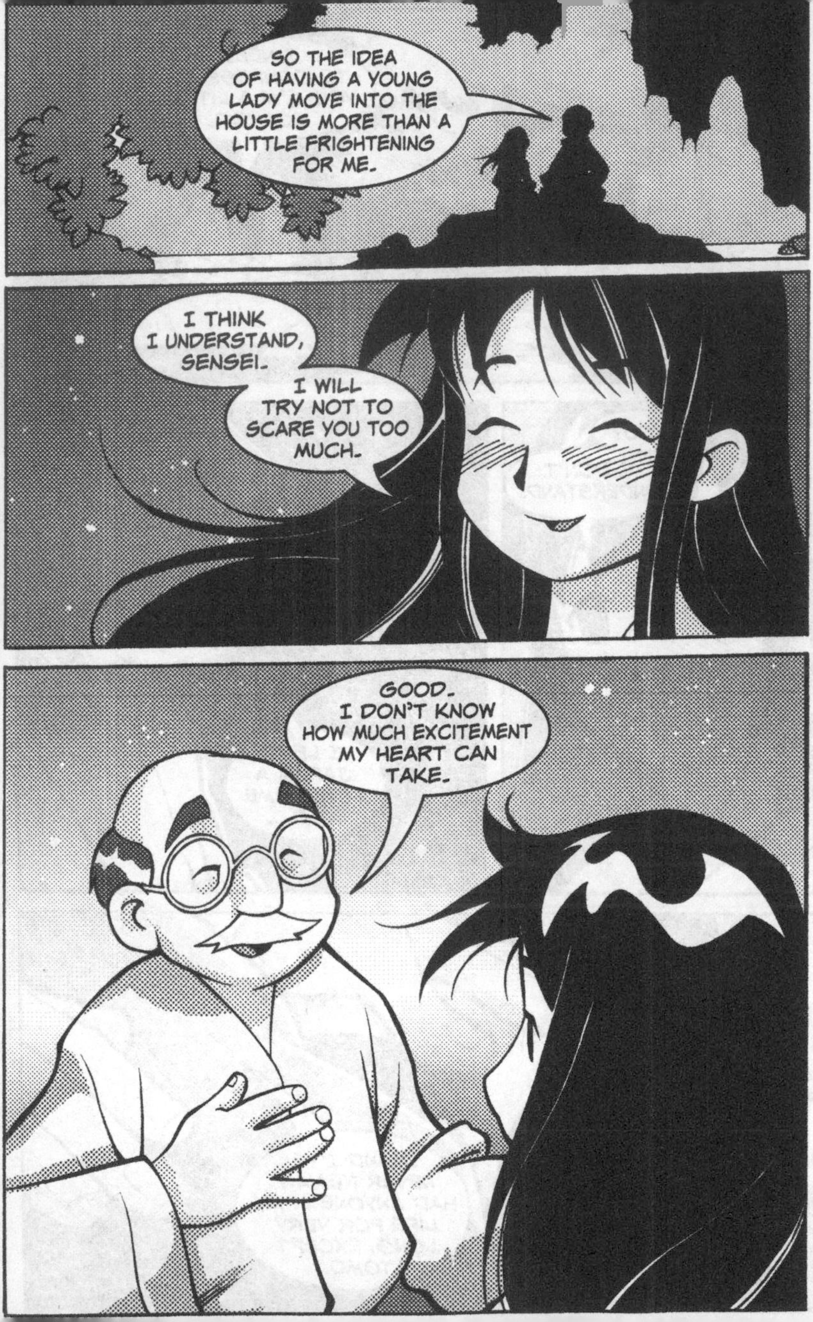
SO THE IDEA OF HAVING A YOUNG LADY MOVE INTO THE HOUSE IS MORE THAN A LITTLE FRIGHTENING FOR ME.
I THINK I UNDERSTAND, SENSEI.
I WILL TRY NOT TO SCARE YOU TOO MUCH.
GOOD. I DON'T KNOW HOW MUCH EXCITEMENT MY HEART CAN TAKE.

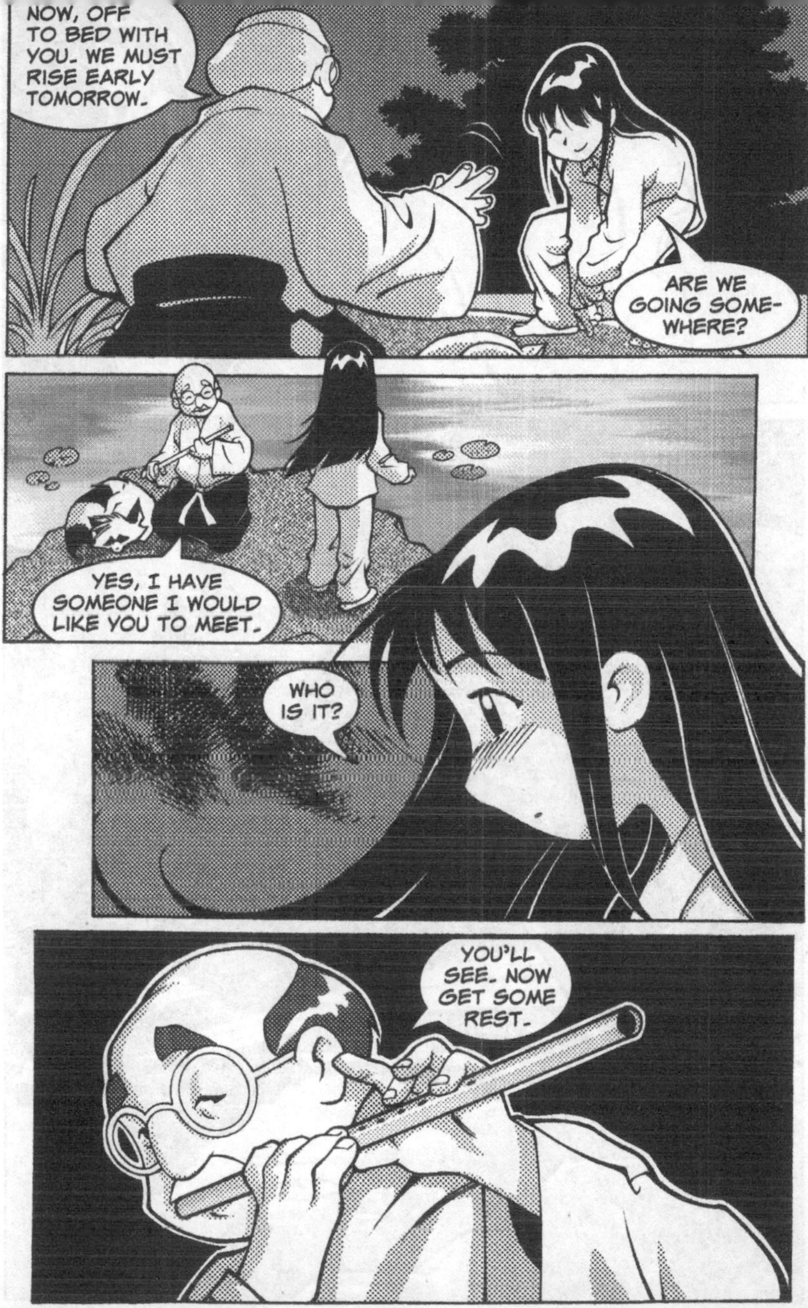
NOW, OFF TO BED WITH YOU. WE MUST RISE EARLY TOMORROW.
ARE WE GOING SOME-WHERE?
YES, I HAVE SOMEONE I WOULD LIKE YOU TO MEET.
WHO IS IT?
YOU'LL SEE. NOW GET SOME REST.

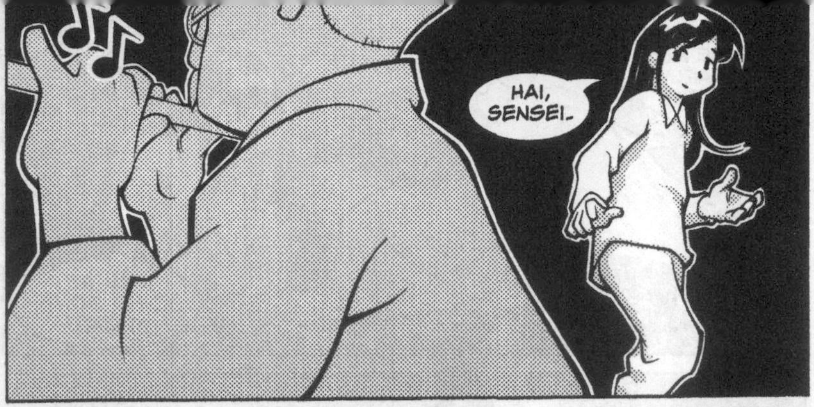
HAI, SENSEI.
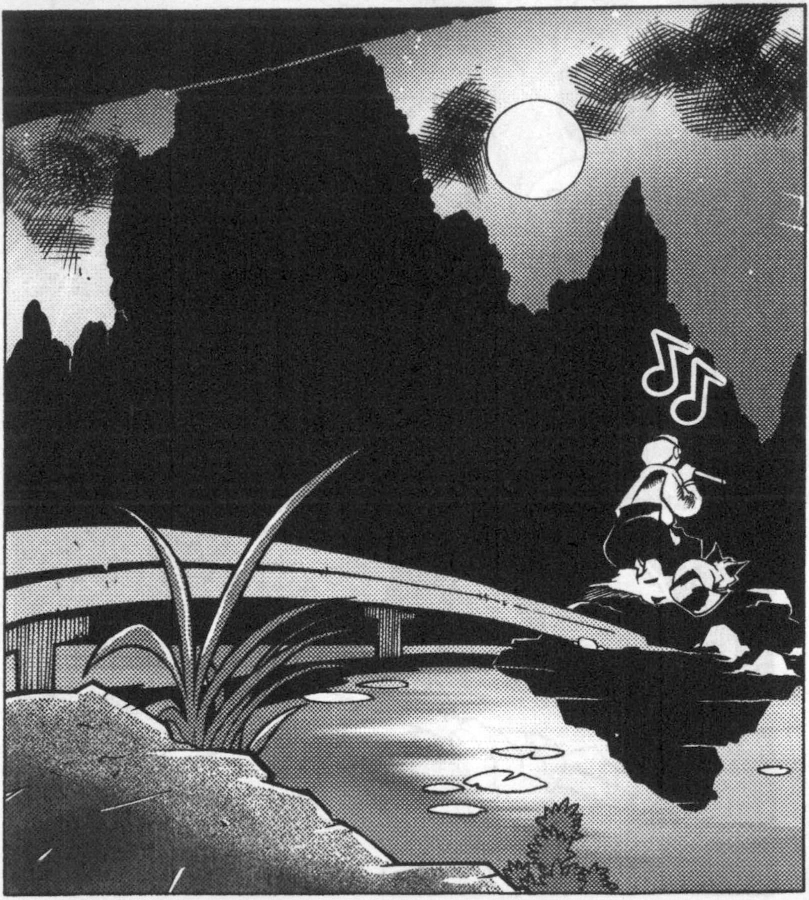

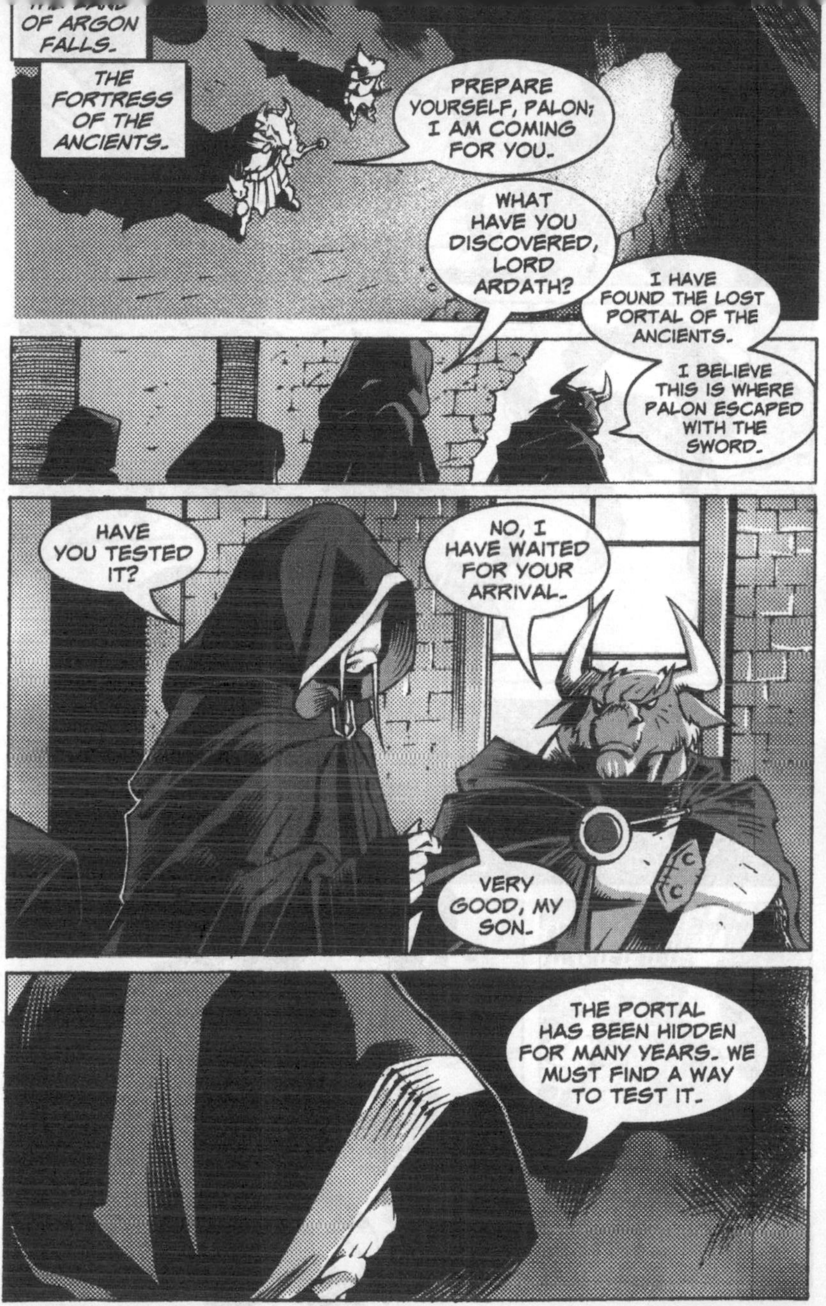
OF ARGON FALLS.
THE FORTRESS OF THE ANCIENTS.
PREPARE YOURSELF, PALON; I AM COMING FOR YOU.
WHAT HAVE YOU DISCOVERED, LORD ARDATH?
I HAVE FOUND THE LOST PORTAL OF THE ANCIENTS.
I BELIEVE THIS IS WHERE PALON ESCAPED WITH THE SWORD.
HAVE YOU TESTED IT?
NO, I HAVE WAITED FOR YOUR ARRIVAL.
VERY GOOD, MY SON.
THE PORTAL HAS BEEN HIDDEN FOR MANY YEARS. WE MUST FIND A WAY TO TEST IT.

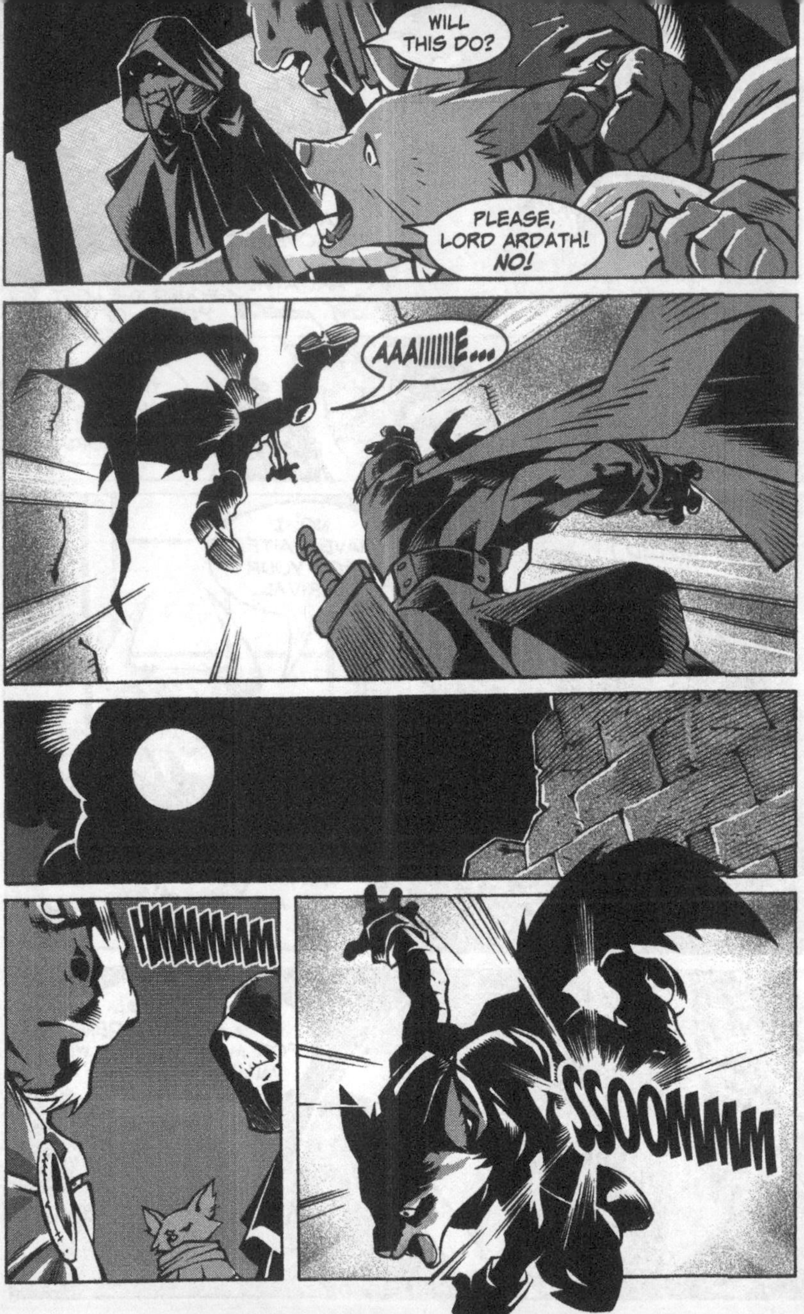
WILL THIS DO?
PLEASE, LORD ARDATH! NO!
AAAIIIIIIE...
HMMMMMM
SSOOMMMM

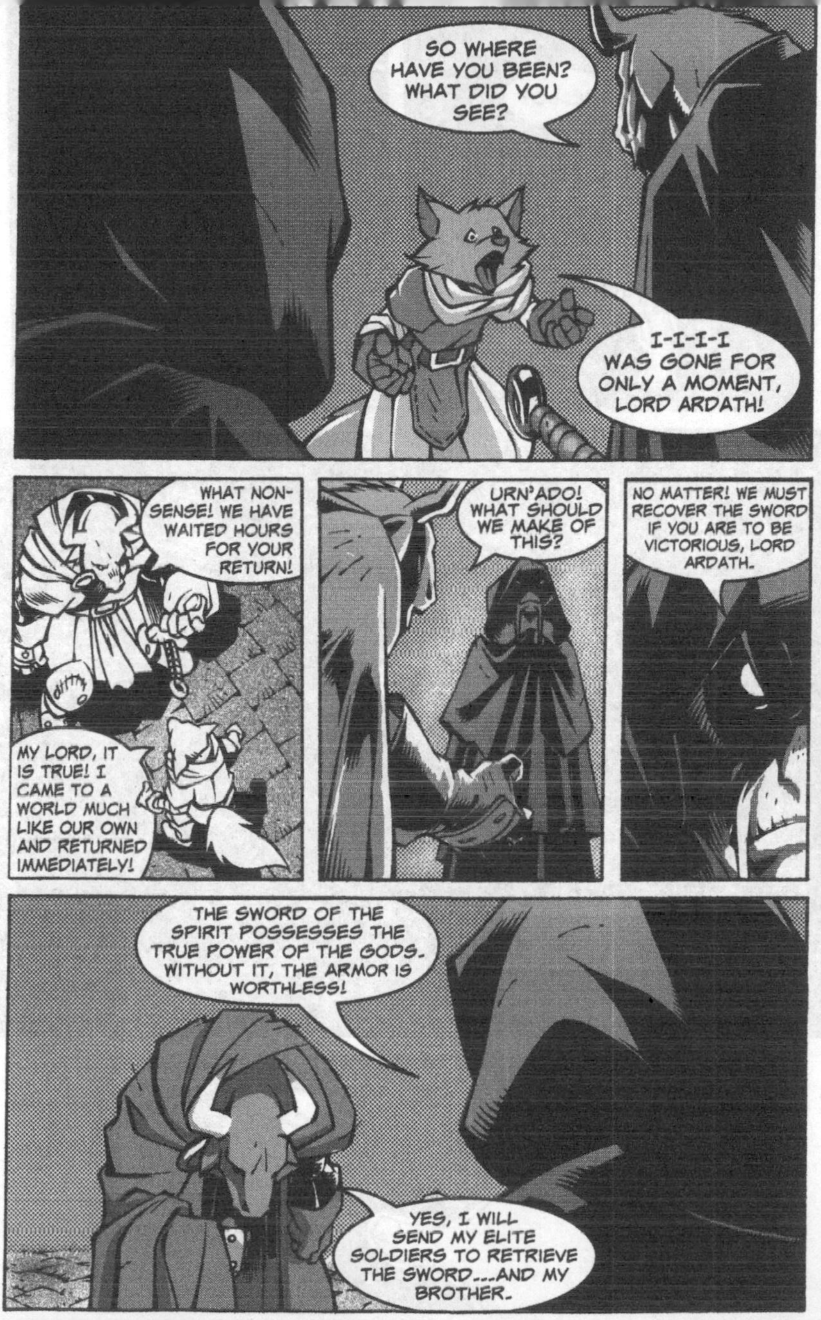
SO WHERE HAVE YOU BEEN? WHAT DID YOU SEE?
I-I-I-I WAS GONE FOR ONLY A MOMENT, LORD ARDATH!
WHAT NON-SENSE! WE HAVE WAITED HOURS FOR YOUR RETURN!
MY LORD, IT IS TRUE! I CAME TO A WORLD MUCH LIKE OUR OWN AND RETURNED IMMEDIATELY!
URN'ADO! WHAT SHOULD WE MAKE OF THIS?
NO MATTER! WE MUST RECOVER THE SWORD IF YOU ARE TO BE VICTORIOUS, LORD ARDATH.
THE SWORD OF THE SPIRIT POSSESSES THE TRUE POWER OF THE GODS. WITHOUT IT, THE ARMOR IS WORTHLESS!
YES, I WILL SEND MY ELITE SOLDIERS TO RETRIEVE THE SWORD...AND MY BROTHER.

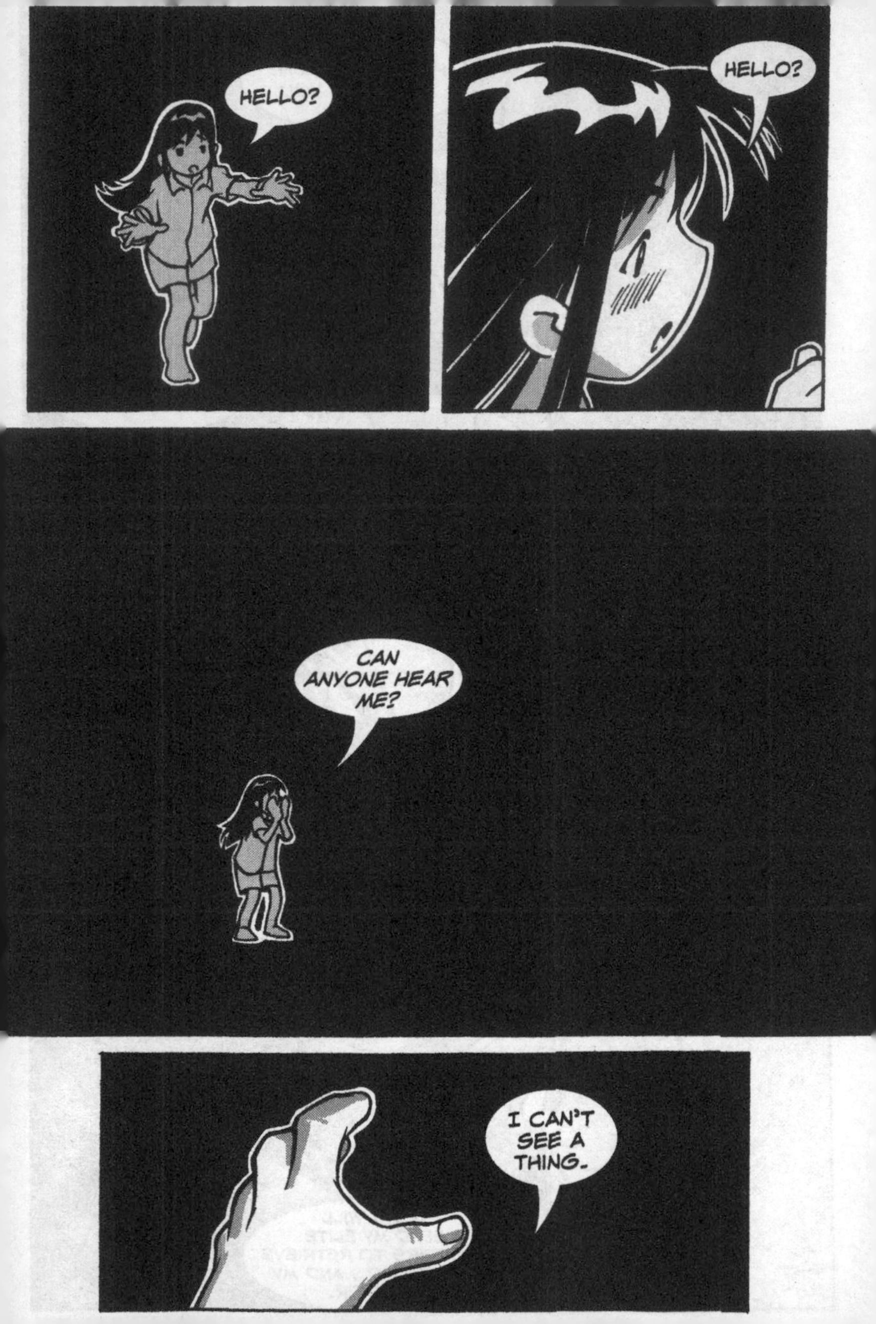
HELLO?
HELLO?
CAN ANYONE HEAR ME?
I CAN'T SEE A THING.

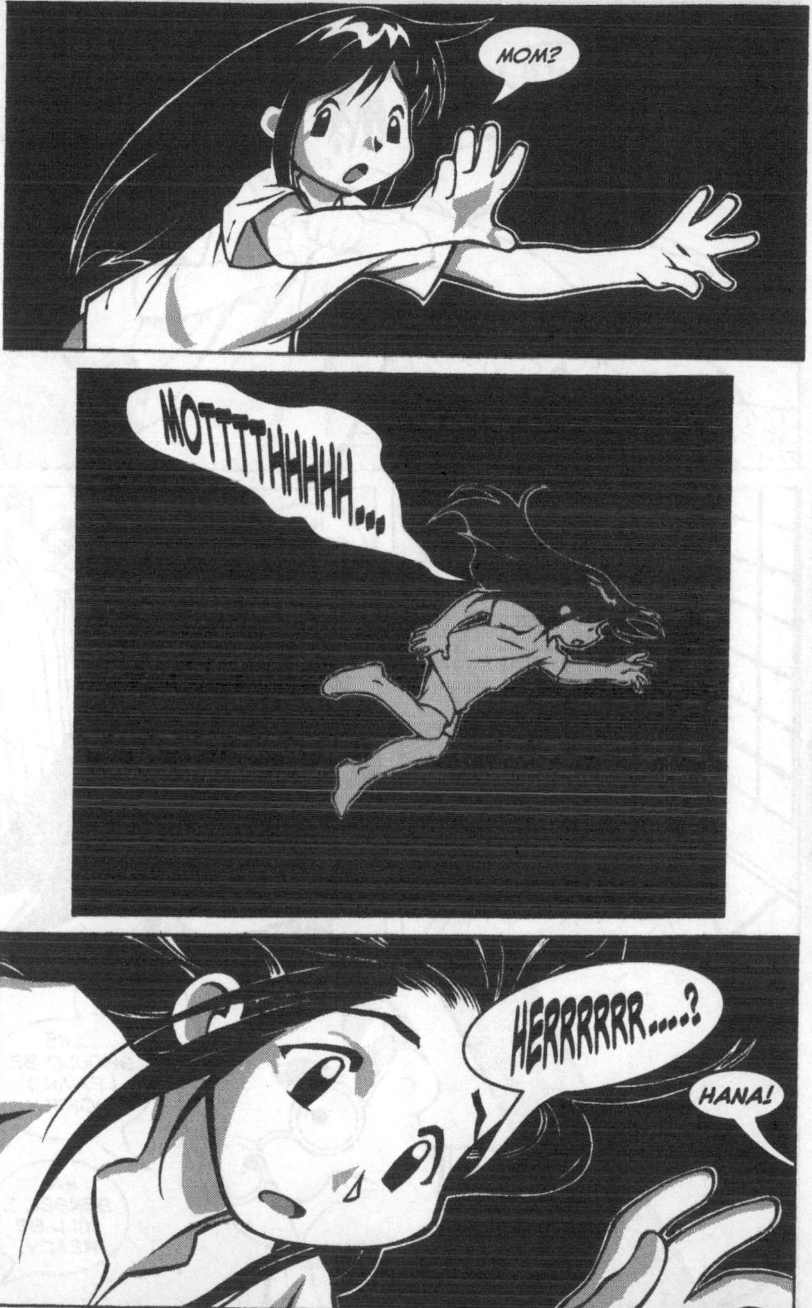
MOM?
MOTTTTHHHH...
HERRRRRR....?
HANA!

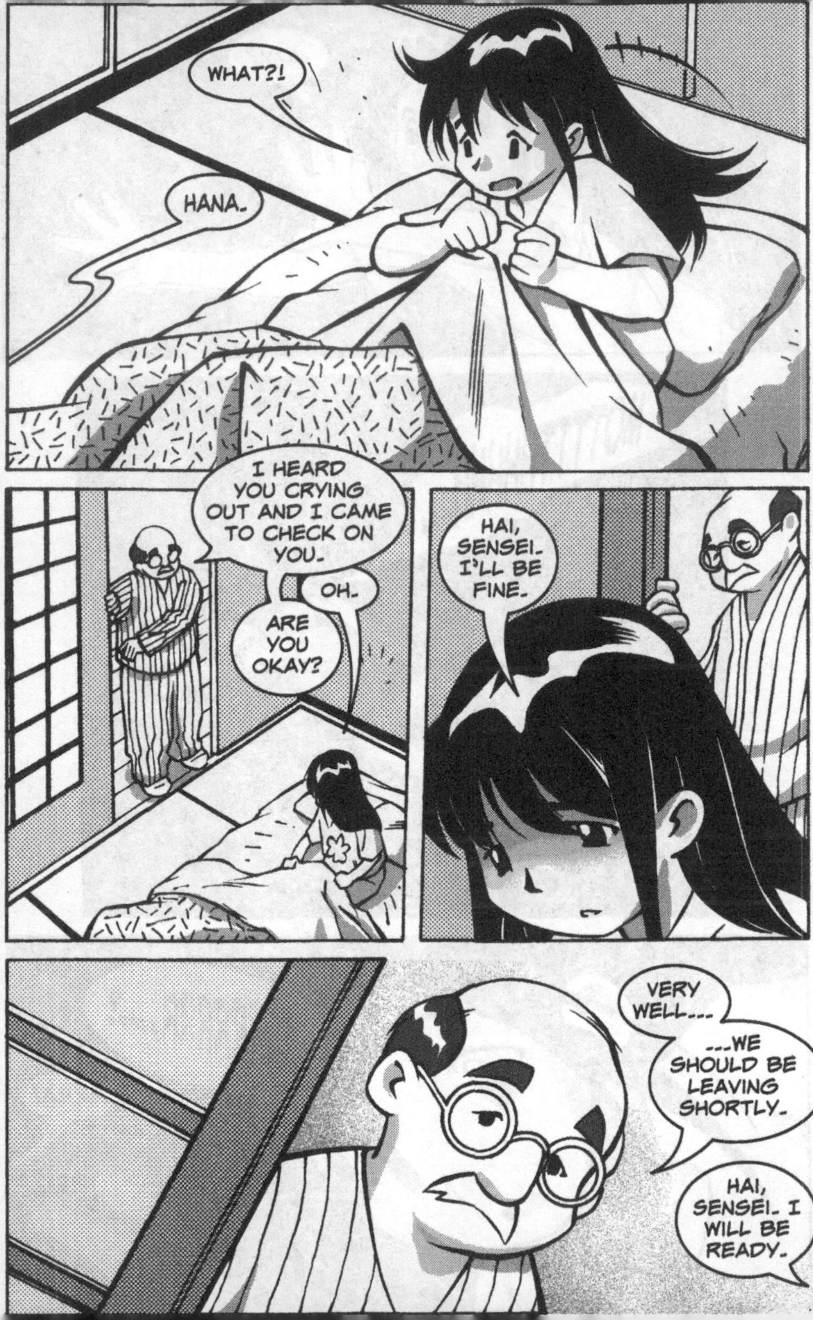
WHAT?!
HANA.
I HEARD YOU CRYING OUT AND I CAME TO CHECK ON YOU.
OH.
ARE YOU OKAY?
HAI, SENSEI. I'LL BE FINE.
VERY WELL...
...WE SHOULD BE LEAVING SHORTLY.
HAI, SENSEI. I WILL BE READY.

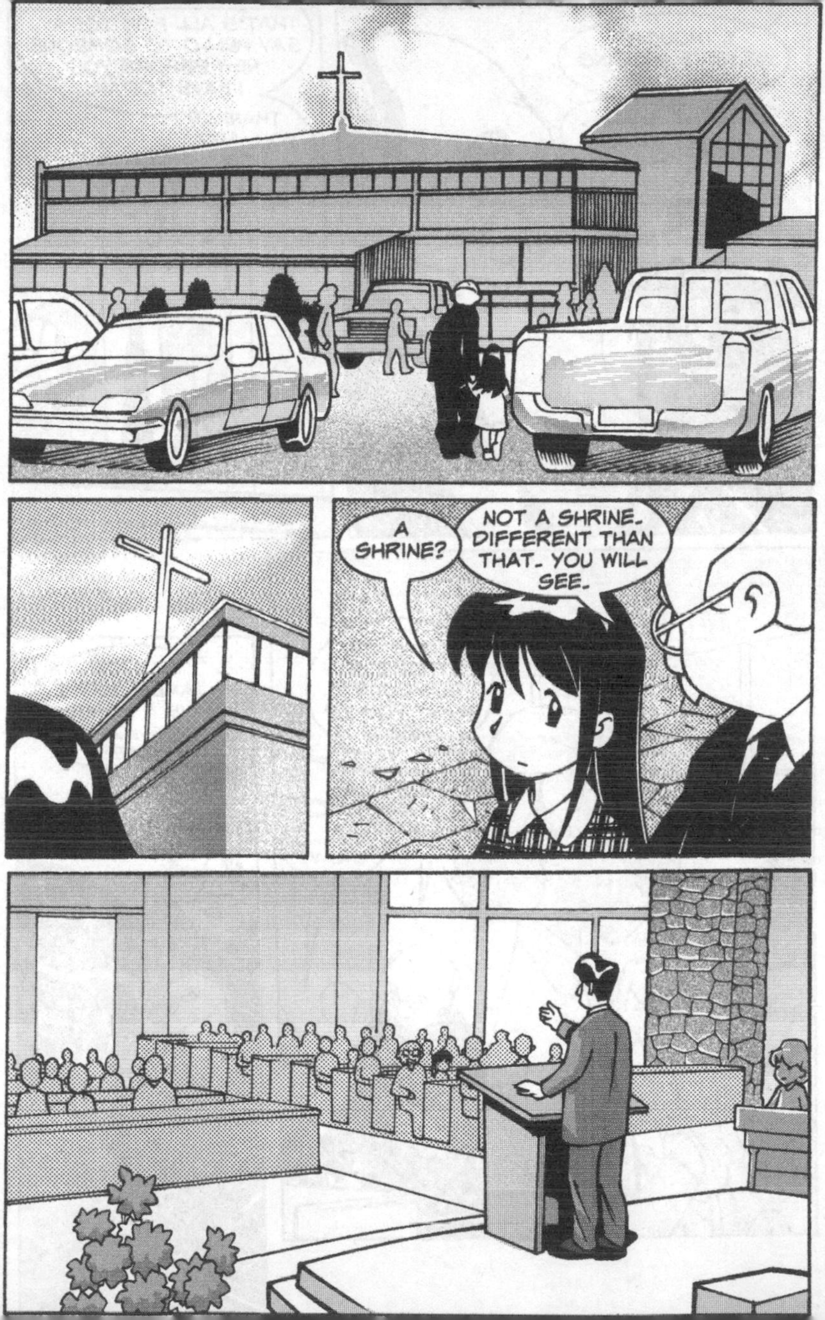
A SHRINE?
NOT A SHRINE. DIFFERENT THAN THAT. YOU WILL SEE.

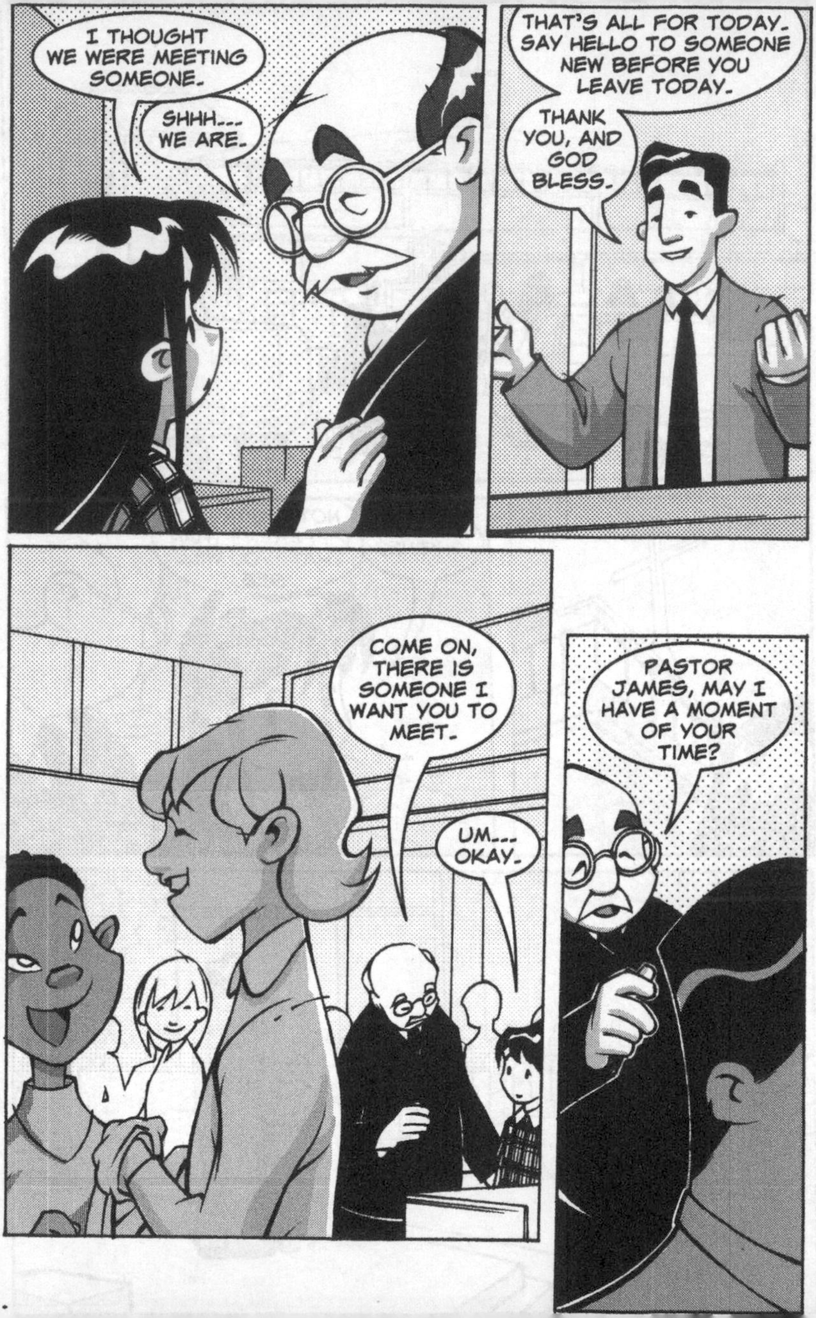
I THOUGHT WE WERE MEETING SOMEONE.
SHHH... WE ARE.
THAT'S ALL FOR TODAY. SAY HELLO TO SOMEONE NEW BEFORE YOU LEAVE TODAY.
THANK YOU, AND GOD BLESS.
COME ON, THERE IS SOMEONE I WANT YOU TO MEET.
UM... OKAY.
PASTOR JAMES, MAY I HAVE A MOMENT OF YOUR TIME?

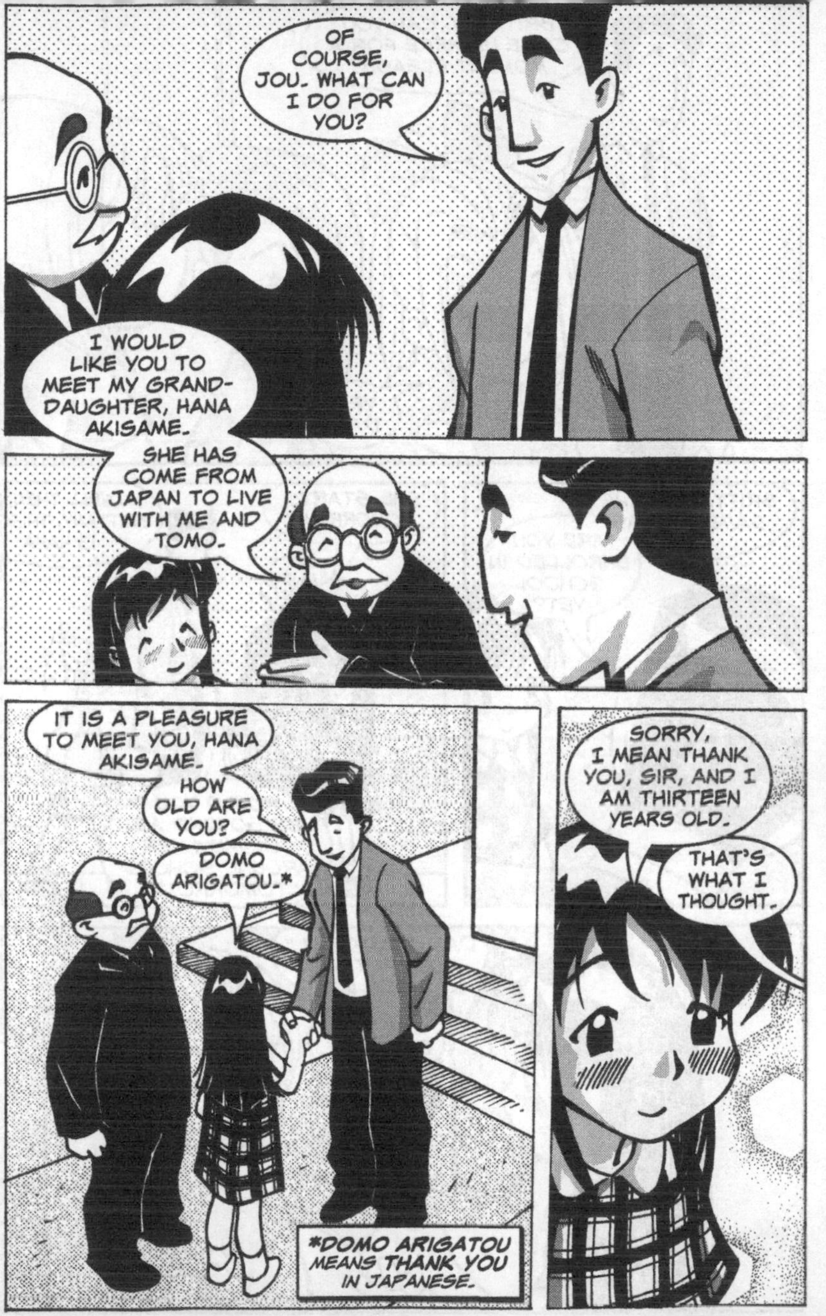
OF COURSE, JOU. WHAT CAN I DO FOR YOU?
I WOULD LIKE YOU TO MEET MY GRAND-DAUGHTER, HANA AKISAME.
SHE HAS COME FROM JAPAN TO LIVE WITH ME AND TOMO.
IT IS A PLEASURE TO MEET YOU, HANA AKISAME.
HOW OLD ARE YOU?
DOMO ARIGATOU.*
*DOMO ARIGATOU MEANS THANK YOU IN JAPANESE.
SORRY, I MEAN THANK YOU, SIR, AND I AM THIRTEEN YEARS OLD.
THAT'S WHAT I THOUGHT.

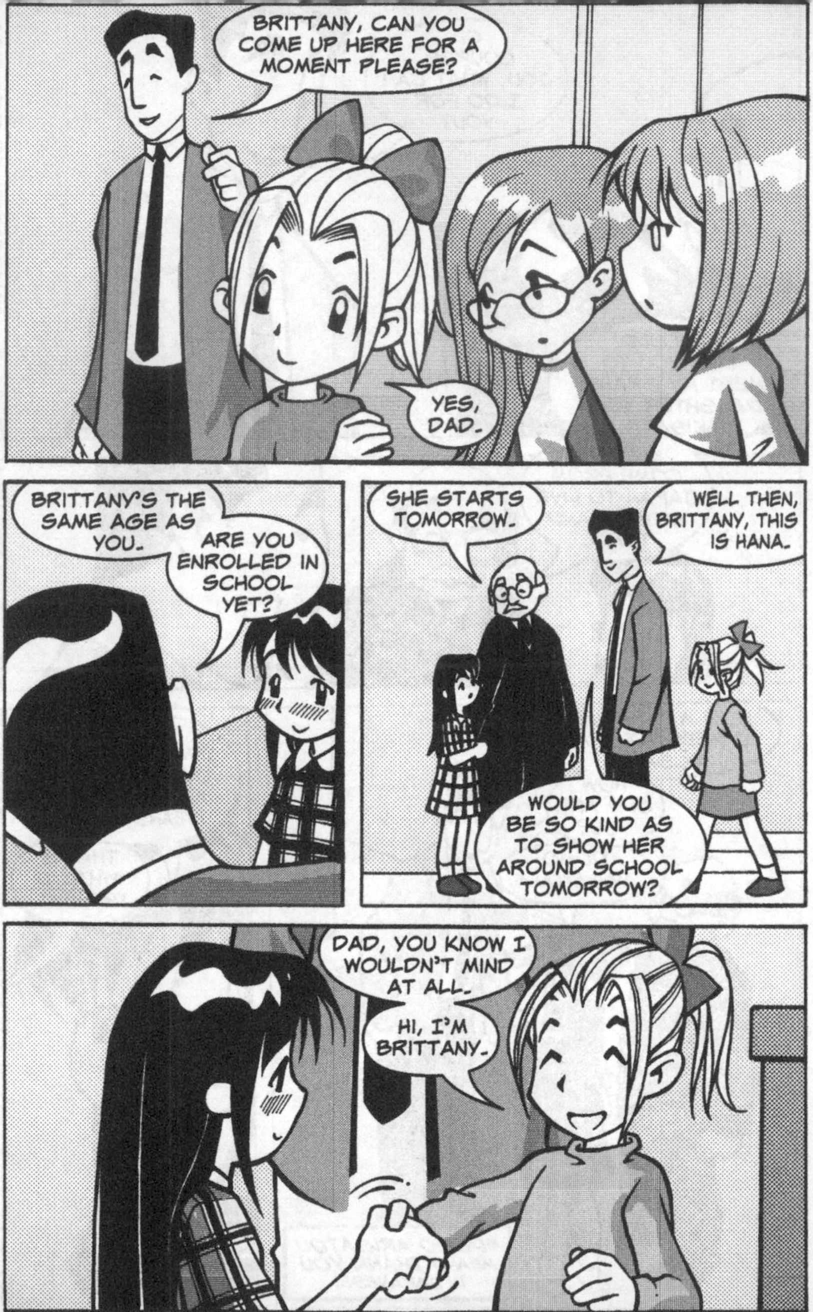
BRITTANY, CAN YOU COME UP HERE FOR A MOMENT PLEASE?
YES, DAD.
BRITTANY'S THE SAME AGE AS YOU.
ARE YOU ENROLLED IN SCHOOL YET?
SHE STARTS TOMORROW.
WELL THEN, BRITTANY, THIS IS HANA.
WOULD YOU BE SO KIND AS TO SHOW HER AROUND SCHOOL TOMORROW?
DAD, YOU KNOW I WOULDN'T MIND AT ALL.
HI, I'M BRITTANY.

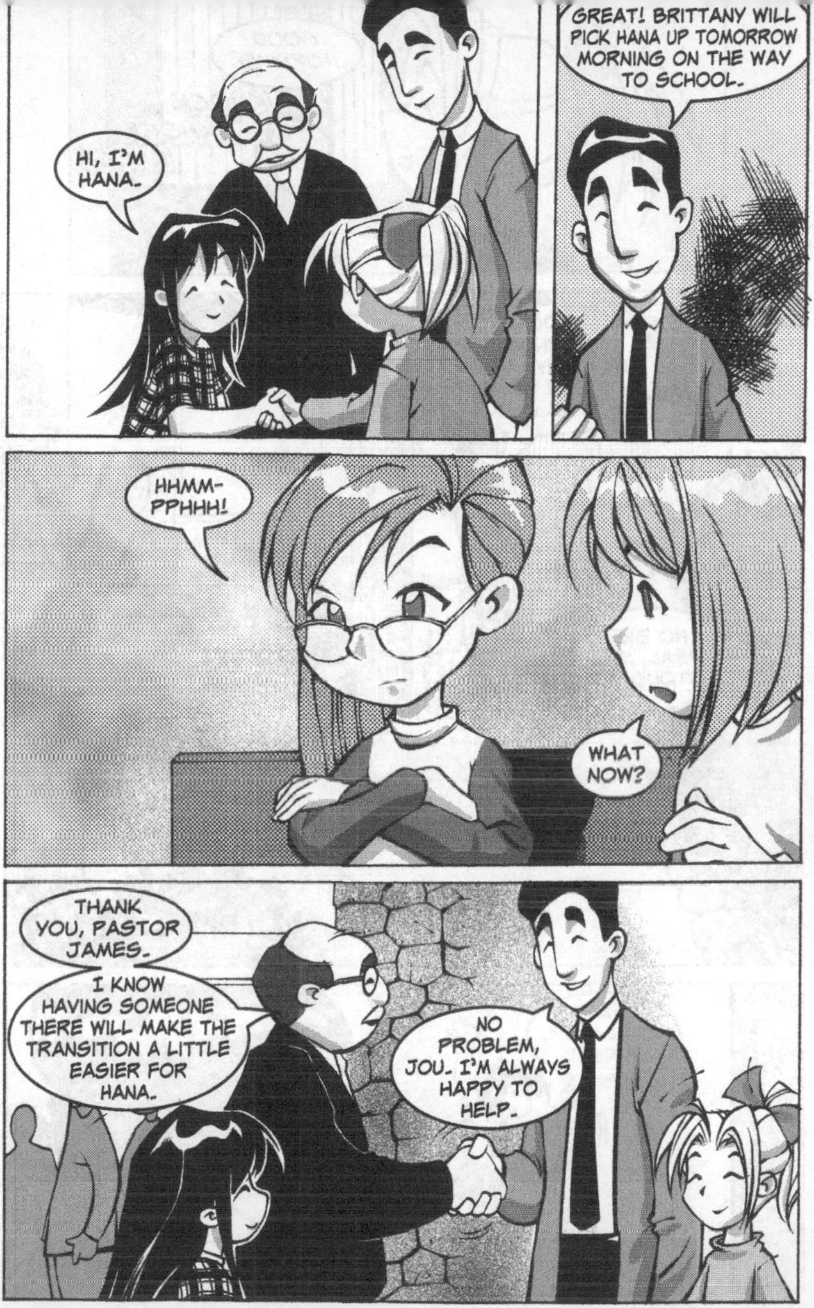
HI, I'M HANA.
GREAT! BRITTANY WILL PICK HANA UP TOMORROW MORNING ON THE WAY TO SCHOOL.
HHMM-PPHHH!
WHAT NOW?
THANK YOU, PASTOR JAMES.
I KNOW HAVING SOMEONE THERE WILL MAKE THE TRANSITION A LITTLE EASIER FOR HANA.
NO PROBLEM, JOU. I'M ALWAYS HAPPY TO HELP.

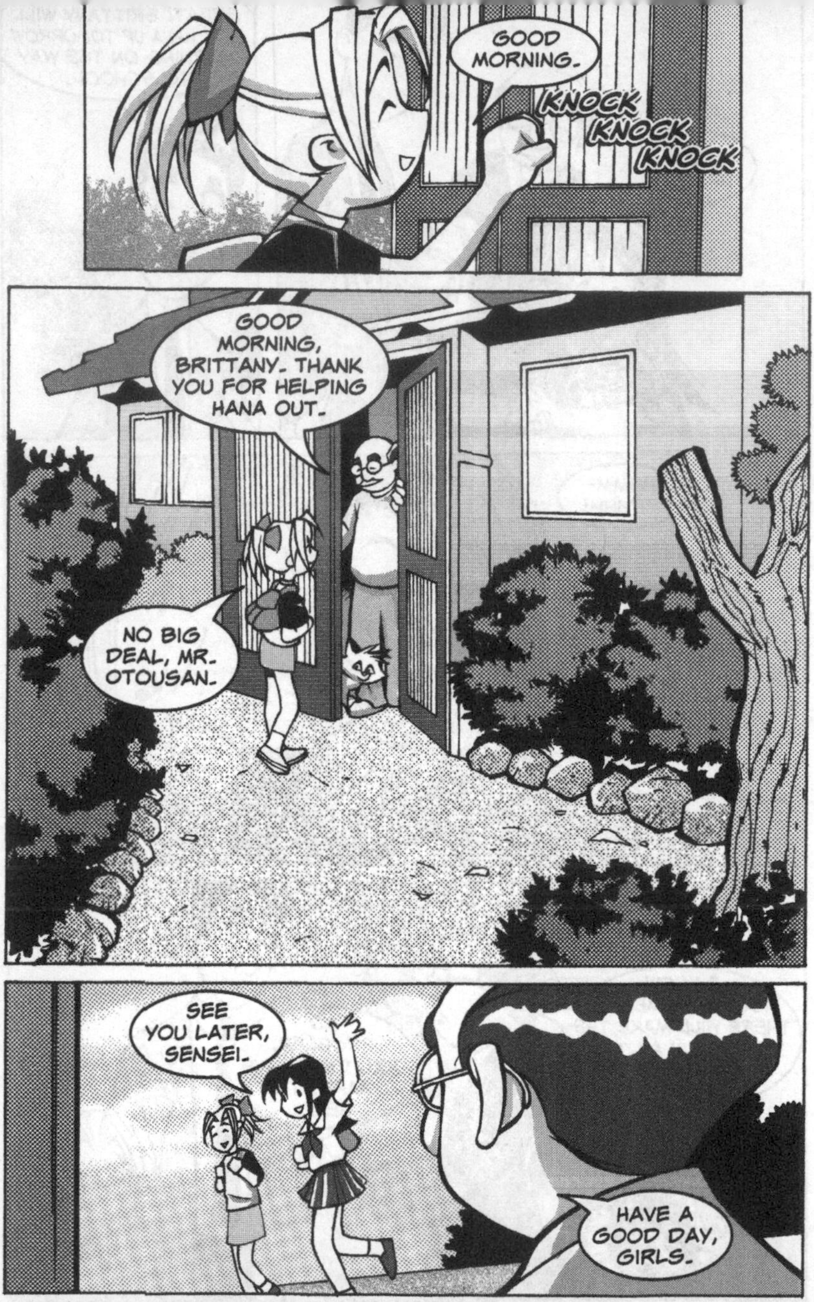
GOOD MORNING.
KNOCK KNOCK KNOCK
GOOD MORNING, BRITTANY. THANK YOU FOR HELPING HANA OUT.
NO BIG DEAL, MR. OTOUSAN.
SEE YOU LATER, SENSEI.
HAVE A GOOD DAY, GIRLS.

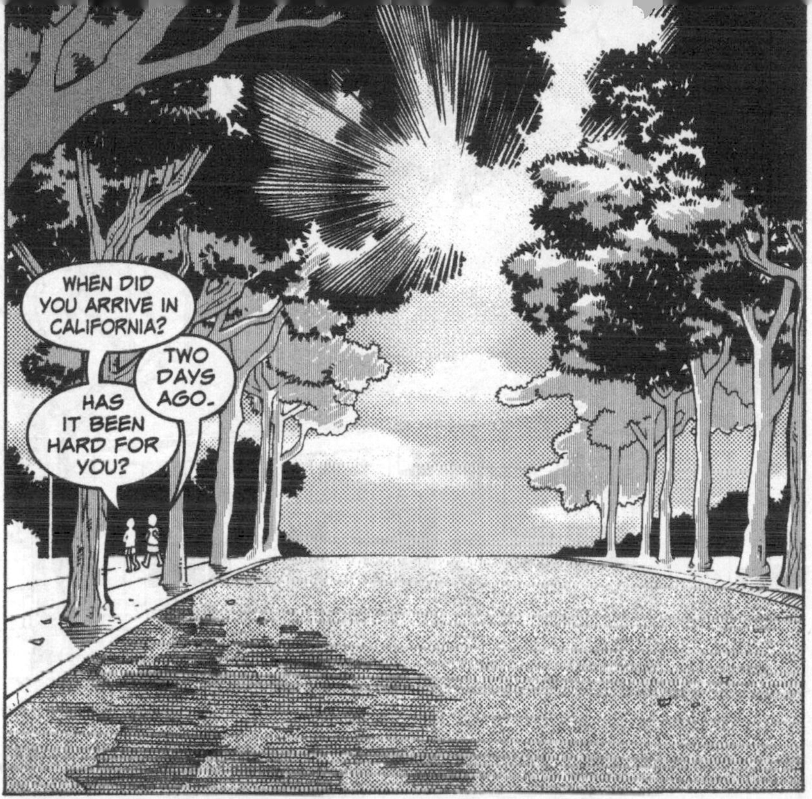
WHEN DID YOU ARRIVE IN CALIFORNIA?
TWO DAYS AGO.
HAS IT BEEN HARD FOR YOU?
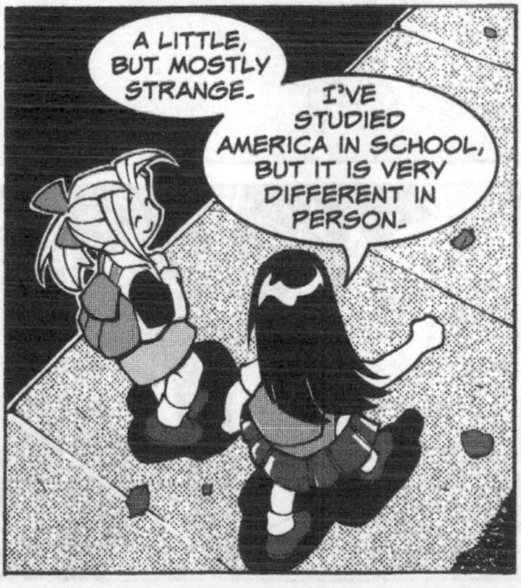
A LITTLE, BUT MOSTLY STRANGE.
I'VE STUDIED AMERICA IN SCHOOL, BUT IT IS VERY DIFFERENT IN PERSON.
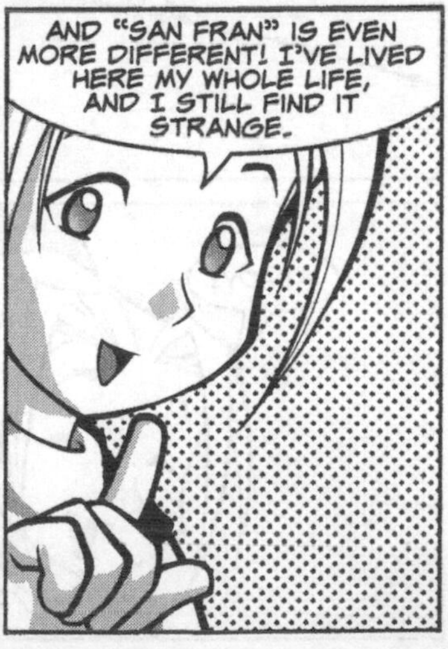
AND "SAN FRAN" IS EVEN MORE DIFFERENT! I'VE LIVED HERE MY WHOLE LIFE, AND I STILL FIND IT STRANGE.

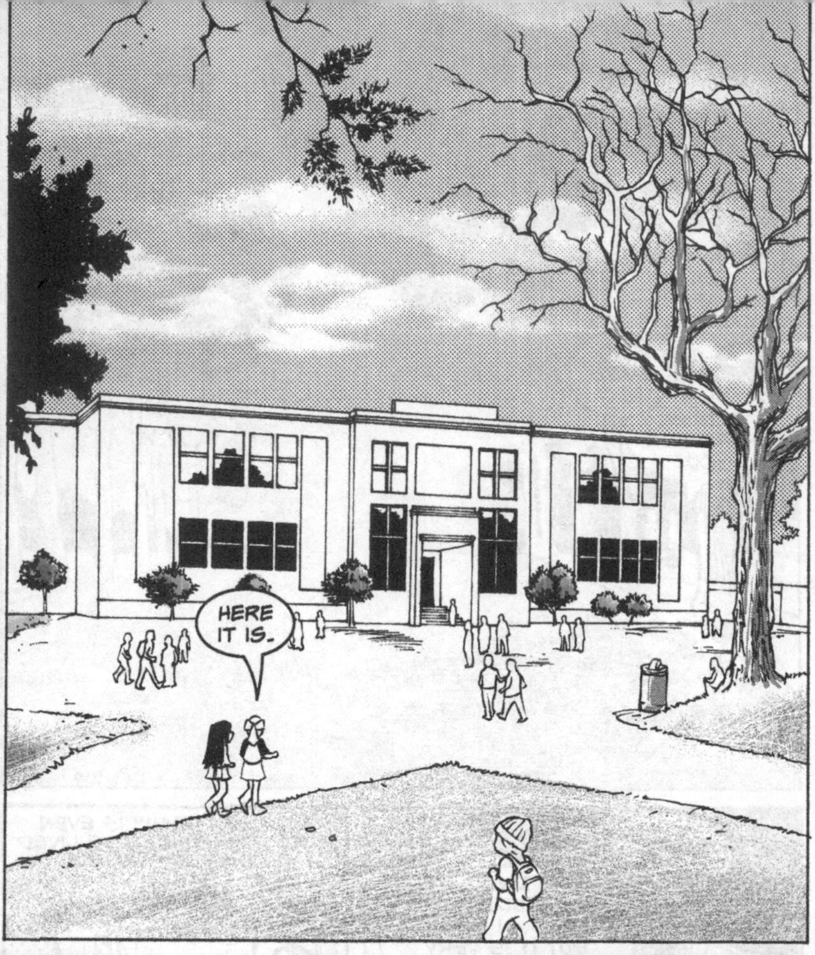
HERE IT IS.

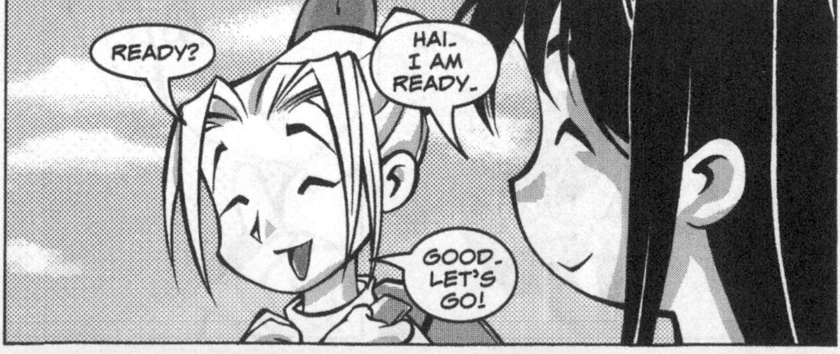
READY?
HAI. I AM READY.
GOOD. LET'S GO!

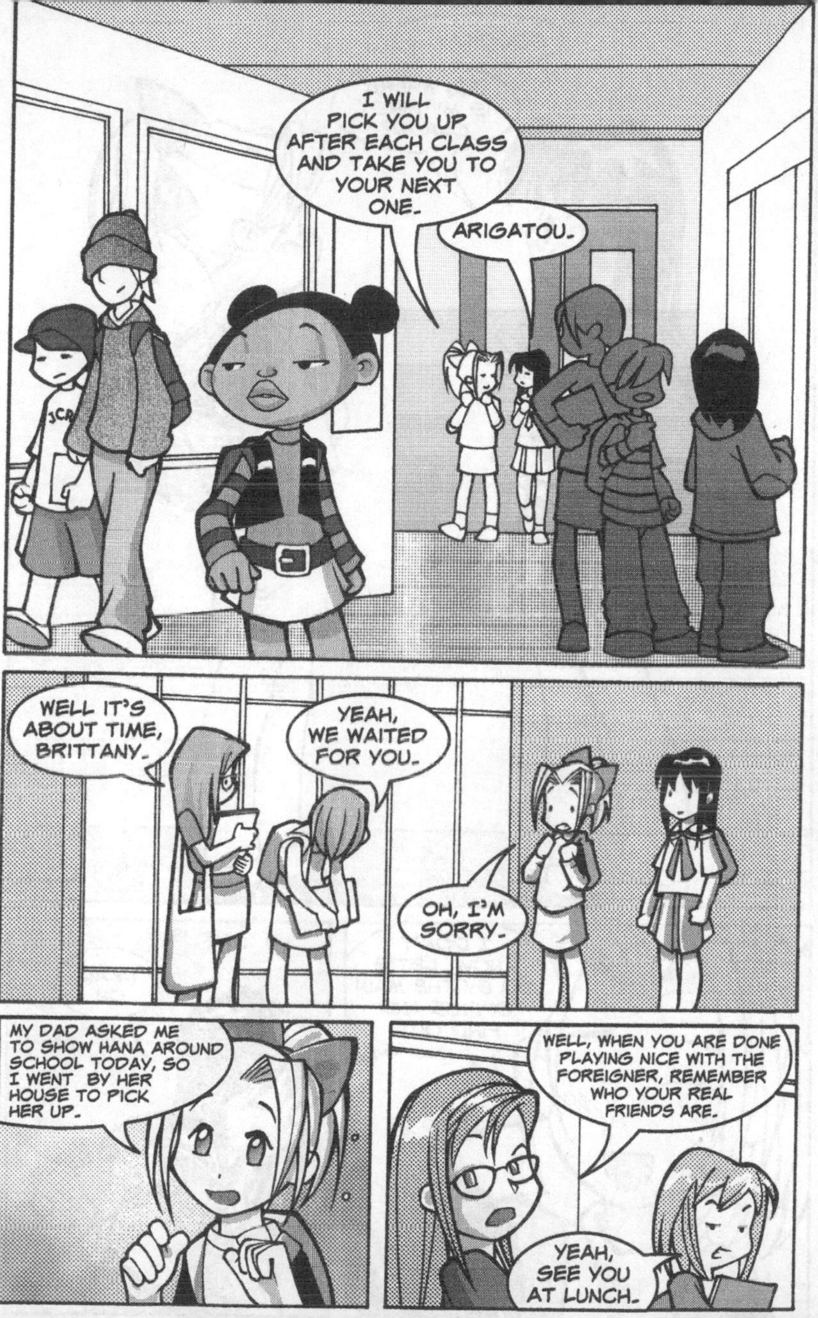

I WILL PICK YOU UP AFTER EACH CLASS AND TAKE YOU TO YOUR NEXT ONE.
ARIGATOU.
JCR
WELL IT'S ABOUT TIME, BRITTANY.
YEAH, WE WAITED FOR YOU.
OH, I'M SORRY.
MY DAD ASKED ME TO SHOW HANA AROUND SCHOOL TODAY, SO I WENT BY HER HOUSE TO PICK HER UP.
WELL, WHEN YOU ARE DONE PLAYING NICE WITH THE FOREIGNER, REMEMBER WHO YOUR REAL FRIENDS ARE.
YEAH, SEE YOU AT LUNCH.

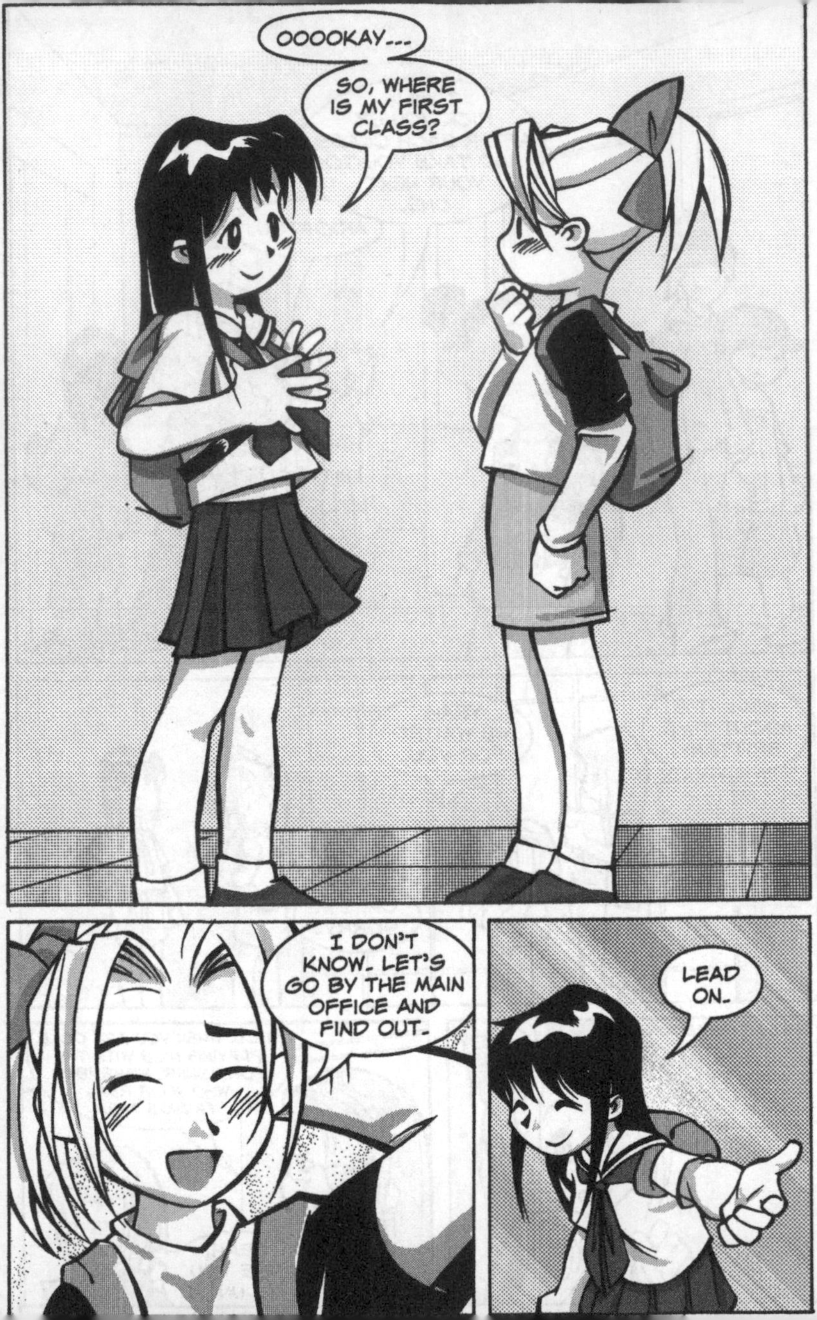
OOOOKAY...
SO, WHERE IS MY FIRST CLASS?
I DON'T KNOW. LET'S GO BY THE MAIN OFFICE AND FIND OUT.
LEAD ON.

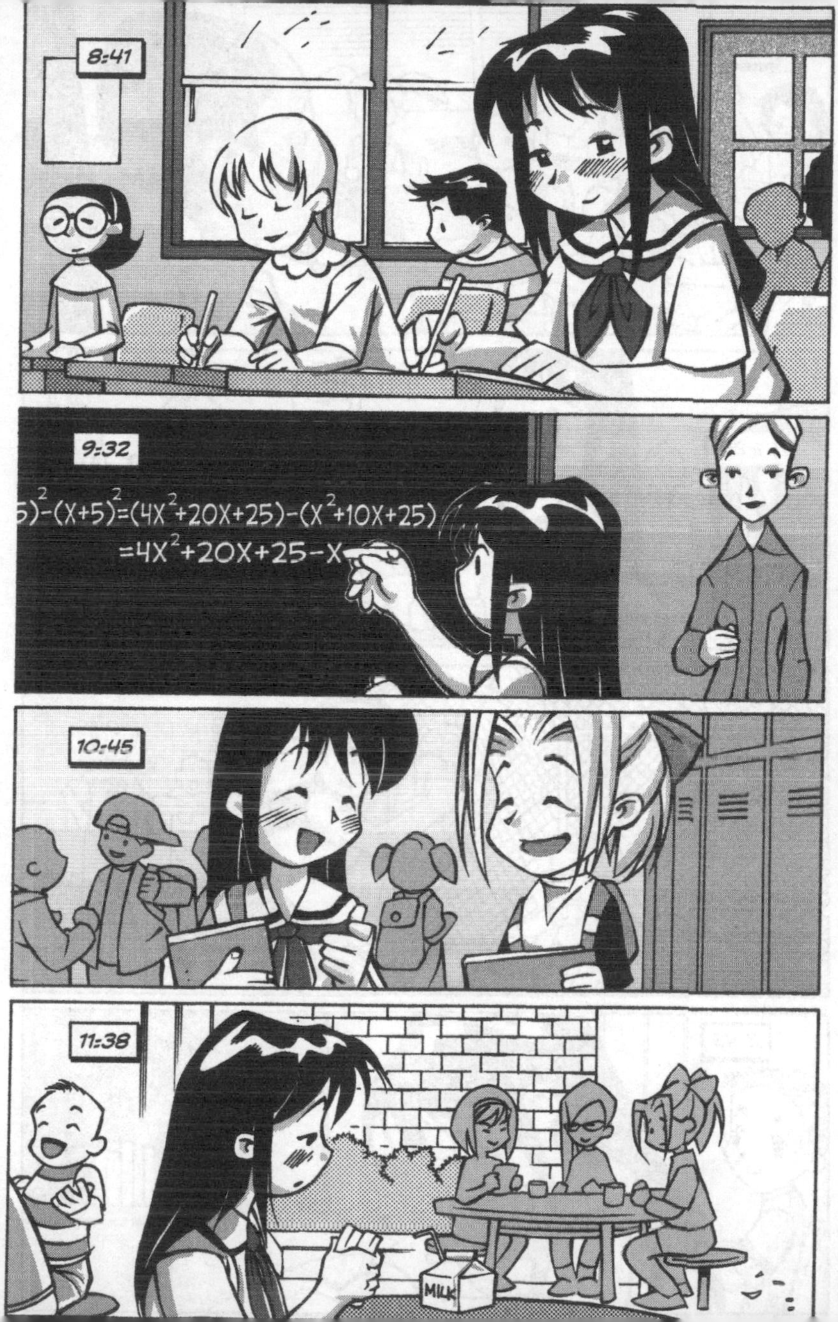
8:41
9:32
5)²-(X+5)²=(4X²+20X+25)-(X²+10X+25)
=4X²+20X+25-X
10:45
11:38
MILK

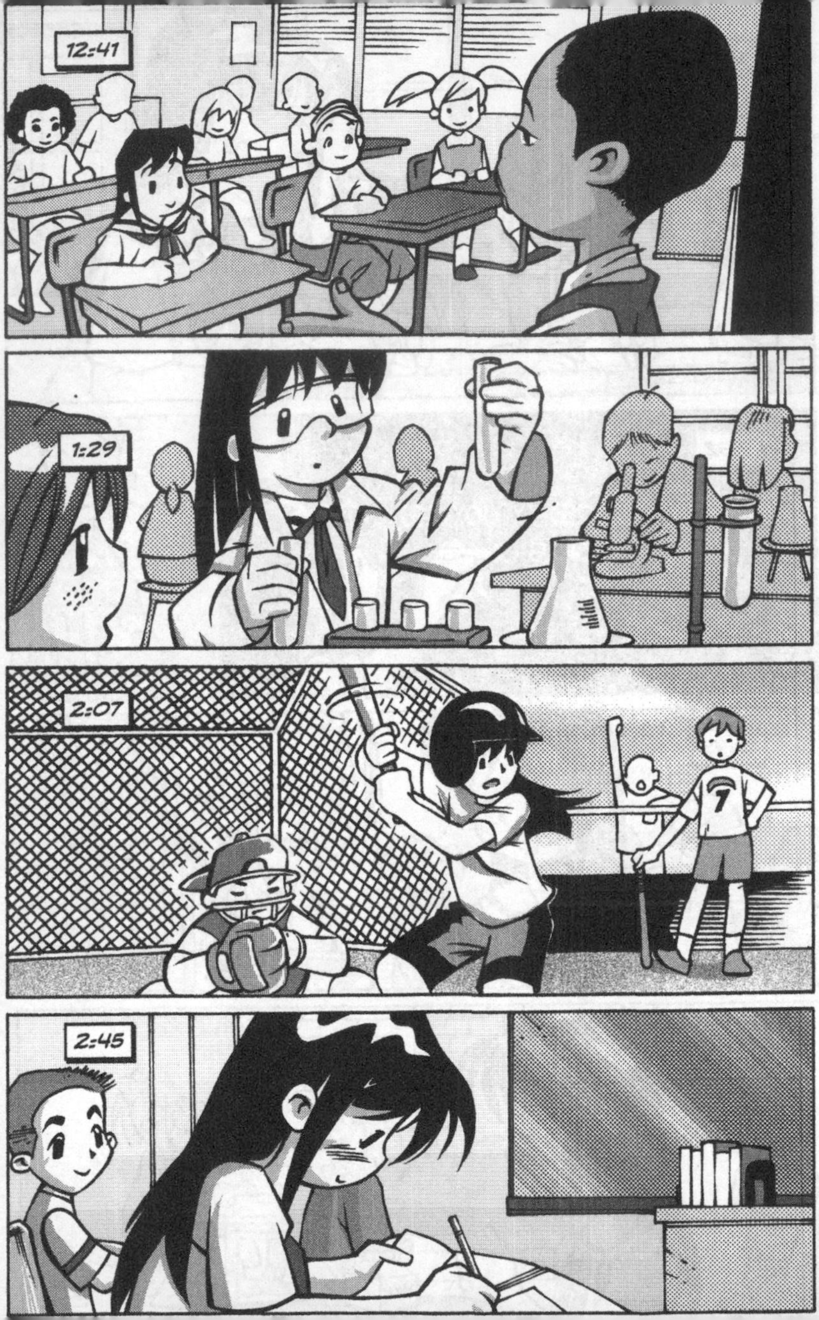
12:41
1:29
2:07
7
2:45

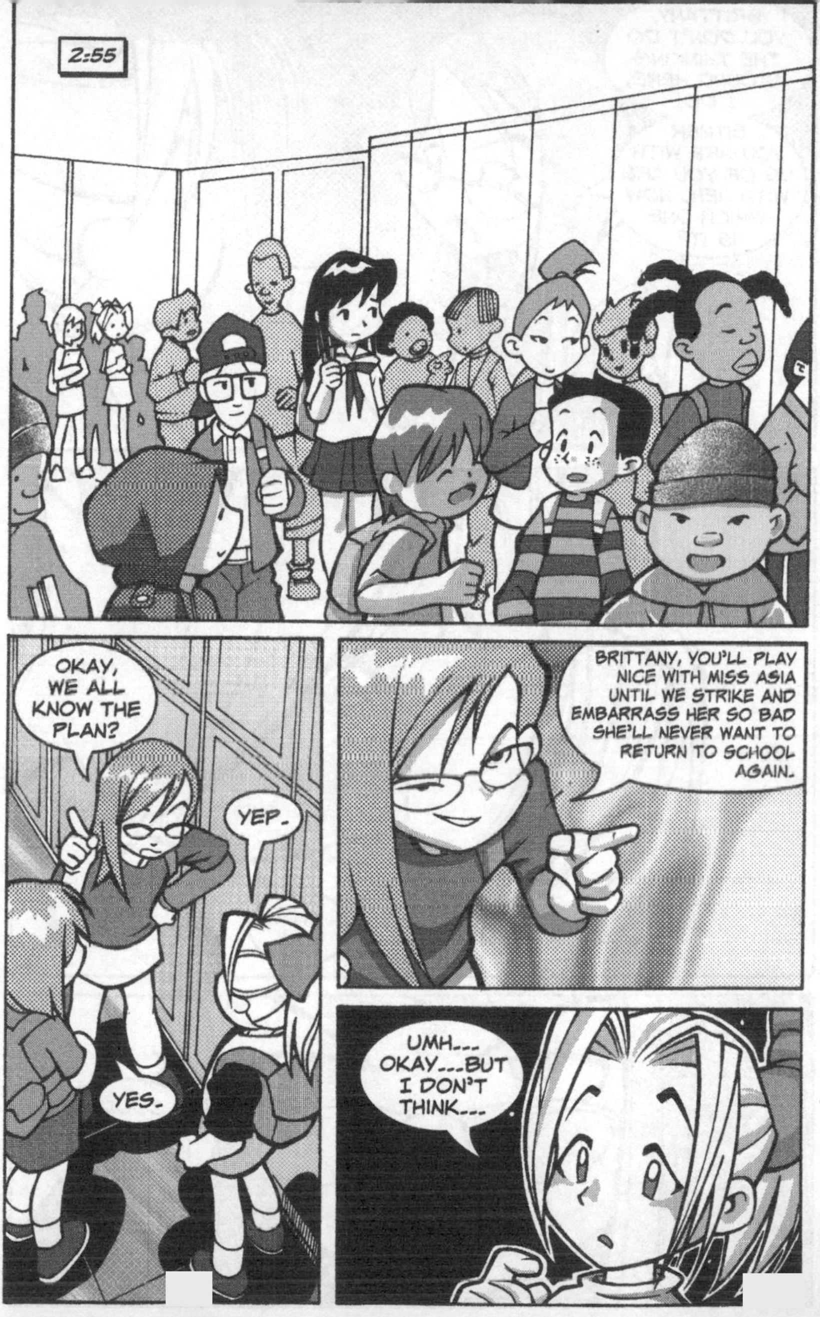
2:55
OKAY, WE ALL KNOW THE PLAN?
YEP.
YES.
BRITTANY, YOU'LL PLAY NICE WITH MISS ASIA UNTIL WE STRIKE AND EMBARRASS HER SO BAD SHE'LL NEVER WANT TO RETURN TO SCHOOL AGAIN.
UMH... OKAY...BUT I DON'T THINK...

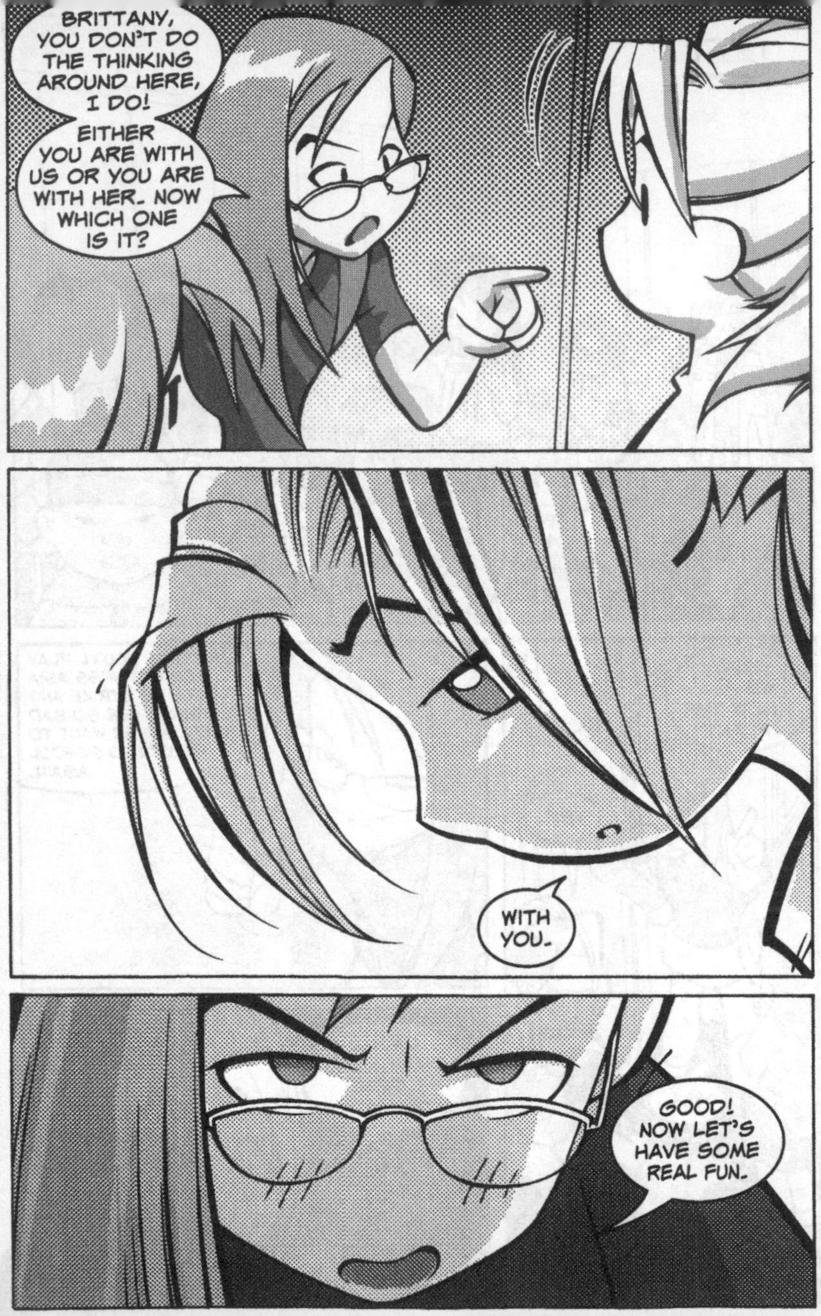
BRITTANY, YOU DON'T DO THE THINKING AROUND HERE, I DO!
EITHER YOU ARE WITH US OR YOU ARE WITH HER. NOW WHICH ONE IS IT?
WITH YOU.
GOOD! NOW LET'S HAVE SOME REAL FUN.

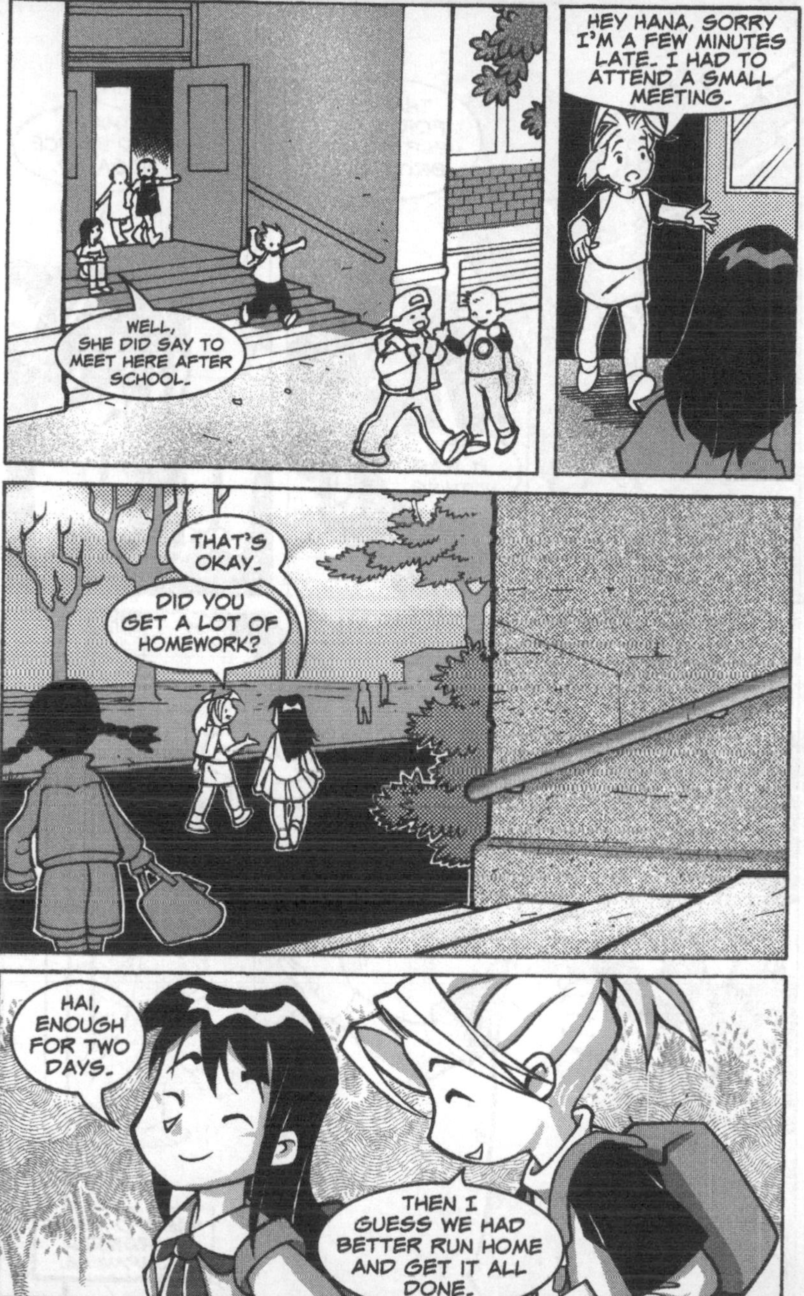
WELL, SHE DID SAY TO MEET HERE AFTER SCHOOL.
HEY HANA, SORRY I'M A FEW MINUTES LATE. I HAD TO ATTEND A SMALL MEETING.
THAT'S OKAY.
DID YOU GET A LOT OF HOMEWORK?
HAI, ENOUGH FOR TWO DAYS.
THEN I GUESS WE HAD BETTER RUN HOME AND GET IT ALL DONE.

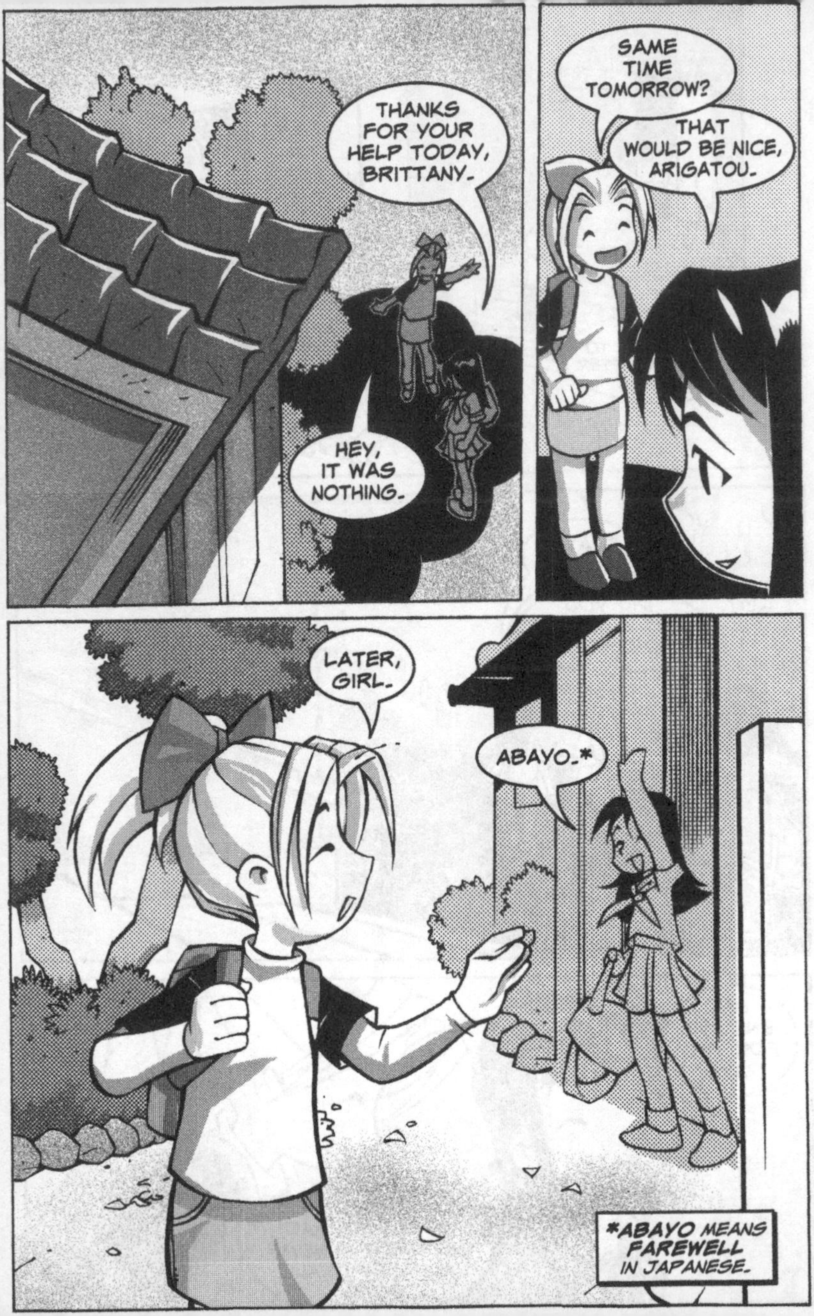
THANKS FOR YOUR HELP TODAY, BRITTANY.
HEY, IT WAS NOTHING.
SAME TIME TOMORROW?
THAT WOULD BE NICE, ARIGATOU.
LATER, GIRL.
ABAYO.*
*ABAYO MEANS FAREWELL IN JAPANESE.

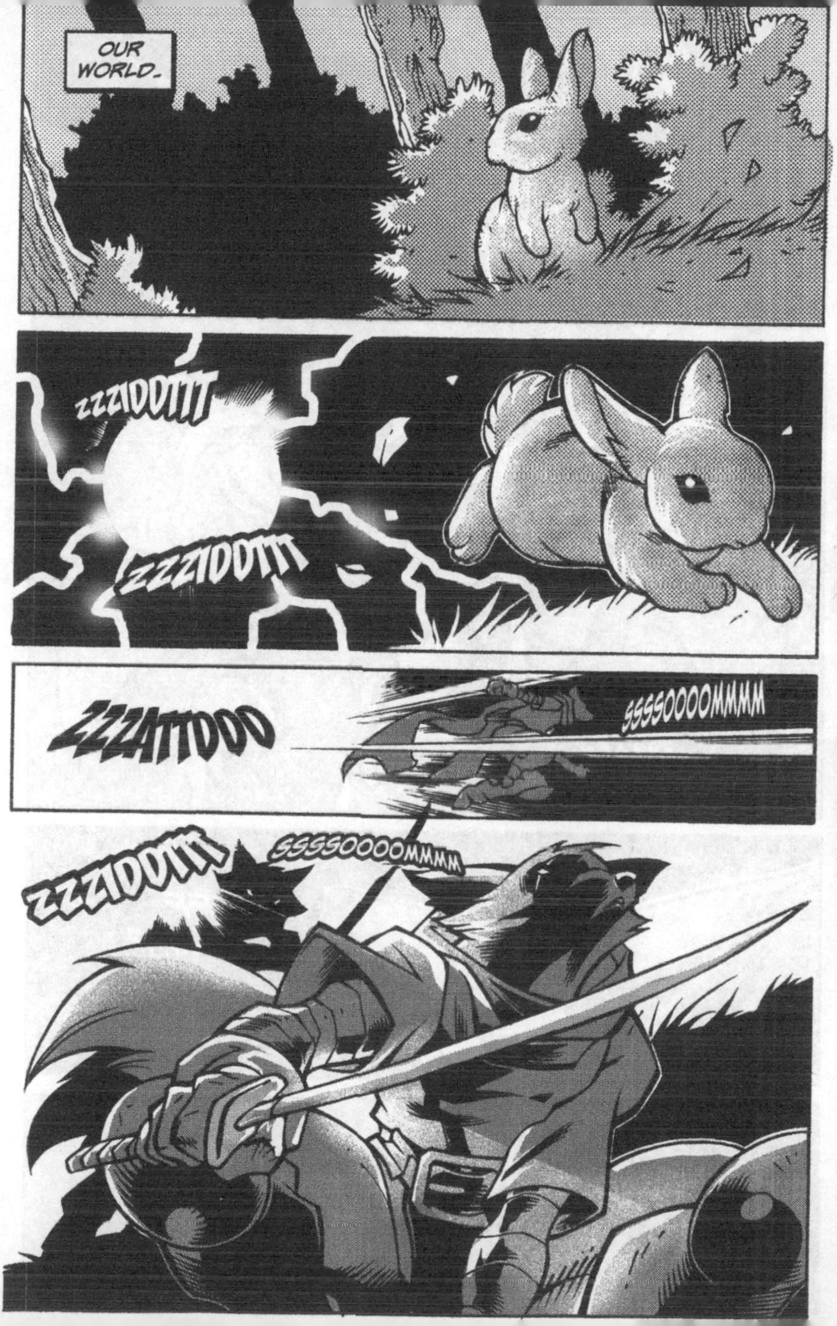
OUR WORLD_
ZZZIDDTTT
ZZZIDDTTT
ZZZATTDDD
SSSSOOOOMMMM
ZZZIDDTTT
SSSSOOOOMMMM

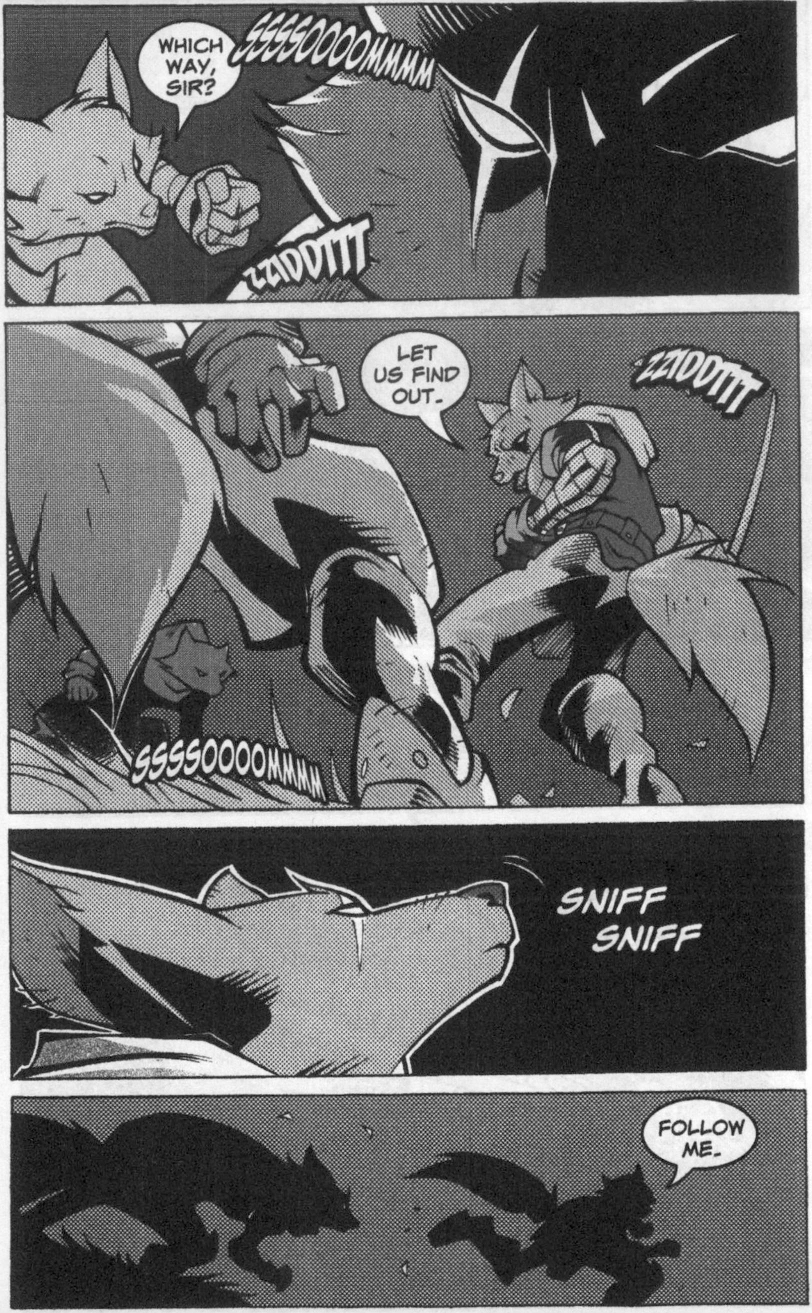
WHICH WAY, SIR?
SSSSOOOOMMMM
ZZIDDTTT
LET US FIND OUT.
ZZIDDTTT
SSSSOOOOMMMM
SNIFF SNIFF
FOLLOW ME.

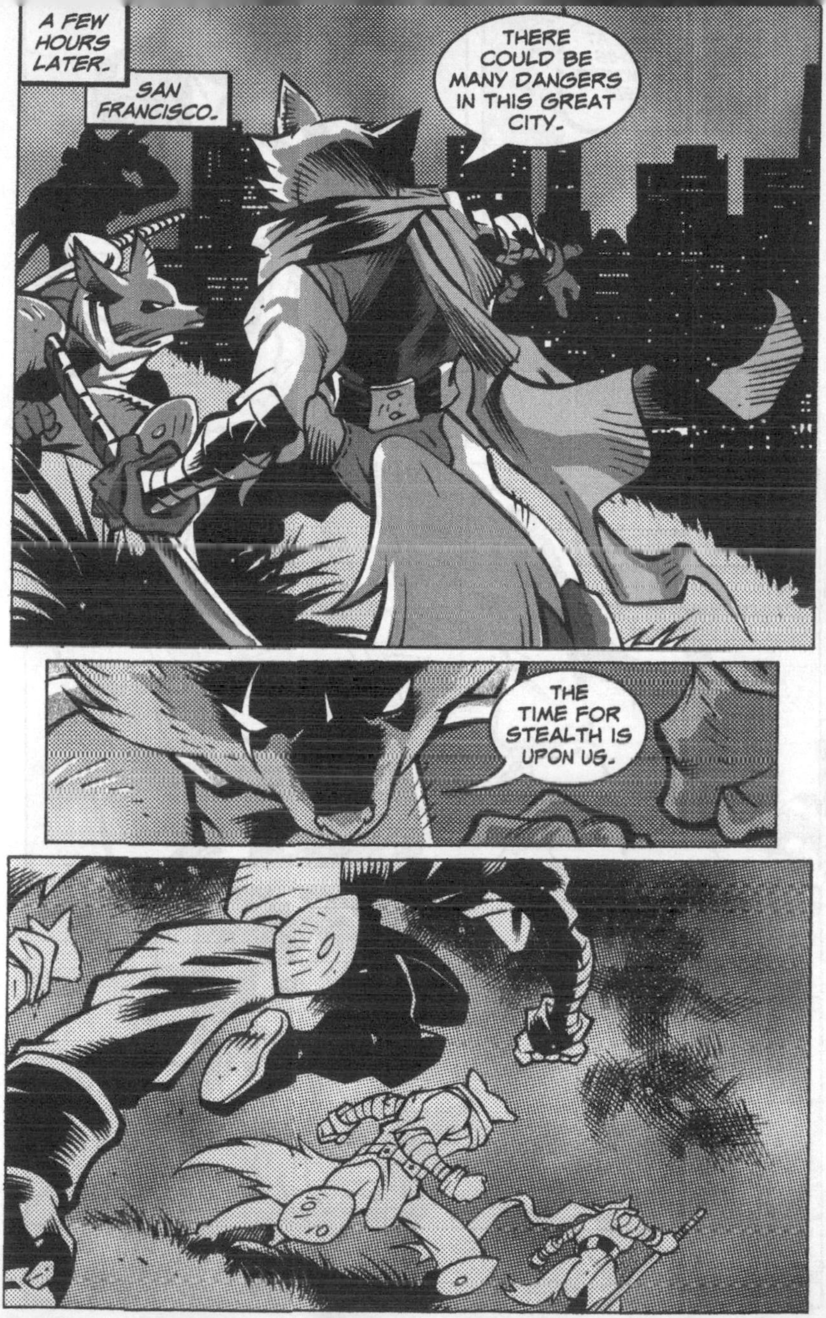
A FEW HOURS LATER...
SAN FRANCISCO...
THERE COULD BE MANY DANGERS IN THIS GREAT CITY...
THE TIME FOR STEALTH IS UPON US...

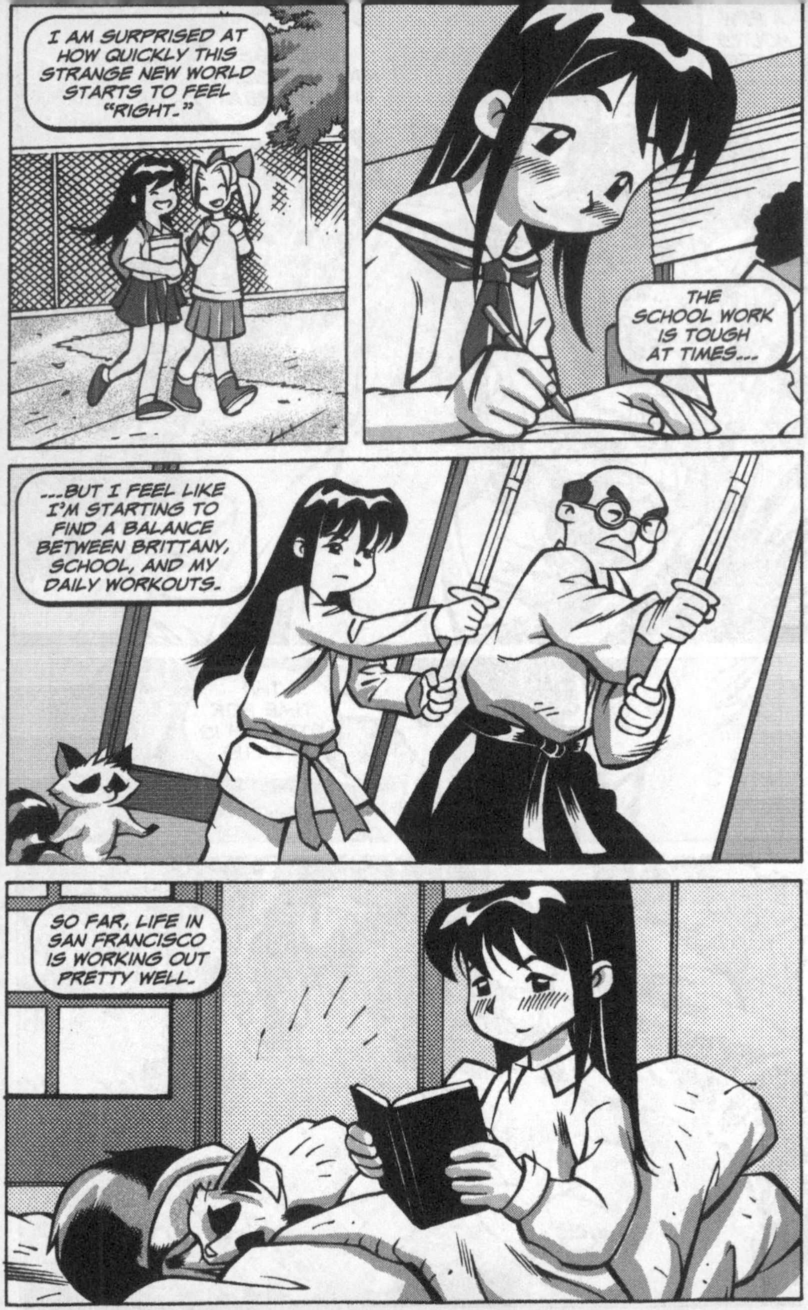
I AM SURPRISED AT HOW QUICKLY THIS STRANGE NEW WORLD STARTS TO FEEL "RIGHT."
THE SCHOOL WORK IS TOUGH AT TIMES...
...BUT I FEEL LIKE I'M STARTING TO FIND A BALANCE BETWEEN BRITTANY, SCHOOL, AND MY DAILY WORKOUTS.
SO FAR, LIFE IN SAN FRANCISCO IS WORKING OUT PRETTY WELL.

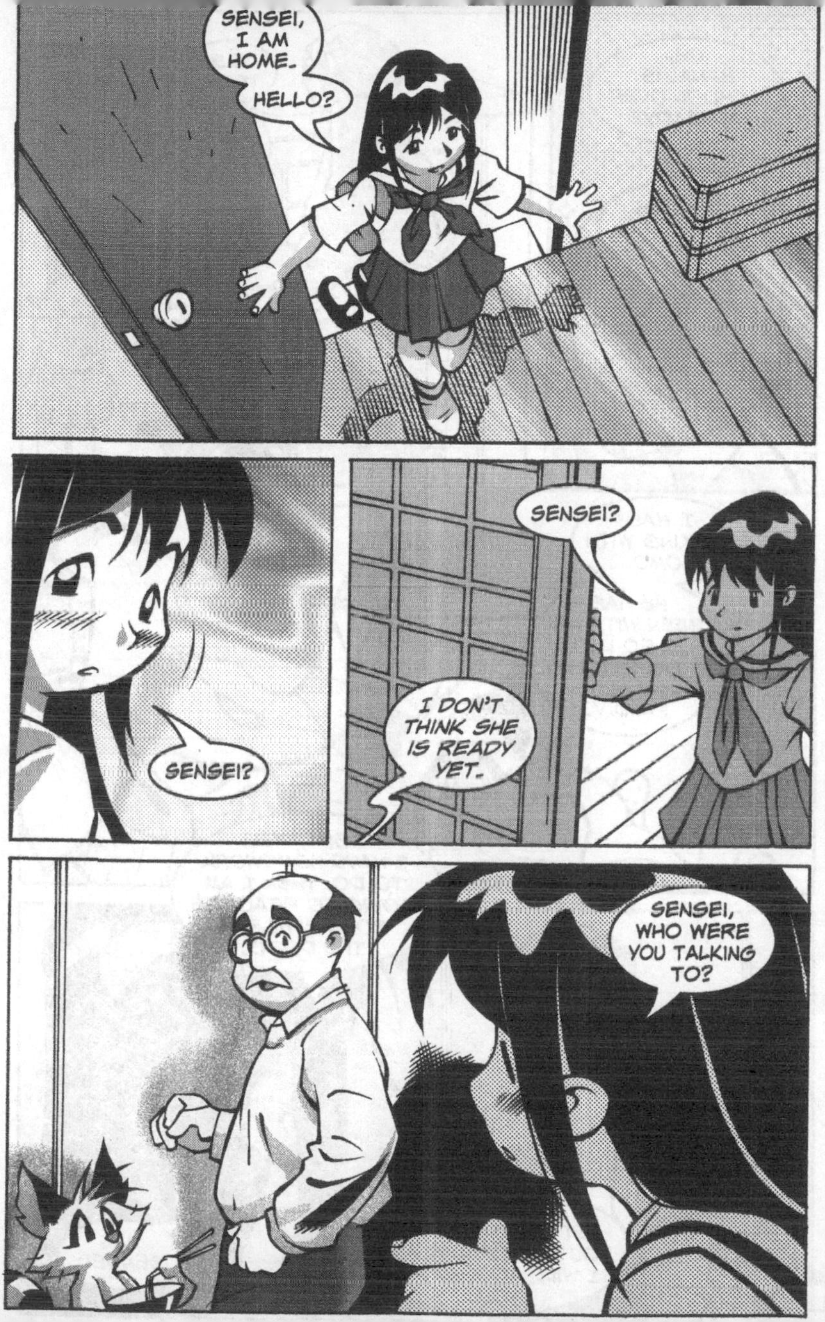
SENSEI, I AM HOME.
HELLO?
SENSEI?
SENSEI?
I DON'T THINK SHE IS READY YET.
SENSEI, WHO WERE YOU TALKING TO?

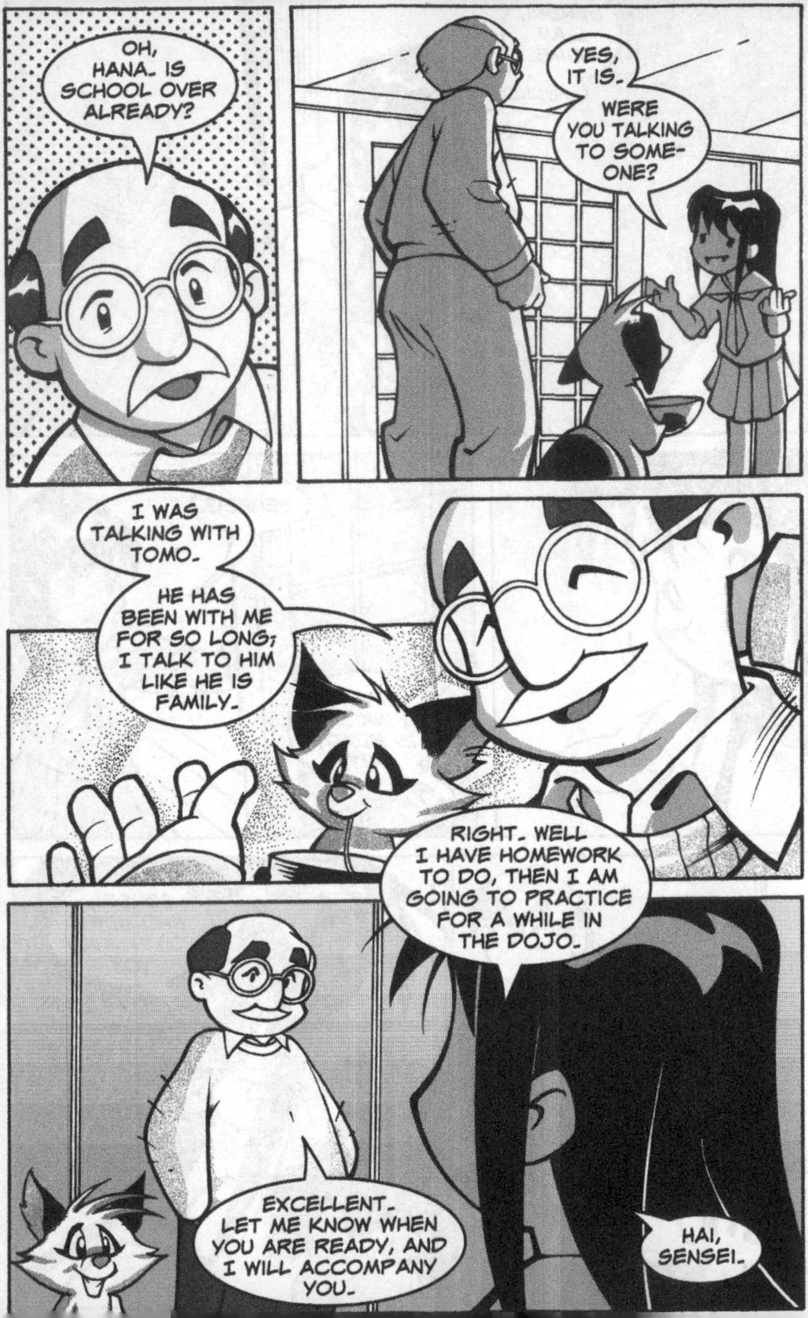
OH, HANA. IS SCHOOL OVER ALREADY?
YES, IT IS.
WERE YOU TALKING TO SOME-ONE?
I WAS TALKING WITH TOMO.
HE HAS BEEN WITH ME FOR SO LONG; I TALK TO HIM LIKE HE IS FAMILY.
RIGHT. WELL I HAVE HOMEWORK TO DO, THEN I AM GOING TO PRACTICE FOR A WHILE IN THE DOJO.
EXCELLENT. LET ME KNOW WHEN YOU ARE READY, AND I WILL ACCOMPANY YOU.
HAI, SENSEI.

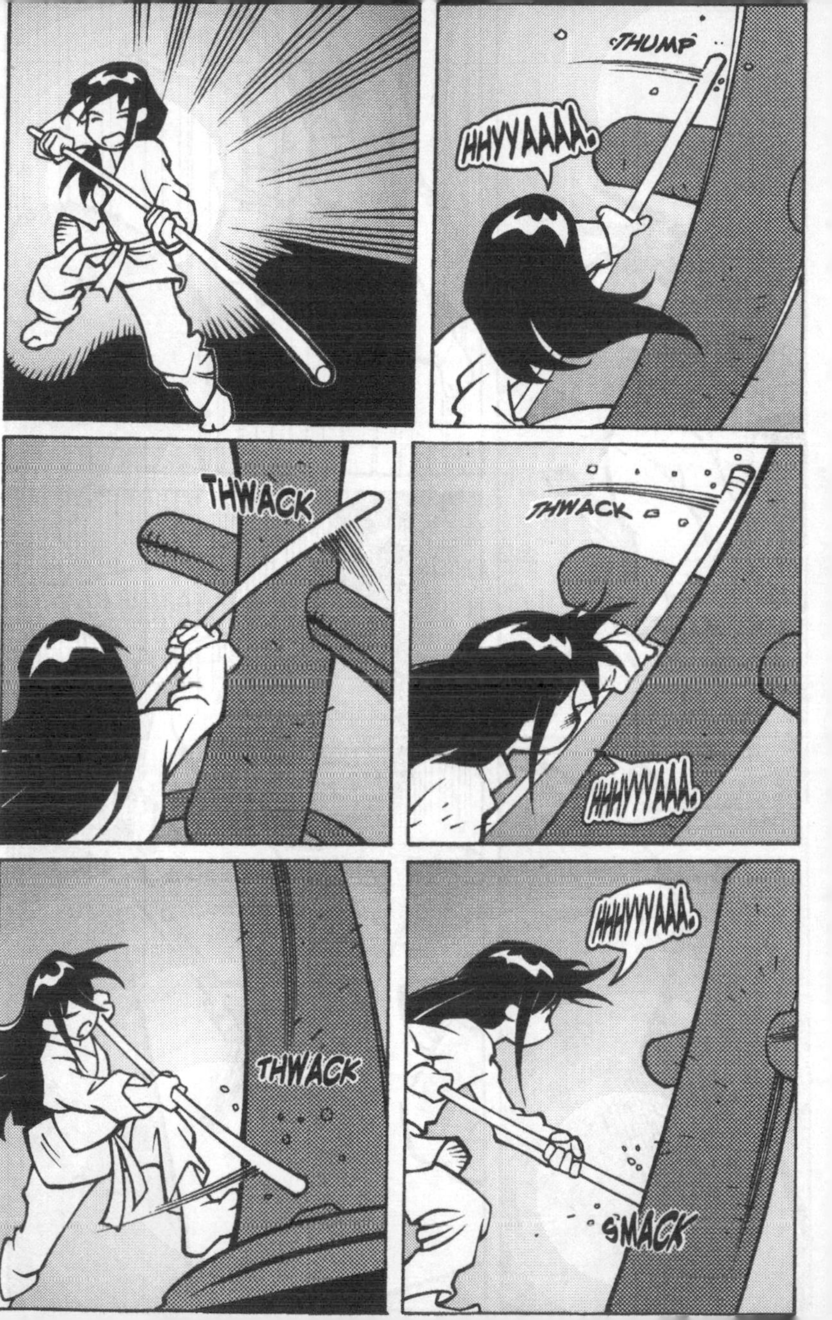
THUMP
HHYYAAAA
THWACK
THWACK
HHHYYYAAA
THWACK
HHHYYYAAA
SMACK

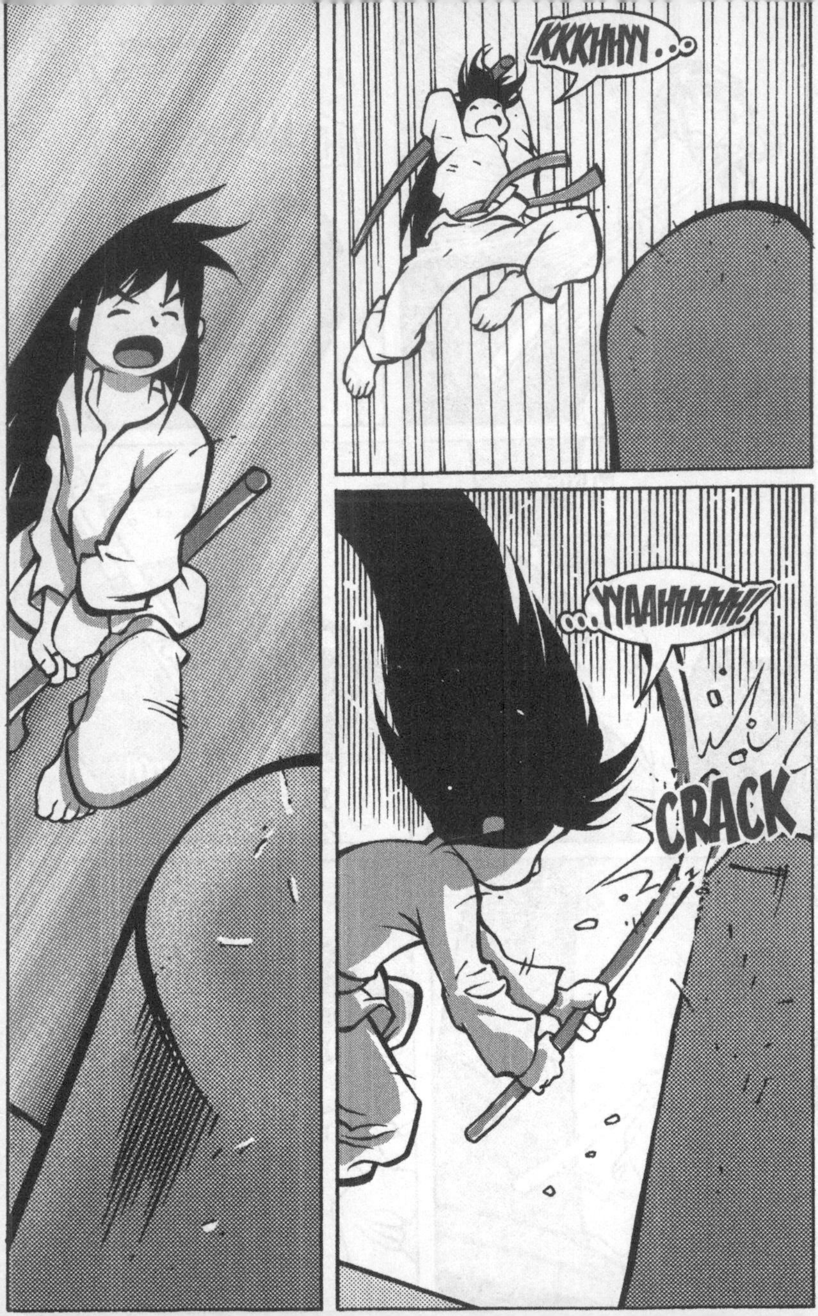
KKKHHYY...
...YYAAHHHHHH!
CRACK

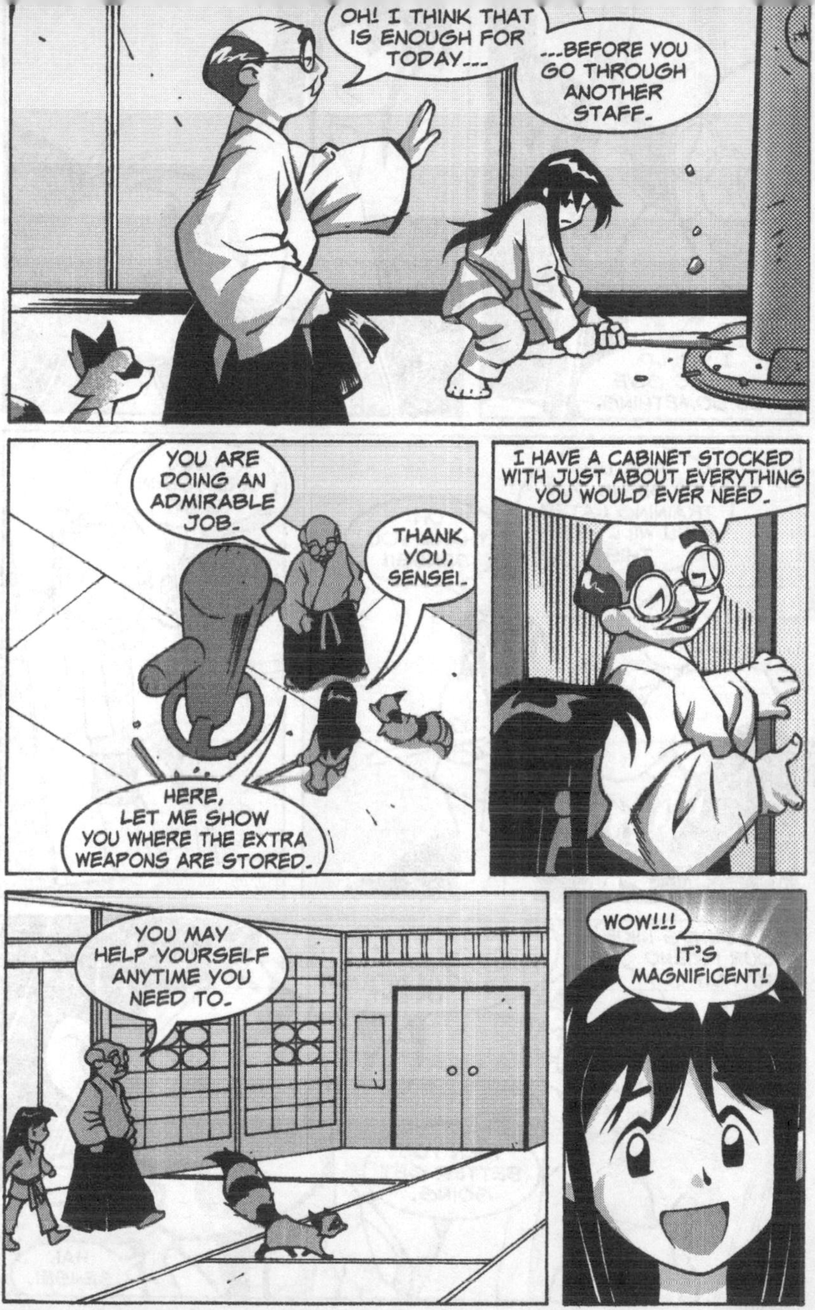
OH! I THINK THAT IS ENOUGH FOR TODAY...
...BEFORE YOU GO THROUGH ANOTHER STAFF.
YOU ARE DOING AN ADMIRABLE JOB.
THANK YOU, SENSEI.
HERE, LET ME SHOW YOU WHERE THE EXTRA WEAPONS ARE STORED.
I HAVE A CABINET STOCKED WITH JUST ABOUT EVERYTHING YOU WOULD EVER NEED.
YOU MAY HELP YOURSELF ANYTIME YOU NEED TO.
WOW!!!
IT'S MAGNIFICENT!

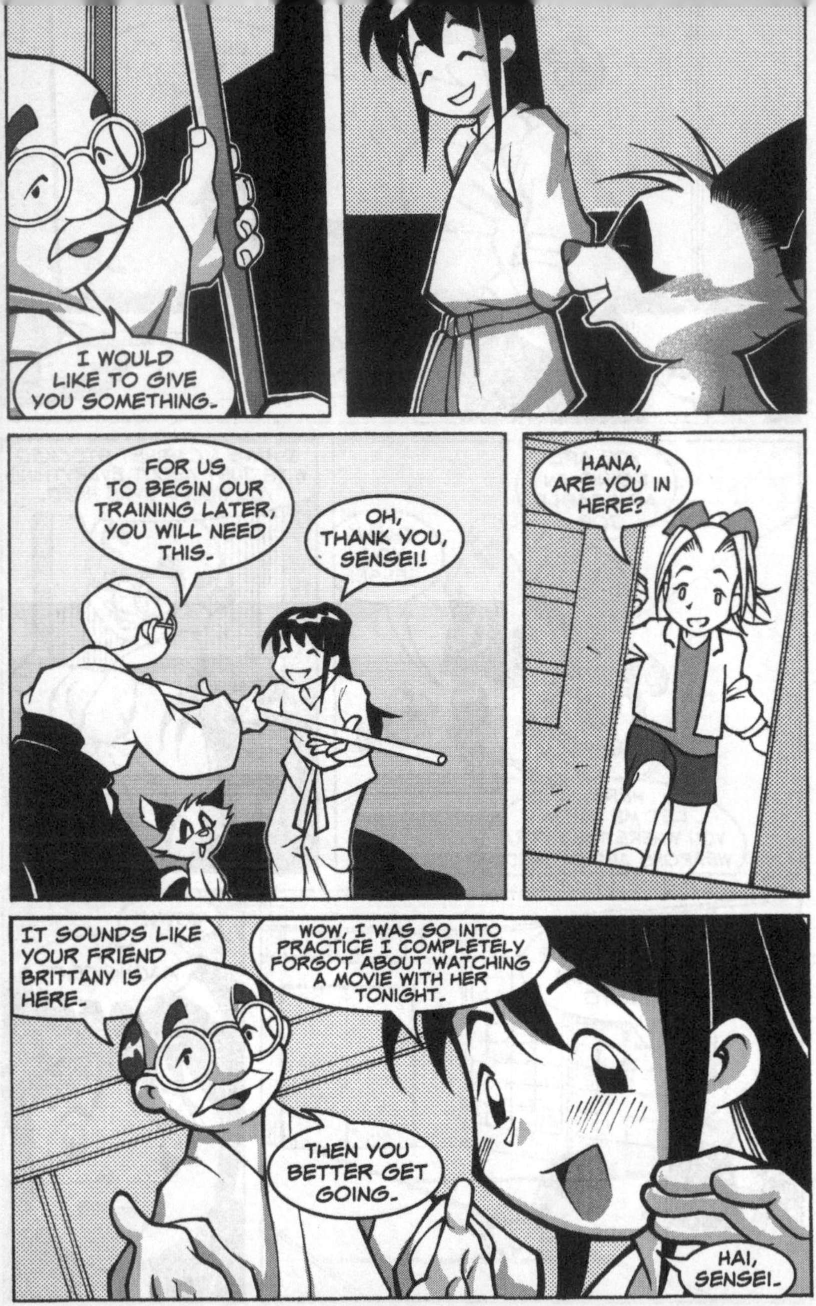
I WOULD LIKE TO GIVE YOU SOMETHING.
FOR US TO BEGIN OUR TRAINING LATER, YOU WILL NEED THIS.
OH, THANK YOU, SENSEI!
HANA, ARE YOU IN HERE?
IT SOUNDS LIKE YOUR FRIEND BRITTANY IS HERE.
WOW, I WAS SO INTO PRACTICE I COMPLETELY FORGOT ABOUT WATCHING A MOVIE WITH HER TONIGHT.
THEN YOU BETTER GET GOING.
HAI, SENSEI.

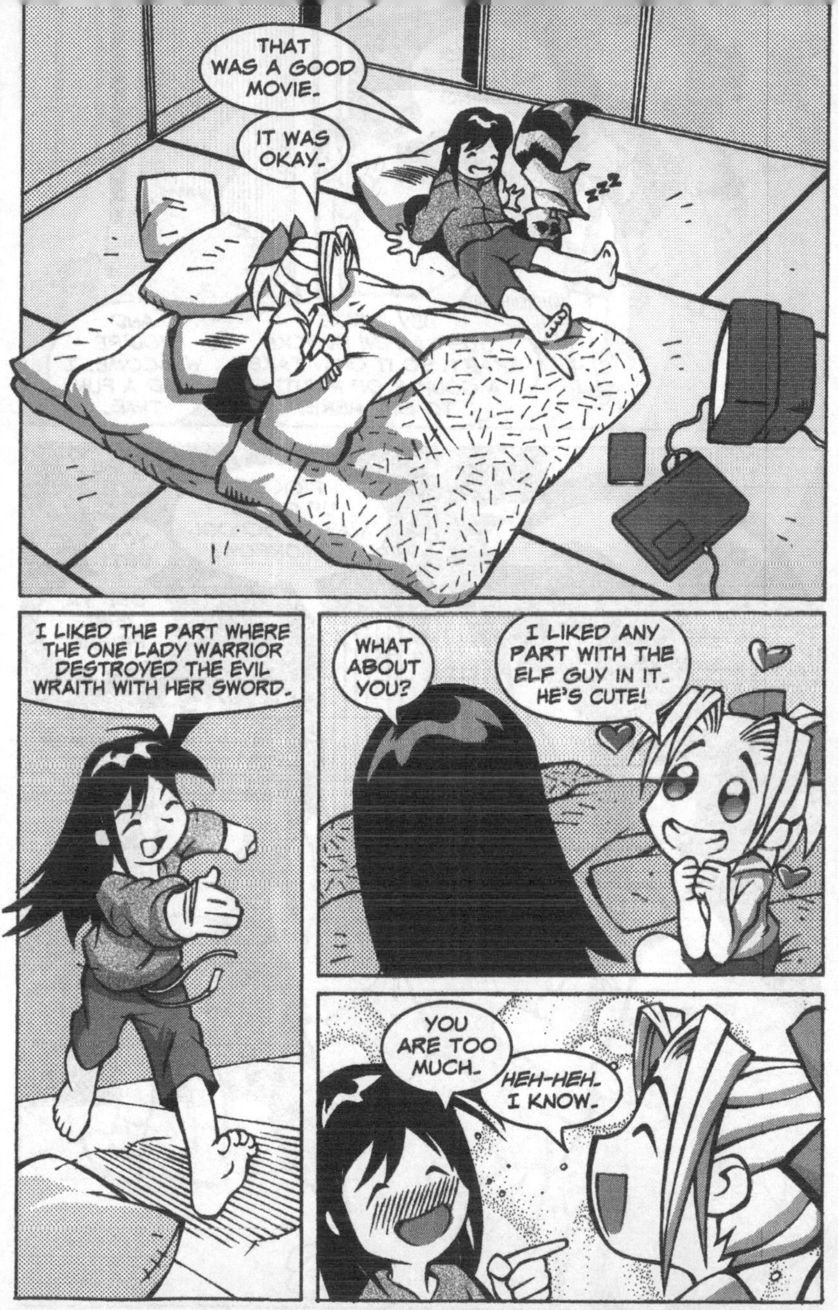
THAT WAS A GOOD MOVIE.
IT WAS OKAY.
ZZZ
I LIKED THE PART WHERE THE ONE LADY WARRIOR DESTROYED THE EVIL WRAITH WITH HER SWORD.
WHAT ABOUT YOU?
I LIKED ANY PART WITH THE ELF GUY IN IT. HE'S CUTE!
YOU ARE TOO MUCH.
HEH-HEH. I KNOW.

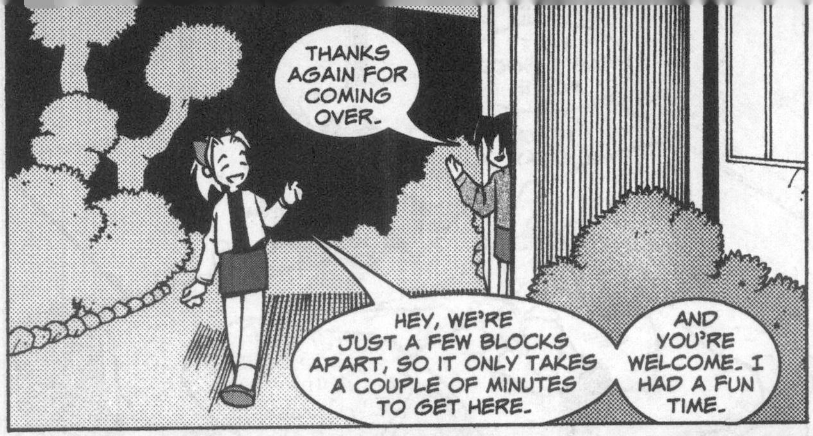
THANKS AGAIN FOR COMING OVER.
HEY, WE'RE JUST A FEW BLOCKS APART, SO IT ONLY TAKES A COUPLE OF MINUTES TO GET HERE.
AND YOU'RE WELCOME. I HAD A FUN TIME.
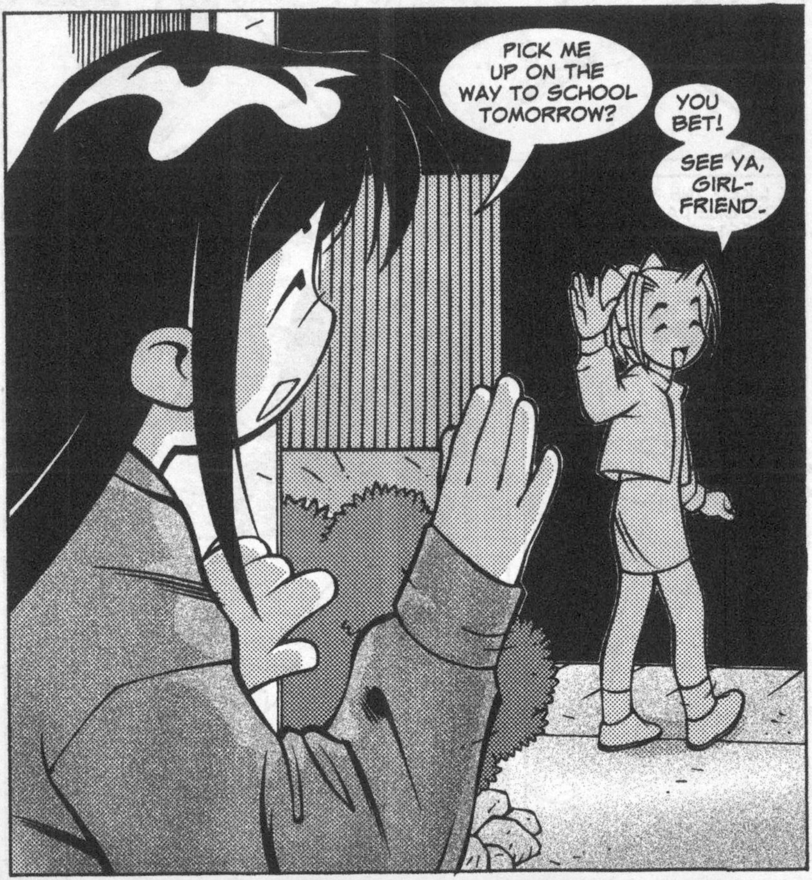
PICK ME UP ON THE WAY TO SCHOOL TOMORROW?
YOU BET!
SEE YA, GIRL-FRIEND.

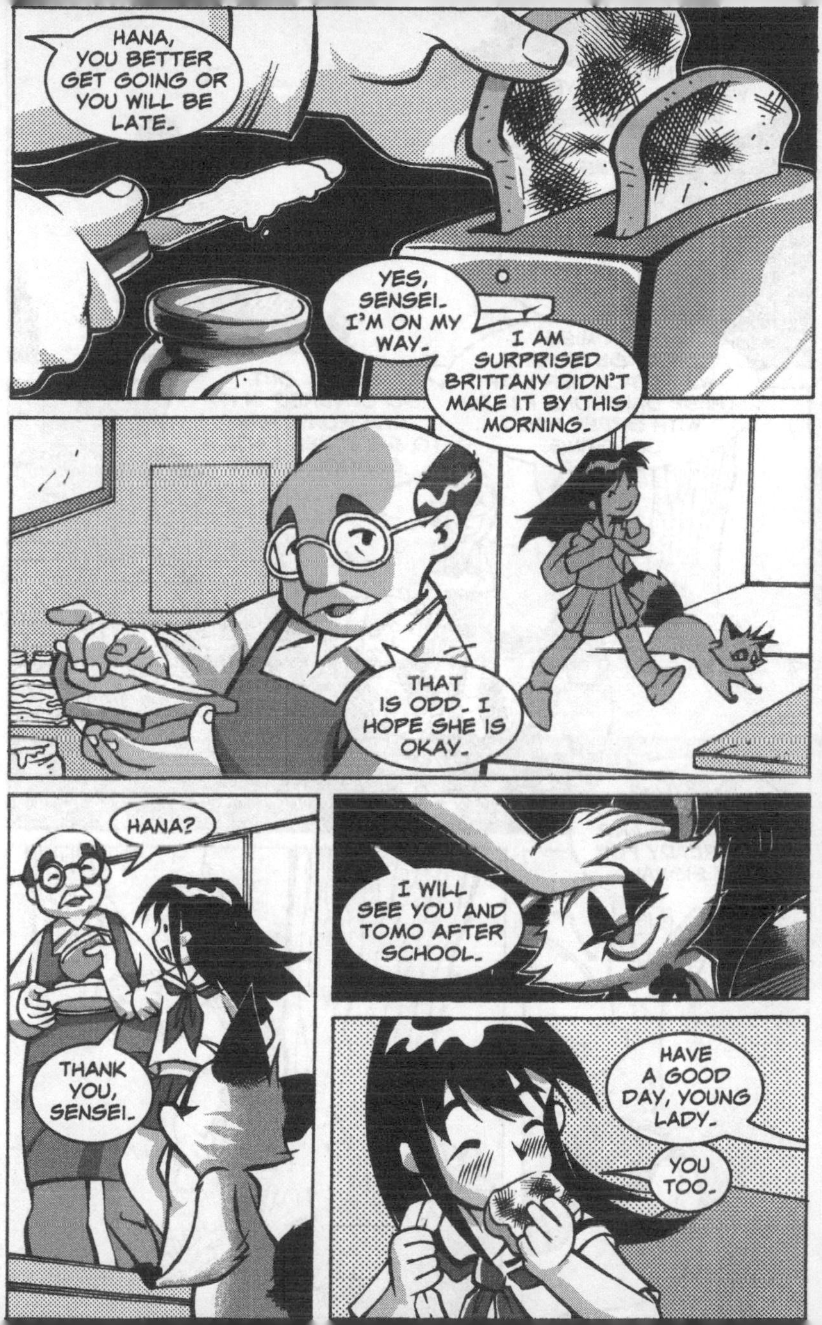
HANA, YOU BETTER GET GOING OR YOU WILL BE LATE.
YES, SENSEI. I'M ON MY WAY.
I AM SURPRISED BRITTANY DIDN'T MAKE IT BY THIS MORNING.
THAT IS ODD. I HOPE SHE IS OKAY.
HANA?
THANK YOU, SENSEI.
I WILL SEE YOU AND TOMO AFTER SCHOOL.
HAVE A GOOD DAY, YOUNG LADY.
YOU TOO.

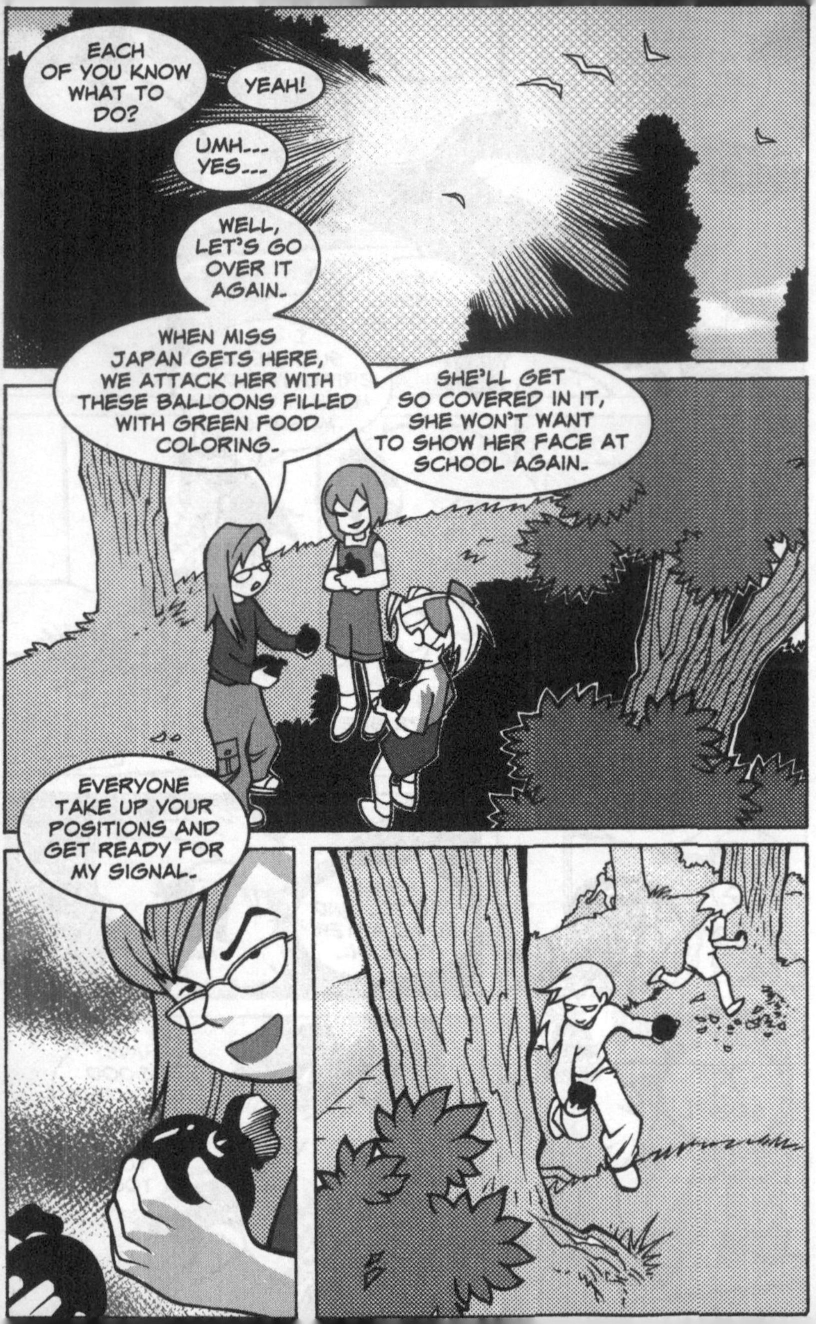

EACH OF YOU KNOW WHAT TO DO?
YEAH!
UMH... YES...
WELL, LET'S GO OVER IT AGAIN.
WHEN MISS JAPAN GETS HERE, WE ATTACK HER WITH THESE BALLOONS FILLED WITH GREEN FOOD COLORING.
SHE'LL GET SO COVERED IN IT, SHE WON'T WANT TO SHOW HER FACE AT SCHOOL AGAIN.
EVERYONE TAKE UP YOUR POSITIONS AND GET READY FOR MY SIGNAL.

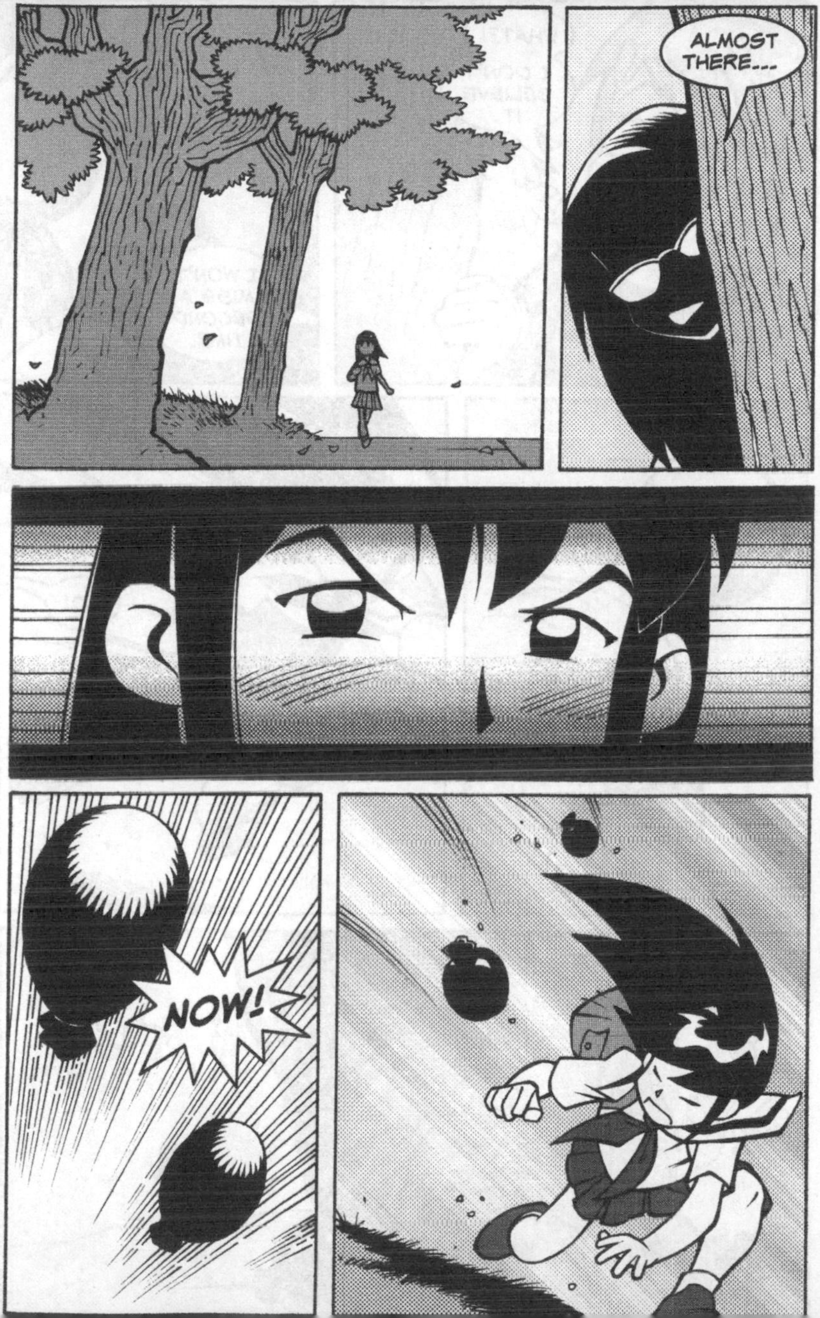
ALMOST THERE...
NOW!

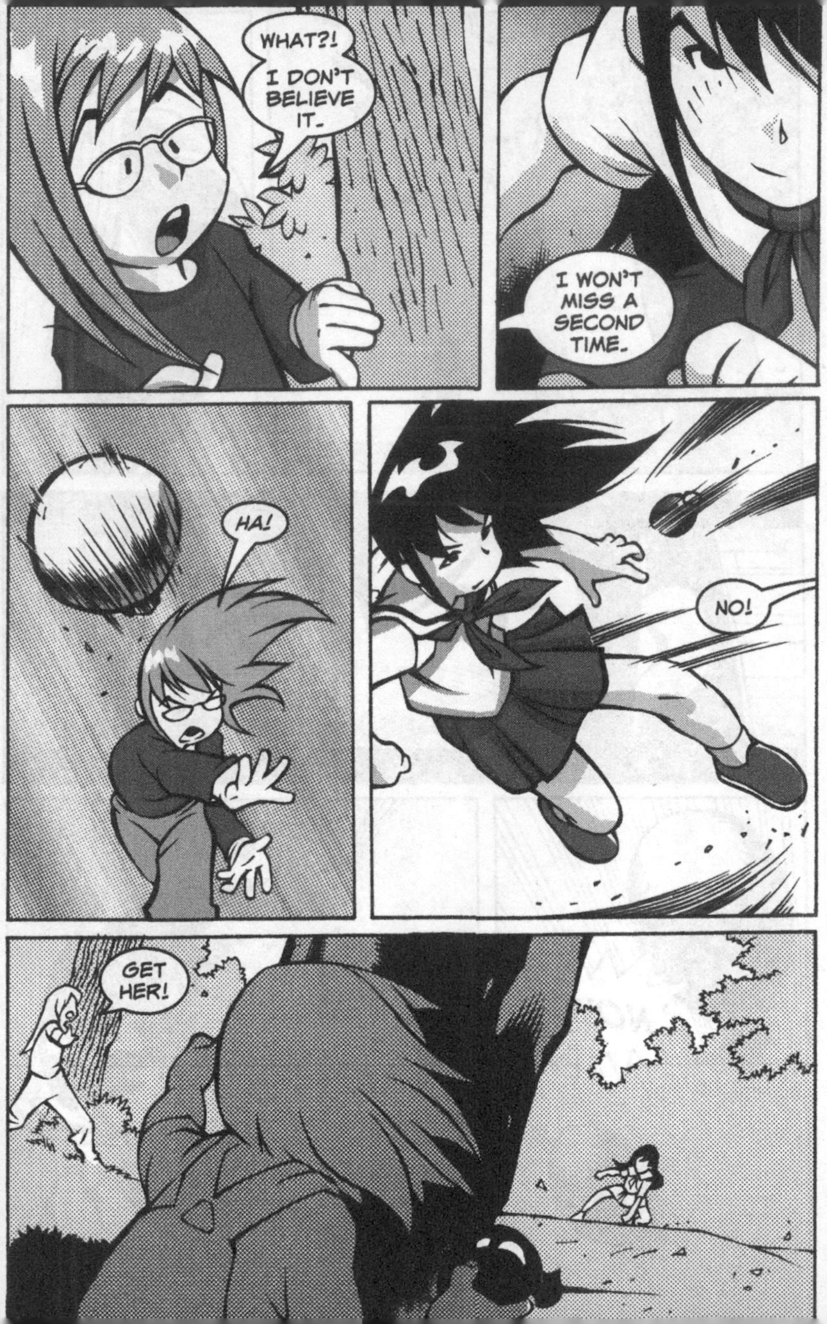
WHAT?! I DON'T BELIEVE IT.
I WON'T MISS A SECOND TIME.
HA!
NO!
GET HER!

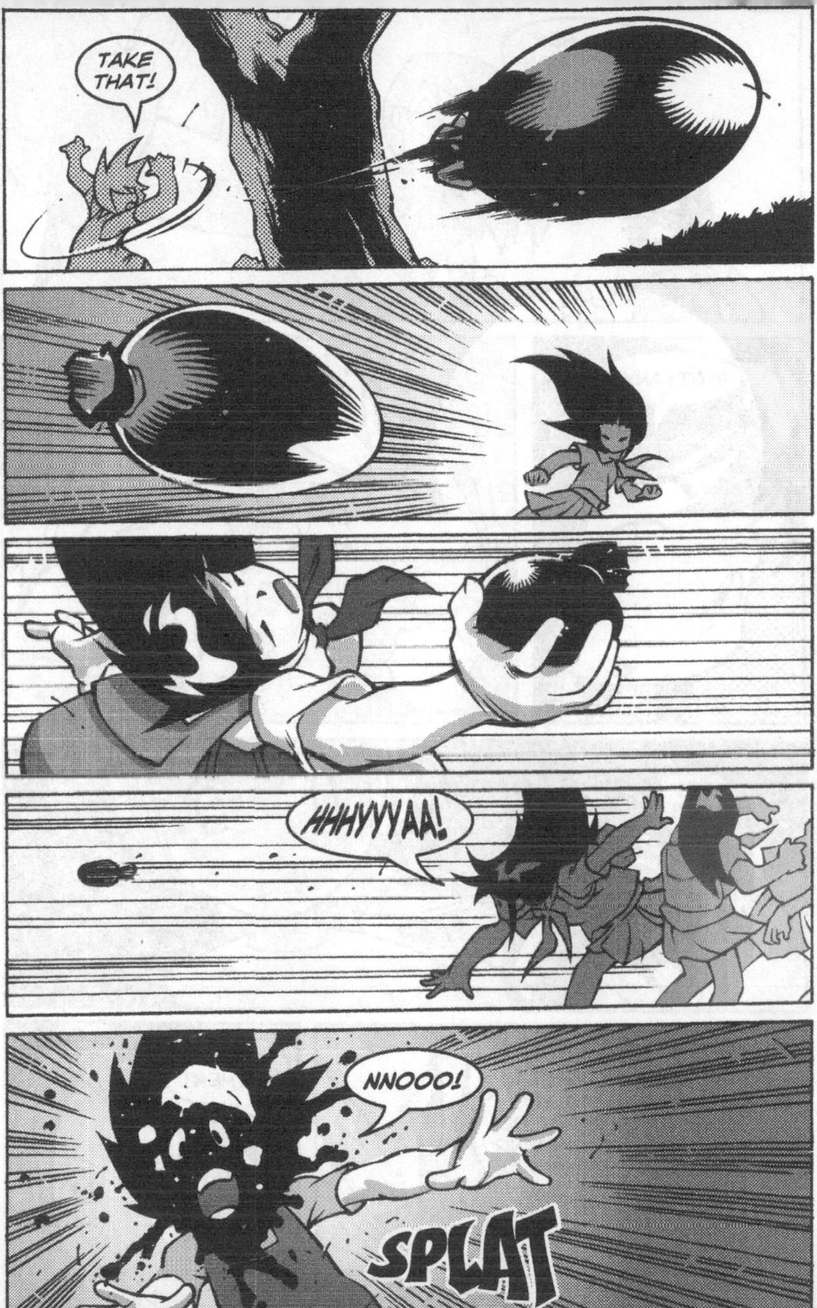
TAKE THAT!
HHHYYYAA!
NNOOO!
SPLAT

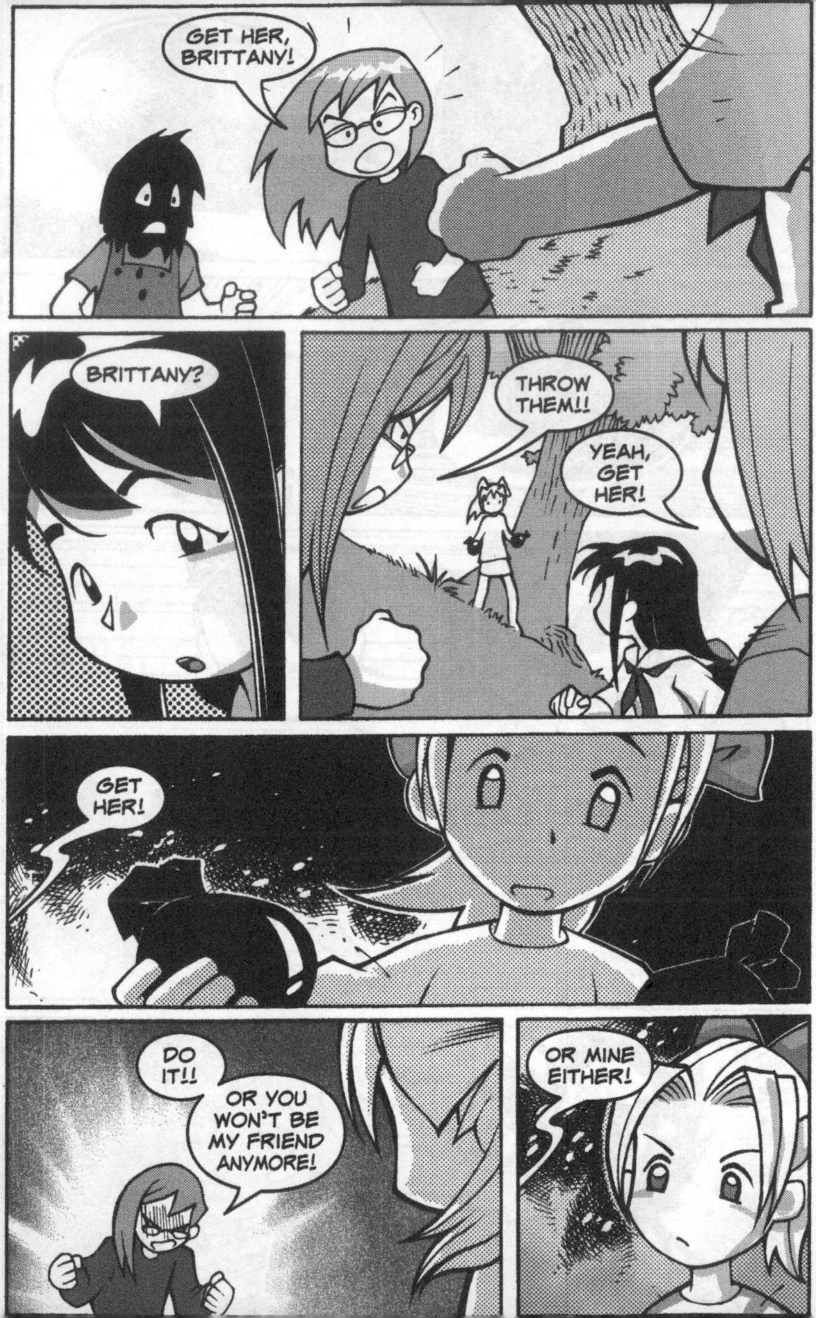
GET HER, BRITTANY!
BRITTANY?
THROW THEM!!
YEAH, GET HER!
GET HER!
DO IT!!
OR YOU WON'T BE MY FRIEND ANYMORE!
OR MINE EITHER!

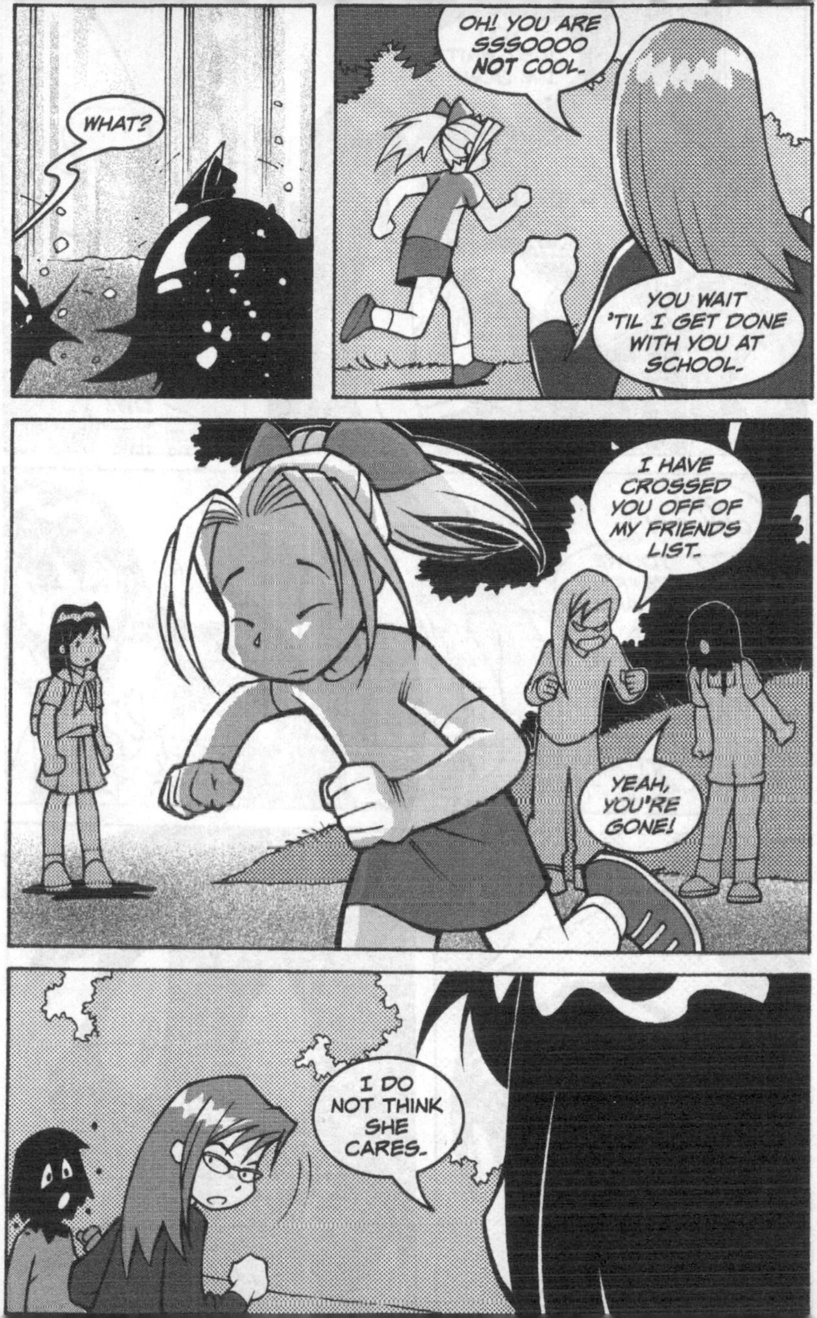
WHAT?
OH! YOU ARE SSSOOOO NOT COOL.
YOU WAIT 'TIL I GET DONE WITH YOU AT SCHOOL.
I HAVE CROSSED YOU OFF OF MY FRIENDS LIST.
YEAH, YOU'RE GONE!
I DO NOT THINK SHE CARES.

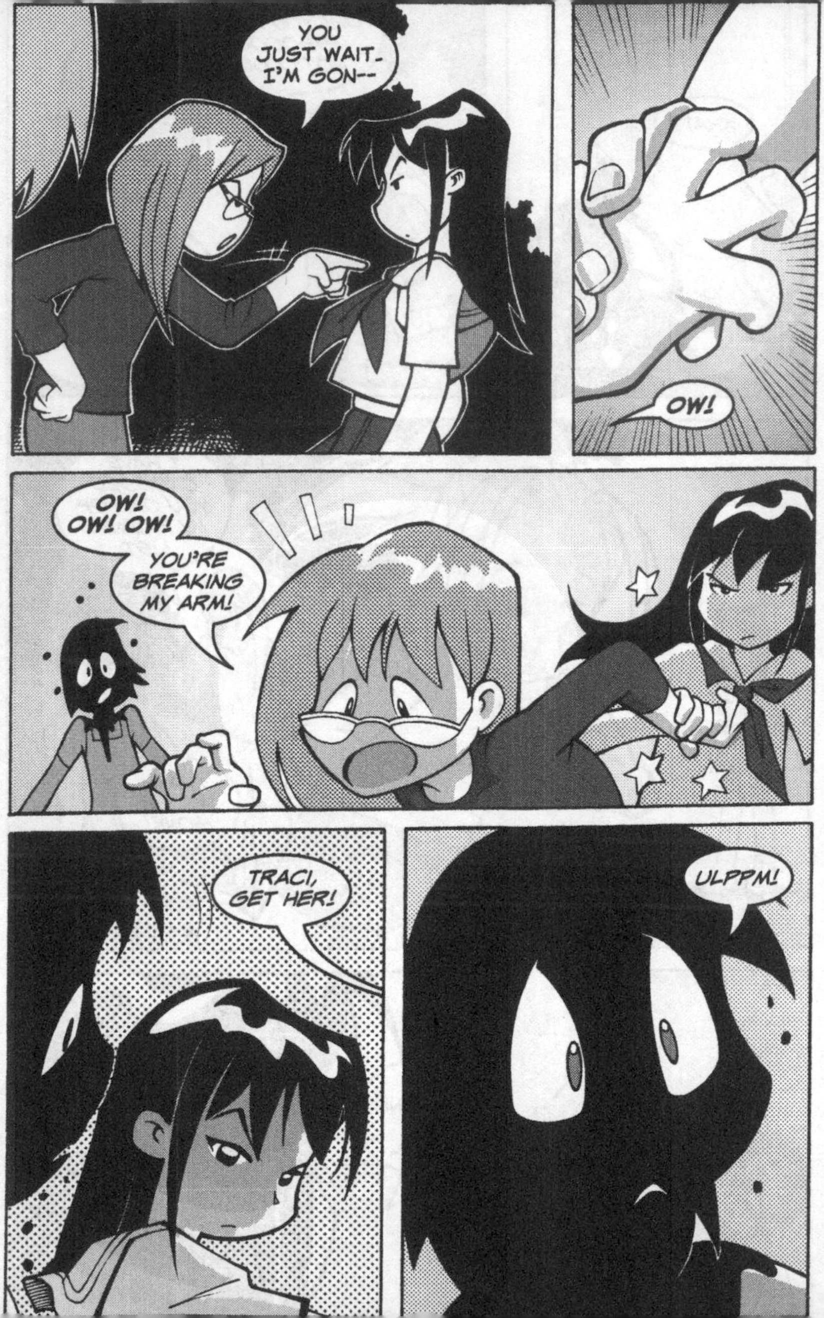
YOU JUST WAIT. I'M GON--
OW!
OW! OW! OW!
YOU'RE BREAKING MY ARM!
TRACI, GET HER!
ULPPM!

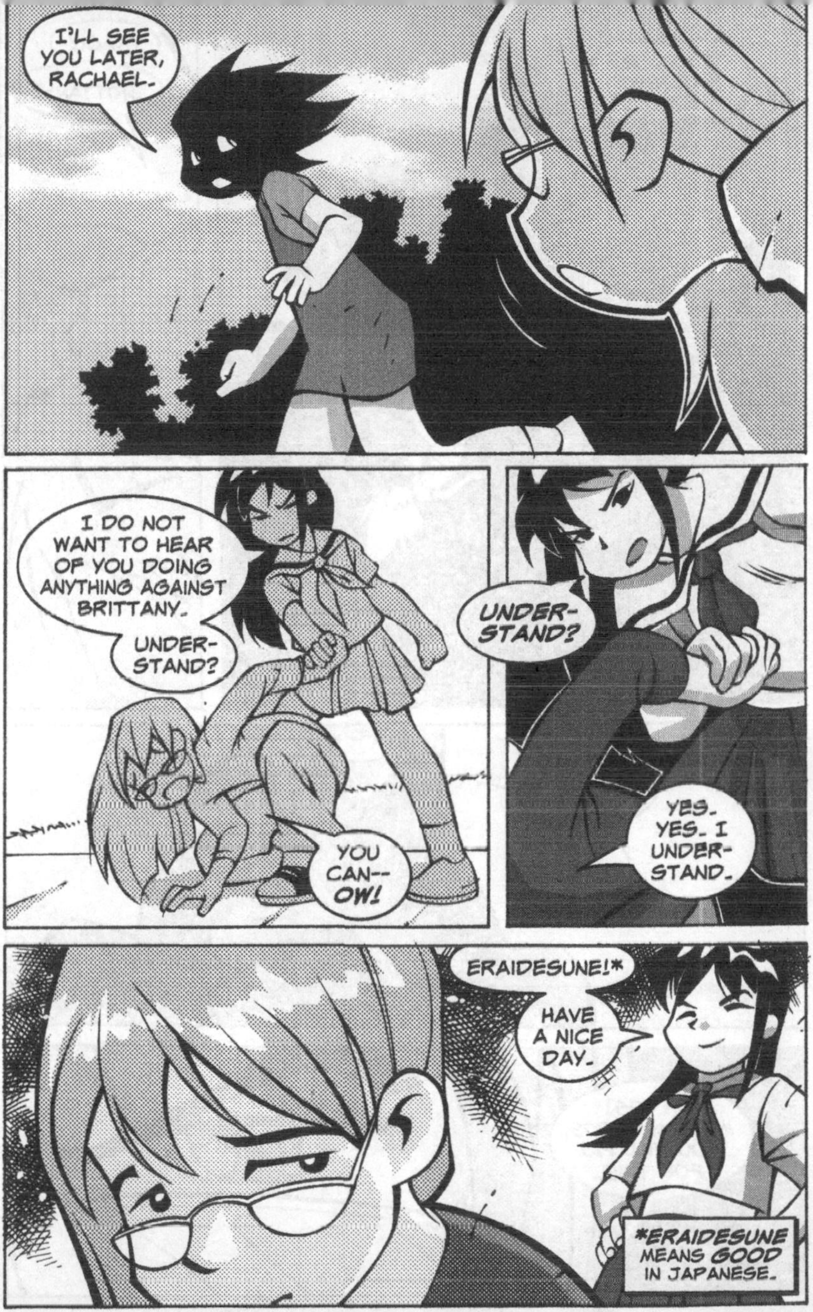

I'LL SEE YOU LATER, RACHAEL.
I DO NOT WANT TO HEAR OF YOU DOING ANYTHING AGAINST BRITTANY.
UNDER-STAND?
YOU CAN--
OW!
UNDER-STAND?
YES. YES. I UNDER-STAND.
ERAIDESUNE!*
HAVE A NICE DAY.
*ERAIDESUNE MEANS GOOD IN JAPANESE.

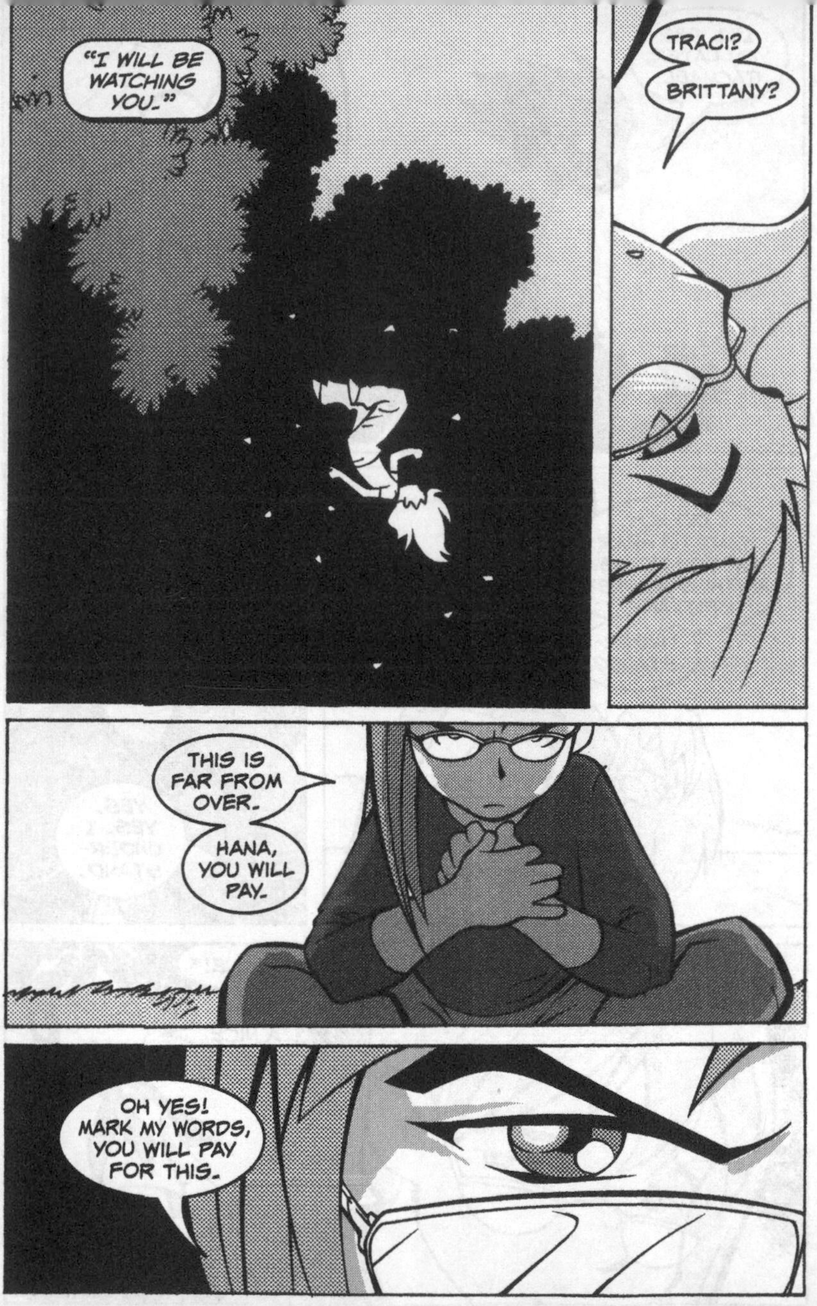
"I WILL BE WATCHING YOU."
TRACI?
BRITTANY?
THIS IS FAR FROM OVER.
HANA, YOU WILL PAY.
OH YES! MARK MY WORDS, YOU WILL PAY FOR THIS.

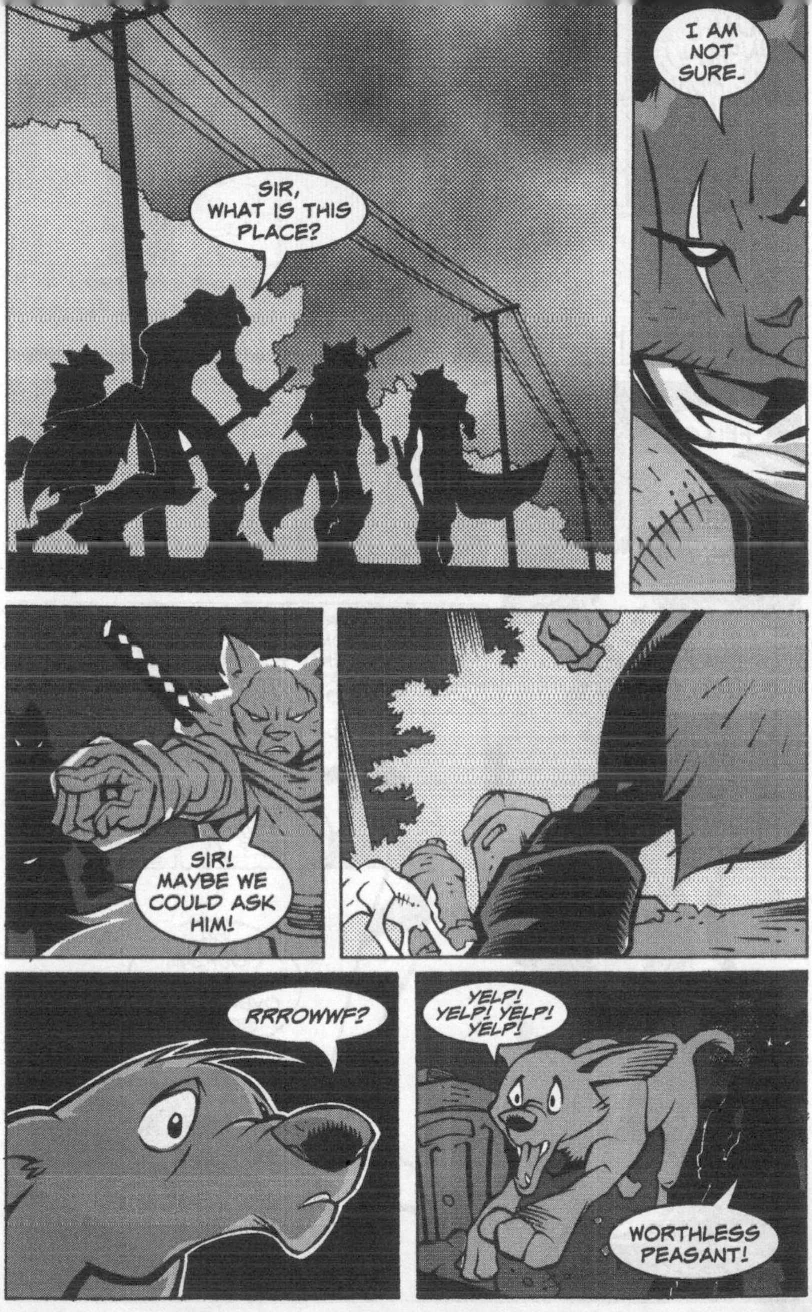
SIR, WHAT IS THIS PLACE?
I AM NOT SURE_
SIR! MAYBE WE COULD ASK HIM!
RRROWWF?
YELP! YELP! YELP! YELP!
WORTHLESS PEASANT!

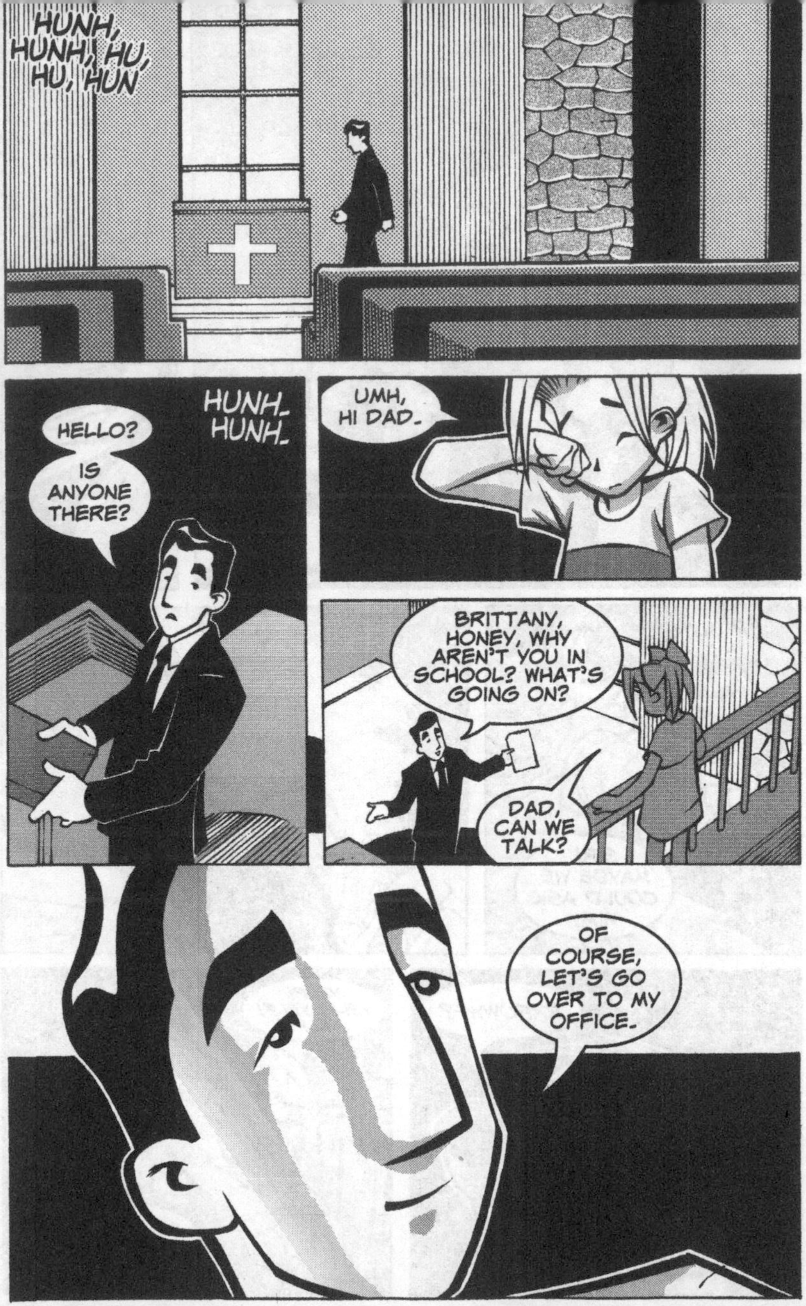
HUNH, HUNH, HU, HU, HUN
HELLO?
IS ANYONE THERE?
HUNH_ HUNH_
UMH, HI DAD_
BRITTANY, HONEY, WHY AREN'T YOU IN SCHOOL? WHAT'S GOING ON?
DAD, CAN WE TALK?
OF COURSE, LET'S GO OVER TO MY OFFICE_

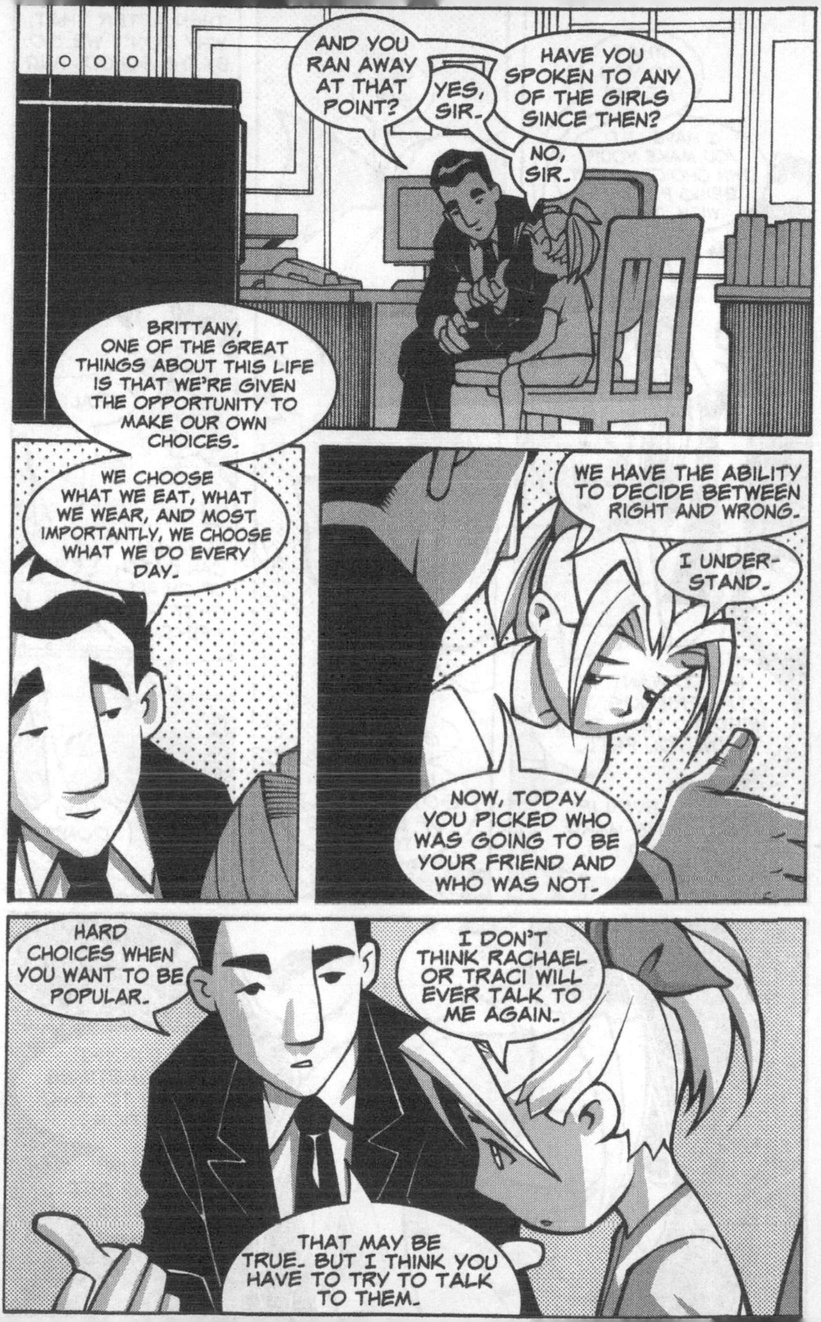
AND YOU RAN AWAY AT THAT POINT?
YES, SIR.
HAVE YOU SPOKEN TO ANY OF THE GIRLS SINCE THEN?
NO, SIR.
BRITTANY, ONE OF THE GREAT THINGS ABOUT THIS LIFE IS THAT WE'RE GIVEN THE OPPORTUNITY TO MAKE OUR OWN CHOICES.
WE CHOOSE WHAT WE EAT, WHAT WE WEAR, AND MOST IMPORTANTLY, WE CHOOSE WHAT WE DO EVERY DAY.
WE HAVE THE ABILITY TO DECIDE BETWEEN RIGHT AND WRONG.
I UNDER-STAND.
NOW, TODAY YOU PICKED WHO WAS GOING TO BE YOUR FRIEND AND WHO WAS NOT.
HARD CHOICES WHEN YOU WANT TO BE POPULAR.
I DON'T THINK RACHAEL OR TRACI WILL EVER TALK TO ME AGAIN.
THAT MAY BE TRUE. BUT I THINK YOU HAVE TO TRY TO TALK TO THEM.

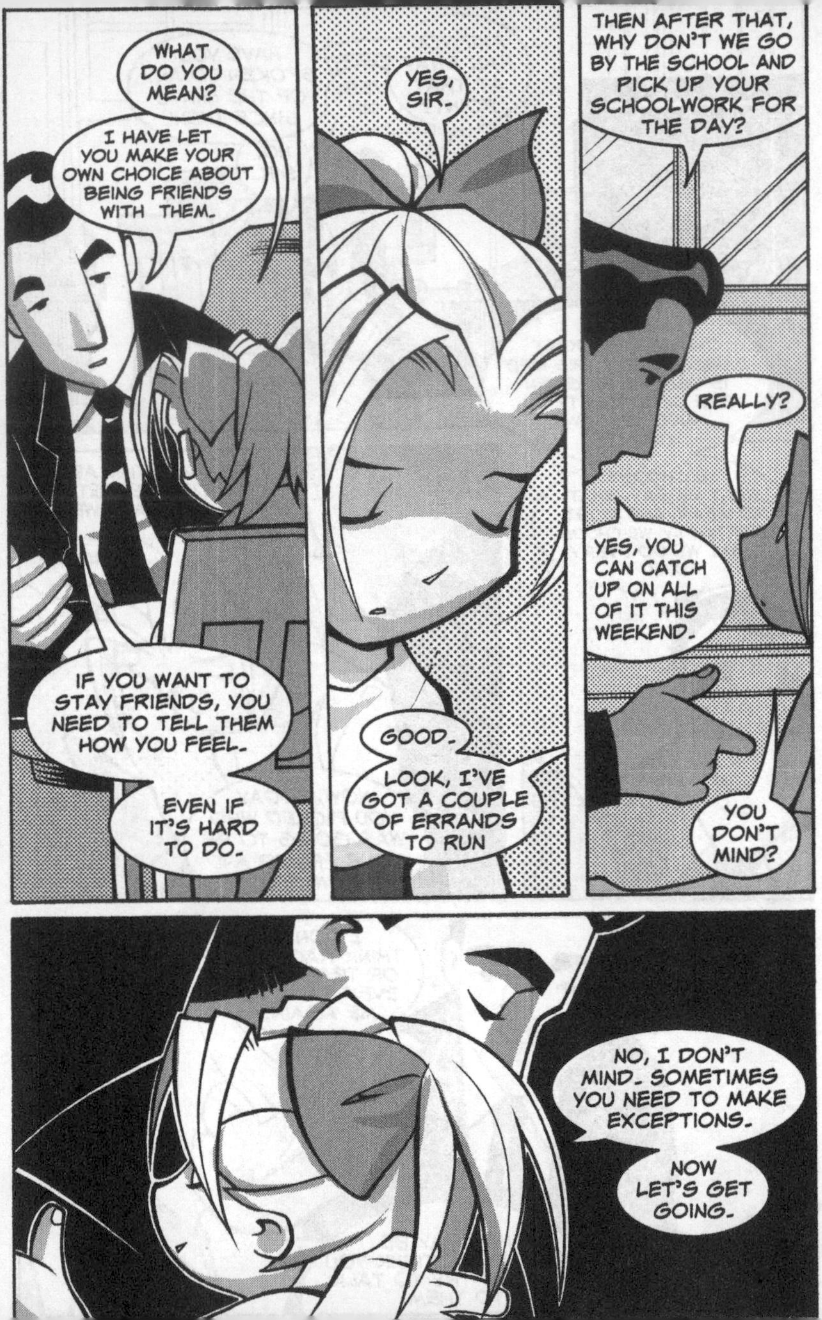
WHAT DO YOU MEAN?
I HAVE LET YOU MAKE YOUR OWN CHOICE ABOUT BEING FRIENDS WITH THEM.
IF YOU WANT TO STAY FRIENDS, YOU NEED TO TELL THEM HOW YOU FEEL.
EVEN IF IT'S HARD TO DO.
YES, SIR.
GOOD.
LOOK, I'VE GOT A COUPLE OF ERRANDS TO RUN
THEN AFTER THAT, WHY DON'T WE GO BY THE SCHOOL AND PICK UP YOUR SCHOOLWORK FOR THE DAY?
REALLY?
YES, YOU CAN CATCH UP ON ALL OF IT THIS WEEKEND.
YOU DON'T MIND?
NO, I DON'T MIND. SOMETIMES YOU NEED TO MAKE EXCEPTIONS.
NOW LET'S GET GOING.

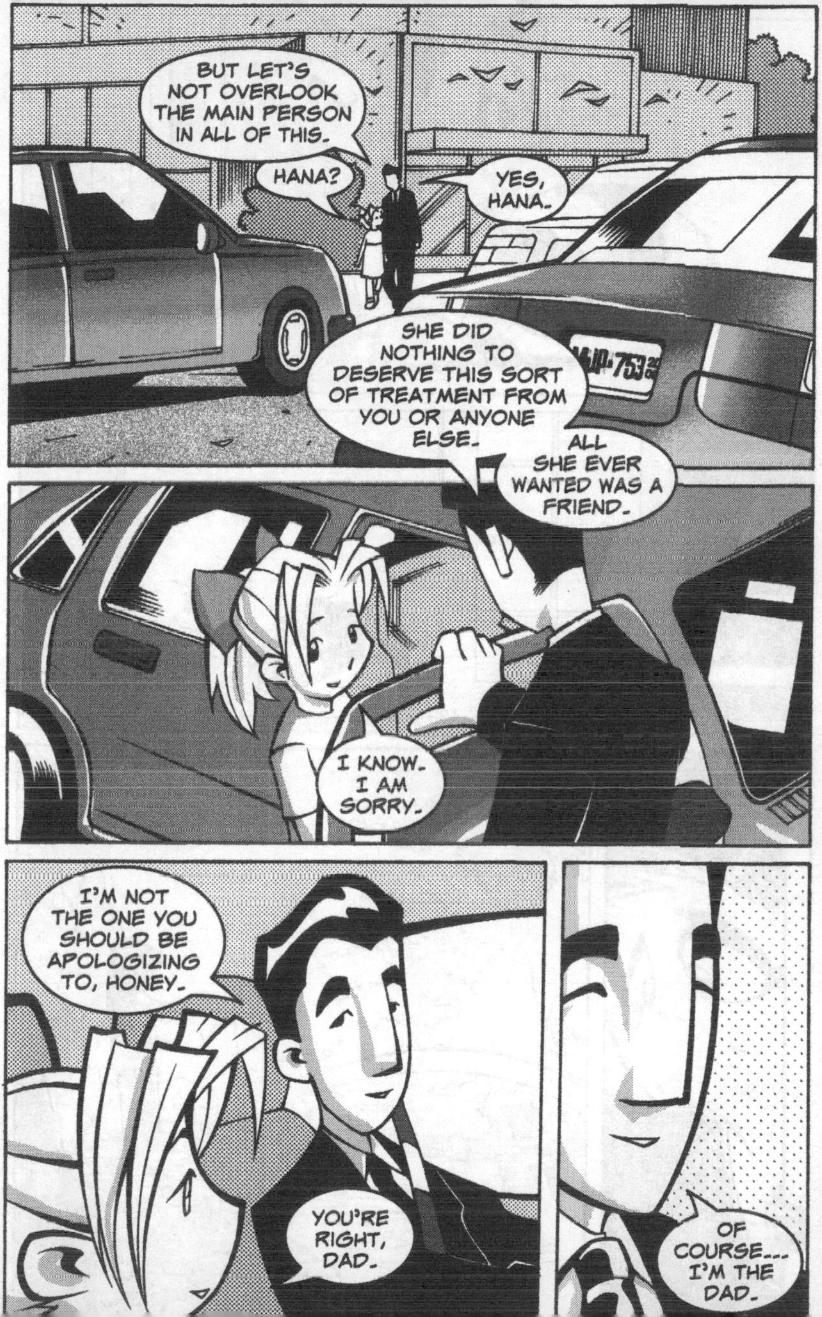
BUT LET'S NOT OVERLOOK THE MAIN PERSON IN ALL OF THIS.
HANA?
YES, HANA.
SHE DID NOTHING TO DESERVE THIS SORT OF TREATMENT FROM YOU OR ANYONE ELSE.
ALL SHE EVER WANTED WAS A FRIEND.
I KNOW. I AM SORRY.
I'M NOT THE ONE YOU SHOULD BE APOLOGIZING TO, HONEY.
YOU'RE RIGHT, DAD.
OF COURSE... I'M THE DAD.

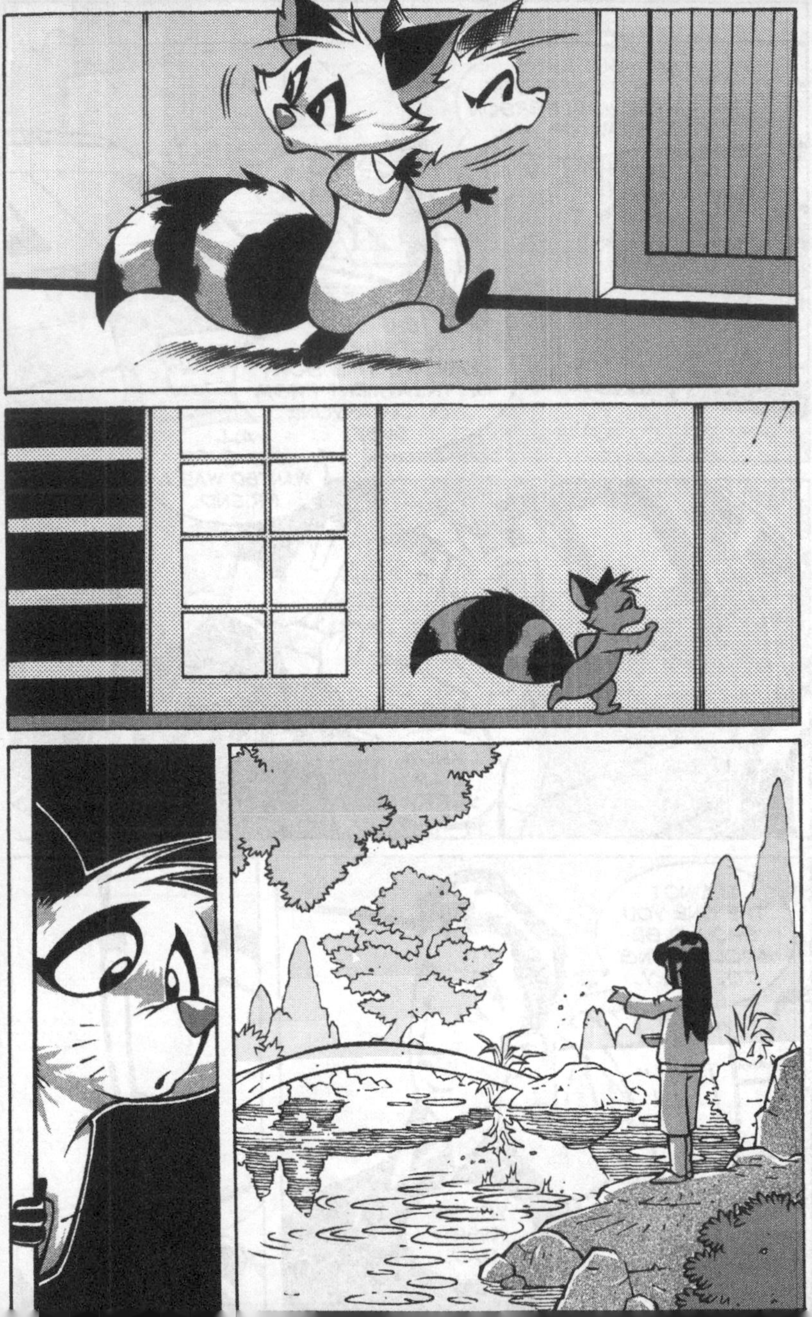

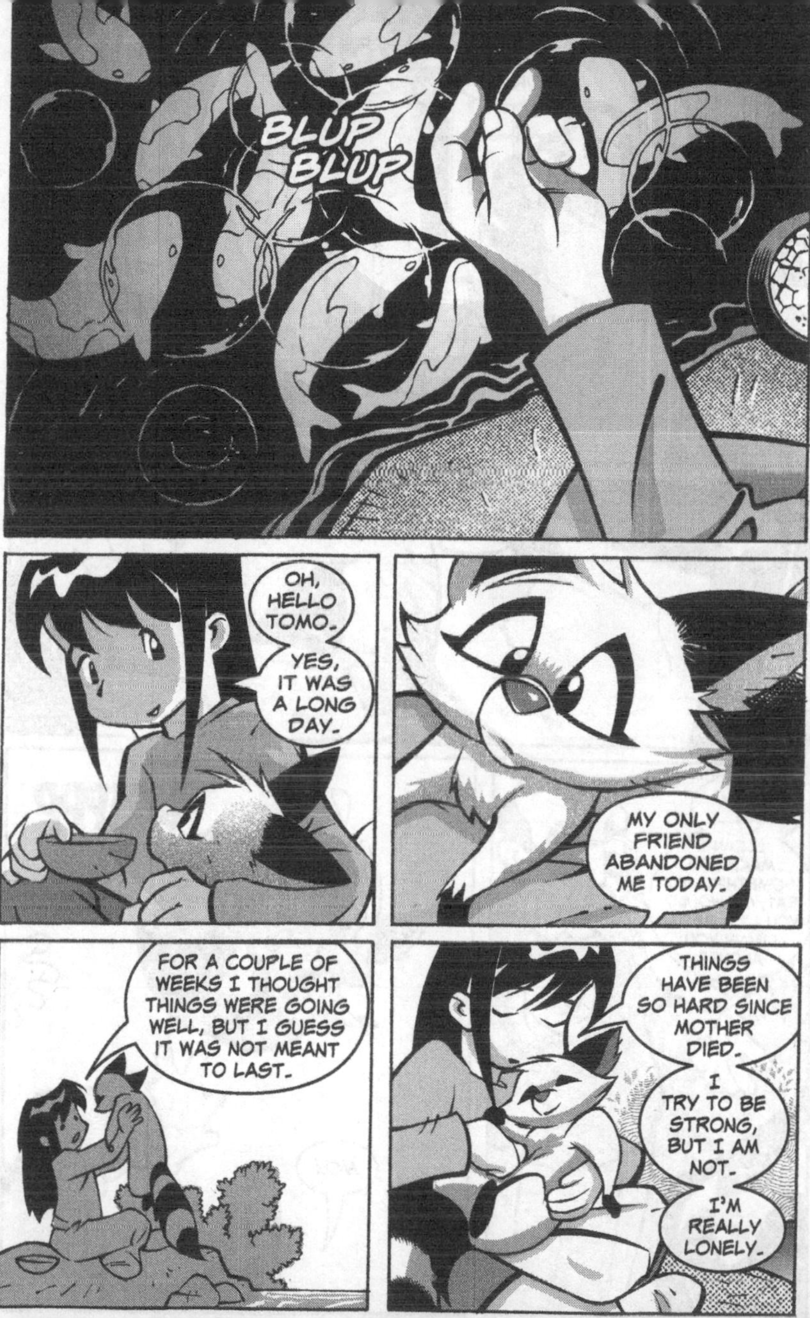
BLUP BLUP
OH, HELLO TOMO.
YES, IT WAS A LONG DAY.
MY ONLY FRIEND ABANDONED ME TODAY.
FOR A COUPLE OF WEEKS I THOUGHT THINGS WERE GOING WELL, BUT I GUESS IT WAS NOT MEANT TO LAST.
THINGS HAVE BEEN SO HARD SINCE MOTHER DIED.
I TRY TO BE STRONG, BUT I AM NOT.
I'M REALLY LONELY.

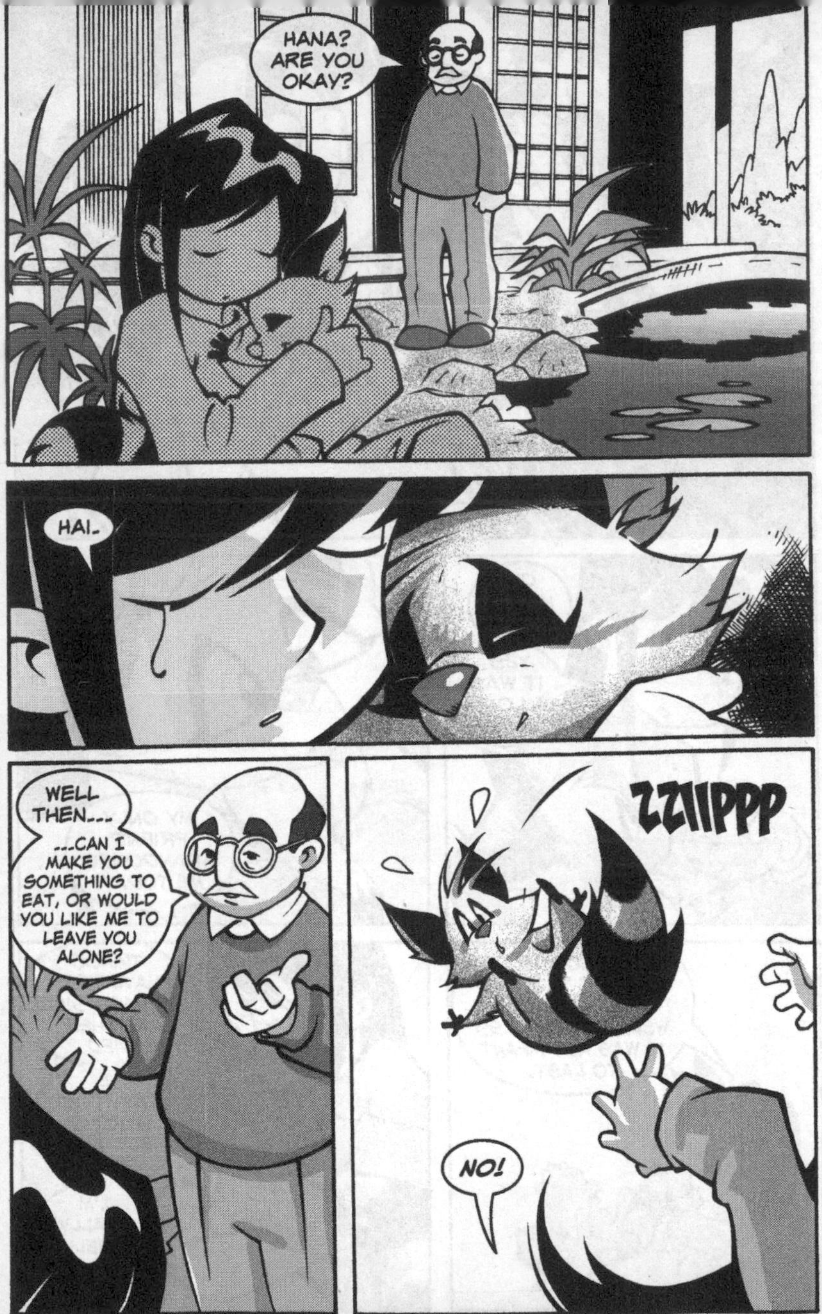
HANA? ARE YOU OKAY?
HAI...
WELL THEN...
...CAN I MAKE YOU SOMETHING TO EAT, OR WOULD YOU LIKE ME TO LEAVE YOU ALONE?
ZZIIPPP
NO!

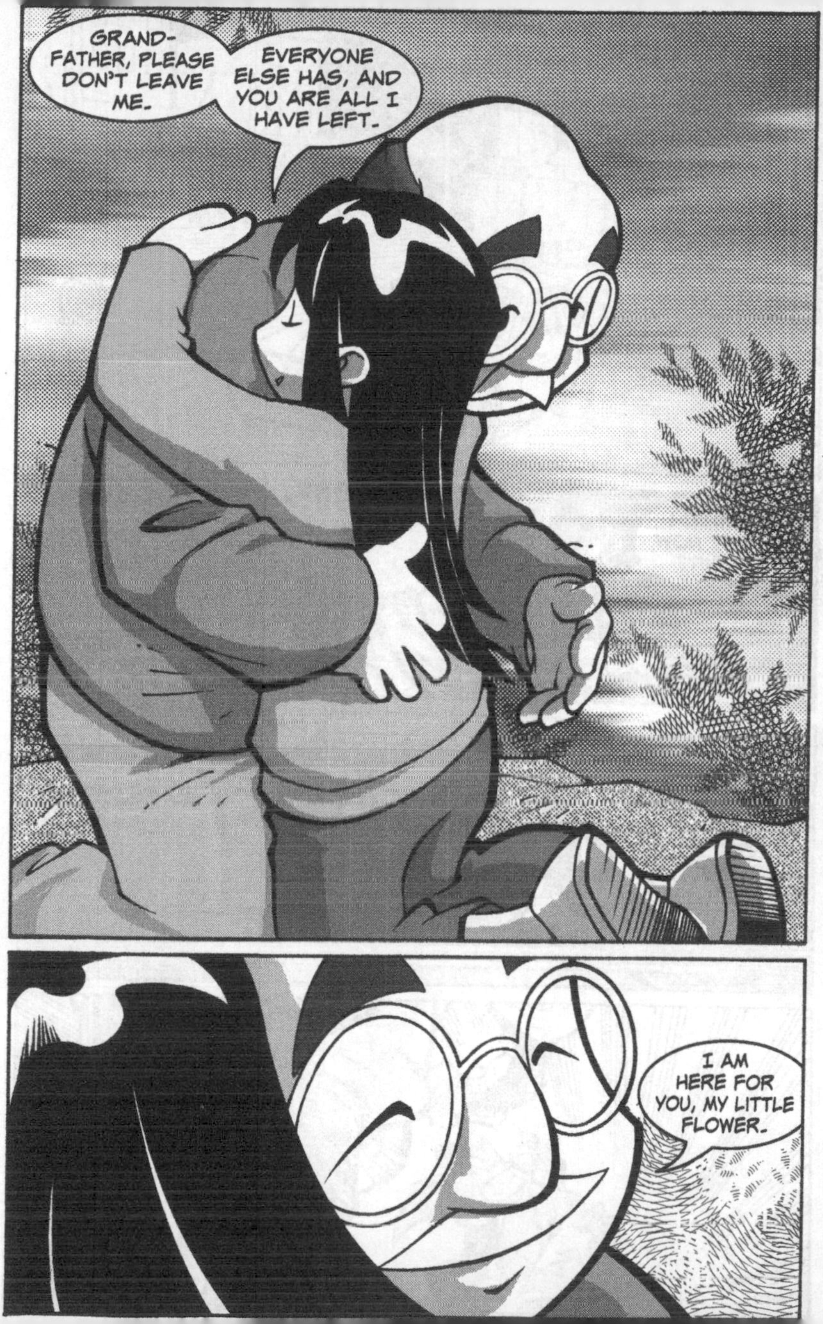
GRANDFATHER, PLEASE DON'T LEAVE ME.
EVERYONE ELSE HAS, AND YOU ARE ALL I HAVE LEFT.
I AM HERE FOR YOU, MY LITTLE FLOWER.

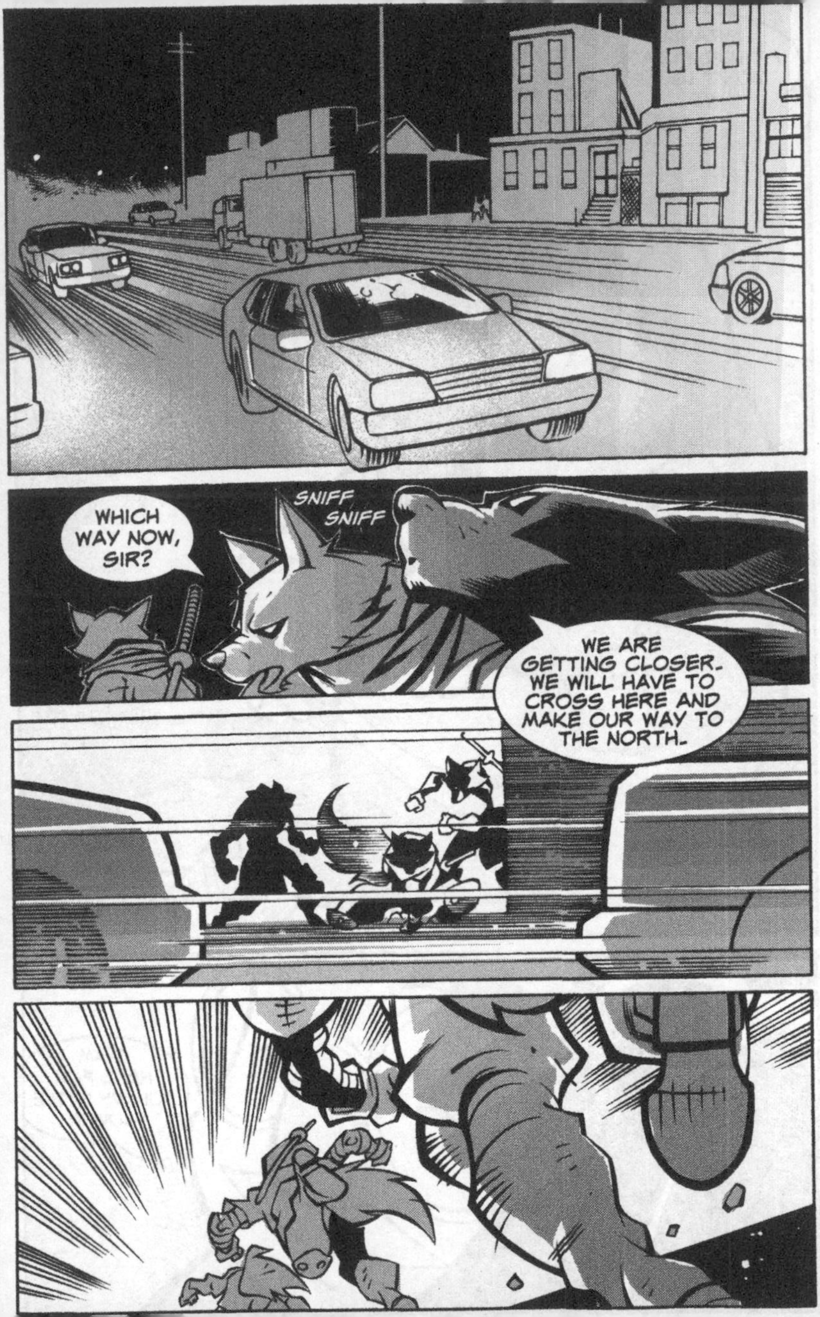
WHICH WAY NOW, SIR?
SNIFF SNIFF
WE ARE GETTING CLOSER. WE WILL HAVE TO CROSS HERE AND MAKE OUR WAY TO THE NORTH.

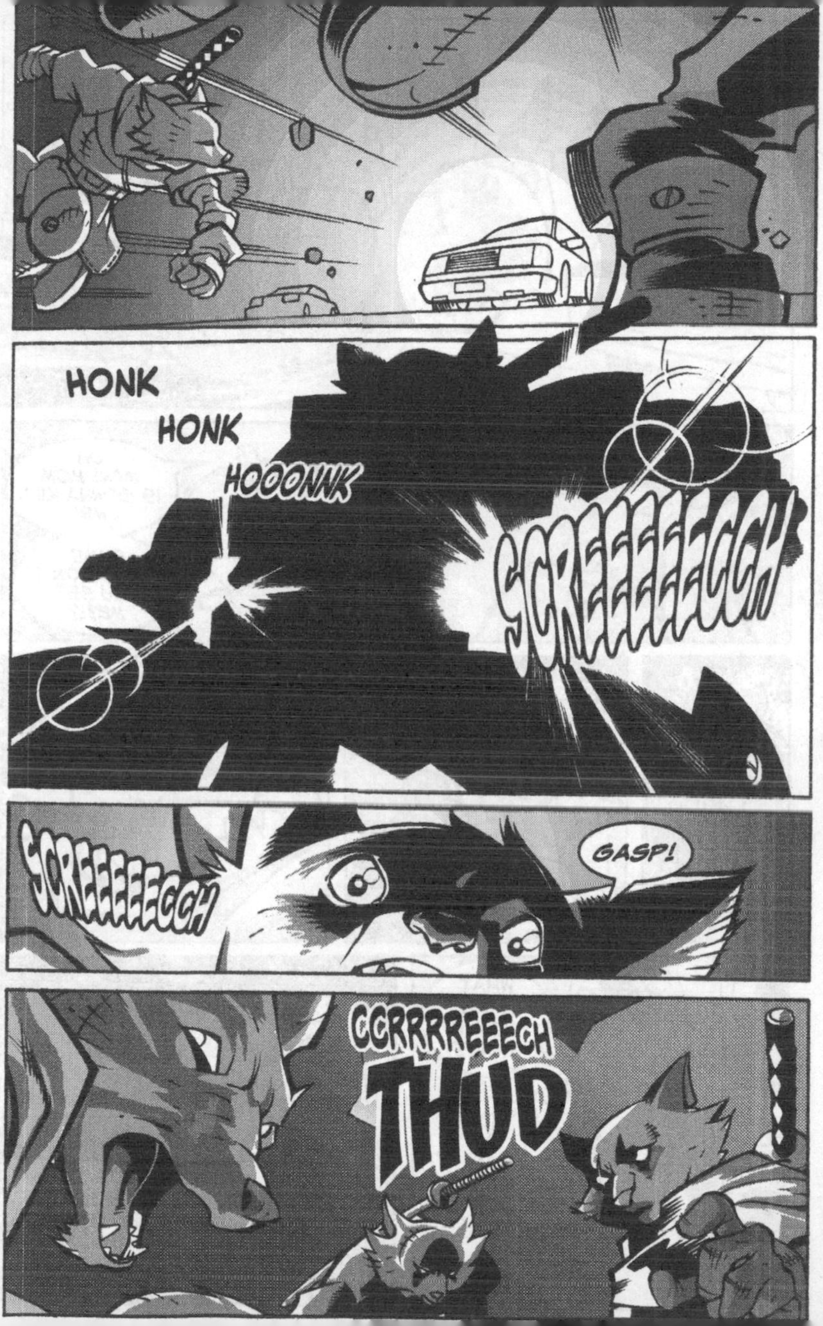
HONK
HONK
HOOONNK
SCREEEEEECCH
SCREEEEEEECCH
GASP!
CCRRRREEECH
THUD

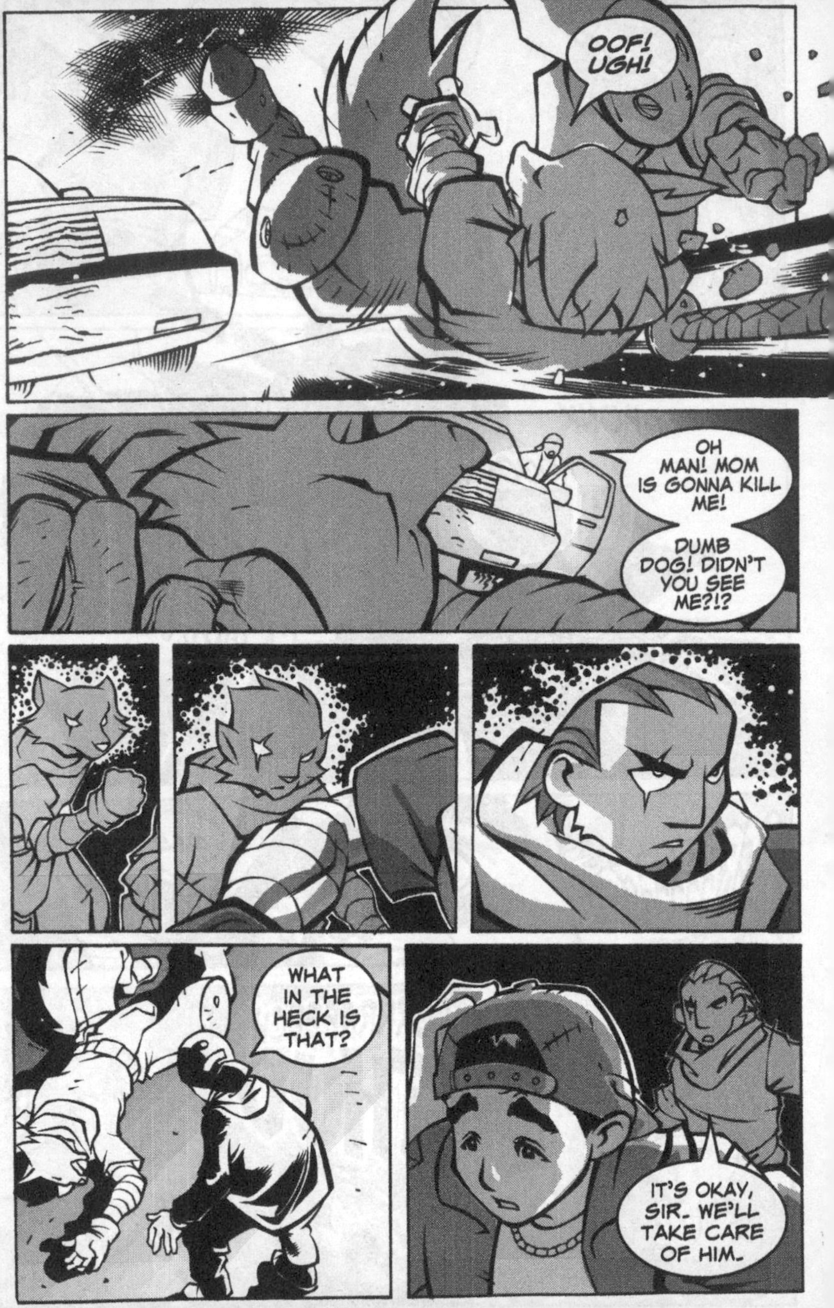
OOF! UGH!
OH MAN! MOM IS GONNA KILL ME!
DUMB DOG! DIDN'T YOU SEE ME?!?
WHAT IN THE HECK IS THAT?
IT'S OKAY, SIR. WE'LL TAKE CARE OF HIM.

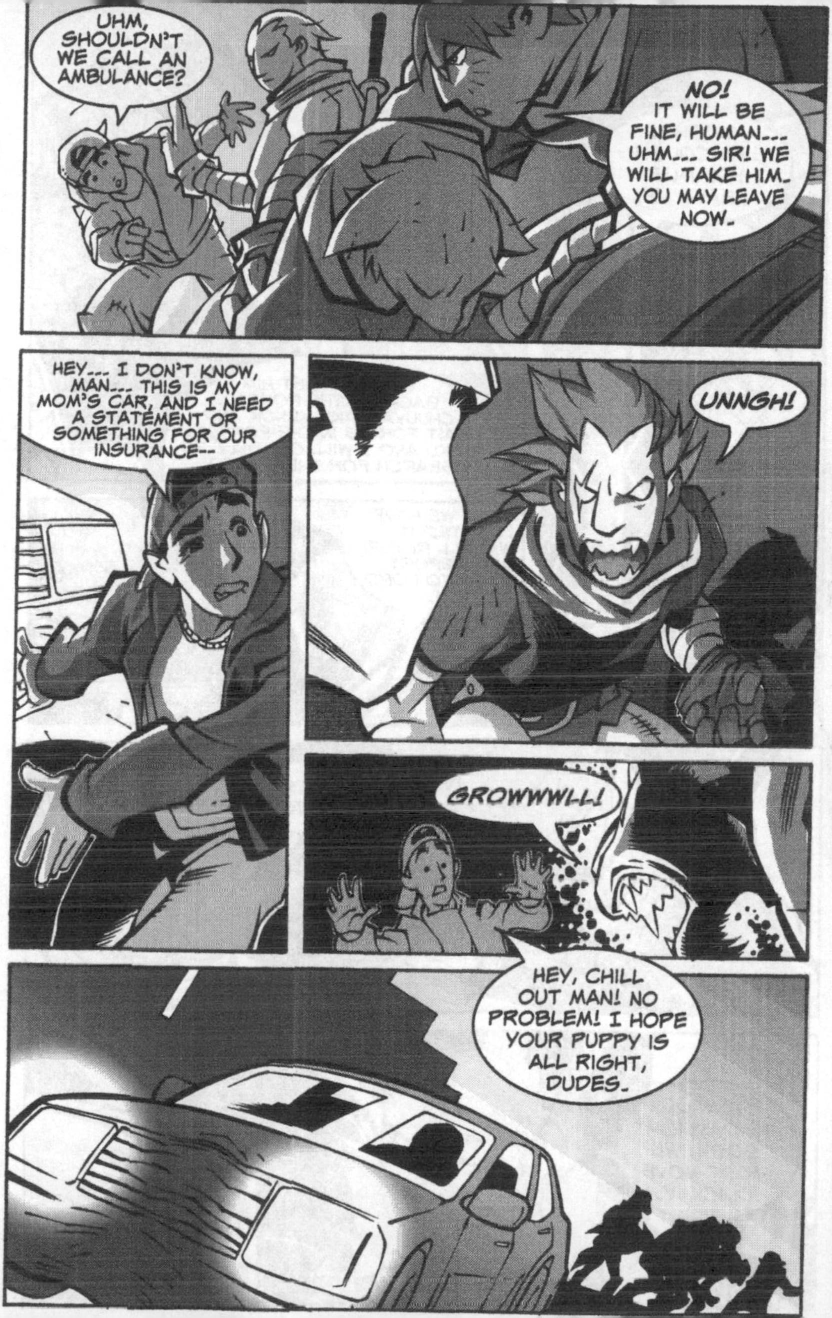
UHM, SHOULDN'T WE CALL AN AMBULANCE?
NO! IT WILL BE FINE, HUMAN... UHM... SIR! WE WILL TAKE HIM. YOU MAY LEAVE NOW.
HEY... I DON'T KNOW, MAN... THIS IS MY MOM'S CAR, AND I NEED A STATEMENT OR SOMETHING FOR OUR INSURANCE--
UNNGH!
GROWWWLL!
HEY, CHILL OUT MAN! NO PROBLEM! I HOPE YOUR PUPPY IS ALL RIGHT, DUDES.

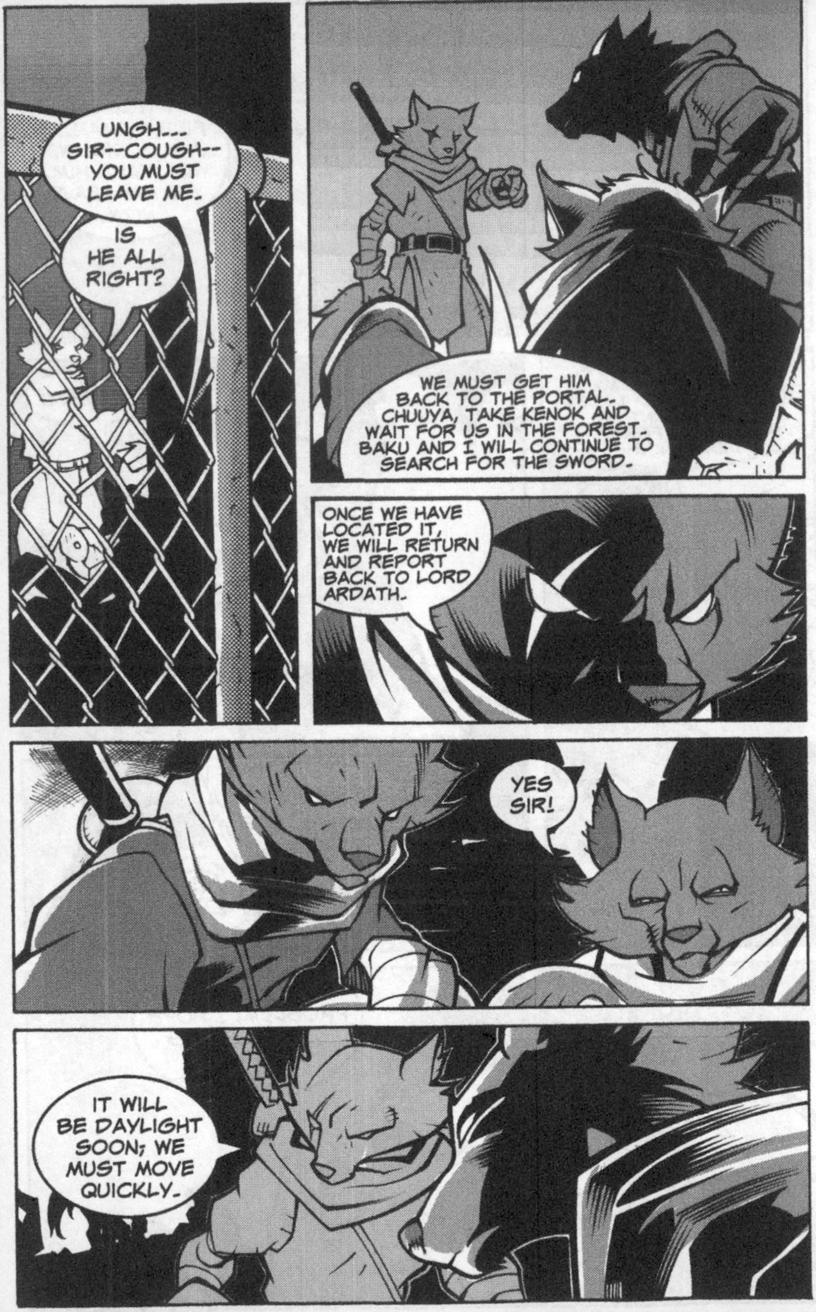
UNGH... SIR--COUGH-- YOU MUST LEAVE ME.
IS HE ALL RIGHT?
WE MUST GET HIM BACK TO THE PORTAL. CHUUYA, TAKE KENOK AND WAIT FOR US IN THE FOREST. BAKU AND I WILL CONTINUE TO SEARCH FOR THE SWORD.
ONCE WE HAVE LOCATED IT, WE WILL RETURN AND REPORT BACK TO LORD ARDATH.
YES SIR!
IT WILL BE DAYLIGHT SOON; WE MUST MOVE QUICKLY.

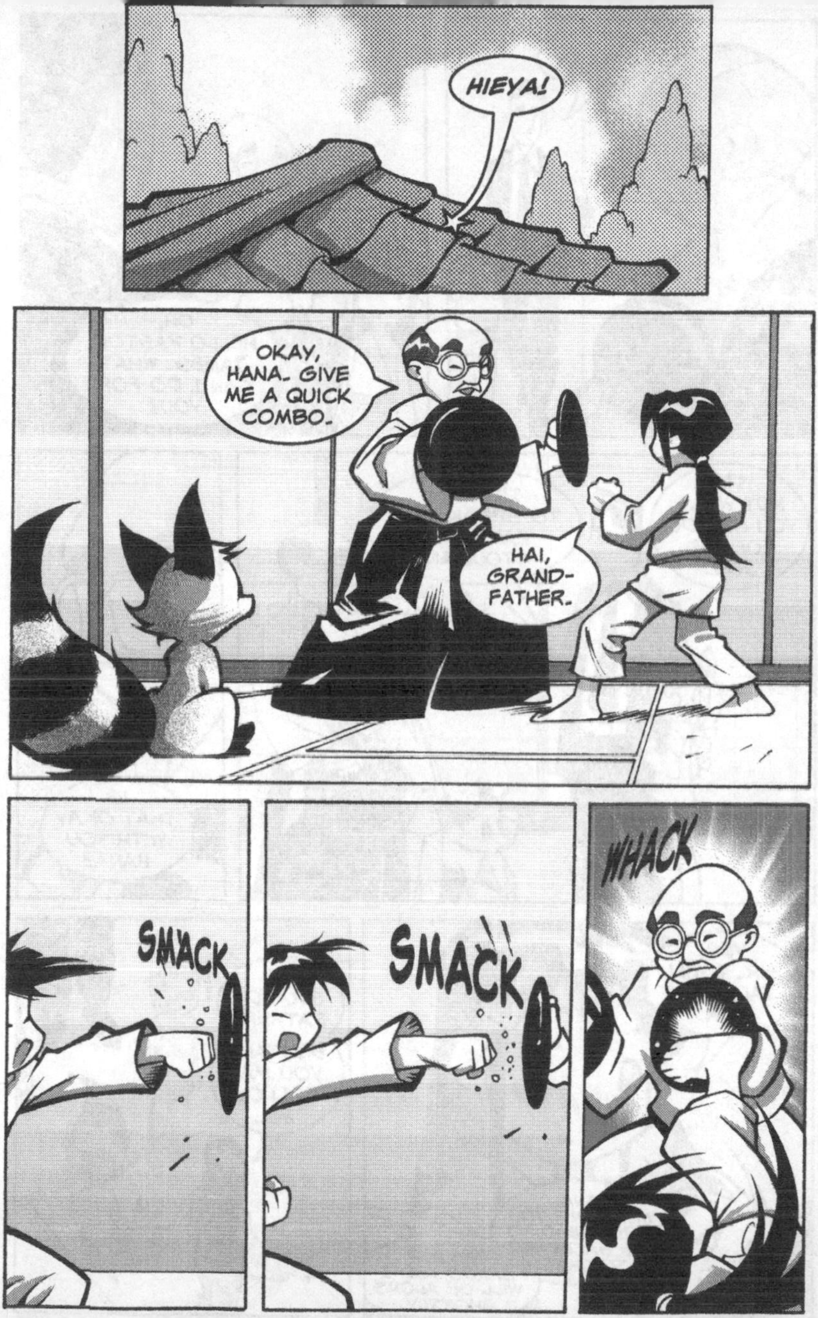
HIEYA!
OKAY, HANA. GIVE ME A QUICK COMBO.
HAI, GRANDFATHER.
SMACK
SMACK
WHACK

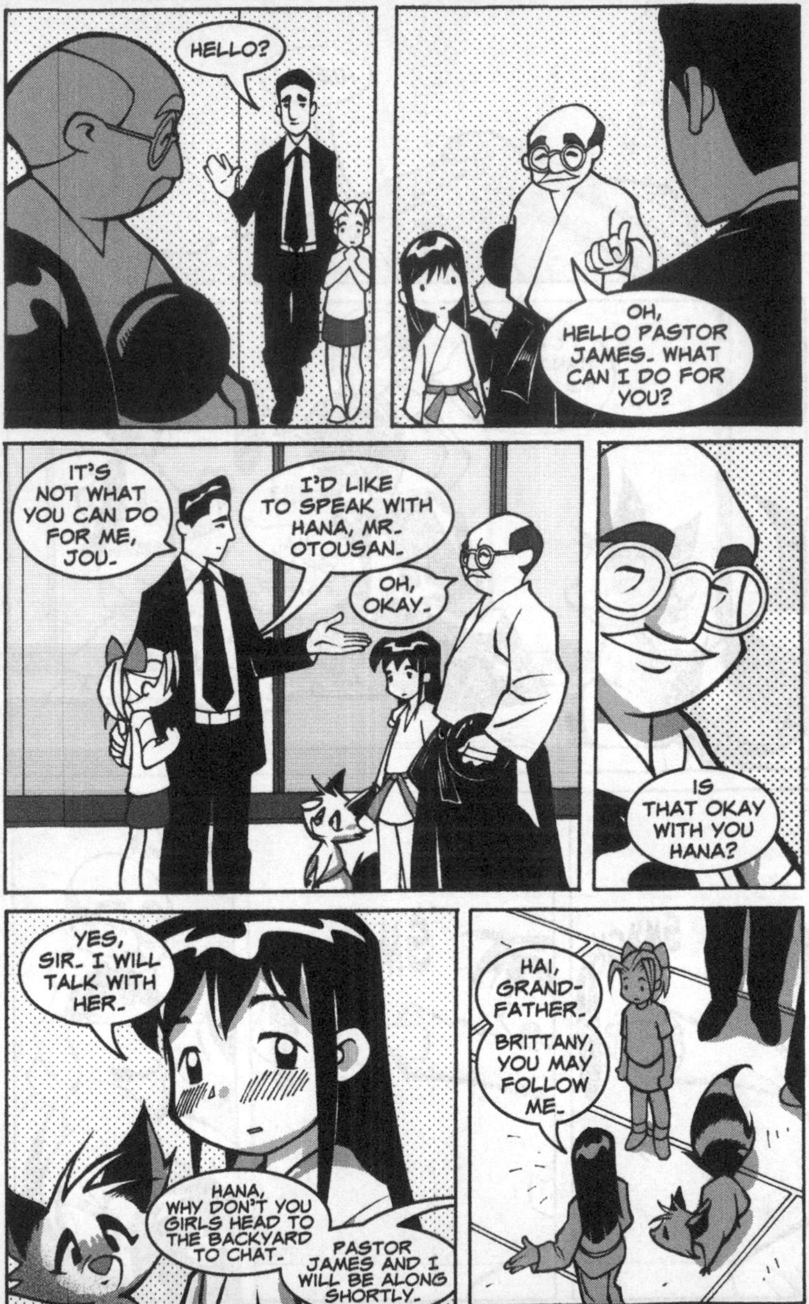
HELLO?
OH, HELLO PASTOR JAMES. WHAT CAN I DO FOR YOU?
IT'S NOT WHAT YOU CAN DO FOR ME, JOU.
I'D LIKE TO SPEAK WITH HANA, MR. OTOUSAN.
OH, OKAY.
IS THAT OKAY WITH YOU HANA?
YES, SIR. I WILL TALK WITH HER.
HANA, WHY DON'T YOU GIRLS HEAD TO THE BACKYARD TO CHAT.
PASTOR JAMES AND I WILL BE ALONG SHORTLY.
HAI, GRAND-FATHER.
BRITTANY, YOU MAY FOLLOW ME.

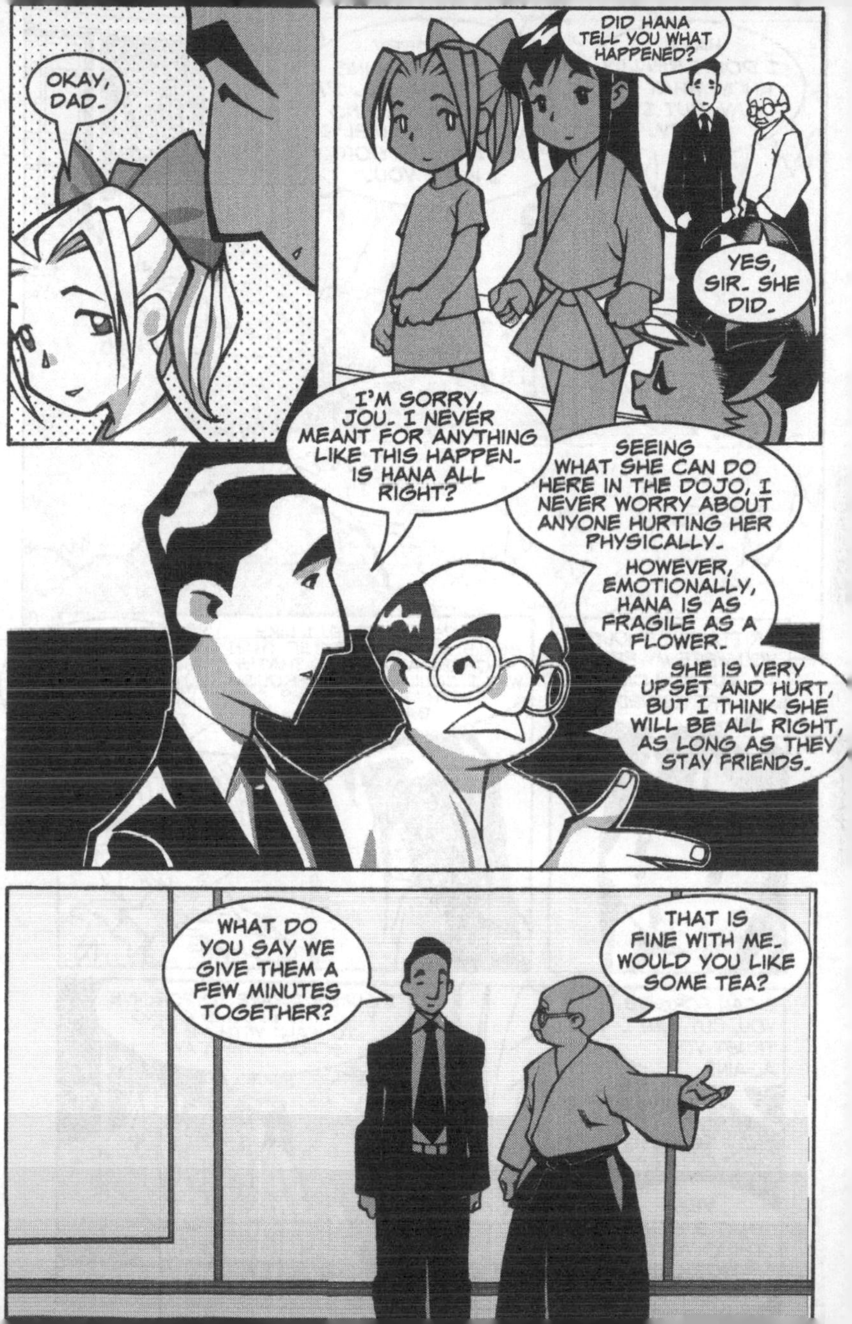
OKAY, DAD.
DID HANA TELL YOU WHAT HAPPENED?
YES, SIR. SHE DID.
I'M SORRY, JOU. I NEVER MEANT FOR ANYTHING LIKE THIS HAPPEN. IS HANA ALL RIGHT?
SEEING WHAT SHE CAN DO HERE IN THE DOJO, I NEVER WORRY ABOUT ANYONE HURTING HER PHYSICALLY.
HOWEVER, EMOTIONALLY, HANA IS AS FRAGILE AS A FLOWER.
SHE IS VERY UPSET AND HURT, BUT I THINK SHE WILL BE ALL RIGHT, AS LONG AS THEY STAY FRIENDS.
WHAT DO YOU SAY WE GIVE THEM A FEW MINUTES TOGETHER?
THAT IS FINE WITH ME. WOULD YOU LIKE SOME TEA?

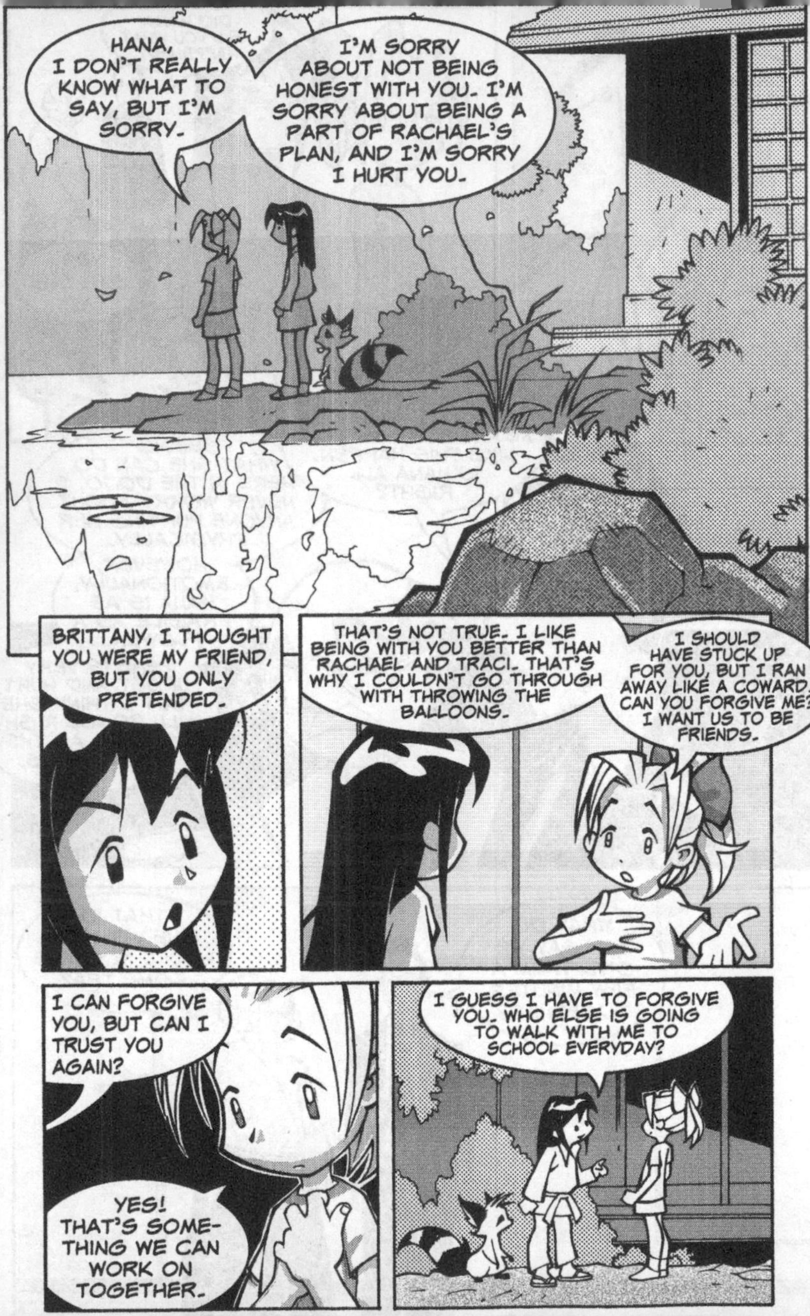
HANA, I DON'T REALLY KNOW WHAT TO SAY, BUT I'M SORRY.
I'M SORRY ABOUT NOT BEING HONEST WITH YOU. I'M SORRY ABOUT BEING A PART OF RACHAEL'S PLAN, AND I'M SORRY I HURT YOU.
BRITTANY, I THOUGHT YOU WERE MY FRIEND, BUT YOU ONLY PRETENDED.
THAT'S NOT TRUE. I LIKE BEING WITH YOU BETTER THAN RACHAEL AND TRACI. THAT'S WHY I COULDN'T GO THROUGH WITH THROWING THE BALLOONS.
I SHOULD HAVE STUCK UP FOR YOU, BUT I RAN AWAY LIKE A COWARD. CAN YOU FORGIVE ME? I WANT US TO BE FRIENDS.
I CAN FORGIVE YOU, BUT CAN I TRUST YOU AGAIN?
YES! THAT'S SOME-THING WE CAN WORK ON TOGETHER.
I GUESS I HAVE TO FORGIVE YOU. WHO ELSE IS GOING TO WALK WITH ME TO SCHOOL EVERYDAY?

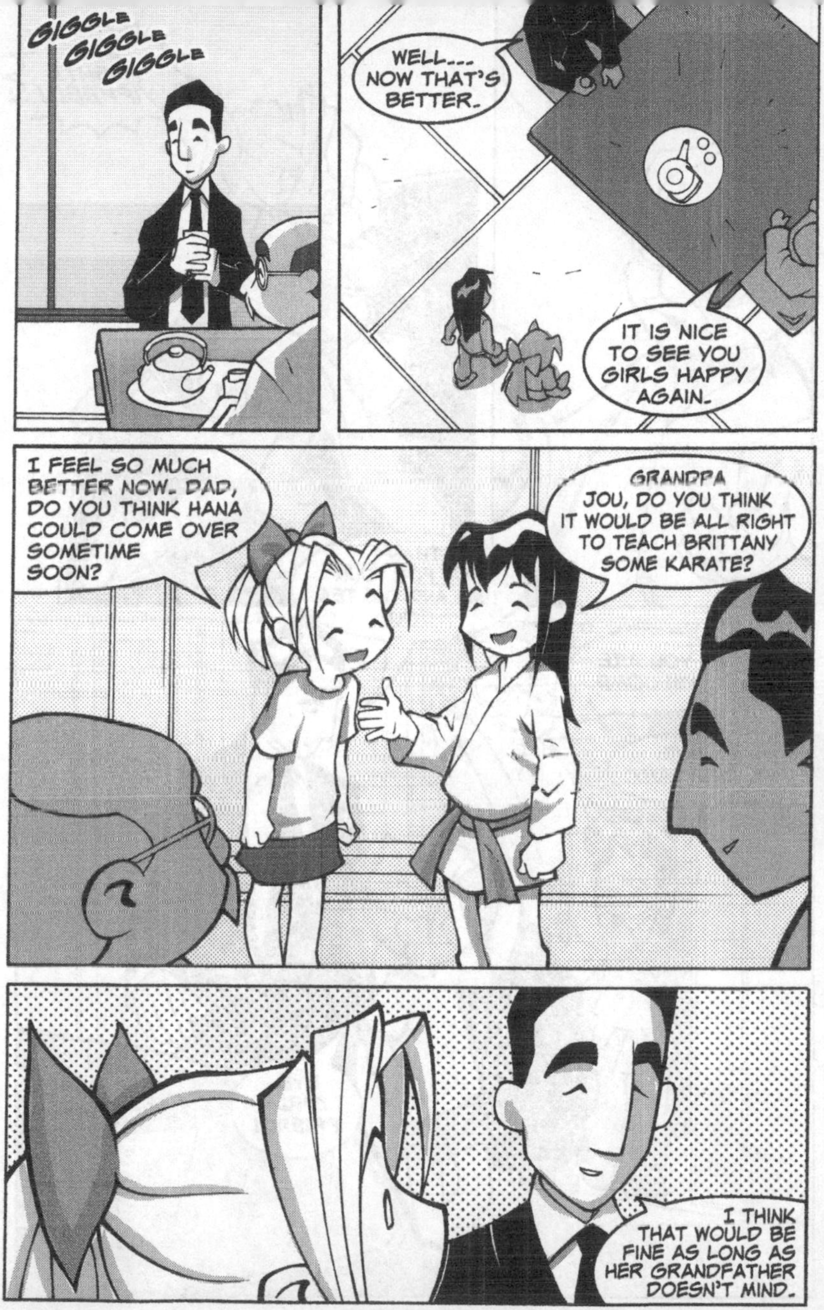
GIGGLE GIGGLE GIGGLE
WELL... NOW THAT'S BETTER.
IT IS NICE TO SEE YOU GIRLS HAPPY AGAIN.
I FEEL SO MUCH BETTER NOW. DAD, DO YOU THINK HANA COULD COME OVER SOMETIME SOON?
GRANDPA JOU, DO YOU THINK IT WOULD BE ALL RIGHT TO TEACH BRITTANY SOME KARATE?
I THINK THAT WOULD BE FINE AS LONG AS HER GRANDFATHER DOESN'T MIND.

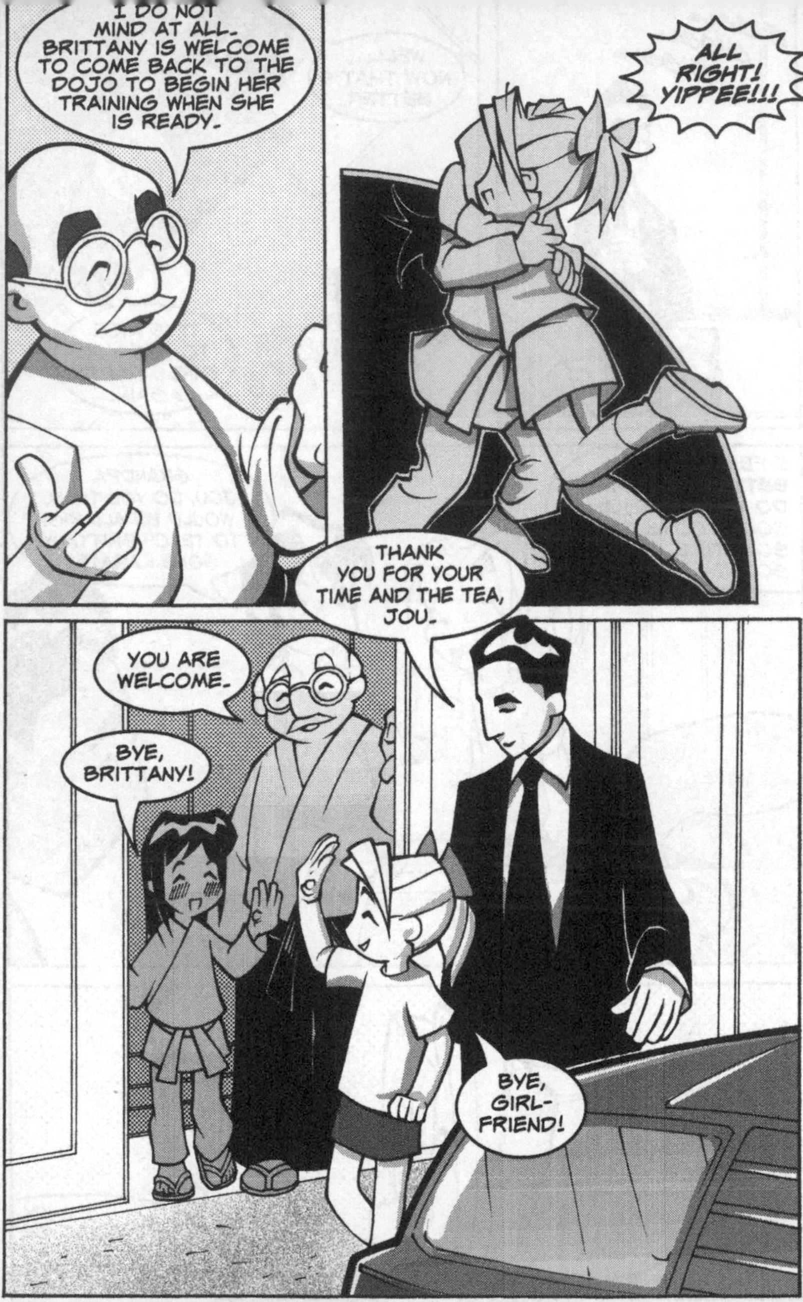
I DO NOT MIND AT ALL. BRITTANY IS WELCOME TO COME BACK TO THE DOJO TO BEGIN HER TRAINING WHEN SHE IS READY.
ALL RIGHT! YIPPEE!!!
THANK YOU FOR YOUR TIME AND THE TEA, JOU.
YOU ARE WELCOME.
BYE, BRITTANY!
BYE, GIRL-FRIEND!

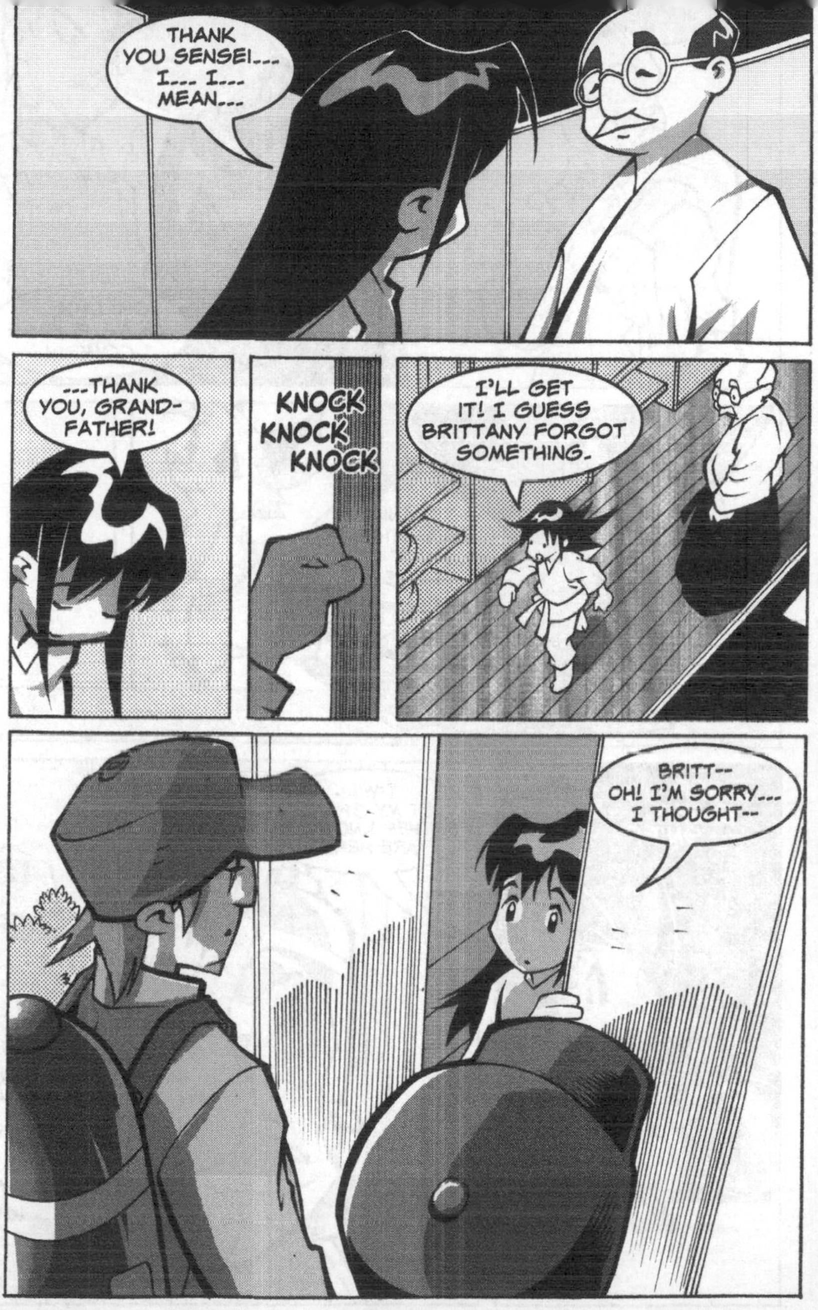
THANK YOU SENSEI... I... I... MEAN...
...THANK YOU, GRAND-FATHER!
KNOCK KNOCK KNOCK
I'LL GET IT! I GUESS BRITTANY FORGOT SOMETHING.
BRITT-- OH! I'M SORRY... I THOUGHT--

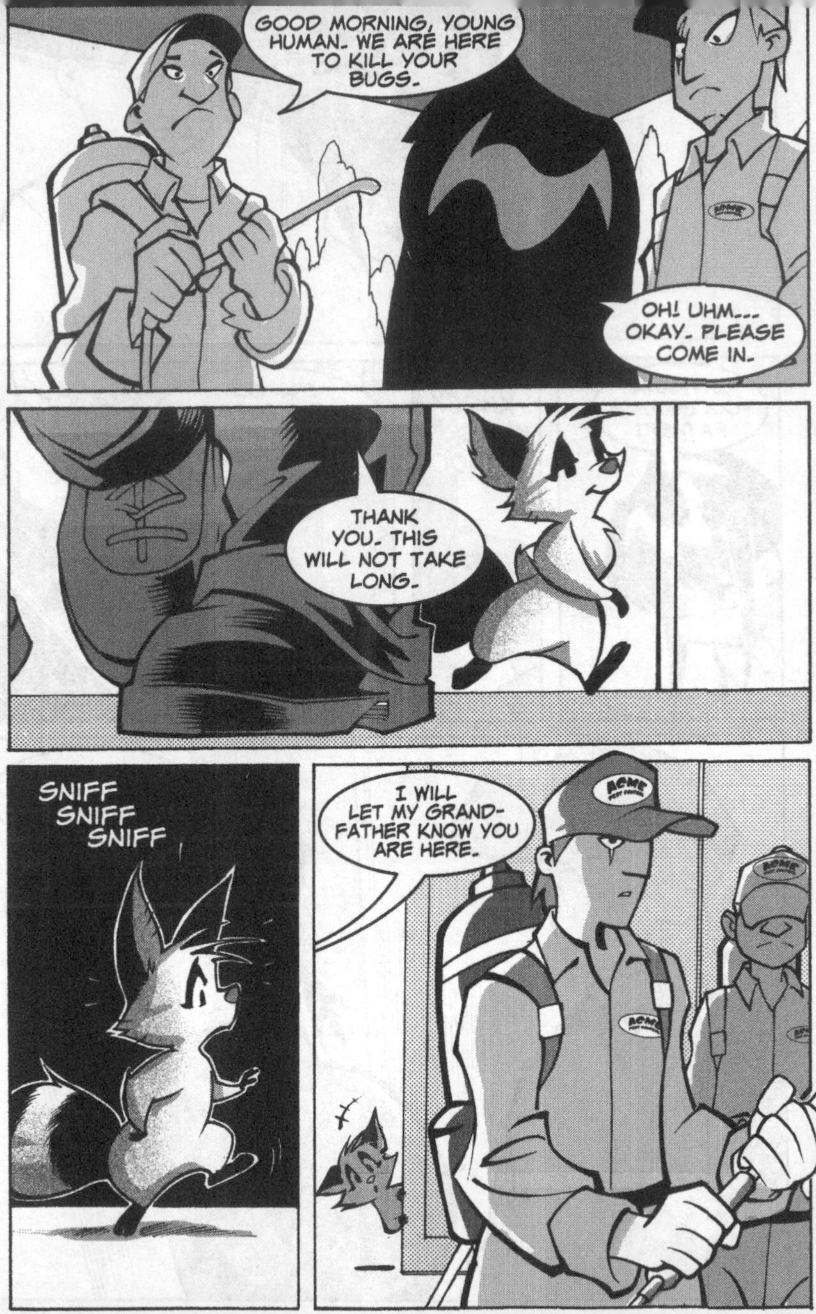
GOOD MORNING, YOUNG HUMAN. WE ARE HERE TO KILL YOUR BUGS.
OH! UHM... OKAY. PLEASE COME IN.
THANK YOU. THIS WILL NOT TAKE LONG.
SNIFF SNIFF SNIFF
I WILL LET MY GRANDFATHER KNOW YOU ARE HERE.

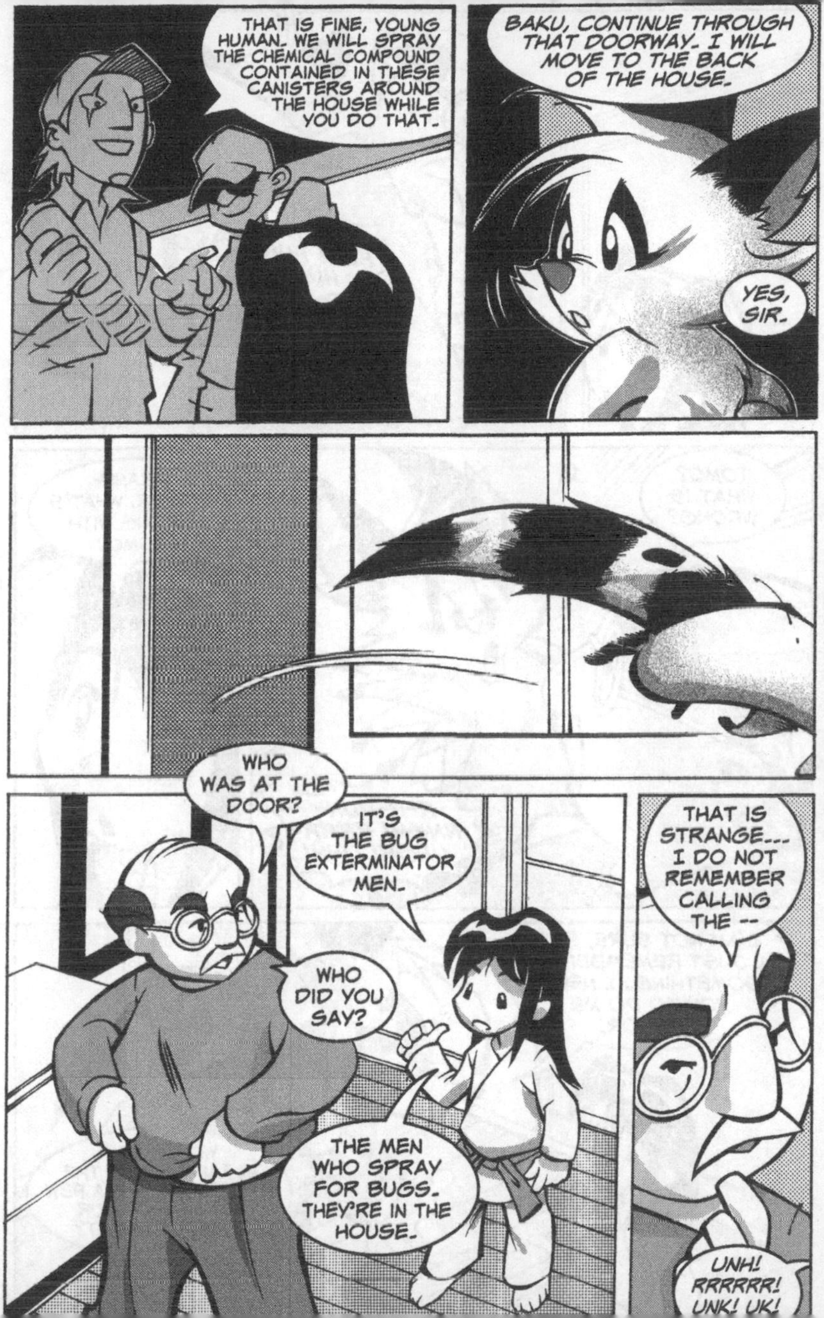
THAT IS FINE, YOUNG HUMAN. WE WILL SPRAY THE CHEMICAL COMPOUND CONTAINED IN THESE CANISTERS AROUND THE HOUSE WHILE YOU DO THAT.
BAKU, CONTINUE THROUGH THAT DOORWAY. I WILL MOVE TO THE BACK OF THE HOUSE.
YES, SIR.
WHO WAS AT THE DOOR?
IT'S THE BUG EXTERMINATOR MEN.
WHO DID YOU SAY?
THE MEN WHO SPRAY FOR BUGS. THEY'RE IN THE HOUSE.
THAT IS STRANGE... I DO NOT REMEMBER CALLING THE --
UNH! RRRRRR! UNK! UK!

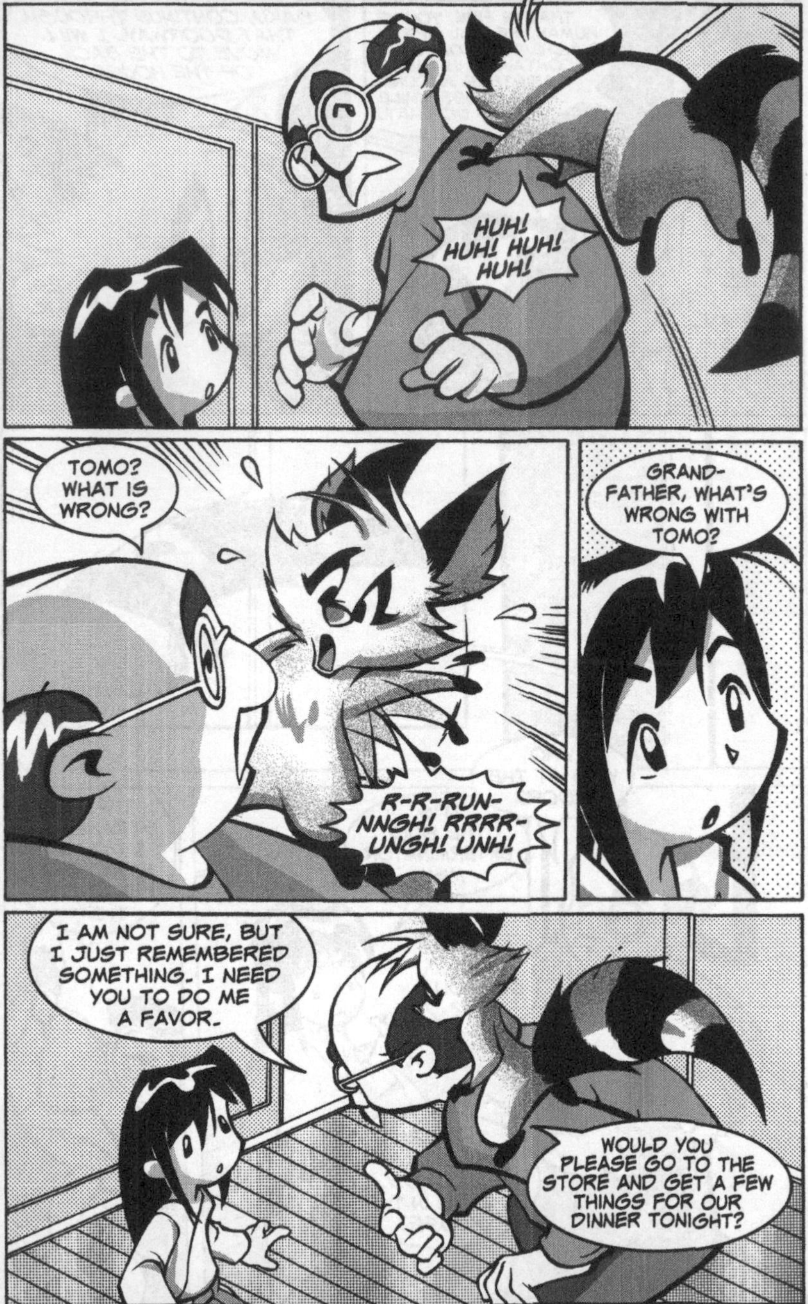
HUH! HUH! HUH! HUH!
TOMO? WHAT IS WRONG?
R-R-RUN-NNGH! RRRR-UNGH! UNH!
GRAND-FATHER, WHAT'S WRONG WITH TOMO?
I AM NOT SURE, BUT I JUST REMEMBERED SOMETHING. I NEED YOU TO DO ME A FAVOR.
WOULD YOU PLEASE GO TO THE STORE AND GET A FEW THINGS FOR OUR DINNER TONIGHT?

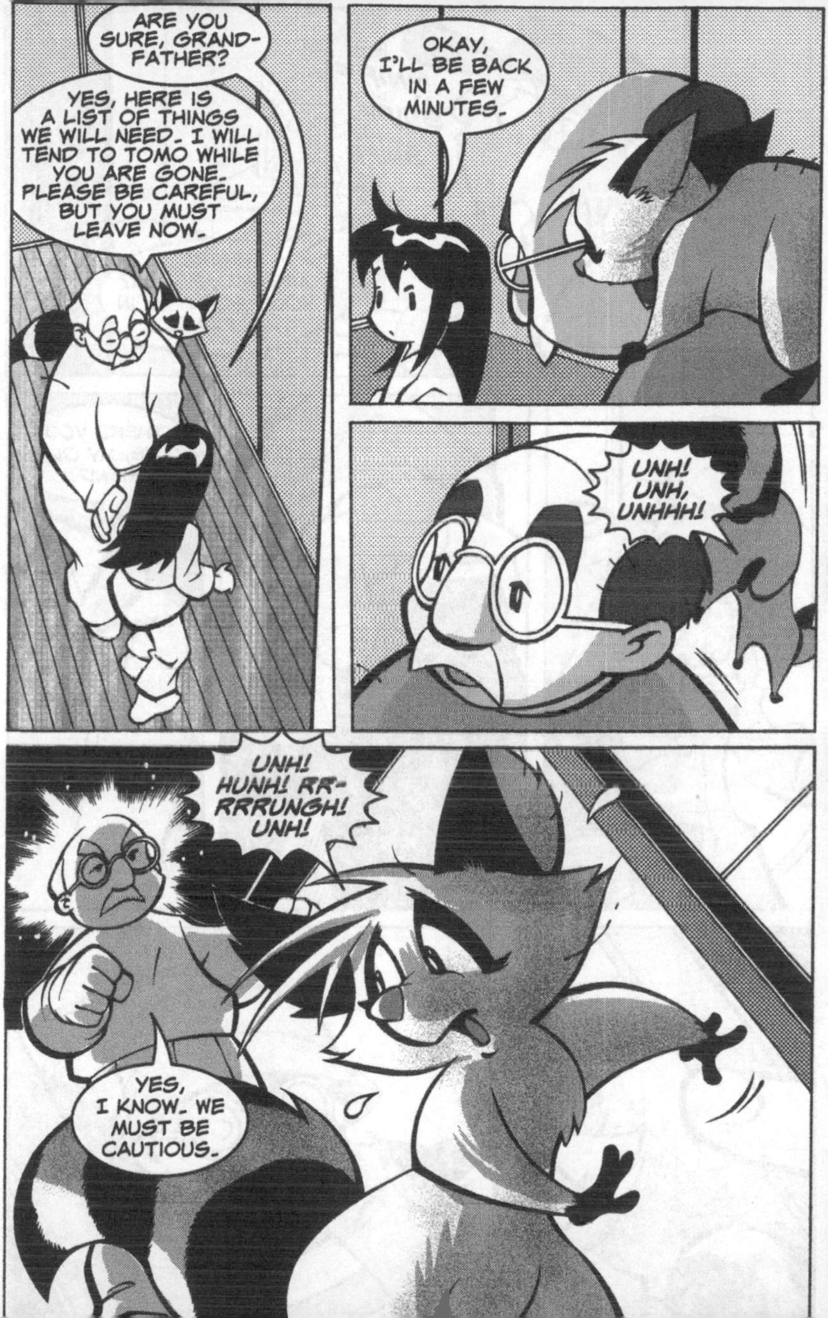
ARE YOU SURE, GRAND-FATHER?
YES, HERE IS A LIST OF THINGS WE WILL NEED. I WILL TEND TO TOMO WHILE YOU ARE GONE. PLEASE BE CAREFUL, BUT YOU MUST LEAVE NOW.
OKAY, I'LL BE BACK IN A FEW MINUTES.
UNH! UNH, UNHHH!
UNH! HUNH! RR-RRRUNGH! UNH!
YES, I KNOW. WE MUST BE CAUTIOUS.

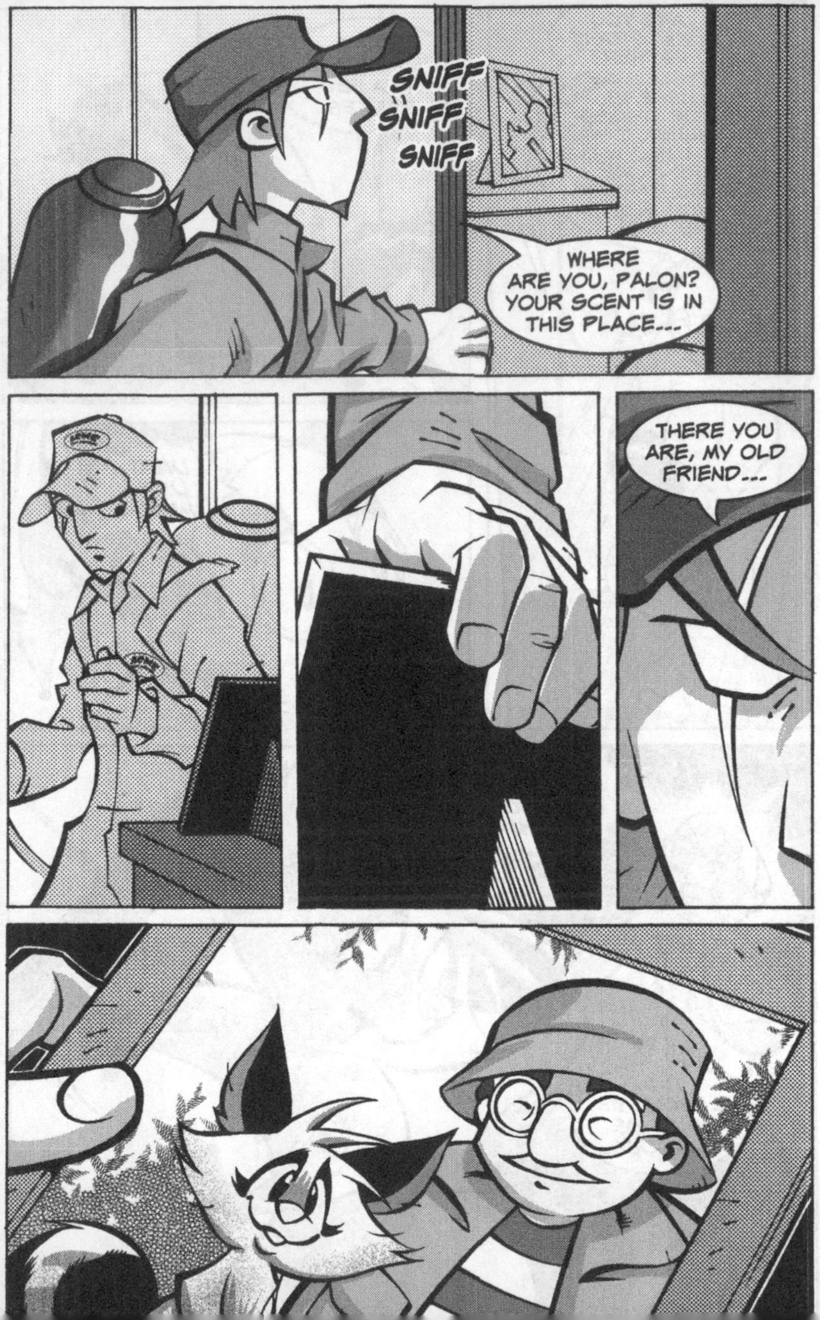
SNIFF
SNIFF
SNIFF
WHERE ARE YOU, PALON? YOUR SCENT IS IN THIS PLACE...
THERE YOU ARE, MY OLD FRIEND...

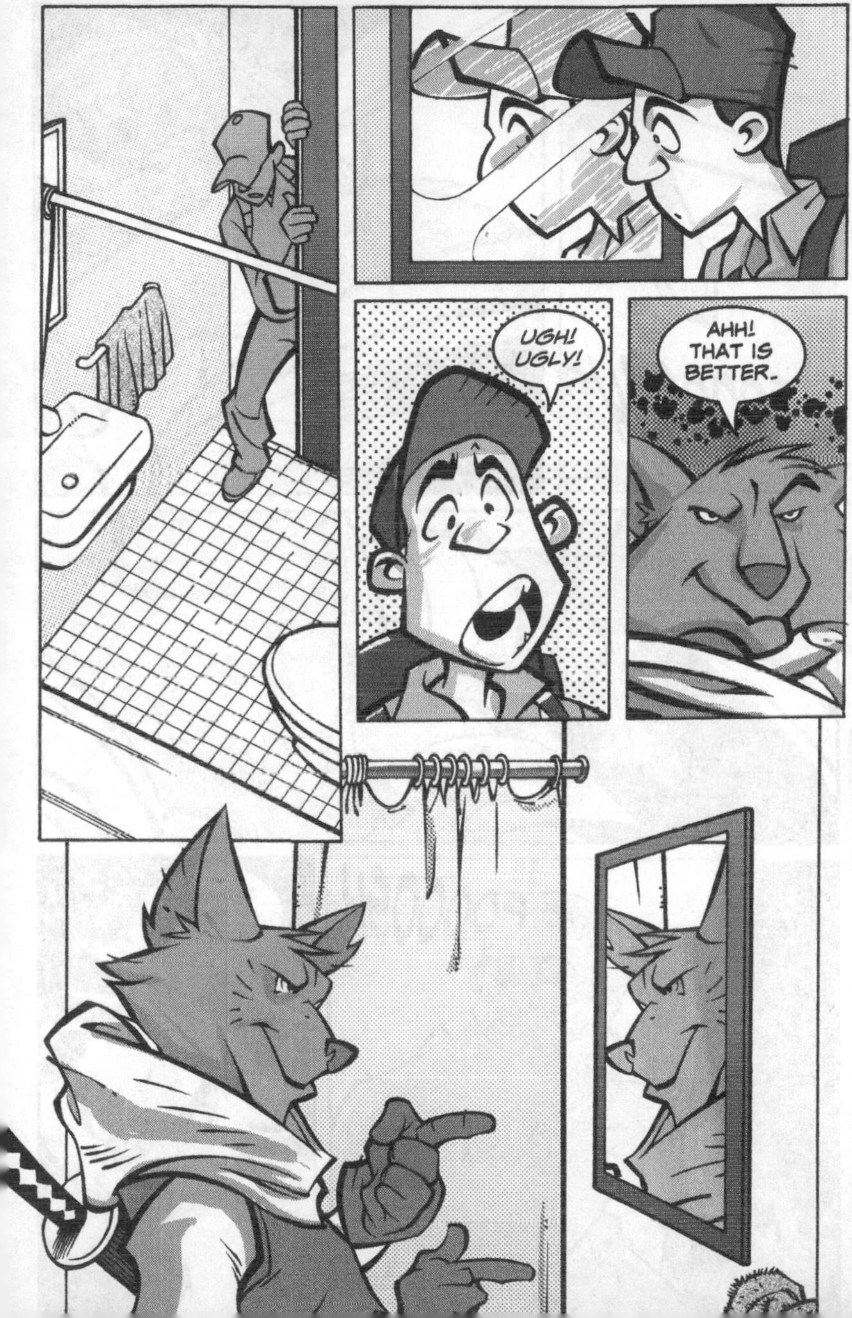
UGH! UGLY!
AHH! THAT IS BETTER.

THUMP

FOOOOSH

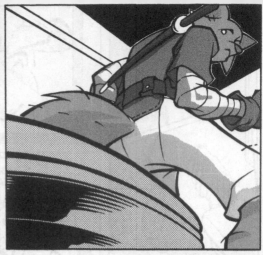

A FOUNTAIN!

FOOOOSH

TOMO... BO STAFF!

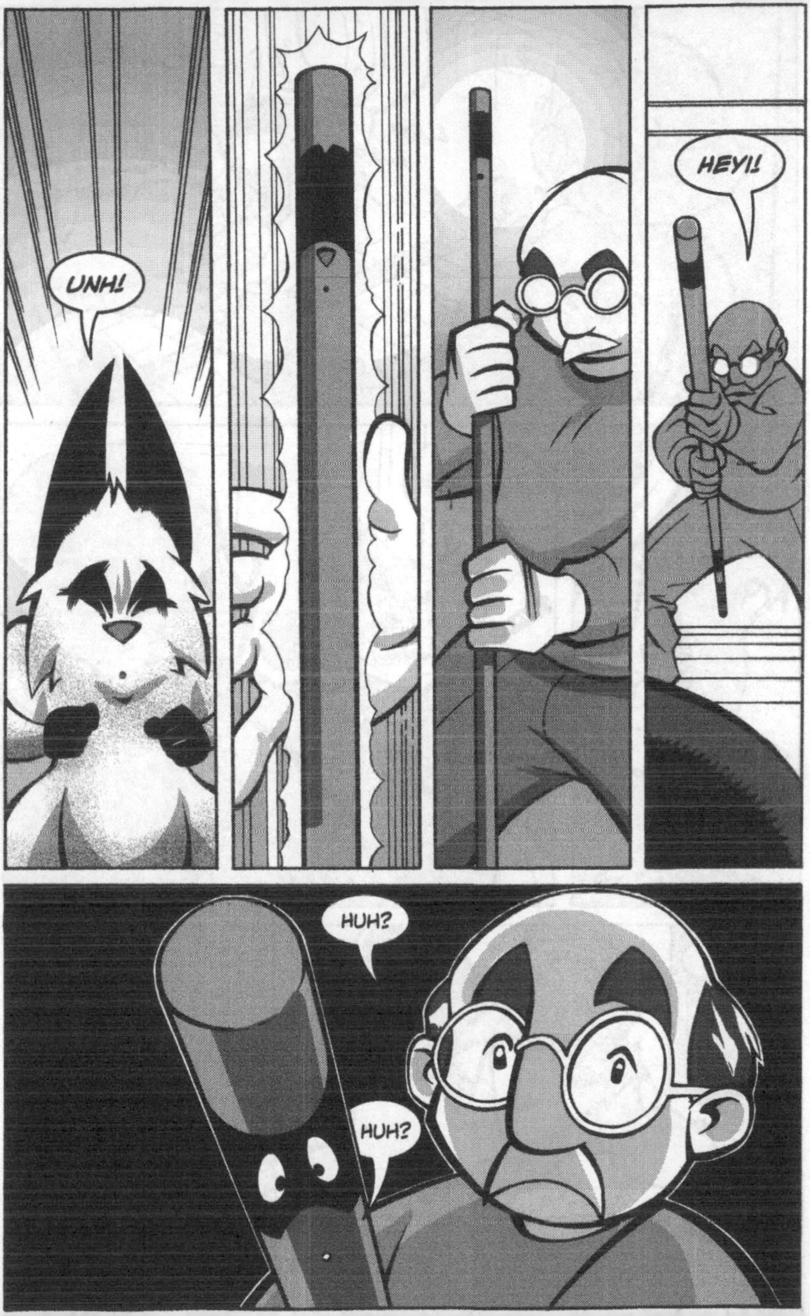
UNH!
HEY!!
HUH?
HUH?

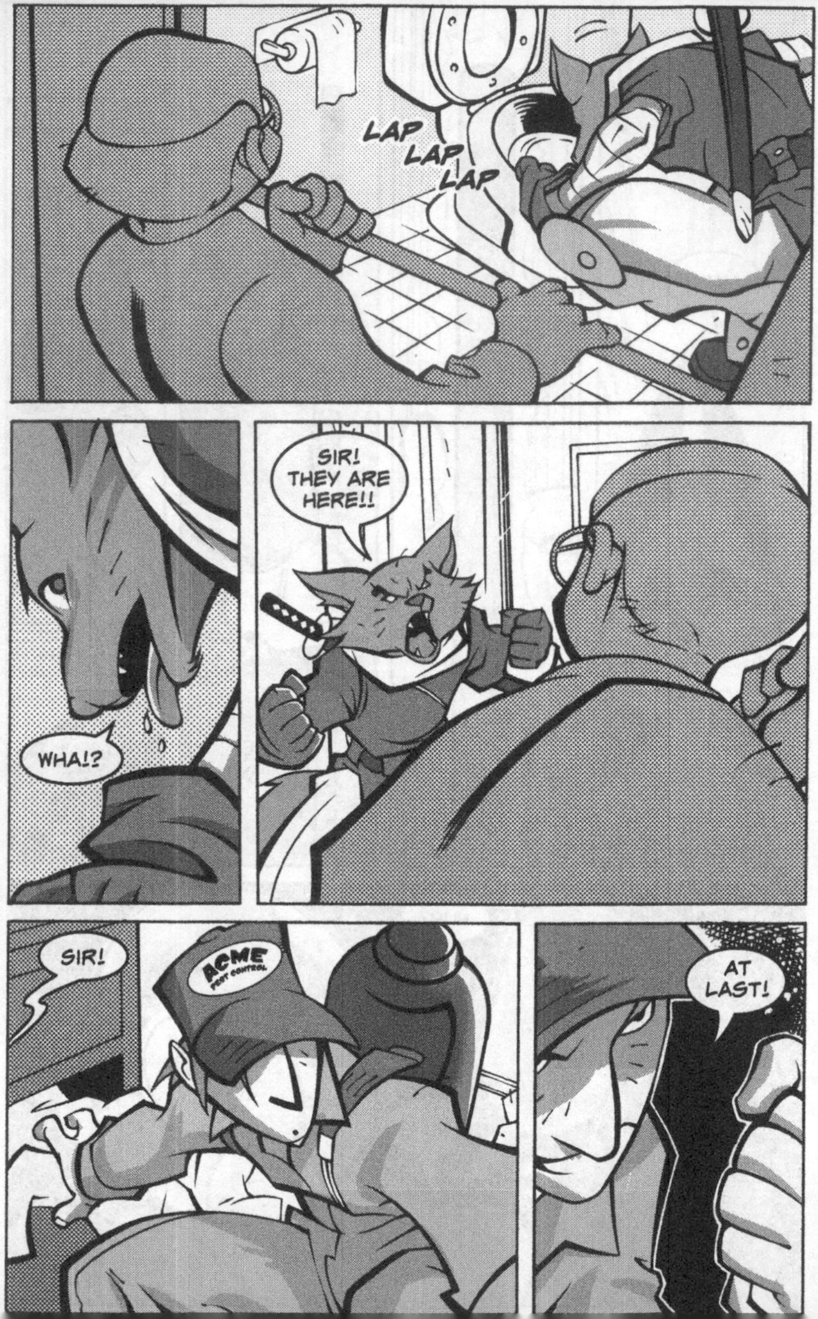
LAP
LAP
LAP
SIR!
THEY ARE
HERE!!
WHA!?
SIR!
ACME
PEST CONTROL
AT
LAST!

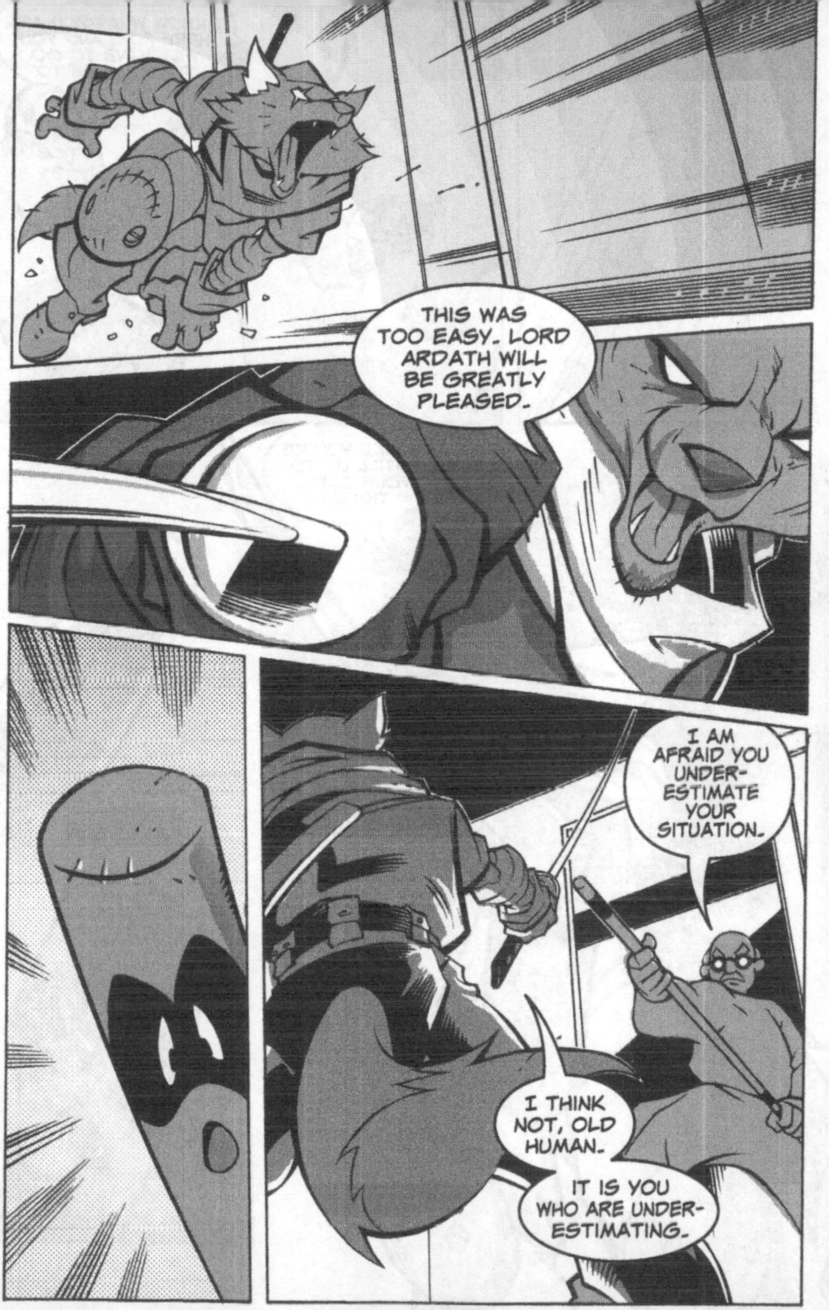
THIS WAS TOO EASY. LORD ARDATH WILL BE GREATLY PLEASED.
I AM AFRAID YOU UNDER-ESTIMATE YOUR SITUATION.
I THINK NOT, OLD HUMAN.
IT IS YOU WHO ARE UNDER-ESTIMATING.

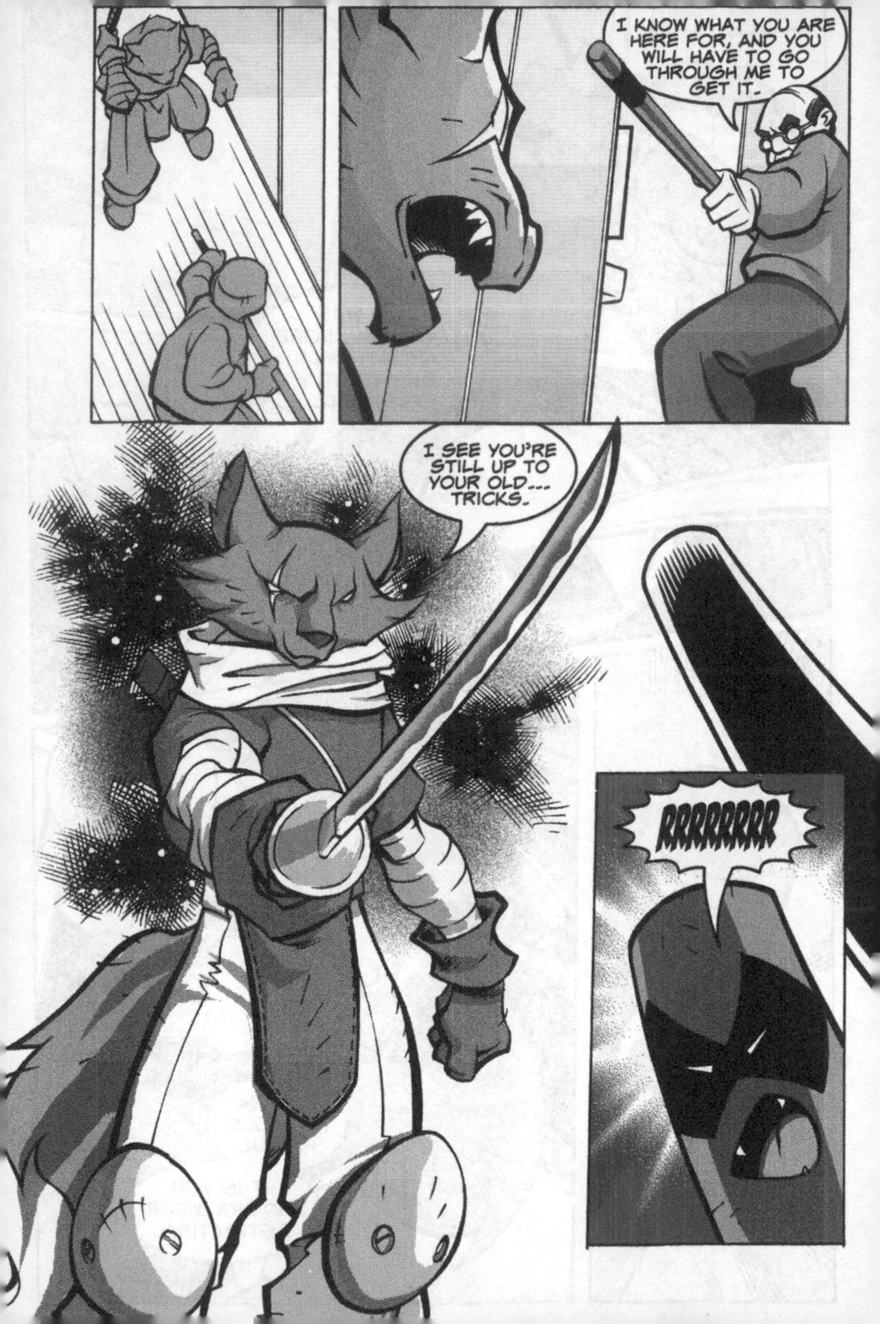

I KNOW WHAT YOU ARE HERE FOR, AND YOU WILL HAVE TO GO THROUGH ME TO GET IT.
I SEE YOU'RE STILL UP TO YOUR OLD--- TRICKS.
RRRRRRRR

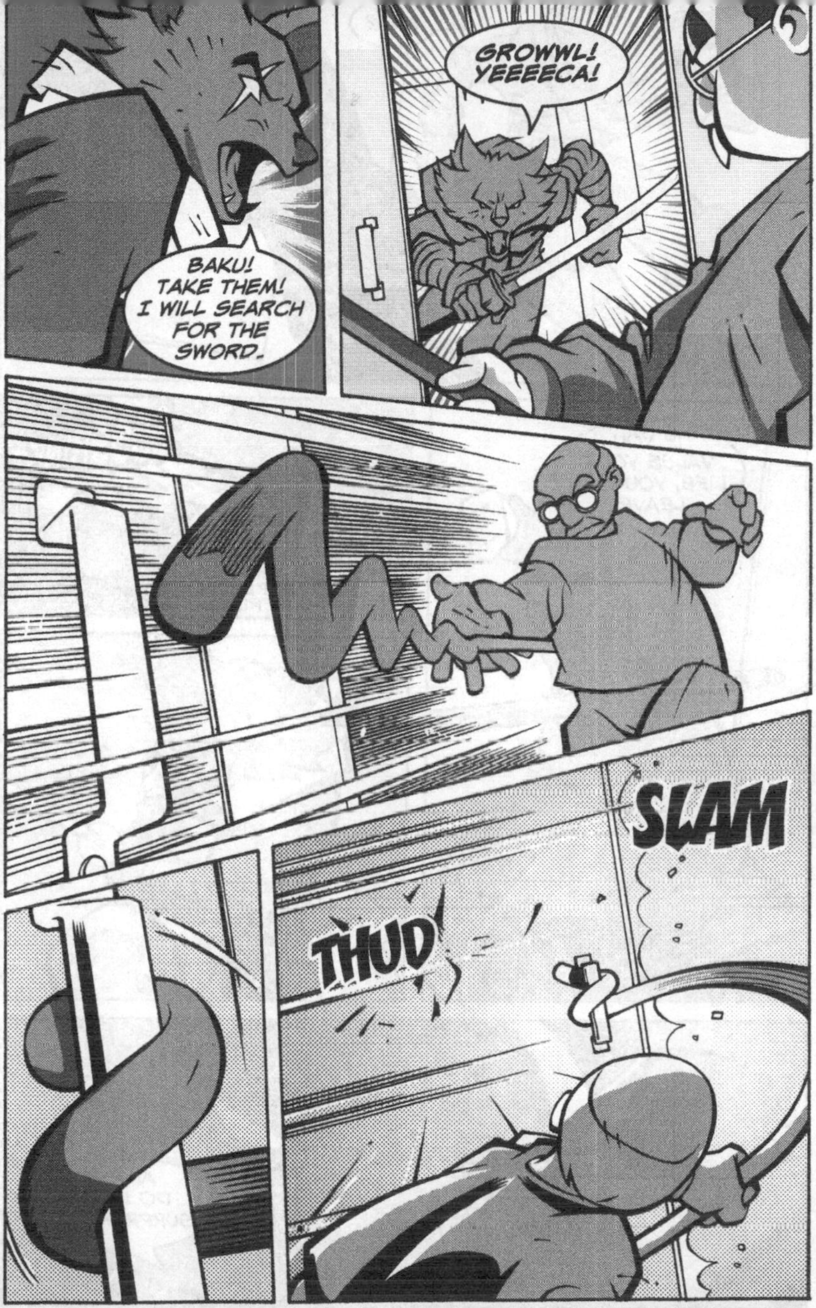
BAKU! TAKE THEM! I WILL SEARCH FOR THE SWORD.
GROWWL! YEEEECA!
SLAM
THUD

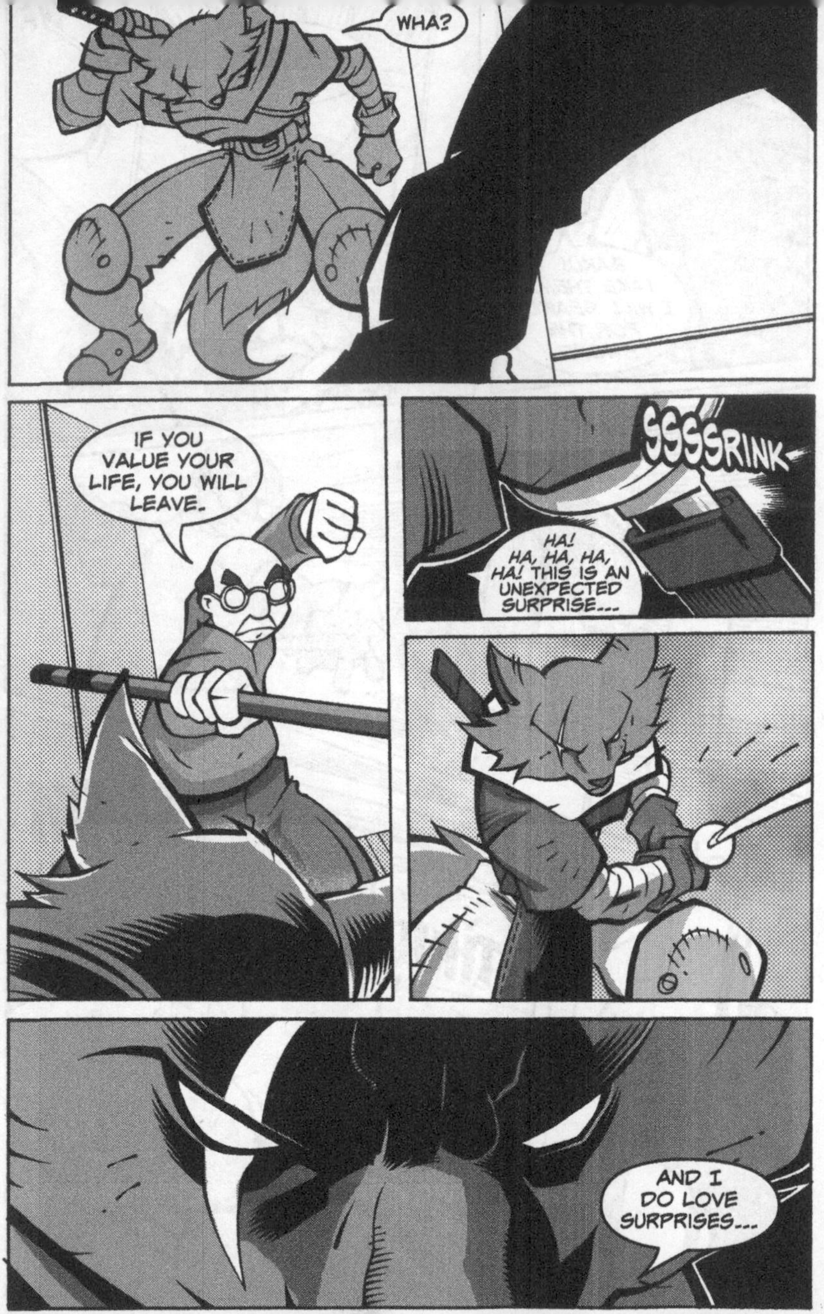
WHA?
IF YOU VALUE YOUR LIFE, YOU WILL LEAVE.
SSSSRINK
HA! HA, HA, HA, HA! THIS IS AN UNEXPECTED SURPRISE...
AND I DO LOVE SURPRISES...

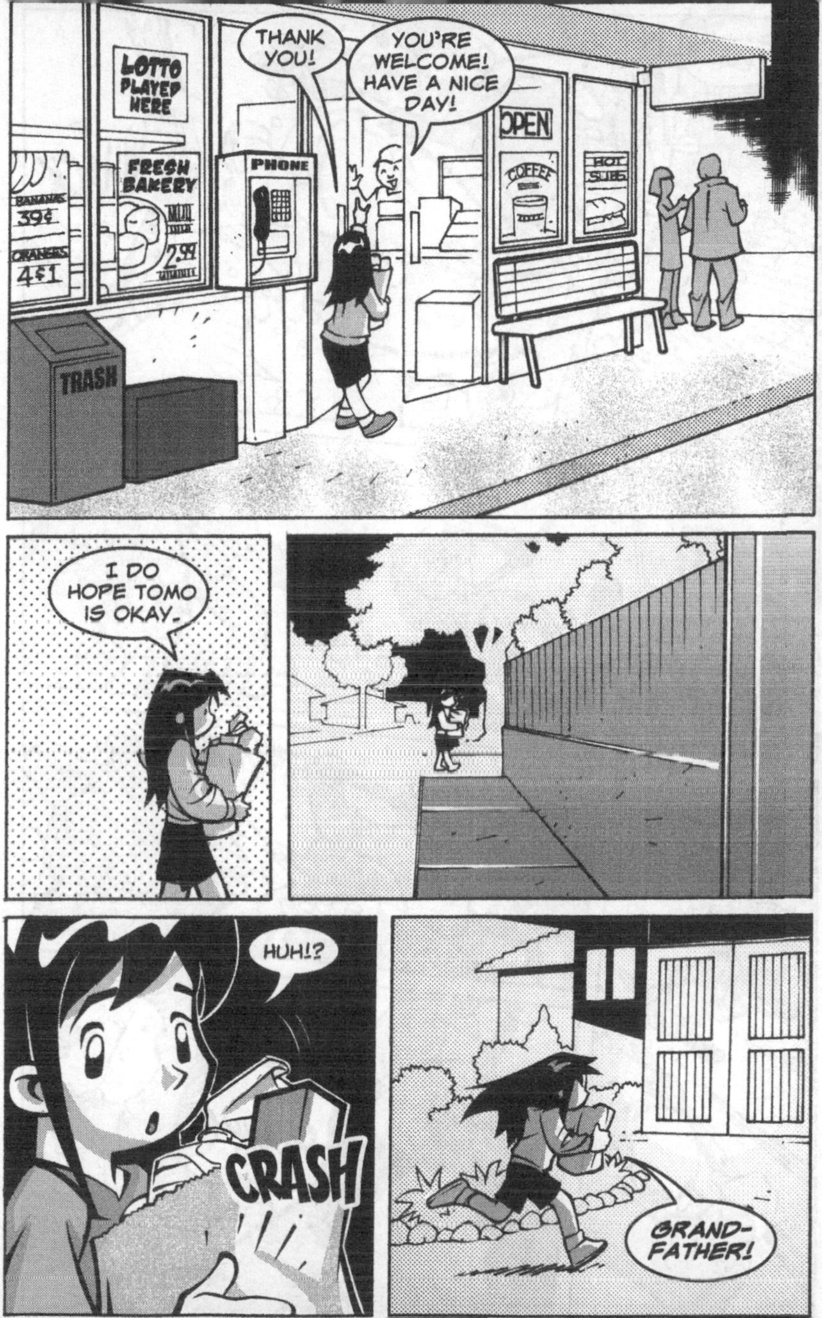
LOTTO PLAYED HERE
FRESH BAKERY
BANANAS 39¢
ORANGES 4$1
2.99
PHONE
THANK YOU!
YOU'RE WELCOME! HAVE A NICE DAY!
OPEN
COFFEE
HOT SUBS
TRASH
I DO HOPE TOMO IS OKAY...
HUH!?
CRASH
GRAND-FATHER!

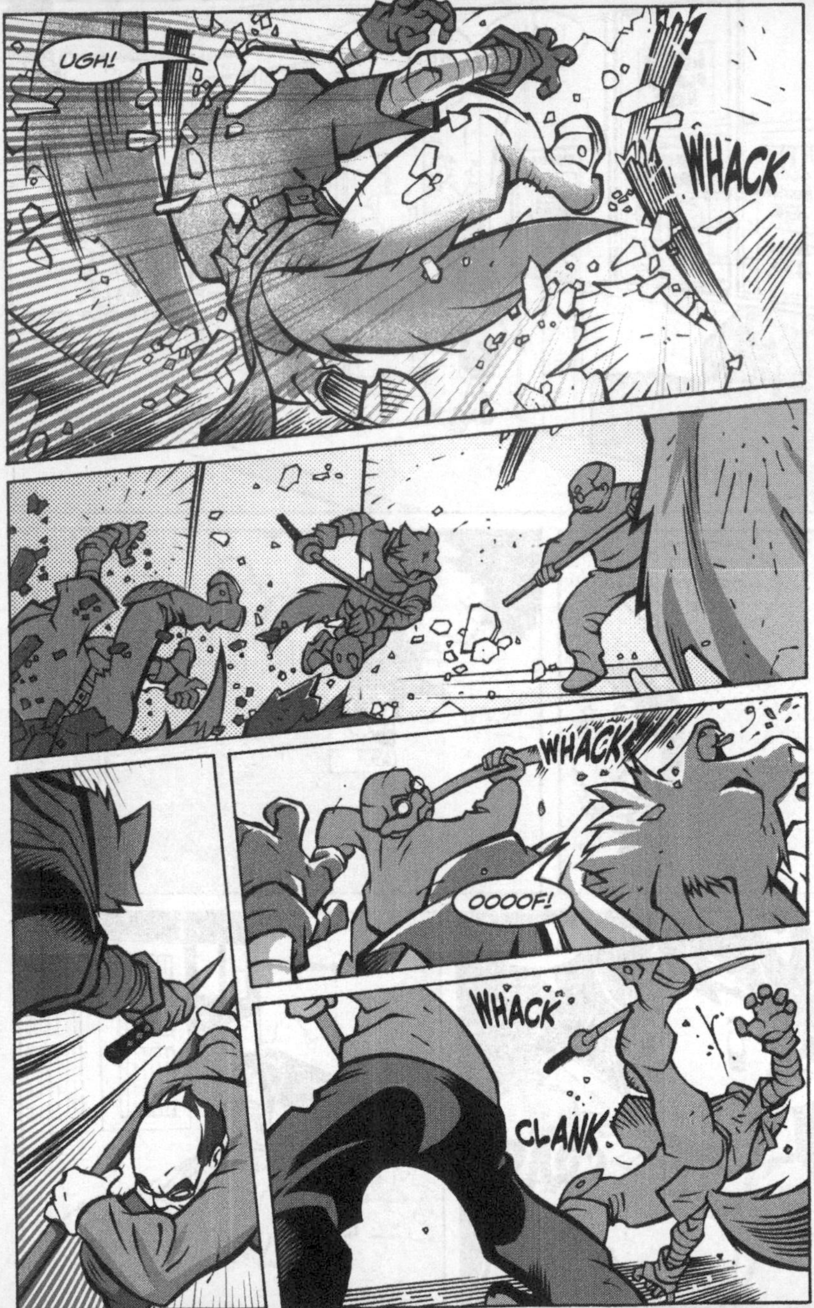
UGH!
WHACK
WHACK
OOOOF!
WHACK
CLANK

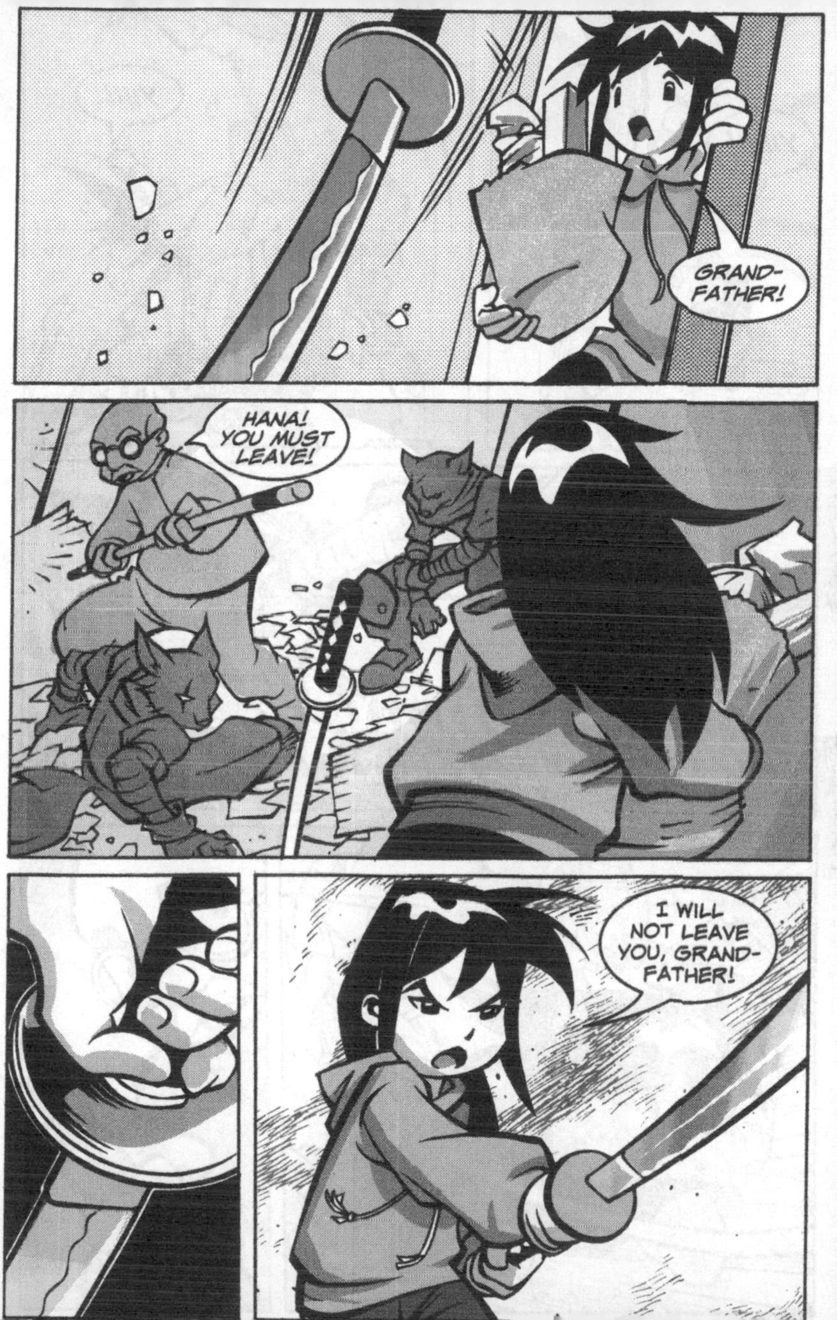
GRAND-FATHER!
HANA! YOU MUST LEAVE!
I WILL NOT LEAVE YOU, GRAND-FATHER!

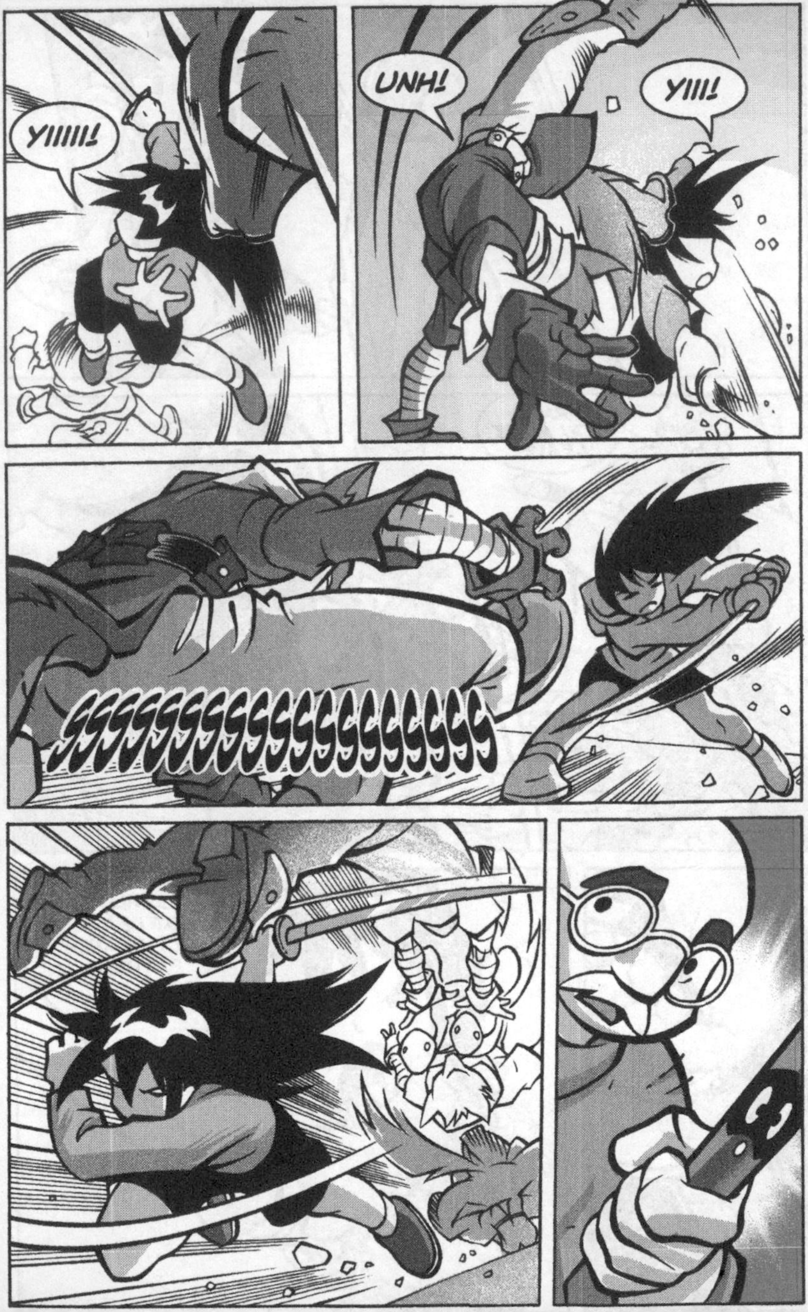
YIIIII!
UNH!
YIII!
SSSSSSSSSSSSSSSSSSSS

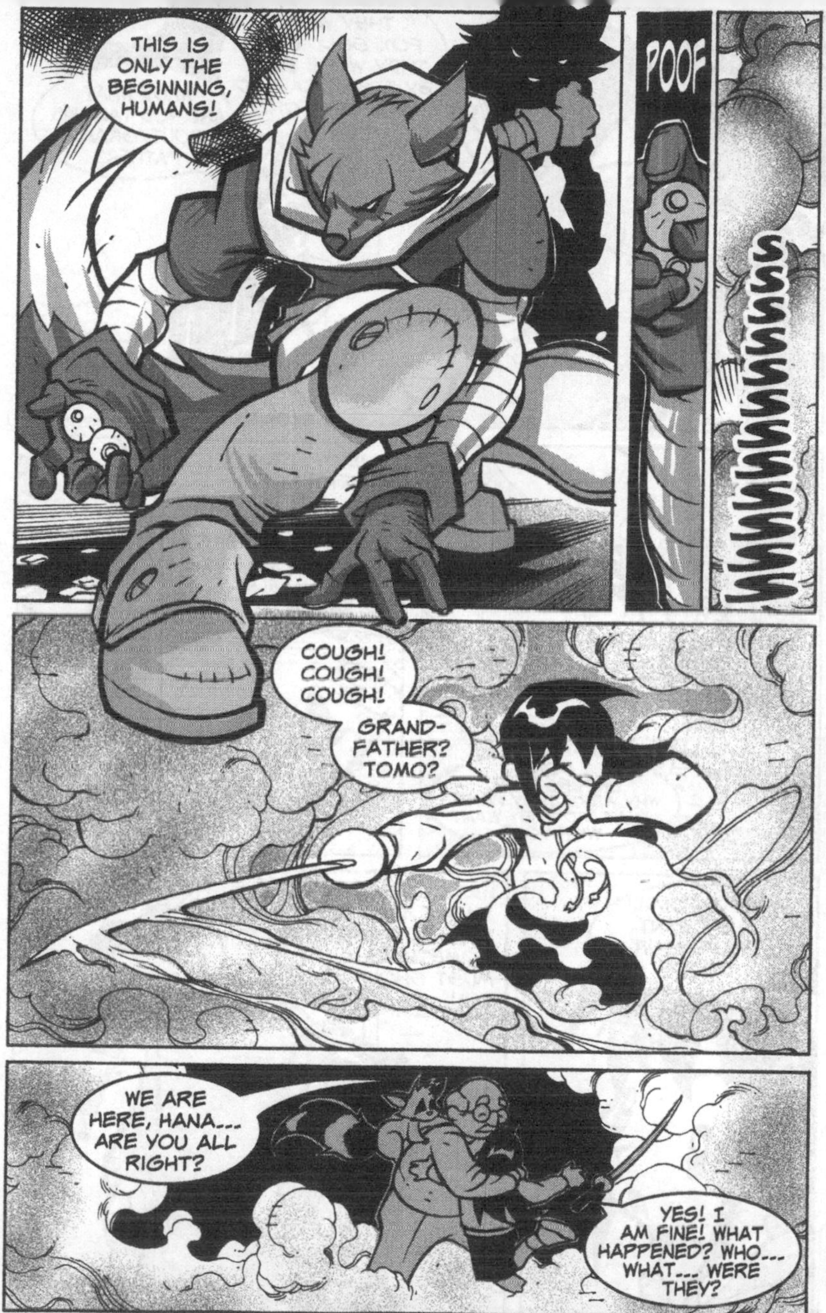
THIS IS ONLY THE BEGINNING, HUMANS!
POOF
SSSSSSSSSSSSSSSSSS
COUGH! COUGH! COUGH!
GRAND-FATHER? TOMO?
WE ARE HERE, HANA... ARE YOU ALL RIGHT?
YES! I AM FINE! WHAT HAPPENED? WHO... WHAT... WERE THEY?

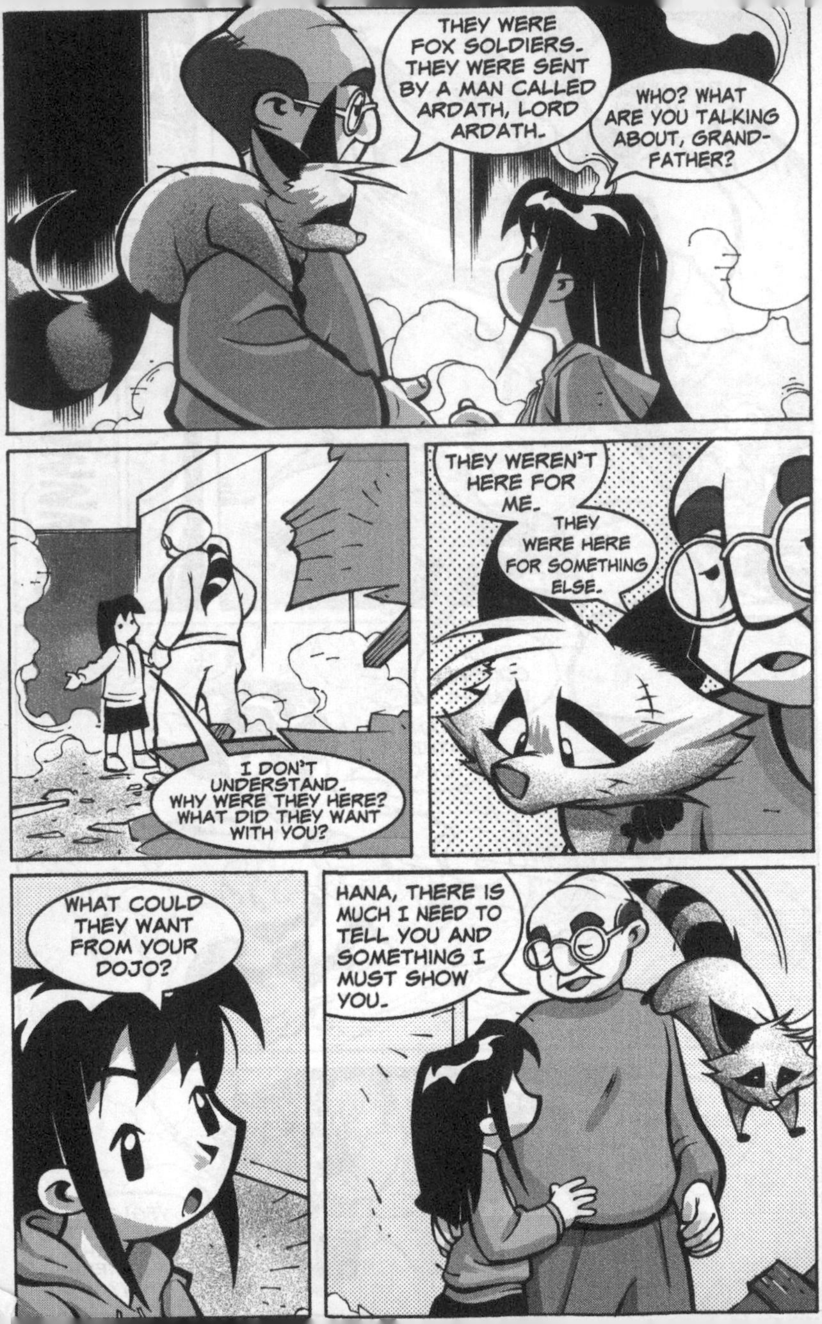

THEY WERE FOX SOLDIERS. THEY WERE SENT BY A MAN CALLED ARDATH, LORD ARDATH.
WHO? WHAT ARE YOU TALKING ABOUT, GRAND-FATHER?
I DON'T UNDERSTAND. WHY WERE THEY HERE? WHAT DID THEY WANT WITH YOU?
THEY WEREN'T HERE FOR ME.
THEY WERE HERE FOR SOMETHING ELSE.
WHAT COULD THEY WANT FROM YOUR DOJO?
HANA, THERE IS MUCH I NEED TO TELL YOU AND SOMETHING I MUST SHOW YOU.

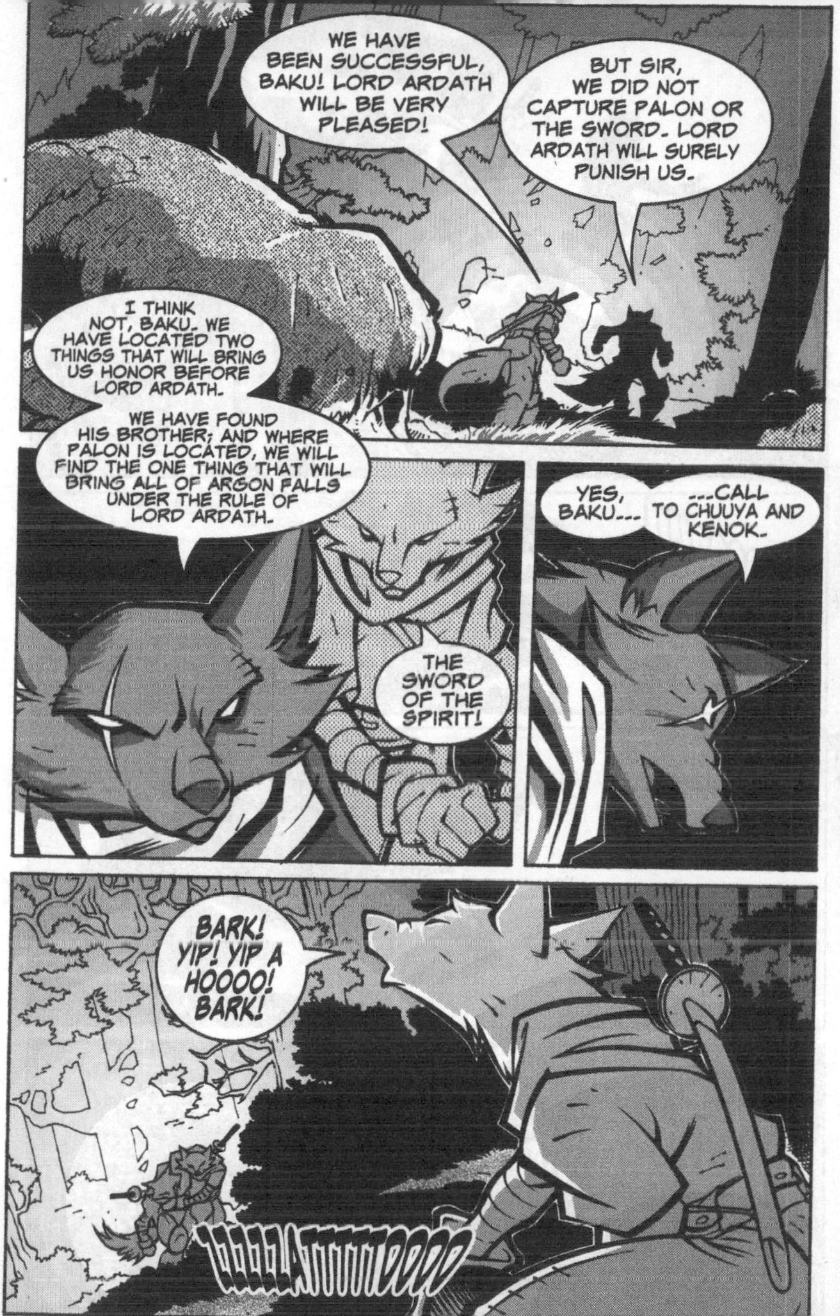
WE HAVE BEEN SUCCESSFUL, BAKU! LORD ARDATH WILL BE VERY PLEASED!
BUT SIR, WE DID NOT CAPTURE PALON OR THE SWORD. LORD ARDATH WILL SURELY PUNISH US.
I THINK NOT, BAKU. WE HAVE LOCATED TWO THINGS THAT WILL BRING US HONOR BEFORE LORD ARDATH.
WE HAVE FOUND HIS BROTHER; AND WHERE PALON IS LOCATED, WE WILL FIND THE ONE THING THAT WILL BRING ALL OF ARGON FALLS UNDER THE RULE OF LORD ARDATH.
THE SWORD OF THE SPIRIT!
YES, BAKU...
...CALL TO CHUUYA AND KENOK.
BARK! YIP! YIP A HOOOO! BARK!

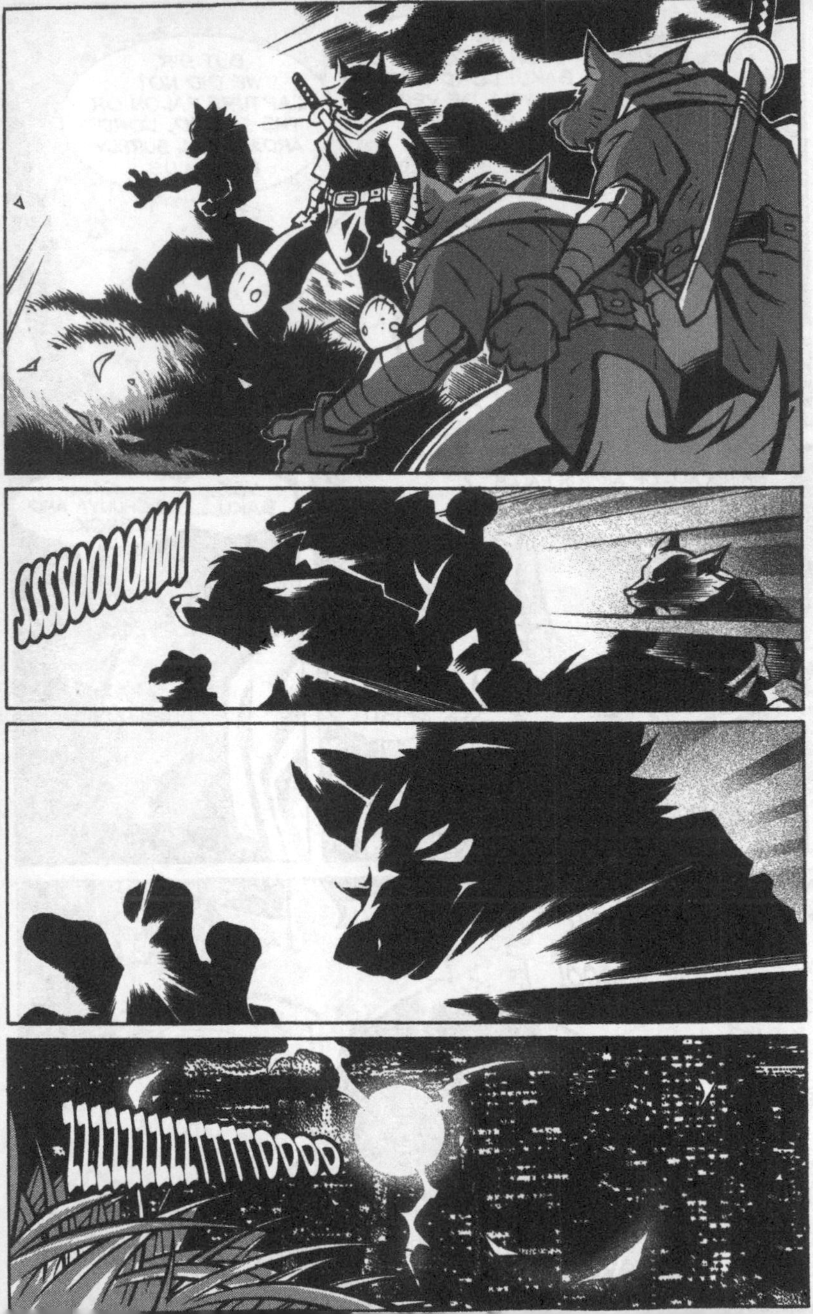
SSSSOOOOMM
ZZZZZZZZZZTTTTTODDD

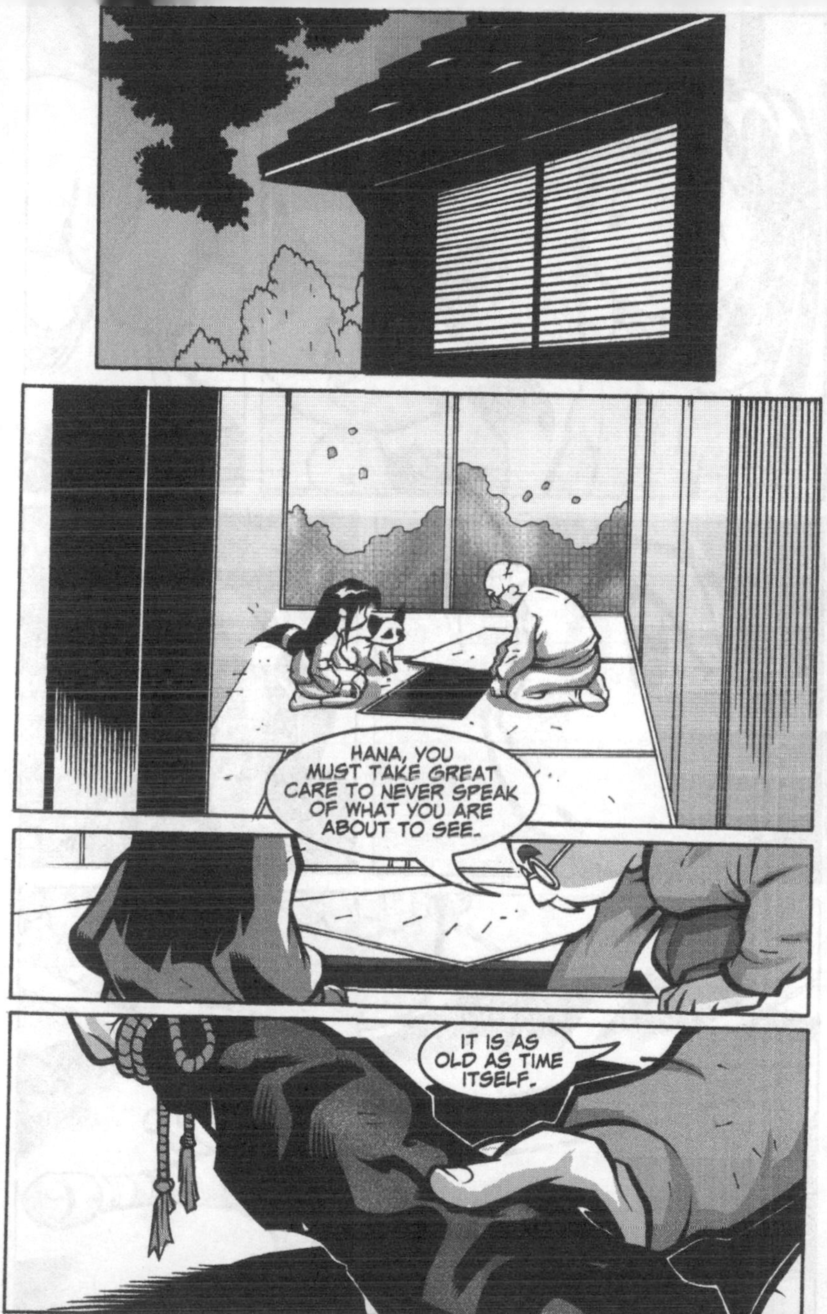
HANA, YOU MUST TAKE GREAT CARE TO NEVER SPEAK OF WHAT YOU ARE ABOUT TO SEE.
IT IS AS OLD AS TIME ITSELF.

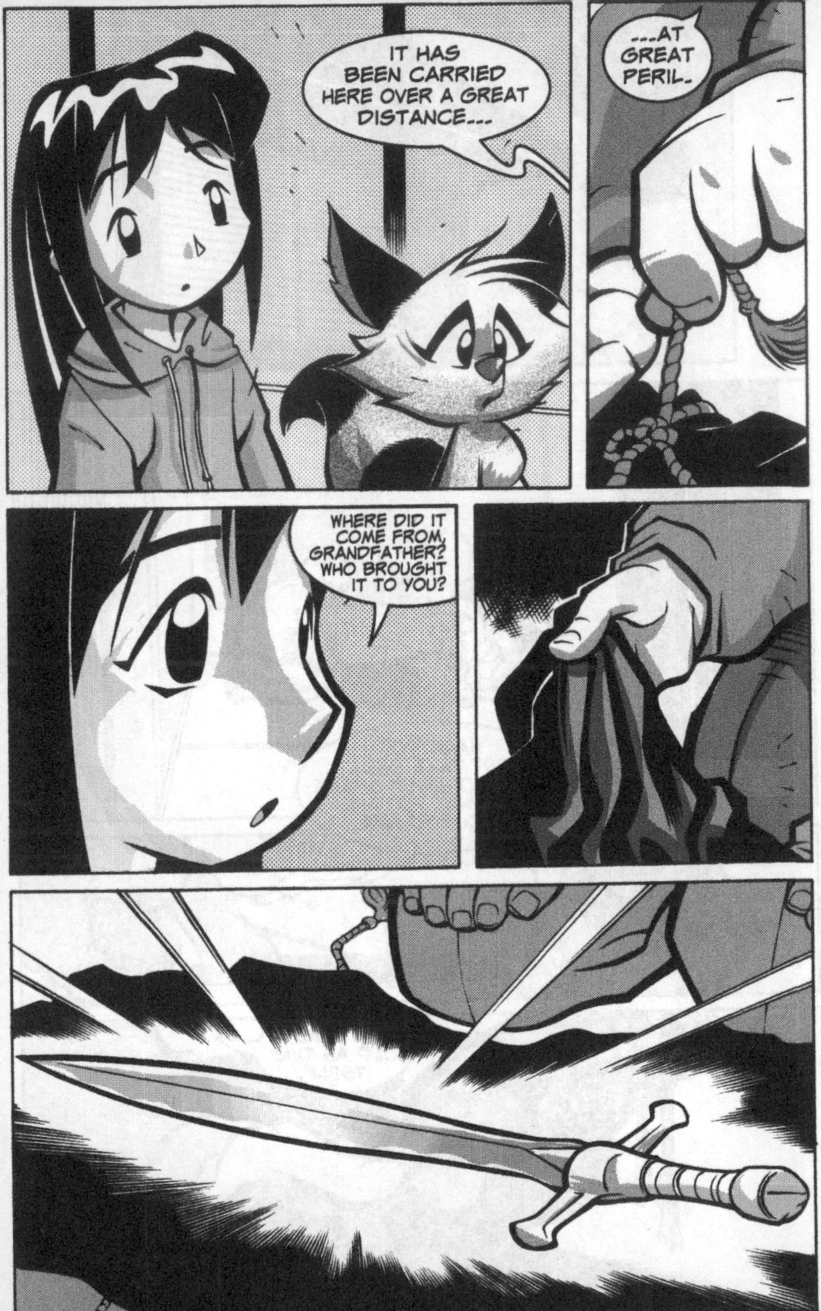
IT HAS BEEN CARRIED HERE OVER A GREAT DISTANCE...
...AT GREAT PERIL.
WHERE DID IT COME FROM, GRANDFATHER? WHO BROUGHT IT TO YOU?

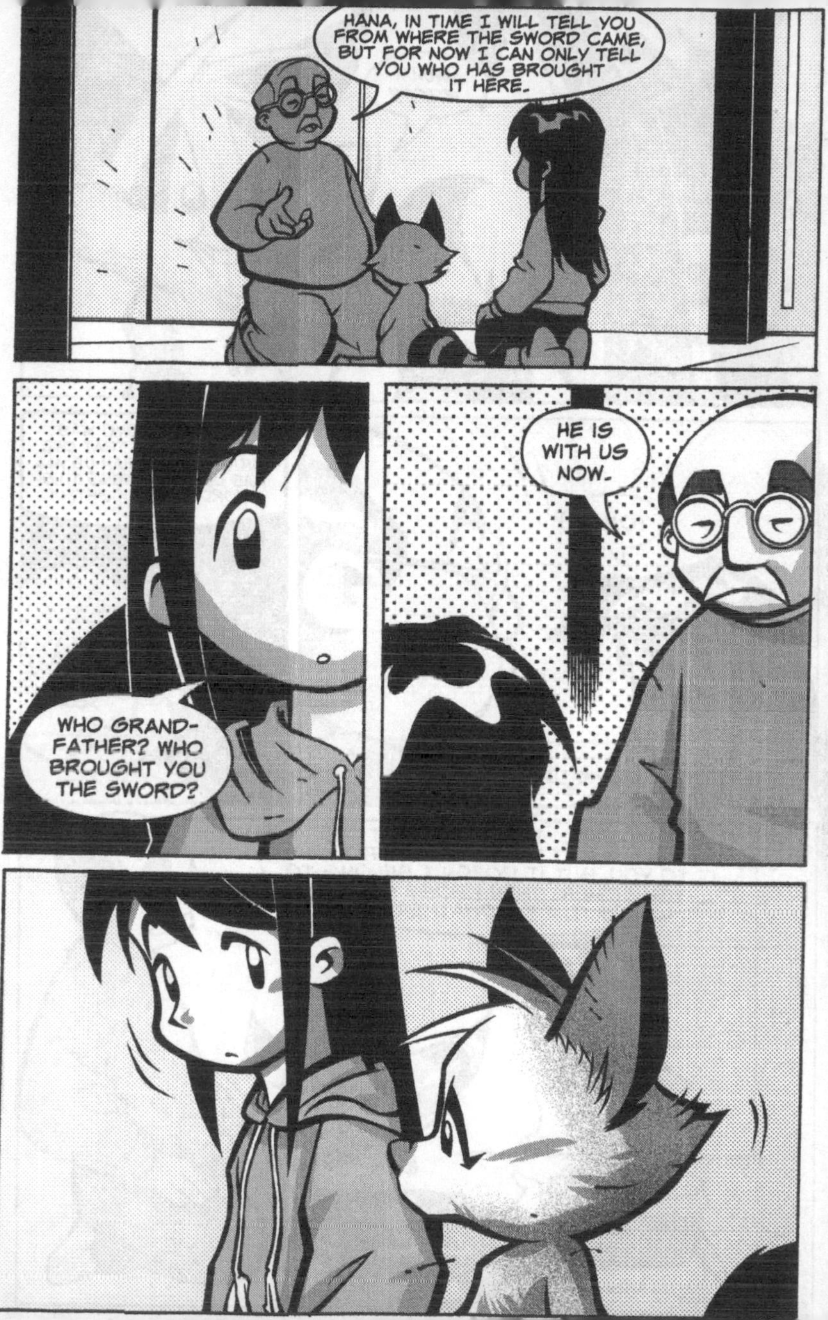
HANA, IN TIME I WILL TELL YOU FROM WHERE THE SWORD CAME, BUT FOR NOW I CAN ONLY TELL YOU WHO HAS BROUGHT IT HERE.
WHO GRAND-FATHER? WHO BROUGHT YOU THE SWORD?
HE IS WITH US NOW.

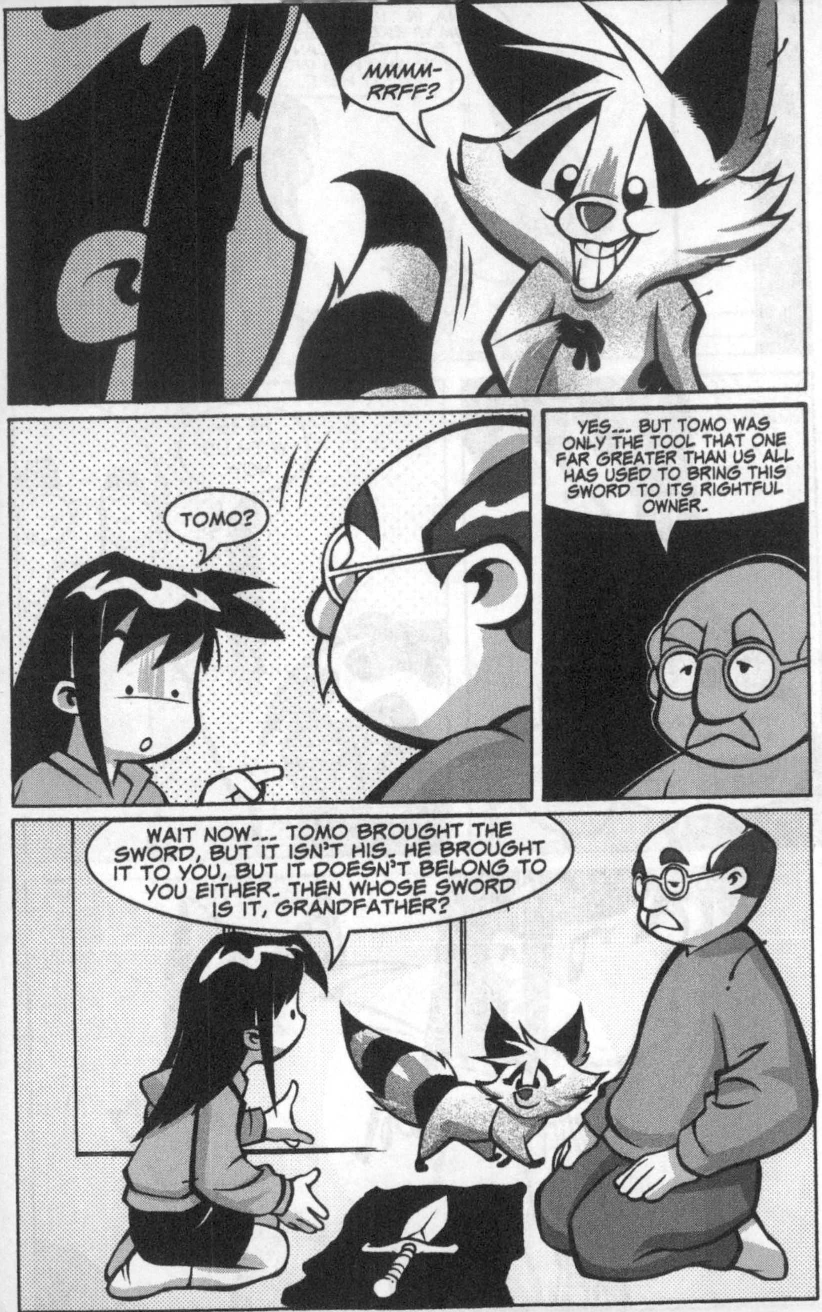
MMMM-
RRFF?
TOMO?
YES... BUT TOMO WAS ONLY THE TOOL THAT ONE FAR GREATER THAN US ALL HAS USED TO BRING THIS SWORD TO ITS RIGHTFUL OWNER.
WAIT NOW... TOMO BROUGHT THE SWORD, BUT IT ISN'T HIS. HE BROUGHT IT TO YOU, BUT IT DOESN'T BELONG TO YOU EITHER. THEN WHOSE SWORD IS IT, GRANDFATHER?

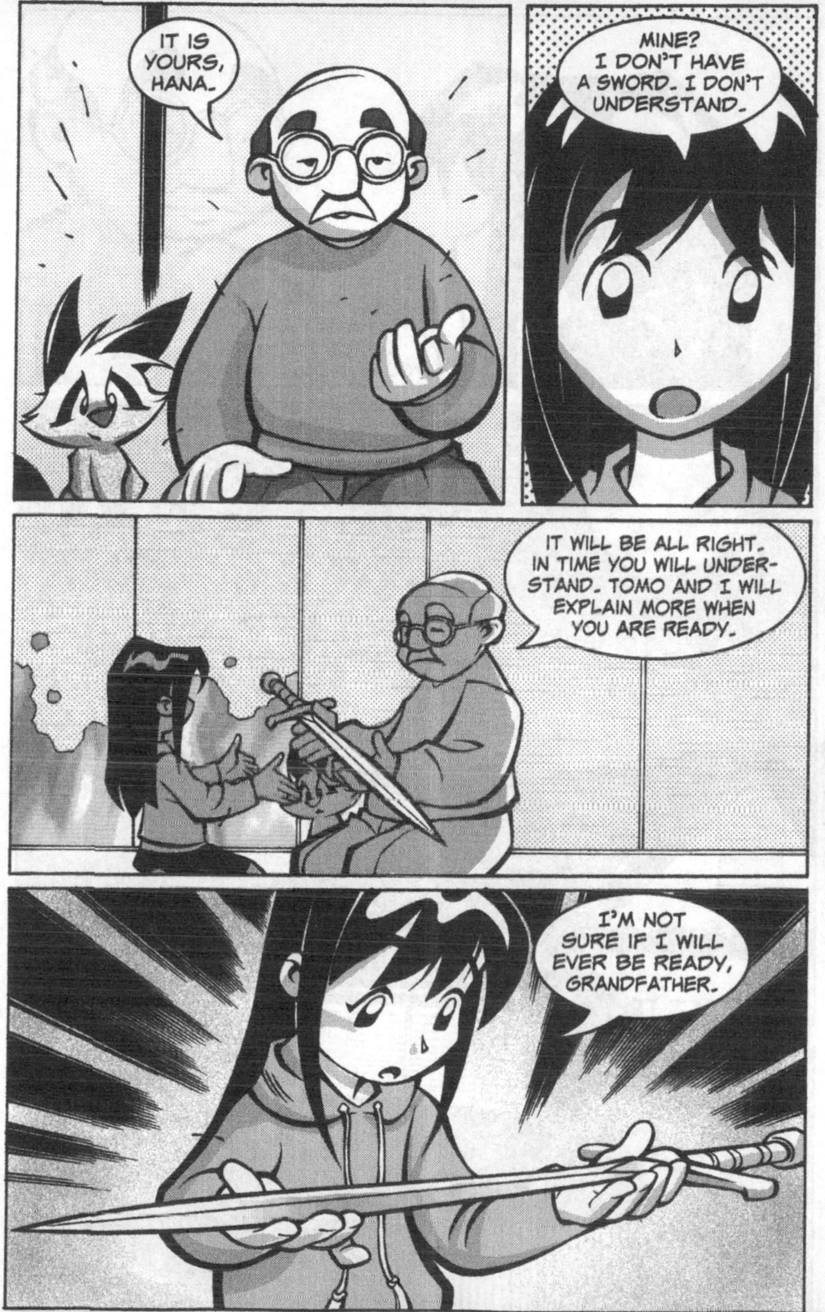
IT IS YOURS, HANA.
MINE? I DON'T HAVE A SWORD. I DON'T UNDERSTAND.
IT WILL BE ALL RIGHT. IN TIME YOU WILL UNDER-STAND. TOMO AND I WILL EXPLAIN MORE WHEN YOU ARE READY.
I'M NOT SURE IF I WILL EVER BE READY, GRANDFATHER.

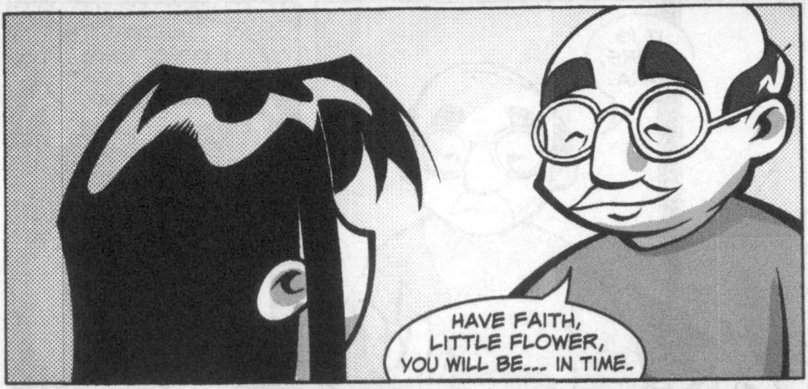
HAVE FAITH, LITTLE FLOWER, YOU WILL BE... IN TIME.
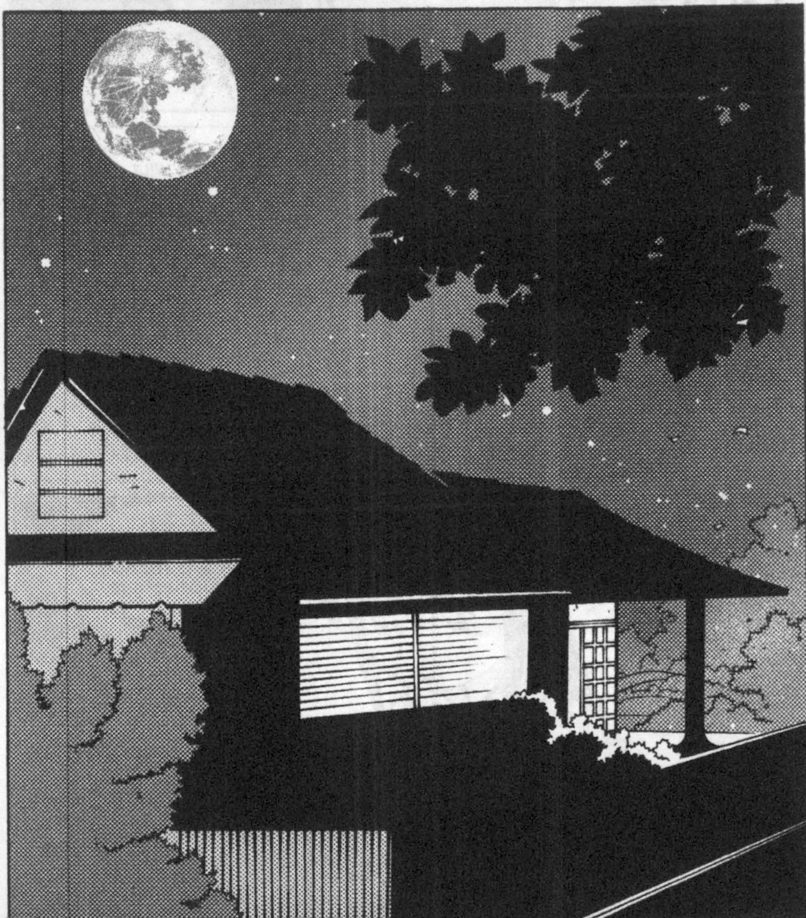

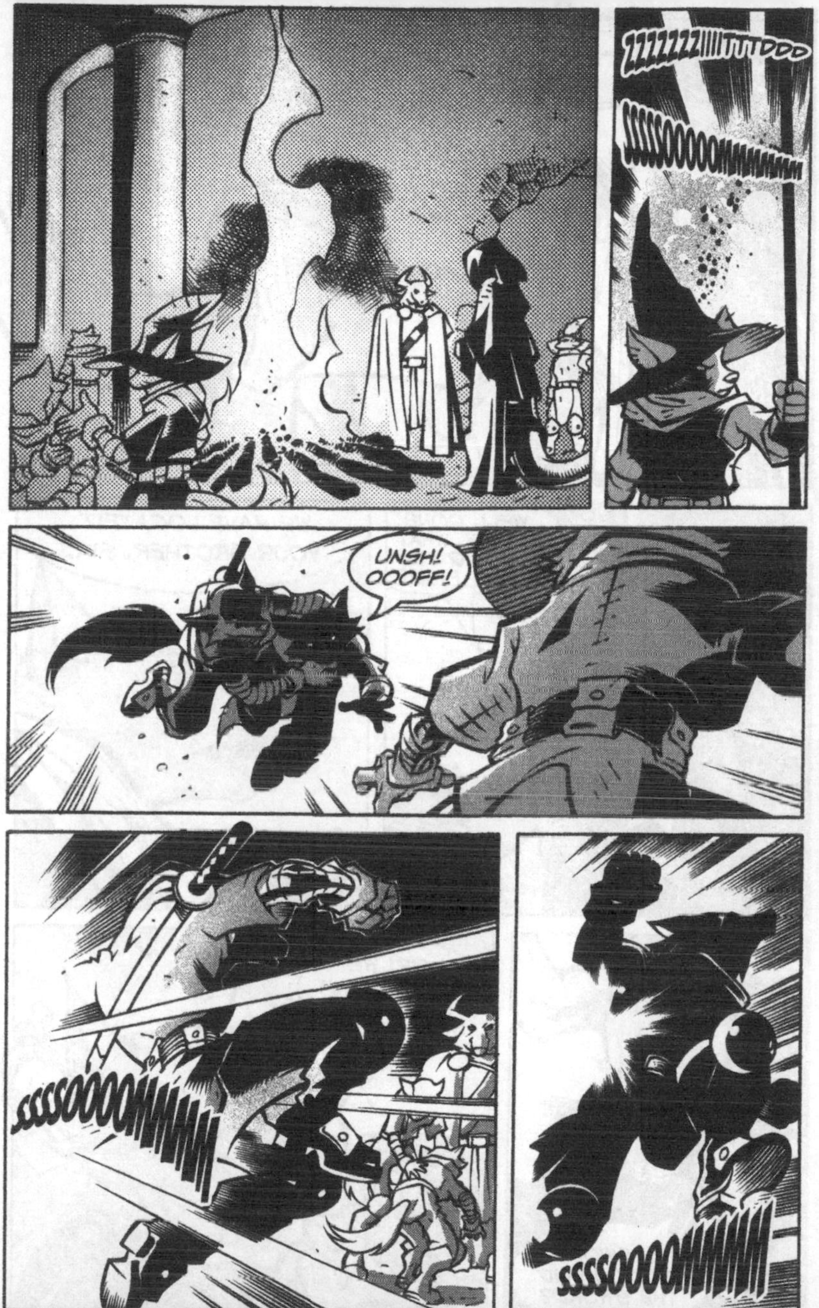
ZZZZZZZIIIIITTTTDDD
SSSSOOOOOMMMMMMMM
UNSH! OOOFF!
SSSSOOOOMMMMM
SSSSOOOOMMMMM

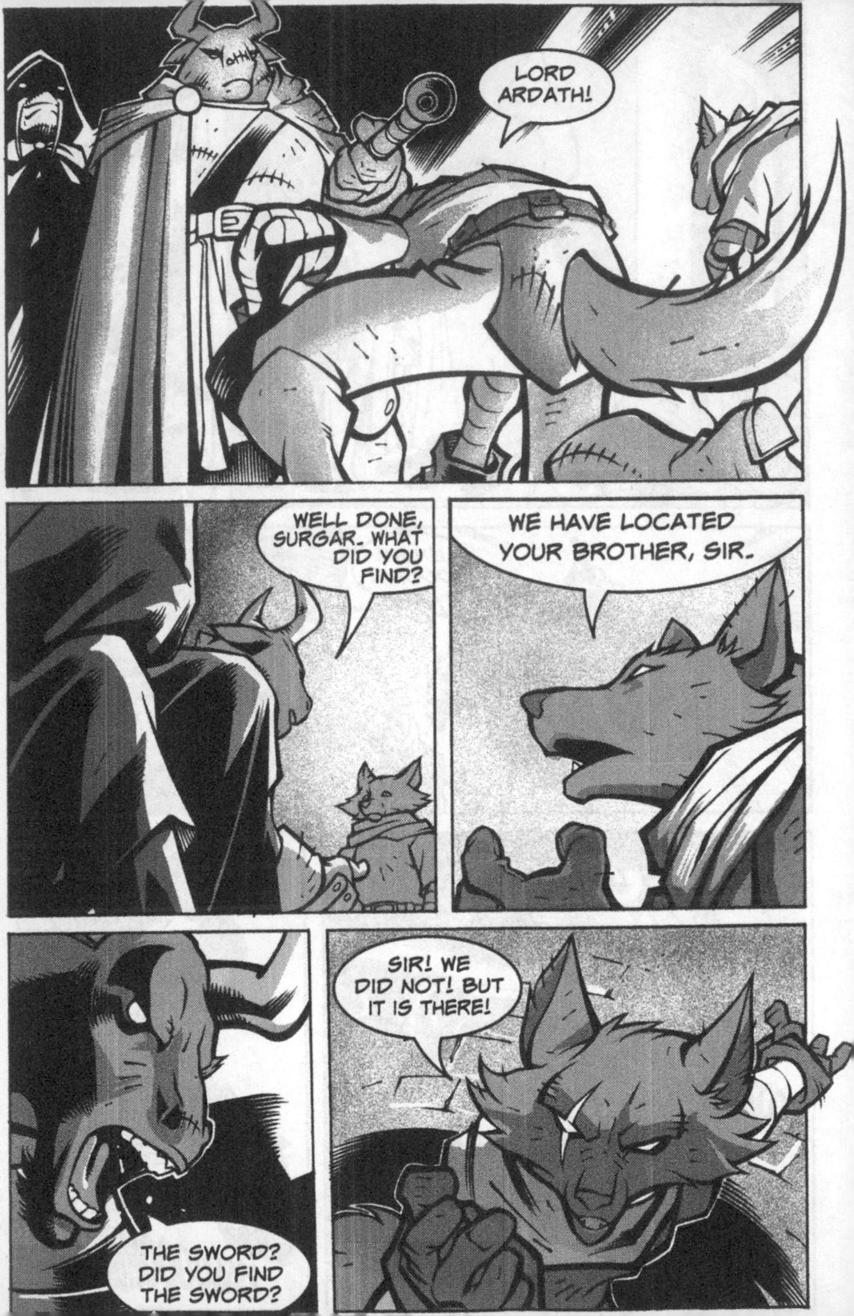
LORD ARDATH!
WELL DONE, SURGAR. WHAT DID YOU FIND?
WE HAVE LOCATED YOUR BROTHER, SIR.
THE SWORD? DID YOU FIND THE SWORD?
SIR! WE DID NOT! BUT IT IS THERE!

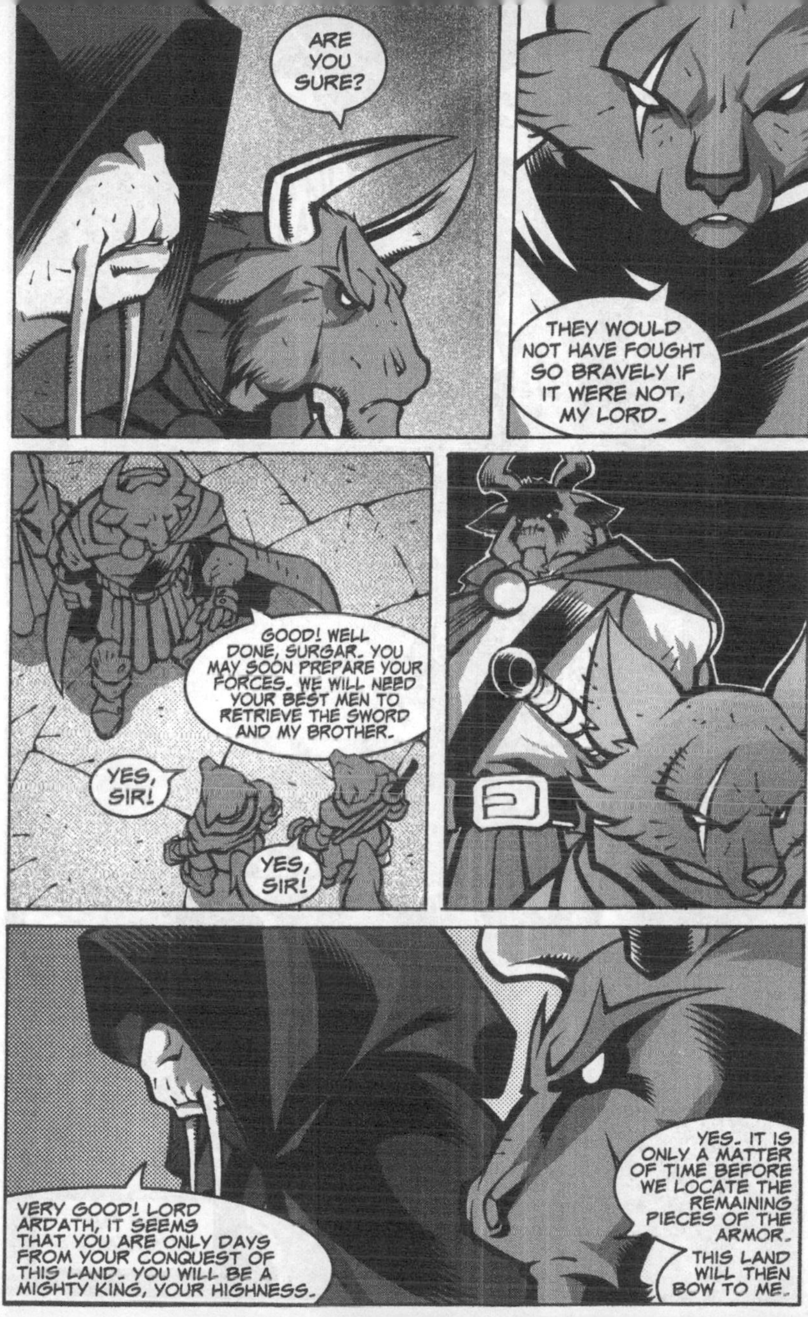
ARE YOU SURE?
THEY WOULD NOT HAVE FOUGHT SO BRAVELY IF IT WERE NOT, MY LORD.
GOOD! WELL DONE, SURGAR. YOU MAY SOON PREPARE YOUR FORCES. WE WILL NEED YOUR BEST MEN TO RETRIEVE THE SWORD AND MY BROTHER.
YES, SIR!
YES, SIR!
VERY GOOD! LORD ARDATH, IT SEEMS THAT YOU ARE ONLY DAYS FROM YOUR CONQUEST OF THIS LAND. YOU WILL BE A MIGHTY KING, YOUR HIGHNESS.
YES. IT IS ONLY A MATTER OF TIME BEFORE WE LOCATE THE REMAINING PIECES OF THE ARMOR.
THIS LAND WILL THEN BOW TO ME.

AND MY BROTHER WILL SEE ME FOR WHO I WAS MEANT TO BE!
KRACKKOW
ARIEL PADILLA '06 + MJASONP
TO BE CONTINUED